TOKIO—PAGODA AND BELL TEMPLE

Japan, Frontispiece.

JAPAN

BY

WALTER DICKSON

WITH **TWO** SUPPLEMENTARY CHAPTERS OF RECENT **EVENTS**

By MAYO W. HAZELTINE

ILLUSTRATED

WILDSIDE PRESS

CONTENTS

LIST OF ILLUSTRATIONS

JAPAN

PREFACE

In the preparation of the following Work the Author has to acknowledge the assistance which he has received from a Japanese gentleman in Yokohama, whose name, for obvious reasons, it is prudent not to mention.

With his knowledge of the history and institutions of his country, the Author was able to fill up the blanks in short notices of history contained in elementary Japanese books. He was further enabled to go over the red-books of the empire which enter into the details of the pedigrees of illustrious families, and into the minutiæ of Government offices.

The supposed unalterable character of these institutions induces those who have any pretensions to learning in China and Japan to master and retain by memory the names and duties of the different offices in the various departments of Government; and they are frequently found to be good authorities upon questions upon which there is no published information.

In the history of the intercourse of the Jesuits with Japan, the letters of the fathers have been almost the only authorities relied upon; while in the more recent events contemporary publications have been used.

In taking notes from the conversation of a Japanese who could speak but little English, in too many cases they were written down in what is known in China as "pigeon English"; and the Author has to acknowledge and regret that in many cases the cramped nature of the notes has not been entirely removed, and for such instances he craves the indulgence of the reader.

HISTORY OF JAPAN

CHAPTER I

THE IMPERIAL FAMILY AND COURT

MAN, in the earlier periods of his existence, when he was as yet putting forth his juvenile strength to subdue creation, was ever inclined to look upon the great forces of nature as difficulties in his path and obstacles to his progress, which, in his more mature strength, he has come to regard as aids to help him, and to cherish as the very means to the attainment of his ends. Such an object of awe to the earlier mariner was the great ocean, when he had no compass to guide him over its unknown and apparently boundless expanse, and with no knowledge of the winds and no experience of the currents. When he had no means of keeping food or fresh water for any great length of time, he was a bold man who would venture far out of sight of land. Provided with the faithful compass, men became bolder; they enlarged their vessels, making longer voyages, until they ran over the length and breadth of the Eastern seas. Still the China Sea, with its typhoons and its monsoons and currents, down to a comparatively recent period, was looked upon as an obstacle which was to be smoothed down and not to be wrestled with. To beat up the China Sea against the northeastern monsoon was considered a rash struggle and a foolhardy waste of time, and in consequence the trade-voyages to China were confined to vessels going up the sea in sum-

(9)

mer with the southerly monsoon and returning in winter
with the northerly.   Obstacles such as these made mariners
unwilling to run the risk of pushing up the sea the length
of Shanghai or Japan, when the time of their return was
a matter of so much doubt.

In the present age, when man is thinking himself of some
importance from the little odds and ends of knowledge he
has stored up, the ocean, instead of being a barrier of separation between islands and continents, has become what the
Mediterranean Sea was to the Old World—a link of connection, a highway of commerce, and steam has become a bridge
by which distant shores have been joined together.   The
world is now finding out that she is one—that the interests of
nations are one, and that no one part of the body can say to
the other, "I have no need of thee."   If Japan has hitherto
felt herself in a position to use such an expression to her
fellow-members of the body cosmopolitan, and the feeling
has been responded to by their acquiescence, the time and
circumstances seem to have arrived when this seclusion is to
be ended.   The distance at which these islands seemed to lie
from the heart of the world's circulation, Europe, has been
almost annihilated, and European nations have through the
settlements in India and China crept up alongside of the isles
of the East.   The difficulties of access have been smoothed
away, her sumptuary laws have been abrogated, while the
produce of her rich soil is daily increasing to meet the demands which are made upon it, and which she is becoming
willing and ready to exchange for that of which she is more
in need.

Steam has been the active agent in bringing about these
changes, causing the pulses of trade to beat with greater
frequency and with increased vigor.   But to any one who
looks below the surface there may be seen other agents at
work, all concurring at this crisis in the world's existence to
produce changes of portentous magnitude.   The discoveries
of chemistry, whether by the aggressive forces obtained in
the manufacture of munitions of war, or by the more widely

extended but silent beneficial operation of such an agent as quinine, steam with all its ramifications of wealth, the telegraph with its tenfold power of convertibility, the discovery of gold at the most remote parts of the world, have combined to produce, by the sudden influx of real wealth, by the intermingling of ranks of men, and by the rapid throwing into men's minds of a quantity of information or of knowledge, a condition of things in the mass which makes that mass kneadable by those who can knead it, and fitted for the reception of any leaven, for good or for evil, which may be mixed with it. The mingling of ranks in the social system, the disturbance of creeds in the religious, the confounding of parties in the political, are preparing the way for some world-wide change, by which old systems are to be done away and new established. It is not working in one nation alone, but in all: it is not confined to Christendom, showing that the time to come is not to be like times past; but that the time is coming when it is possible for one person to aim at one rule over the whole world. This change is coming up like the rising of water. It may overwhelm all existing things like a wave. Some call it Progress, others Democracy, but, whatever it be, it is evident that every existing institution is to get such a shaking that only the things that cannot be shaken will stand.

All national institutions having, or pretending to have, order, will probably have to undergo this trial; and when it comes the whole remains of the feudal system will be tested: monarchies, the peerage, tenures of land, orders in the Church, and, above all, the question of primogeniture, cannot fail to be put on trial. The different sections in the religious and political world seem gradually separating themselves into two large parties, the one standing for the *vox Dei*, the other holding the *vox populi* to be the *vox Dei*—the one believing that power comes from above, the other that power comes from below.

The leaven is working in the minds of men, whether they will it or not; and no nation will feel the effects of this fermentation more than Japan. Above all nations, she to this hour retains her feudal system intact. She must learn, as others have in past times and may have to learn again, at the expense of revolution and blood. The people are already being stirred, and dare to question. The nobles are beginning to quake, they know not why, in the face of changes which are being forced upon them. The very throne of the emperor is being searched and shaken.

In order to understand where the weakness of a building lies, or how it is likely to fall down, it is first necessary to know how it is constructed; and in order to comprehend the changes which events may bring about in Japan, some idea must be formed of the government of the country. Without some knowledge of the framework of the constitution, it is difficult to understand the relative position of men, or to appreciate the operation of external agents upon the system of the empire, whether that operation work by a slow process of leavening from within, or by a violent concussion from without.

The aim of the author in the following pages has been to give some idea of the framework of the constitution of Japan. Having resided for some little time in the country, he was enabled to get what seemed to him a clearer glimpse of the working of the different parts of the machinery of State than was to be gained from any of the able works published on the subject. The time at his command was too short, and his knowledge of the language too limited, to enable him to do more than prepare a sketch which may serve a temporary purpose, before works of greater research and fuller information are produced.

The position of the Emperor (Spiritual Emperor, as he is sometimes erroneously called), as the first in the empire, must be recognized; the office held by the Temporal Emperor, the Shiogoon (or Tycoon, as he has been named), must be correctly and distinctly understood before the nature of the rule in the empire can be comprehended. It is further essential that the student should be acquainted with the rank and position of the nobility or nobilities of the empire (for of these there are two classes)—that of Miako at the court of the Emperor, the Koongays; and that at Yedo at the court of the Shiogoon, the Daimio, and beneath them the Hatta-moto. Without some knowledge of these the reader is lost in a maze of unmeaning names and titles; but with a slight acquaintance with the rank, offices, and names of these nobles, he is able not only to follow the thread of history, but to understand the intricacies of current events.

A description of a picture by a native artist, seen by the author of this volume, may give some idea of the relation in which these dignitaries stand the one to the other. The upper half of the picture represents the Shiogoon or Tycoon at the palace in the capital, Miako, making his obeisance and performing homage before his liege lord the Emperor, seated in the great hall, Shi shin den, of the palace. The upper part of the Emperor's person is concealed behind a screen of thin slips of bamboo hanging from the roof. The throne is three mats, or thin mattresses, placed one above the other upon the floor. There is no chair or support to the back. On each side of the Emperor sit on their knees on the floor the high officers of his court. Before him is seen the late Shiogoon, kneeling and prostrating himself, with his head to the floor. Behind the Shiogoon are his high officers Stots-bashi and the great Daimio Owarri, both in a similar position of prostration; while beneath, in the open court, are military officials of the Imperial Court standing or kneeling. This picture represents accurately a fact, and what appears to be a correct illustration of the ideas of the people of Japan with regard to the relative status of the Emperor and the Shiogoon.

It may almost be a matter of wonder that so little was known of Japan until the advent of the Portuguese. Men were in old times adventurous travelers, and yet, except what is contained in the pages of Marco Polo, written in the thir-teenth century, nothing more was known of the existence of the country. The Buddhism of India had permeated China, Corea, and Japan, but it brought nothing back. Moham-

medanism, at an early stage, reached China, and gained
many converts, and the Arabs carried on an extensive trade
with China and the Eastern Isles; but neither by their writings nor by the early native accounts do they seem to have
reached the shores of Japan, or, at least, ever to have returned from them.   This may perhaps be attributed to the
wars of the Crusades, which appear to have lighted up such
a fierce feeling between the Christian and the Moslem as to
have proved a barrier to the inquisitiveness of the former
in his investigations regarding the East.   When the Portuguese, in the beginning of the sixteenth century, had pushed
their discoveries and trade as far as Malacca, and thence to
China, it was to be expected that such adventurous seamen
as they then were would, before long, solve the question of
a people living under the rising sun.   It is fortunate that,
among the lawless buccaneers and pirates, as they evidently
were, on those seas during his time, one man, Mendez Pinto,
should have been found with the zeal to write some account
of the doings on the Sea of China, and to lift the veil which,
until he wrote, hung over the events which he records.   That
the latter part of his narrative, relating principally to China,
should have been called mendacious, is not to be wondered
at.   But all that he relates with reference to Japan is not
only corroborated by a closer acquaintance with the country
and people, but also by the native historians in their accounts
of the arrival of foreigners in the country, as well as by the
letters of the Jesuits who visited Japan very shortly after it
was first discovered by the Portuguese traders.

Subsequently to the period at which Mendez Pinto wrote,
the history of foreign relations with the country is kept up
by the letters of priests and Jesuits who occupied Japan as
a field for the spread of Christianity.   In the "Histoire de
l'Eglise du Japon" there is an excellent summary of occurrences connected with the Church, its missions, its successes.
its difficulties, its martyrs, and its enemies, together with a
glance at events in Japan during the most eventful crisis in
the history of the country.   After the expulsion of the Jesuiti

and Roman Catholic doctrines from the empire, there are accounts from time to time published by the officers connected with the establishment kept up by Holland at Nagasaki. Caron, Fischer, Meylan—but, above all, Kæmpfer and Thunberg, and Titsingh and Klaproth—and, in our own times, Siebold—have done much to elucidate the manners and customs and natural history of Japan.

Kæmpfer has given a most interesting and instructive account of what he saw in the country during a long residence, and upon more than one progress to the courts at Miako and Yedo. His delineation of the manners and customs of the people of Japan will remain as a memorial of a state of things seen under circumstances not likely to occur again. But the work was published by another after the death of the author, and, in consequence of this, many of the names of men, places and things are nearly unintelligible. Kæmpfer's work is well known to the Japanese, having been translated or repeatedly copied in manuscript, and is known as "Su koku rong." It is an interdicted book, and only recently a man was punished upon being detected in the act of copying the translation. The translation by Klaproth of the "Annales des Empereurs de Japon" is a most valuable work, and contains a wonderful amount of information, being, as it were, the complement of Kæmpfer's work, drawn entirely from books and not from personal observation.

The natives of Japan appear to have an intense love and reverence for their own country, and every individual in the empire seems to have a deep and thorough appreciation of the natural beauties and delights of the country. To this the genial climate, the rich soil, and the variety of the surface contribute. The islands lie at such a latitude as to make the air in summer warm without being hot, and in winter cold without being raw. The soil, as in all recent lava soils, is of a rich black mould, raising the finest crops of millet, wheat and sugar-cane, and when supplied in unstinted profusion rearing splendid timber, or capable, when

nearly entirely withdrawn, of keeping life and vigor and
seeding power in a pine tree of two inches in height. The
trees have a tendency to break out into excrescences from
plethora. The variety of surface arises from the great
height to which the mountains rise in an island which at
no part presents so great a breadth as England, and yet
slopes gradually from the mountain tops to the sea. Some
of these ridges appear to rise to the height of Mont Blanc,
one of them, Fusiyama, being upward of thirteen thousand
feet in height, and it would appear that other ranges are
higher. The great beauty of Fusi (*pah rh*, not two) consists
in its rising singly out of a low country with a beautifully
curved sweep to a conical apex; and the atmospheric effects
changing from hour to hour, as it is seen from thirteen
provinces, give such a variety to this single object that it
is rightly called by a name to express the feeling that there
are not two such in the world. The variations of atmospheric density make it look at one time much higher than at
another. It may be seen with its head clear in the blue sky
rising out of a thick base of clouds—or the clouds rise and
roll in masses about the middle, leaving the gentle curve to
be filled up by the mind's eye from the base to the apex.
Again, the whole contour, in a sort of proud, queenly sweep,
stands out against a cloudless ether, or with a little vapor
drifting to leeward of the summit giving the appearance
of a crater—or, after a cool night in September, the eye is
arrested by the appearance of the bursting downward of a
flattened shell, the pure white snow filling the valleys from
the top, the haze of the morning half concealing the hill beneath. Every hour brings a change upon a landscape which
consists of a single object which the lover of nature can
never weary of admiring, in a climate where seventy miles of
atmosphere does not obscure the larger features on the face
of the mountain even to the naked eye. How often would
such an object be visible in the climate of England?

The first settlement of inhabitants upon an island is always
a subject of interesting speculation and inquiry. The insu-

lar position gives an idea of a definite time or period at which the peopling of a large island must have taken place. The freedom of possession of boundless wealth presents every inducement to the immigrant to remain, while distance and difficulties repel the idea of return. In Japan this immigration may in all probability have commenced by a gradual spreading from the north of inhabitants of Manchuria through the islands of Saghalien and Jezo to those of the Japanese group.

During the earlier periods of a nation's existence, the art of writing has been generally kept in the hands of men who have devoted themselves to a life of retirement and seclusion from the strife and temptations of the outer world. These have been found among the priesthood, and it has been their business or their amusement to gather up and commit to writing what had been up to the time current as oral tradition in regard to prehistoric occurrences. Men are forced by reasoning to refer the appearance of their first ancestors to a creation by, or procession from, a Divine Being. At the same time, those who have wielded the power of writing, and thereby reached and influenced a larger circle of their fellowmen, have generally endeavored to clothe the deities from whom they profess to have sprung with virtues which were to be emulated by their descendants, or to inculcate through them, by precept, a purity of moral conduct to be practiced by their followers.

The group of islands generally included under the one name Japan was known in remote times by a variety of names—"Akitsu sima, Toyo aki, Toyo ashiwarra no nakatsa kooni." "Wo kwo," the country of peace, is used by the Chinese for Japan. "Ho," pronounced "Yamato," and used for one province, is frequently applied in Japan to the whole country.

The name Nippon—Nits pon—"Yutpone" in Cantonese, "Jih pun" in the Mandarin dialect, by which the whole empire is now known—is of Chinese origin, and has probably been conveyed to the country by the first Chinese settlers.

Denoting, as the name implies, that it is the country where
the sun rises, the idea must have originated with the people
to the west. "Hon cho," another name by which it is
known, conveys the same idea, "The beginning or root of
the morning." The name "Yamato," peaceful, harmoni-
ous, was more likely to have originated with the natives.
"Akitsu sima" implies that the island resembles a dragon-fly
in shape, and was at first applied to Kiusiu alone. "Shin
koku," a name by which the Japanese speak of their own
empire, means the land of spirits; and a similar idea is conveyed by the name "Kami no kooni." "Awadsi sima" refers to the supposed origin of the islands from mud or froth,
and is still applied to the large island lying between Nippon
and Sikok.

Some of these names probably retain the old words used
by the original inhabitants of the country translated into
Chinese by the new immigrants. To these newcomers it
was no doubt a work of pleasure to gather up what stores of
tradition were floating among the inhabitants of the country,
and, adding thereto much from their own imagination, to
compose a mythology suited to the genius of the people.
This mythology, which we may suppose to have been composed by some of the Chinese *literati* about the court, had
for its object the elevation of the reigning family, and the
assertion for that family of a divine origin and divine ancestry. It is worthy of note that these divine ancestors were
known at a very early period by Chinese names, that of the
mother and founder of the imperial family being "Ten sho
dai jin"—the "great spirit of the celestial splendor of the
sun," four distinct Chinese words.

According to this mythology, the heavens and the earth
having formed themselves out of nothing, gave forth a spirit
—a "kami"—who was the father of a line of seven generations of spiritual beings who ruled the universe as it then
was, during a period extending over millions of years, ending in a male and a female, respectively named Issanaghi
and Issanami. These seem equivalents to or representatives

of the male and the female principles which, according to the Chinese, pervade all animate creation.   They are allegorically represented as producing the islands of Japan, the mountains, seas and other natural objects therein.   Subsequently a daughter was brought forth, "Ten sho dai jin," who is the spirit of the sun; and another, "Tsuki no kami," the spirit of the moon.   These divinities are of no further importance in history than as serving to make a line of ancestry for the reigning family.   At the time when, according to tradition, the genealogy merged in mortal men, the country was found to be peopled, and there is no attempt to show whence these people came, though described as hairy, uncivilized, and living in the open air.   These myths are generally of a Buddhistic origin, and were probably brought over or invented by some missionary of that religion at an early time, when the influence of India operated strongly in the spread of its doctrines.   This influence is shown to this day in the repetition of prayers in an unknown language, and the retention of an Indian alphabet and writing—the Sanskrit or Devanagari—in all the religious works of Japan.

Some of these divinities are so frequently heard of, and representations of them, in pictures and carvings, are so common, that even a slight acquaintance with their names and attributes is useful.   The different Buddhas are worshiped; Compera; the five hundred "Rakhan" or "Lohon"; the "Kwanon," or goddess of mercy; and the "Stchi fuku jing," or seven gods of riches.   These last are generally drawn or carved on a boat, with emblems around them of long life, etc. —the stork, tortoise, a deer, a bag of money, a fir-tree, a bamboo, a crystal ball, a fish.   Their names are —Hotay Daikoku, Yaybissu, Benten, Gayho, Bistamong, Fukowo kojiu.   But the religion is more or less pantheistic, and there are many other gods and divinities, even down to shapeless stones.

To "Ten sho dai jin" is attributed the origin of the imperial house, as is shown by the words of the Emperor, in a letter recently written on the political position of affairs, "I am grieved, standing as I do between 'Ten sho dai jin' and my people."

In the fifth generation after "Ten sho dai jin" was born "Zinmu" or "Jin mu" (Chin: Shinwu—*i.e.*, spirit of war). He was the first of the earthly or human rulers. He is said to have been born in Fiuga, a mountainous province on the east side of Kiu siu, on the west coast of the Boo ngo Channel. This part of the islands is well suited for trading purposes, and it is also well adapted for the landing of an invading force, and it is not unlikely that Zinmu either originally came from China, or was the son of some Chinese who had settled there, and who started thence on a design of conquest. At the time when he set out upon his career, the people of the country are said to have been hairy and uncivilized, but under the rule of a headman in each village. The Japanese have to this day a great contempt for the people of Yezo, who may be thus described, and they allege that similar tribes occupied the whole of the islands, and that they were gradually driven back before the armies of Zinmu. It is more likely that they were conquered, and gradually amalgamated with their conquerors by the intermarriage of these with native females, and that in this way, and by the effects of the warm climate of the south, they lost that hirsute appearance which is so characteristic of the people of Yezo.—Aino, the name given to the hairy inhabitants of Yezo by the Japanese, means "between," and has reference to a contemptuous idea of the origin of these people from a dog.—There are two strongly-marked varieties of feature in Japan, which are always strikingly portrayed in their own pictures. There is the broad flat face of the lower classes, and the high nose and oval face of the higher. The difference is so marked as to be some argument in favor of a previous mixing of two different races; the one of which had extended southward from the Kurile Islands and Siberia, hairy and broad-featured; while the other had originated from the south, with Indian features and smooth skins.

The Japanese themselves do not pretend that there is any

native documentary evidence in support of their history at the date of Zinmu, and the best writers allow that no writings prior to the seventh century are authentic. The introduction of Chinese letters into Japan is generally attributed to Onin, a learned man who came from Corea about the year 285 A.D. But prior to the date of Onin, many of the names of offices and officers were Chinese. It is hardly credible that, with the communication which is known to have existed at different times between Japan and China, and also with Corea, there should have continued for so long a time such complete ignorance. More than one embassy had resided at the court of China for months. The Chinese annals speak of an embassy during the reign of the Han dynasty, A.D. 238, when China was divided into "three kingdoms." The ruler of Woo, one of these three, proposed to invade Japan, but the expedition miscarried. Nearly two centuries before this, in A.D. 57, an embassy was sent from Japan to China by Sei nin, which arrived at the court of Kwang ou, of the Eastern Han dynasty, in the last year of his reign. It is unlikely that, residing as such an embassy must have done for a considerable time at the court of China, they should not have brought away some knowledge of letters or some instructors in reading and writing. This Corean, Onin, may have been brought over to replace or to reteach what had been lost: for in more recent times it is known that, after the long civil wars of the fifteenth and sixteenth centuries, so little attention had been given to the instruction of youth that only two men were found in the empire competent to teach the written language.

We may be permitted to believe that much of what became tradition had at one time been committed to writing, and that, corroborated as it is at some points by Chinese history, there is a foundation for much of that part of history subsequent to the time of Zinmu, for the support of which there existed, when writing recommenced, no documentary evidence.

THE EMPEROR OF JAPAN

The line of gods carried on through godlike mortal descendants was prolonged in ordinary mortals, the first of whom was Zinmu. It is of little consequence by whom this pedigree was written or invented. It evidently was solely written for the then *de facto* rulers of the land. It does not pretend to deal with the people of Japan, or with the mode in which the peopling of the empire took place, but simply invents and details a divine pedigree for one family. At the time when this family is first heard of, the islands of Japan are acknowledged by Japanese historians to have been already peopled and divided into villages, each under some municipal rule.

The reign of Zinmu is the era of Japan, and is placed at 667 years before Christ. Setting out from Miazaki in Fiuga, on the east side of the island of Kïusiu, he with troops under his command gradually overran that island, and the adjoining one of Sikok, together with the west half of the island of Nippon, as far as the province of Mino to the east of Miako. Coming from the most rugged and comparatively barren province in the empire, he was attracted by the beauty and desirableness of the country around Miako. He settled at a place named Kashiwarra or Kashiwabarra, a site near the city of Narra, about fifteen miles from the present capital. This choice of a site has been ratified by every succeeding emperor, the Kio or capital ("King," Chinese) of the empire having been frequently changed, but never removed to any great distance from the spot originally selected by Zinmu.

In truth, the site is in every way most suitable for the capital of the country. It is, geographically, nearly in the center of the islands which constitute the empire. From the port of the capital, Osaca (or Naniwa, as it was named of old), a great fringe of the coast of the three islands in almost landlocked waters is accessible to ships without their venturing into the open sea. To this port a large body of water is rolled down by the confluence of several rivers, which at one time were dispersed into several mouths and branches; but by labor these have been collected and confined within two outlets. There is, in consequence, a large extent of alluvial ground producing rice and wheat for a numerous population. The inland water communication extends to the large lake Owomi—upward of sixty miles in length and eighteen in breadth; and thence, with an interval of a few miles only of land-carriage, to the port of Tsurunga, on the northern coast; while to the southeast, the natives report that there is uninterrupted water-communication to Owarri, and thence to Sinano, and, with a short interval of land-carriage, even to Yedo—whence, again, it extends northward by rivers and canals to the vicinity of Nambu. The city of Miako of the present day stands on a plain, among hills clothed with wood, where art has done what it could to assist nature in the completion of landscape scenery, of the beauties of which the natives speak with rapture. During twenty-four centuries, members of the family of Zinmu have sat upon the throne, and during that long time the palace has been only at short intervals removed to any considerable distance from the site on which it at present stands.

The imperial residence in Japan is a very different structure from anything that European ideas of palaces would expect, being chiefly built of wood and other materials so inflammable that a palace has been reconstructed and destroyed within a year. When we read of each emperor, at an early date, building a palace for himself, it is not to be supposed that these were either expensive or very durable buildings. Each emperor seems to have occupied a different habitation from his predecessor, removing from one site to another, but generally keeping within the province of Yamashiro, or that adjoining, Yamato. Kwanmu, in the year 794, built a palace on the site where the present city stands, and since his time Miako has been always looked upon as the metropolis.

The palace of the Emperor of Japan is called, as a whole, "Kinri go sho." Though built of fine and expensive timber, it presents no appearance of that outward splendor which is generally considered by us to be necessary to an imperial residence. The roofs of the buildings are said to be white. It is surrounded by a common inclosure of wooden boarding. This inclosure is pierced by several gates. These entrances are graduated, and the settlement of the gate by which a great man shall make his entrance or his exit is a matter of no small importance at court. These gates lead into a large open space; in this is another inclosure (with other gates), in the center of which stands the wooden building, the "Shi shin deng," or imperial office, in which the emperor receives the highest officers of the empire. This he appears to do almost in the open air. The emperor does not sit upon a throne or chair, but is slightly raised above the floor—three of the ordinary mats of the country, and placed one above the other, being used as a throne. To the back of this public office is the residence or private apartments of the emperor; and behind these are the female apartments of the empress, the empress-mother, and other high ladies.

The "Shi shin deng" (Ch. "Tsz shin tien") faces to the south, to the large outer gate, the "Yïo may mong"; within this is another gate of a red inclosure, the gate of the sun, "Hi no go mong." On passing through this, the large wooden-pillar-supported hall, with its roof with immense eaves, is seen raised from the ground upon a lower framework of wood. Before it stand an orange and a cherry tree. Between these, six steps lead up to the wooden gallery or veranda, which goes round the hall under eaves projecting five or six feet from the supports. A low balustrade surrounds this veranda. Under this large canopy of roof, almost in the open air, the Emperor sits while he receives homage. The "Shi shin deng" occupies the red inclosure, having on the east side a small wooden building for covering the car used in processions; to the east of that is the building in which the "three jewels" are kept, the "Naishi dokoro."

Within the "Shi shin deng" all extraordinary formal business of importance is transacted. The Shiogoon here presents himself to the Emperor. In the long hall to the west of the "Shi shin deng," the "Say rio deng" ("Tsing liang tien") or "Hiru no ma," the mid-day room, ordinary business is transacted. Immediately in the rear of the "Shi shin deng" is the "Nai go bansho," or inner hall for business. To the east side, and overlooking the garden, is the "Tsunay no goteng," or hall of meeting, or drawing-room. Behind, in the "Ko ngo sho," the Emperor's son and heir lives; here also are the apartments of the elder women. "Nanga Hashi no Tsubo nay" is the room in which levees are held, where rank is given, and degradations or punishments are awarded. Formerly all the offices of the different departments of government were in the neighborhood of the palace, but outside, at a distance of one "cho," or 120 yards.

At the back of all are the female apartments. On the east side, outside of the inclosure, is the Gakumonjo, or imperial school.

To the southeast of the whole is another inclosure, the "Ko een go sho," the palace of the Emperor after he has abdicated, when he is known as Kubo, covering a space of ground nearly as large as the palace inclosure. Adjoining this, and immediately to the south, is the residence of the father or predecessor of the abdicated emperor. He is known as Sento (Tsin tung). To the southwest is that of the empress dowager, and the females of the old emperor's court. The Shi sin wo, or four royal families, are located in the neighborhood, while all around are the residences, with inclosures of ground, belonging to the "Go sekkay," or "five assisting" families. Among these also is found a small inclosure, the residence of the Sho shi dai, the envoy of the Shiogoon at the imperial court.

Except the greater elevation and whiteness of the roofs, there is nothing to distinguish the palace from the adjacent streets. That the Emperor should be thus housed probably involves a great state principle. The houses of Daimios and

high officers are built in a much more durable manner. The
Shiogoon's residences at Osaka, Miako, Yedo, and other
places, are generally built more like fortifications or places
of great strength. In similar style are raised the houses,
palaces or forts of the Daimios in their respective provinces.
It cannot, therefore, be from any fear of earthquakes that
this style of a plain wood-and-paper house is adopted, but it
is probably founded on the same principle as that on which
the imperial pedigree is drawn up; viz., with the view of
giving to it the appearance of a temple, and surrounding the
Emperor with the circumstances and attributes of a god.

This palace in Miako appears to be the only one now used
by the Emperor. He is supposed to move from it temporarily
only upon rare occasions. When he is obliged to change his
residence, as when the palace is burned down, he occupies
apartments in some one of the many temples in the neighborhood. Any display of splendor in building is reserved
for the Shiogoon, who has several palaces of great size and
strength, as at Miako, Osaka, Fusimi, Yedo, Kofoo, Soonpoo,
all of which are laid out on the plan of forts, and built with
a view to defense from military attacks.

It has been stated, and often repeated, that the Emperor
of Japan sits on a throne all day without moving his hands,
or even his eyes; that he is treated as a god, and that his
subjects believe that the empire totters if he is unsteady.
These are the exaggerations of the lower classes. There
is no doubt that he is treated with the greatest reverence
and respect—that he is, as it were, an ideal abstraction, a
thing apart, necessary to the empire—that he is the Lord's
anointed, and not to be touched, and that no subject, however great he may be, or however firmly he may have
grasped the power of the empire in the convulsions of a
revolutionary period, may contemplate placing himself upon
that seat; and we shall find that two of the greatest men
who rose to the highest power did not dare to take such a
step, though one, and perhaps both, proposed it to himself,
and broached the idea to his followers. Though Nobunanga

set up a representation of himself to be worshiped, he did not set aside the Emperor; and though Taikosama proposed to depose the Emperor, his followers would not allow it, or at least dissuaded him from making the attempt. Still the Emperor is not altogether looked upon as the spiritual being he is generally represented in modern books. Indeed, in the first periods of the history of the country the head of the empire was the commander, the leader of the army. Zinmu led his army to victory; and long after him the Empress Jinku Kogoo led her army into Corea. Her son Osin, better known by his posthumous title of Hatchimang, was at the head of his army. But where there is no enemy to fight, the post of commander-in-chief soon falls into abeyance. Japan has long been in this position—of having no enemy to watch or to attack. Such a position entails, almost of necessity, the creation of a duality or double power. The weak condition to which the imperial court descended, after it had been denuded of its power, and after the command of its armies had fallen from the hands of scions of the blood-royal into those of other families, was followed by convulsions, civil wars, and bloodshed, till the people returned to a state of ignorance, and the fields to barrenness; but this seems only a consequence of having no enemy, no near neighbor with whom, by a process of constant watching and battling, as in Europe, the sinews of a nation are strengthened, and national feeling is concentrated into a unity.

The annals of the emperors show that, for long after the time of Zinmu, his successors took an active part in the politics, the wars, and the intrigues of the state. It is not a matter of wonder that the hands which held the scepter should have become feeble during the fierce civil wars which raged in the sixteenth century. The country would seem to have been driven by necessity to have two emperors—or, at least, two opposing interests; and when the hereditary commander-in-chief had in turn become a nonentity, one adventurer after another started up—first, Nobunanga; secondly, Taikosama; thirdly, Iyeyas, all able men. The first

battled with the Buddhist priesthood, the second turned his
arms against Corea, the third, the ablest of all, devised that
dual system of seemingly divided empire, by which the power
of the executive remained in the hands of the Shiogoon at
Yedo, while the source or fountain of honors remained with
the Emperor in Miako.   The configuration of the islands prevents their being cut into two empires; it remained for Iyeyas
to devise a dual system by which peace has been preserved
in a remarkable way for two hundred and fifty years.

   As to the titles by which the Emperor is known, these are
drawn in most part from the Chinese, and denote, in language suited to Oriental ideas, the illustrious position which
he holds.   The names express the idea that he reigns by
divine right.   The oldest of these titles seems to be Mikoto.
This is a Japanese word meaning "venerable," and translated into Chinese, "tsun."   The word Mikado is more commonly used now, and is translated by the Chinese "Ti," or
emperor.   The word "O" or "Wo" is the Chinese "Wang,"
emperor; and the word "ten," or heaven, is commonly
added—"Ten wo," the heavenly ruler; or the combination
"Owo," or "Oho-wo," meaning the great ruler, in which
sense "Dai-wo" is also used.   "Tenshi" is the "tien-tsi" of
China, the son of heaven.   "O-ooji," the great family, is
sometimes applied to the Emperor.   The common people talk
of the Emperor as "Miyako sama," in contradistinction to
"Yedo sama," the Shiogoon, the Lord of Yedo.   "Ooyay-
sama," or the superior lord, is also used.   "Dairi," made
up of two Chinese words signifying the inner court or "the
interior," is equivalent to the word "the court" in English,
and seems to include the residences of the royal families and
higher nobility.   It is, however, sometimes applied to the
Emperor himself, and sometimes to the palace as a building.
The first word, "dai" is written both "great," *ta*, and "inner," *nai*.   The latter seems the more common.   "Gosho"
is a word sometimes applied to the palace, at others to the
Emperor and the government.   The word "in," or "een,"
is a Buddhist word, added to the posthumous name of some

of the deceased emperors instead of "Ten wo." In addition
to these, other names are used, as "Kwo tei," or ruler of the
people, "Chokku," etc.

From the earliest period in the history of Japan, mention
is made of three things which necessarily appertain to the
person who sits upon the throne. They seem to be looked
on as symbols of the imperial power, as palladia of the empire. In one of the treatises upon the Emperor's court it is
said of these mysterious emblems: "In that early time the
heaven-illuminating god arrived at Kashiwabarra, then the
capital, and placed an eight-cubit mirror and a grass-shaving
sword in the palace, on the throne of the Emperor, and these
received such homage as was rendered in the early times.
The efficacy of the god was very great, so that the Emperor,
dwelling with this god (these divine symbols), was, as it
were, equal to a god. Within the palace these things were
laid up, that the divine power might remain wherever these
things were. At that time (two high officers) regulated the
sacrificial rites and ceremonies until the tenth emperor, who,
fearing the sacredness of the divine presence, took these two
efficacious symbols, the sword and the mirror, and put them
away in another place, which was the origin of the idea of
the Emperor sitting like a god in the place of a god."

In this quotation only two things are mentioned—the
sword and the mirror. A third is spoken of sometimes as a
ball of crystal, at others as a seal, "sinji." Klaproth calls
it a ball of greenstone with two small round holes. The
three things go by the name of "Sanjoo no jinji." During
the long and bloody wars between the emperors of the north
and south, in the sixteenth century, the former, who resided
in Miako, and finally established himself on the throne, was
not considered incontestably emperor until he obtained possession of these three sacred symbols. Though the emperor
of the south was hard pressed, and almost a refugee in the
mountains, he kept possession of them, and finally concluded
a truce, delivering them up to his opponent, emperor *de
facto*. On one occasion the three precious jewels were stolen,

and after being kept several months were recovered or sent
back.   On several occasions they have narrowly escaped
destruction by fire, and in the year 1040 A.D. the mirror was
broken by the heat; but the pieces were recognized and
placed together.   Within the last few years (in 1851) they
were again nearly exposed to a similar chance of destruction,
but were saved by Hoongay Hashimoto, who brought them
out at the risk of his life.

In Japan it is usual to perform a ceremony at the time
when the boy assumes the *toga virilis* and becomes a man.
The age at which this takes place is not settled, and seems
to vary from the tenth to the fifteenth year.   The eldest son
of the Emperor undergoes this operation (known as "Gem-
buko"; Ch., "yuen fuh") about the age of ten or eleven,
when he, according to the custom, receives a new name.
His hair is shaved off in the manner usual with men, and he
assumes a dress.   In all families the occasion is an important
one, and in the case of the son of the Emperor, the heir-
apparent, it becomes national.   At the inauguration of the
Emperor (according to Klaproth) his height is measured with
a bamboo, which is deposited in one of the great temples in
the province of Isse until his death, when it is removed to
another, and revered as a spirit.   With the bamboo of the
reigning Emperor are deposited a straw-hat, a grass rain-
mantle, and a spade, emblems of agriculture, held in Japan
as an occupation second only to that of the soldier.

The Emperor is said to have his eyebrows shaved, and to
blacken his teeth every morning, which operation is effected
by a mixture of sulphate of iron and some astringent bark.
The state dresses of the Emperor are generally of very rich
strong silk of a bright green color.   The shape, the color, the
pattern are all fixed, and not left to choice.   His under garments are of white silk, and called "mookoo"; and this is
the part of his dress which he never wears twice.   Besides
being changed every morning, there are other occasions during the day in which necessity demands a change.   These
white silk dresses are the perquisites of one of the servants,

and are sold by him in Miako. The Emperor always uses cold water for bathing. The cups which he uses for his meals are also broken; but when it is remembered that the Chinese and Japanese style of eating requires only one cup, and this perhaps not a very expensive one, the total does not amount to a large sum in the annual budget. He is said to devote his time to business matters, with discussions upon history, laws, and religion. In times past he has taken but little part in the business of the country; but his share in this is every year upon the increase, and he is courted by those who see in what direction political power is tending. The power of conferring titles and rank may have given him an amount of occupation and an acquaintance with mankind which would hardly leave him the nonentity he has generally been described. Twelve days of the month are set apart for conversations and discussions upon the history, laws, and religion of Japan. Such spare time as he has is devoted to the composition of poetry, with music and chess. The Emperor is supposed to move out of his palace and the grounds and gardens adjoining only twice a year—once during spring, and once in autumn—when he goes in a covered car, inclosed by semi-transparent screens of bamboo, drawn by large bullocks, to visit the environs of Miako. This procession is known as "Miyuki" or "Gokowo."

On this state procession the Emperor is accompanied by all the high officers in Miako. He does not always strictly adhere to this rule of seclusion, however. Twenty-five years ago Kokaku was in the practice of walking about the town with his son, afterward Jin-ko, dressed like a common man. The excuse for this was that his palace was being rebuilt, after having been burned down. After the Emperor has abdicated no restrictions are placed upon him.

The Emperor, like the majority of his countrymen, is a vegetarian in his diet, and, in addition, only eats fish. At one time such animal food as venison was considered fit for royalty; but the story goes that the Emperor Ssu-jio heard one evening a doe crying plaintively for her mate. On the succeeding morning he came to the conclusion that some venison for his breakfast was the missing lover; and, ever since, venison has not been included among the dainties of the royal kitchen. In his time the Emperor and all his court began to wear the stiff-starched ample robes still used, and the long "kio" or train, which was introduced to prevent the feet of the retreating courtiers being seen. On leaving the presence of the Emperor, officers walk backward on their knees.

Some writers have alleged that the Emperor is looked upon as a god, and that the people think that he goes in the eleventh month to the meeting of the spirits, the "kami." This meeting is believed by the lower classes in Japan to take place during the eleventh month in the province of Idzumo, at the temple of Oyashiro, which temple is thus honored because the first spirit dwelt there. At this meeting the spirits arrange the sublunary and mundane business of Japan for the subsequent eleven months. The inhabitants of Idzumo call this month "Kami ari tski," or the spirit month. All the other provinces call it "Kami nashi tski," the month without spirits. The Emperor is supposed to be above all the kami or spirits, inasmuch as he can confer honors upon the dead; but he is not looked upon as above the "Tento sama," or Lord of heaven, showing that a lower position is assigned to the kami (or "Shin" of the Chinese) than to the highest deity. But no one of any ordinary education in Japan believes that the Emperor goes to this meeting of spirits; these ideas, like many others similar in China, are only current among the least educated of the people. During this month, when the spirits are so occupied, none of those ceremonies in which their assistance must be invoked, such as marriages, adoptions, etc., take place; no prayers are offered, as the spirits are supposed to be engaged. At this meeting they arrange all the marriages which are to take place during the ensuing year. Each individual in this world, male and female, is supposed to have a thread of existence, "yeng." The spirits take the pairs of threads of those who are to be

joined in martimony and knot them together. So we speak
of marriages being made in heaven while the hymeneal knot
is tied on earth. From this the month is called "Yeng
moosoobi tski"—*i.e.*, Tie-the-knot month.

Abdication from positions of active life is very common
among all ranks in Japan. No position seems to be more
easily renounced than that of the occupation of the throne.
In a country where the heir may have the misfortune to be
brought up in the lap of luxury, and amid sensual excite-
ments and indulgences of every kind, it is not surprising that
the irksomeness of his position should make the holder sigh
to be relieved from it, or that vigor of mind or body is only
to be found in those cases where, the heir-apparent having
been cut off, the successor has been adopted at a late period
of his life, having been reared without the expectation of
subsequent elevation. After the Emperor has abdicated he
is named "Tai sho ten wo"—equivalent to "His most exalted
and sacred Majesty." At the present day, upon his taking
this step, should he devote himself to religion and become
"Fo wo," his head is shaved, and he retires to a monastic
life, and generally occupies the temple Ninaji or Omuro in
the neighborhood of Miako.

The Japanese are unostentatious in their customs, and
in the treatment of their great ones after death are singularly
undemonstrative. Considering that all the rites connected
with the dead are after the Buddhist ritual, and that the
Chinese devote so much money and soil to the tombs and
monuments of their ministers and great men and women,
something of the same veneration might be expected in
Japan. But, on the contrary, the tombs are generally very
small unpretending structures, consisting of a basement,
upon which a single stone is erected of no great size. Such
is the tomb of Yoritomo, the great hero, in the neighborhood
of Kamakura; and such, we are told, are the tombs of the
emperors. They are covered over with a roofing of straw,
to keep before their countrymen and subjects the remembrance of their primeval simplicity.

As to the succession to the throne, the laws or regulations in Japan do not seem to be very decided. The frequent abdication of the ruler gives the opportunity for securing that his successor shall have all the weight and assistance that the predecessor can give to overcome the pretensions of rival claimants. When the death of the Emperor has suddenly left the throne vacant, the eldest son is supposed to be the rightful heir. But when, as frequently has happened, his mind and body have been enfeebled by dissipation, and he has neither wit nor vigor to seize the reins of power, he has too often been supplanted by the ambition of a brother, or a wife of his father. When the Emperor leaves only a daughter, she is married to a member of the four imperial families, and her husband in that case becomes Emperor. In reality, the most powerful party about the court, when any difficulty occurs, puts in and supports the member of the imperial family most favorable to their continuing in power.

The genealogy of the Emperors is considered true and authentic as published in the Red Book of the empire; the pedigree of the Shiogoon is looked upon as made up. The former is to be found fully detailed from native sources in the works of Klaproth and Kæmpfer. The "Oon jo may rang" is the title of a small book giving the pedigrees and crests of the Emperor's family, and of the koongays or nobility. Two crests or coats-of-arms are used by the Emperor —the one, "kiku," for outside imperial government business, like the flower of a chrysanthemum, with sixteen petals; the other, the "kiri," is used for the palace matters personal to the Emperor and his family. No notice seems to be taken of the common assumption of the imperial crest, but no one dares to use the crest of the Shiogoon except by permission.

The following sayings give some idea of the reverence with which the Emperor is spoken of: "Mikado ni ooji nashi," is a saying to express that the Emperor is of no family. "Tenshi foo bo nashi"—"The Emperor has neither father nor mother.'' ''In heaven there is one sun, on earth there is one Emperor,'' is a Confucian saying in accordance with the ideas of the country. ''O wo wa jiu zenn, kami wa ku zenn''—'The power of the Emperor is as ten, that of the gods as nine''; implying that more reverence is due to the Emperor than to the lesser spirits, and that he has more power. ''The Emperor all men respect, the Shiogoon all men fear.'' ''Heaven is his father, earth is his mother, his friends are the sun and moon.'' Such ideas are taken from the Chinese classics.

The Emperor marries one wife, who is the Empress. He is allowed by the laws of the country to take twelve concubines, who are generally the daughters of the poorer nobility. The throne can be, and has frequently been, occupied by a female. The Emperor is supposed to receive, as an allowance from the Shiogoon, 100,000 kobangs, equal to $350,000 per annum. This he receives from the Yedo government, but he probably has a large revenue from land in the ''Go ki nai'' or ''Go ka koku,'' or five provinces. He is said to complain of the duties from foreign trade not being paid into his treasury, inasmuch as when the trade was conducted formerly by the Portuguese at Sakkye, the Emperor received the duties; but as Yokuhama is out of the Gokinai, the Shiogoon prefers that the duties should flow to Yedo. These five provinces are frequently spoken of by the writers of the sixteenth century as the Tensee—heavenly or sacred soil. They are Yamashiro, Yamato, Setsu, Kaawdsio, and Idzumi. The whole empire is spoken of, as in China, as all under heaven—''Tenka.''

Two officers in the Emperor's palace are appointed from Yedo—two Hattamoto, or inferior barons—to superintend the disbursement of money, and to keep accounts of the money paid by the Shiogoon's government. These men have fifty soldiers under them. Under them are nine ''Toritsungi,'' generally men of some rank and position.

The Emperor's own private establishment consists of the following officers:

1. Makanye Kashira, generally a Hattamoto, who keeps the accounts of the imperial table and pays the money.

2. Kye mon tskye, called "Kimsakye," two Hattamoto, who go to buy the provisions for the palace.

3. Go zembang, six men, whose business is to examine the Emperor's food.

4. Shuri siki, five men, to look after the buildings; generally Miako men of old families.

5. Makanye kata, six men, whose duty is to say what, and how much, is to be purchased for the palace.

6. Gim miakoo and Itamoto—of the former three, of the latter seventeen—head cooks and ordinary cooks.

7. Kangay bang, keepers of the keys, seven men.

8. Sosha bang, messengers.

9. Tskye bang or Kashira, three men, lower messengers.

These are all given in the official list as the ordinary household in daily attendance on the emperor.

After his death an honorific title is given to the deceased Emperor, by which he is subsequently known in history.

THE SHI SINWO, OR FOUR IMPERIAL FAMILIES

The "Shi sinwo" ("sz tsan wang") are "four imperial relatives," or royal families of Japan. This name denotes four families of imperial descent set apart, with allotted residences and revenues, as supporters to the imperial family. The families are cadets of the royal line descended from junior branches. From among the members of these four families, in case of failure of male heirs of the body, an heir to the throne, or a husband to the Princess Imperial, is to be sought.

In Japan all ranks are under laws more or less strict, and from such the imperial family does not escape. The succession to the throne, at all times an object in Eastern countries for daring ambition to aim at, and a fruitful source of revolution and misery to the people, is regulated and guarded in Japan on a basis wide enough to secure a succession, and preserved by such safeguards as to put it out of the power of collaterals to hope for success from intriguing ambition. One of these safeguards is supposed to be in the Emperor's being allowed to take twelve concubines over and above his lawful wife, the Empress. These are generally daughters of men of high rank about the court, and the son of any one of them, if there is no son by the Empress, may succeed. If there be a daughter, she marries one of the members of these four families, and he becomes Emperor. Jinko, the father of the late Emperor, succeeded in this way. His father, Kokaku, was a member of the royal Kunnin family, and married the only daughter of the Emperor, and so became Emperor. He had a concubine, the daughter of Koongay Kwadjooji. The wife and the concubine had each one son. Satchay no mia was the son of the wife, and heir-apparent to the throne. But the concubine was a fierce, jealous woman, and determined that her son should succeed, and she poisoned Satchay. It was the duty of the Shiogoon's envoy, Sakkye, to inquire into the reports that were circulating; and having done so, he discovered the truth, and put the concubine into confinement. But, though the Emperor was much distressed, he loved her too well and insisted on her being released. The government at Yedo heard of what had happened, and required the envoy to give his reasons for releasing her, when she had committed so heinous a crime. He committed suicide. Her son, Jinko, it is said, always paid the Empress the greatest respect, and would never see his own mother afterward.

But even with this wide matrimonial basis allowed to the Emperor, there may be a failure of heirs direct. These four families are therefore established as a further safeguard to the succession.

They take their names from collateral branches of the imperial house, being originally the families of younger sons of previous Emperors. At present there are only two families of Sinwo, two having become extinct by failure of heirs. They are, however, only dormant, as it is a part of the policy of the state that these families should be in existence, and it is in the power of the Emperor to put one of his sons into, as it were, the extinct family—that is, to call him by the name and give him the revenues belonging to the house, which revenues have been accruing until the family is re-established.

The four families are called collectively Shi (four) sin (relations) wo (imperial). The sons of these families are called Sinwo O'nkatta, or O'nkatta sama [O'nkatta is used as an address of respect to ladies, and also to Sinwo and high officers in personal attendance on the Emperor], and from these sons a successor to the Emperor may be taken.

The names of the four "families" are—1, Fusimi; 2, Arisungawa; 3, Katsura; 4, Kunnin. Of these the two last are the dormant houses. The revenues of these two houses are managed by factors or agents, and the fourth is said to be very wealthy.

The heads of the two existing families are:

1. Fusimi no mia, who has a nominal revenue of 1,016 koku * of rice; but he has probably twenty or thirty thousand koku. The present man is a Koboong of Jinko the late Emperor.

This "boong" is a voluntary union between two persons, and is quite different from adoption. It is more of the character of a Masonic connection. In the relation of a child he is called Koboong; of a father, Oyaboong; of brothers or sisters, Kiodaiboong: and this connection is a very common tie between two individuals in Japan, as well as in China, to help and assist each other. It runs through all ranks and both sexes. It is a connection which may be as easily severed as it is made, but it is often strictly adhered to. It is

---

* The koku, or "stone," contains 5.13 bushels; is the measure by which revenue is estimated; is the standard value of the country; and is generally considered equivalent to one gold kobang. The only invariable standard of value in the world is the average amount of food that will suffice to keep a man in health—a pound varies, the other does not.

generally made by drinking formally out of the same cup, each taking half of the liquor. It may be severed by cutting off the queue, or simply by formally intimating that it is at an end.

2. Arisungawa Nakatskasa no kio, or head of the Central Board. His nominal income is 1,000 koku, but his real revenue is much larger.

3. Katsura; the revenue is 3,006 koku.

4. Kunnin; the revenue is nominally 1,006 koku.

In these families there is generally a sufficient number from among whom to select a successor in case of the death, or what seems more common in Japan, the abdication and retirement, of the Emperor. But, at the same time, the arrangement has its disadvantages. It places a number of men and women of all ages in a very high position, with apparently no occupation for their leisure time. These men might become troublesome in the state by carrying on intrigues for their own advancement and for the gratification of their ambition. Within the last few years much disquietude has been caused by one of the Sinwo engaging in intrigues to upset the reigning Emperor. A means has been arrived at for at once giving these persons income, business, position, and at the same time getting them out of the way.

The Buddhist priesthood was at one time a very powerful element in the country. The number of priests was very great, and the revenues of the monasteries were enormous. By their wealth, and from among their vassals, they were able to keep up a respectable army; and not by their vassals alone—the priests themselves filled the ranks. The different sects built magnificent temples, and these were endowed with ample lands. Immediately before the period of the advent of the Christians in the sixteenth century, the power of the priesthood seems to have reached its highest point. Nobunanga, who at one time was inclined to favor the foreign priests, had always a great jealousy of, and bore a great ill-will to, the Buddhist priesthood. He destroyed their temples, killed their priests, and confiscated their revenues, and thus gave a blow to their power from which they have never recovered, and under which they are withering more and more every day.

In Japan, a man while a priest, after having shaved his head and taken the vows, is supposed to be out of the world, and it is then much easier to keep a certain amount of surveillance over him, and to see that he is attending to his duties, and is not engaged in political intrigues.

Of the larger Buddhist temples of different sects, fourteen are retained as having the largest rev nues; and whenever a male member of the royal family is unprovided for he is put in as head abbot or bishop of one of these temples. They are generally appointed while children, and brought up to the position; and as the revenues of the office have thus time to accumulate, the reverend holder has sufficient for his wants and those of a respectable retinue. They are then called Sinwo Monzekke (Muntsih).

1. The first is Rinnoji Monzekke, or abbot of Rinoji temple. The temple over which he is abbot is To yay zan, in Yedo. The first high-priest put into this was Koboong of Iyeyas, then Shiogoon. The revenue amounts to 13,000 koku of rice. The holder is of the Arisungawa family, and is of the first rank and second degree. He is known as "Kwan rayee no mia" (from the nengo, or date, of his appointment), and Yedo no mia or Ooyay no mia. In 1860 the incumbent was very old, and a boy, Gofutay, of the Fusimi family, was appointed assistant and successor.

2. The second is Ninaji no mia, otherwise called Omuro. The income is 1,502 koku. The incumbent is of the Fusimi family. He is head of the Singong sect, and was appointed to the office in 1843, when four years of age. To this temple the Emperor generally retires should he become a priest after abdication.

3. Dai Kakuji, otherwise called Sanga, is vacant.

4. Mio ho in, at Hiyayzan, a large temple near **Miako**. The Monzekke is of the Kunnin family. He is head of the Tendai sect of Buddhists, and is known as Tendai zass.

5. Sho ngo in no Monzekke is head of the Yamabooshi religion. He is of the Fusimi family, with an income of 1,430 koku. His temple is at Omine Honzan.

6. Sho ko in; vacant, but the revenues are held by No. 5.

7. Say ray in Monzekke: is known as Awata Mia. He is of the Fusimi family. The income is 1,330 koku.

8. Chi wong in Monzekke, of the Arisungawa family. The temple is in Miako, and he is the head of the Jodoshiu sect of Buddhists.

9. Kwajooji is vacant.

10. Itchi jo in Monzekke. The temple is in Narra, and is very old. Held by one of the house of Fusimi.

11. Kaji ee Monzekke, of the Tendai sect. Of the family of Fusimi, with an income of 1,600 koku.

12. Manjo in Monzekke is vacant.

12. Bissa mondo Monzekke is also vacant.

14. Emmang in Monzekke, commonly called Medora, in the province of Owomi, is also vacant.

All these bishoprics, as they may be called, are held, or may be held, by Sinwo or sons of Sinwo.

But as it is in many countries, both European and Eastern, as necessary and as difficult to dispose of the females of high families as the males, they also are in many cases provided for.

There are twenty-four temples or nunneries which are, or may be, under the superintendence of daughters or relatives of the four royal families.

1. Daijoji, in Miako; of this temple a daughter of the Emperor was formerly abbess.

2. Hokio ji.

3. Dan kay in.

4. Ko shio in.

5. Ray gan ji, held by one of the Fusimi family, who has the title of Nio-wo, or Queen of Nuns.

6. Yenshoji, in Narra, the ecclesiastical metropolis of Japan.

7. Rin kinji.

8. Chiu goji and sixteen others of lower class. Many of them are, however, unoccupied; partly, perhaps, from want of ladies of the royal family to fill them, and partly from failure of zeal for the Buddhist religion all over the country.

The laws with reference to the perpetuity of the vows of these priests and priestesses do not seem to be very strict, as we find that, when opportunity offers, the garb is thrown off, the hair is allowed to grow, and he or she mixes again in the world in whatever capacity their worldliness, their ambition, or their sense, has prompted them to desire.

It has been stated that the Emperor, as the fountain of honor, reserves to himself the sole right of conferring titles and rank. This reservation throws great political power into his hands, the acquisition of title and rank being, with rare exceptions, an object of the highest ambition to a Japanese. The amount of business connected with this power is great, and may be said to have been for many years the sole occupation for the Miako court. A special office and officers are set apart within the palace inclosure for carrying on the correspondence and settling disputes connected with the department.

RANKS OF MEN IN JAPAN

Every individual in Japan, whether noble, priest or peasant, is supposed to know the rank in which he stands relatively to those about him. The marks of respect to superiors—which in degree appear excessive to Western nations—are graduated from a trifling acknowledgment to the most absolute prostration. When two men or women meet, the first point to be ascertained seems to be, which of the two is to make the acknowledgment of the social position of the other. This state of things is supported by law as well as custom, and more particularly by the permission given to a two-sworded man, in case of his feeling himself insulted, to take the law into his own hands. What would be irksome to us seems to become easy and a matter of course in Japan; and though, no doubt, the assumption of position is often the source of brawls and fights, the system works more smoothly than might have been expected.

The custom of wearing two swords was introduced in the sixteenth century. The old Miako nobility do not adopt the custom—civilian Koongays wearing no sword, and military only one as of old. All Japan is divided into two classes: those who have a right to wear two swords, the "Nihon sashi shto" or "two-sworded man," called also "Yashiki shto" or castle retainers; and those who have no such right, the "Matchi shto" or street man (otherwise called Chonin). The latter class comprises merchants, artisans, workmen, etc., who work at some trade, but possess no ground; and also Hiaksho, farmers who do not trade, but farm or rent ground. In some cases individuals of these classes can wear two swords. The "swordless man" in Yedo pays rent for his ground, house and shop. The "two-sworded man" pays no rent and no taxes, because he is not allowed to trade. In Yedo, parts of the town are known as "Matchi tsuchee," street ground, and other parts as "Yashiki tsuchee," castle ground. Persons living on the former can open shops and trade; in the latter this is not allowed. This last two-sworded class is known as "Samurai" (Ch. Sz), which may be translated "an officer and a gentleman," and is an important distinction conferring valuable rights and privileges at the expense of the rest of the community.

This division of the people into two classes is a measure issuing from the executive at Yedo, the Shiogoon's government, rather than from Miako. The Samurai class may be said to include the Koongays, the Daimios, the "Jiki sang," who are the officers and sub-officers in the service of the Shiogoon; the Byshing—*i.e.*, officers in the service of Daimios; and such Chonin as are doing duty as officers in some large town, such as Osaka or Miako, and are always spoken of in connection with the city—as Osaka chonin, for instance. The term "Samurai" is applied more particularly to all below the fifth rank, military or civilians who are not merchants or artisans. There are others who have the right to wear two swords, such as Goshi, large farmers or landed proprietors whose ancestors were Daimios. These are strongest in the provinces of Kahi, Etsjiu and Dewa, some being very wealthy—as Homma in Dewa, and Hanagura in Etsjiu. The Samurai who have the right to wear two swords assume the right of giving two swords to their attendants; and this right, once assumed, is not readily relinquished, seeing that a two-sworded man has the privilege of traveling at a much cheaper rate than other members of society, pays no tolls or taxes, and not infrequently pays nothing for food and lodging, their power being so great that they are feared, if not in actual attendance upon some superior. These men are frequently dismissed by, or voluntarily leave the service of, their Daimio or master; but as those who are so dismissed are often brawlers, they retain their swords, and gain a living by their becoming a terror to quiet people. They are said to be "floating," without any attachment, like straws on a stream, and are thence called "Ronin" or "floating-man." These men are most imperious and domineering toward others not having the same privileges as themselves, and this power compels wealthy traders and others to enroll themselves in the retinue of some Daimio, or take some other roundabout mode to prevent themselves being insulted. This is not the character of every Ronin, many of whom are respectable members of society, holding their privileges in abeyance until called upon to give feudal service by some superior.

The people of Japan are divided generally into the following classes:

1. Koongays, or Miako nobility.
2. Daimios, or Yedo nobility.
3. Hattamoto—Lower Daimio class.
4. Hiaksho—Farmers and landed proprietors without rank or title.
5. Shokonin—Artisans, carpenters, etc.
6. Akindo—Merchants.
7. Kweiamono—Actors, beggars, etc.

8. Yayta—Tanners, shoemakers, leather workers, skinners.

Beneath these are prostitutes, and all connected with them, who are considered beasts, or on a level with them.

In opposition to the name of "Koongay" (Kung kia), "exalted house," the nobility of Miako, the Daimios and officers of the Shiogoon's court, are called "Jee ngay" (Ti hia), meaning persons low, on a level with the ground, the latter not being recognized by the Emperor as feudal lords further than as servants of his servant, "Tokungawa"—*i.e.* the Shiogoon.

The Japanese titles and classification of officers have been taken generally from China. As in China, all the officers honored with titles by the Emperor, or performing duties about the court, are divided into classes or ranks. In China the Mandarins are divided into nine classes. Each of these classes is again sub-divided into a first and secondary division. The same division and sub-division are found in Japan, with this difference, that there are six classes, each sub-divided into four ranks. The word used for rank is I, otherwise called Kurai. This is the Chinese word Wai. The six ranks in order are, Itchi-i, Ni-i, Sanm-i, Shi-i, Go-i and Roko-i. Each of these is divided according to the Chinese classification into two, the "shio" (or "jio") and the "jiu," corresponding to the "ching" and the "tsung." These are sub-divided again into two—upper and lower— "jio" and "gay," the Chinese "shang" and "hia." The full description of men of the first and second ranks would be respectively "Jo itchi-i no jio" and "Jo itchi-i no gay" —the "no" meaning "of." The minor divisions "jio" and "gay" are not much used in the higher ranks until the highest is reached, an honor now reserved only for the dead. Indeed, all below Shi-i, or the fourth grade, are commonly known now by a general name, "Sho dai boo" ("Chu ta fu"). The higher classes wear at court distinguishing dresses and colors, or devices upon black dresses, and they are entitled in virtue of their rank to have a spear carried before them when moving about officially. Officers are presented at court, both at Miako and Yedo, according to their rank, not according to the importance of their office. Few of the Daimios are higher than the first sub-division of the fourth rank. The Shiogoon himself is elevated from one rank to another by the favor of the Emperor, at times not rising higher than the first sub-division of the second class. To attain such rank at the imperial court is the great object of ambition in Japan, and next in importance is the acquisition of a title conferred by the Emperor. But as some titles, though not recognized at court, are used by the Daimios as holding territory under the Shiogoon, there is a distinction observed between the two. The holders of titles conferred by the Emperor are known as "Kio kwang" (King kwan) or imperial officers, while the Daimios are known from their territorial appellations as "Kooni kami" (Kwoh shau), or keepers of the provinces. An imperial title in the address is always placed before the territorial title.

THE KOONGAY

After the Emperor and royal families, the first in rank in the state are the Koongays. Until further light be thrown upon Japanese history, the remote origin of this class will be somewhat obscure, some tracing their pedigree back upward of 1,500 years. Many of the Koongays are descendants of younger sons and cadets of the imperial family branching off at former periods, while the surnames of some of the other families are as old as historic records. In all probability their forefathers came over to Japan at the time of its invasion and conquest by Zinmu, and being the assistants, brothers in arms, and mainstays of his throne and power, the soil about the center of the empire was divided among them, and they thenceforward became the nobility of the court of the Emperor. So long as the empire was under one emperor who ruled vigorously, this aristocracy seems to have existed in the central provinces as feudal lords, much in the same way as the Daimios of the present day. But when the vigor of rule relaxed, and power fell into the hands of a commander-in-chief, or mayor of the palace, with uncertainty in the rulers, there followed division in the aristocracy. Previous to the beginning of the fifteenth century, the western part of the empire was all that was known to any who could throw light upon its position by writing. The large tract of country to the north and northeast of Yedo, called the obscure or unpenetrated way, was comparatively unknown and uninhabited, and was divided into four or five large territories, under princes who seldom heard of, and more rarely visited, the court at Miako. The dissensions and struggles for power between the two powerful families of Heji and Genji gave rise to a nearly continual state of civil war for upward of 200 years. During the Onin war families were destroyed, territories were lost, might was everywhere right, and though several of the oldest and noblest families among the Koongays retained their honors and titles and places about the court, they lost their property, and many have ever since remained at the lowest ebb of poverty.

Those few noble families which had previously to this period of civil war divided among themselves the places and titles of the court, were denuded of their splendor; but their representatives continued to struggle on with poverty, proud in the possession of an ancient lineage, and of their names being enrolled as nobles in the Great Book of the empire. These are the Koongays of the present day. They are not all in this state of poverty, many of them being well off, and some very wealthy; but others are very poor, and eke out the scanty subsistence given them by the Emperor by painting, basket-making, and other manual employments, affording, in their persons, their poverty, and their pretensions, ample scope for the pen of the native caricaturist. The names, history, and pedigree of the Koongays are enrolled in the Great Book of the empire, the equivalent to the Heralds' Office or Patent Office of England. A book, the

"Koongay no Kayzu," or Pedigree of the Koongays, is printed in Japan, giving all these particulars, and is generally by the natives considered authentic. The names of Daimios (as such) are not so enrolled; they have no patents of nobility from the Emperor, and the "Hang campu," giving the pedigree and history of the families of Daimios, is regarded as anything but authentic, and is looked upon as in many cases made up by individuals to conceal the origin of the family.

The Koongay class includes all the illustrious families of Japan. In common estimation the Daimios are far below this class; and even the Shiogoon, though he is feared as the head of the executive, is. looked upon as comparatively a parvenu.

The class is divided into two, an older or higher, the "Koongio," and a lower, or more recently created, "Ten jio bito" (Tien shang jin). "Koongio" (Kung hiang) is a name which includes all the officers of the first, second and third ranks. All of the fourth rank and below are called "So shing," in which are included "Ten jio bito," "Sho diabu," and "Samurai." The appellation "Mayka" (ming kia) seems to denote that the bearer is a civilian. All the higher offices in the state are filled by Koongays, but only five families are eligible to fill the highest. These five families are known as the "Go sek kay" (Wu ship kia), or "Shippay kay," or "Sessio no eeyay," helper of emperor—lit., to take the handle—"the five assisting families." They are: 1, Konoyay; 2, Koojio; 3, Nijio; 4, Itchijio; 5, Takatskasa. If the highest offices under the Emperor (as those of "Dai jio dai jin," "Kwanbakku," or "Sessio") be vacant, no one who is not of one of these five families is eligible to fill such office.

In regard to rank at court, the Koongays generally stand in the lower class of the first, or in the second or third rank. They are known at Miako by their dress. For a long time past they have had little power, and were of little importance; but since the commencement of foreign relations the political tide has rather flowed toward Miako, and from Yedo, and they have increased in political power as well as in wealth, as the Daimios and office-seekers of Yedo endeavor to obtain the objects of their ambition through the influence of their poorer brethren in Miako. The poverty of most of the class prevents them entering upon an enervating life of dissipation, which too often saps the vigor of the constitution of the Daimios, and they are able to take a part in the discussion of political subjects. Many of them fill the more or less nominal offices of government in one of the eight great boards of the empire; and this amount of occupation, together with writing imaginative pieces, keeps their minds in a sufficient state of activity.

In addition to the distinctions of rank in Japan, there is also the distinction into families or clans, great importance being attached to a family name. The feuds between rival families have in past times rent the empire to pieces. The Emperor is said to have no name; but some of the cadets, offshoots from the imperial line, have founded lines of their own, taking root and flourishing as distinct families. In this way have been derived the lines known as the "Say wa Genji," the "Ooda Genji," and the "Murakami Genji." These are descendants of younger sons of emperors of these names. But among all the families of Japan, the first place is held by that of Fusiwara, in length of pedigree, in the honors held in past ages, and in the present position of the family. During every period in the annals of the empire, members of this family have filled the highest offices, civil and military, of the state. But it has, perhaps, shone more in civil employment than in military. The "five families" of the Sekkay mentioned above belong to the clan Fusiwara. Other families have risen at different times to the highest pinnacle attainable by subjects, but after a time they have gradually fallen back into comparative obscurity. Ninety-five of the Koongays call themselves of the clan Fusiwara. In very remote periods the family of Nakatomi seems to have held the highest rank, absorbing by its members, at one

3

time, all the offices of religion. Only one Koongay family, Fusinami, now represents this old clan. In point of antiquity, if not of luster of name, the Sungawara family, commonly called Kwang kay, ranks only second to Fusiwara. The members of this family are rarely found in military employment, generally filling the offices of teachers or lecturers on history or religion.

The "Gen kay," otherwise called "Minnamoto," are more illustrious as military men. Seventeen families of the Koongays belong to this clan. All the Minnamoto Koongays are descended from younger sons of former emperors. One of these, the "Say wa" Minnamoto, assert that their line is the same as that of the present imperial dynasty of China, who are descendants of the Emperor Say wa, or "Tsing wa," whence the "Tsing" or "Ta Tsing" family, which emigrated from the north of Japan several centuries ago.

The Taira, or He kay, the great opponent of the Gen kay (otherwise known as Heji and Genji) during many years of civil war, includes five familes.

Nishika koji, of the Tanba clan, is said to represent one of the emperors of China of the Eastern Han dynasty, who was driven from China and took refuge in Japan.

A new creation of Koongays is very rare. About 1830, Kitta koji (of the clan Oway), whose family for three generations had filled the office of Kurodo, was elevated to the rank.

The names of Koongays are, in many cases, derived from the street or place where they originally lived, as Itchi jio, No. 1 Street.

There are in all 137 Koongays.

There is assigned to each Koongay an annual revenue calculated in koku of rice. This, in most cases, implies so much ground held of the Emperor. The total sum divided among these noble families does not amount to that allowed to a third-rate Daimio. But though several of these nobles are miserably poor, and have probably little to live upon besides the rice which is given them by the Emperor, there are some among them who have other sources of wealth. In old times the Koongays possessed large landed property; but in the wars of the He kay and Gen kay, Kiomori, the leader of the former, despoiled them, and the divided portions of these lands were seized by whoever had the power. Some still retain extensive landed property, but the majority have fixed salaries, which they receive at the Emperor's hands. Residing near the court, and often connected with the Emperor and high officers by marriage, the poorest may possess some influence, and this frequently contributes to swell their incomes. This influence is courted by the Daimios at a distance, who, aspiring to rank or titles, purchase the assistance and influence of the Koongays, such as it may be, by solid presents. The higher class, who really have much power, in this way become very rich. The little land which belongs to them may, by taxes, duties, or customs, produce much more than the exact number of koku of the original calculation. Thus the seaport town of Itami stands on the ground of Konoyay dono, and he levies a tax upon the exports and imports; and, in addition to the customs, he receives the duties upon all the saki or spirit distilled between the towns of Hiogo and Osaka, and this is the great distilling district for the whole country. Having acquired money, he lends it out at Oriental rates of interest to the Daimios, who are too often in need of ready money, so that he is a very wealthy man. The Koongays have not the large expenses which drain the purses of the Daimios; having comparatively few retainers, they are not obliged to make the ostentatious display which brings the Daimios to poverty; nor have they the same number of establishments to keep up at different places. All this contributes to make the upper class of Koongays, already powerful by rank, position and influence, substantial in their independence. The poorer class eke out their existence in a variety of ways, honorable enough, but not contributing much in the way of worldly wealth. Assukayee teaches playing at "mari," a sort of football, which is a fashionable game at court, and which is probably derived from the Chinese shuttlecock, varied according to the difference in the style of boots and shoes. In playing at this game in Miako, the court turns out in gorgeous dresses. Jimio-in and others teach writing. Sono dono teaches the science of dwarfing trees, and the art of arranging flowers in flower-holders. At both of these the Japanese excel. In the former they display a wonderful power over nature, and in the latter a highly cultivated taste. A fir-tree has been seen in perfect vigor, bearing a cone, and eight years old, and only an inch in height. Rayzay teaches poetry and composition. Sijio dono teaches the art of dressing dinners and cookery, which is considered in Japan the occupation of a gentleman. When an artist has prepared a dinner, and laid it out, it is common for the public to go to see it as a work of art. Yamashima and Takakura superintend and teach the art of dressing and of etiquette. Tsutchi Mikado teaches and explains what is known in China as the "Ta kih," the ultimate cause of things, the immaterial principle of the Chinese philosophers, as contained in and exemplified by a series of diagrams; and, as an astrologer, divines into futurity. Others paint, and sell their works of art, or teach painting. The poorer individuals who receive rice also get the Emperor's cast-off outer garments. Their daughters are in the habit of going to the families of the Daimios as governesses (and are commonly known by the name of "jorosama"), to teach the young ladies and gentlemen the customs and language of the court. Of these ladies there are generally one or more at the residence of the Shiogoon in Yedo. They sometimes act in the capacity of spies as well as of governesses; and, having much influence, they are sometimes feared as *censores morum.*

Under the five Go sekkay nearly all the Koongays are classed into five divisions; and in his relation to his head, each Koongay is known as "Monrio" or "Sorio"—one division under each of the five.

If any of those in a position of Monrio have any business

with the court, such must be dispatched through his head, who then communicates with the Emperor.

It has been shown that the Sin wo and sons of the imperial families are provided for by absorption into the higher offices of the priesthood, and to fill the seats in, and receive the revenues of, the richer abbeys and monasteries. In a similar way the sons of the Go sekkay and higher Koongays (known as Kindatchi) are provided for. There are six richly-endowed temples whose revenues are respectively enjoyed by a member of one of these families. These men are known by the name of "Sekkay Monzekke."

If a Daimio happens to meet the norimono or sedan-chair of a Koongay upon the highroad, he must wait with all his retinue till the latter shall have passed. Koongays usually blacken their teeth and shave the eyebrows, and do not follow the usual custom in shaving the head. Civilians do not carry a sword; military carry one called "tatchi." In ordinary times a Koongay is not likely to be put to death, however great may be his crimes; but he may be ordered to shave his head and enter a monastery, or may be confined to a room in his own house.

It is not easy to ascertain what was the exact position of the Koongays in the times before the great civil wars of the thirteenth and following centuries. The empire seems to have been divided at that time very much as it is now, into one large central court at the metropolis, with a number of smaller courts in the provinces, each ruled by its lord, king, Daimio, or dynasta, as they have been called. The court of the Emperor always remained at Miako. There he was surrounded by the members of the old families, among whom he distributed honors. There was to be seen a supposed prefect form of government, the history of which is written in the "Annals." Probably in each of the lesser courts—such, for instance, as that of Satsuma, Mowori, and other wealthy lords—the same form of government was carried on in a miniature scale; and, so far as can be gathered from history and native historical maps, the extensive territories belong-

ing to these lords were always under the entire rule each of
its own master, and acknowledging no right in the central
court (so long as that master did not in any way come into
collision with the general good of the empire) to interfere
in any way with what passed within these territories. The
imperial court, in its executive form, was confined to the
provinces around Miako—the Gokinai. The annals of the
Emperors are devoted in the main to the occurrences which
took place within these provinces, detailing the names and
families, the titles, ranks, and history of the men who in
that court were looked upon as great and eminent. Of
these, the more prominent were brought forward and advanced by the Emperor in hereditary rank and title above
their fellows—these were the Koongays; while the territorial
lords were only known by their family names, or the name
of the provinces over which they ruled, and were only expected to come once a year to Miako, in order to pay their
respects to the Emperor. It is not to be expected but that
differences would arise among these territorial lords, some
more or less powerful; ambition and lust of wealth or power
would soon find a cause for a quarrel, and this would light
up a civil war. In such cases, the Emperor and the officers
of the imperial court were looked to as the arbiters or um-
pires, and acquired and retained so firm a position in the
machinery of the State and in the minds of the people as to
withstand all the shocks which have at different times so
frequently and rudely put one down and set up another of
these provincial powers.

CHAPTER II

THE EIGHT BOARDS OF GOVERNMENT

HAVING given above a sketch of the ranks eligible in old times to fill the offices of government, a step will be gained by obtaining some insight into the means by which that government was carried on. The arrangements are of very ancient date, and seem to have been more or less in actual use until the separation of the empire into two at the end of the sixteenth century. At that time the executive department of the empire was entirely removed to Yedo, but the shadow or the skeleton of the defunct body was allowed to remain in Miako. The offices which had of old conferred power, and demanded exertion in fulfilling the duties, were now only empty names—honorific appellations; the power of conferring these nominal offices being all that remained to the Emperor of his former greatness. Still the retention of the power has not been without its use. Though the actual power has been in the hands of the Shiogoon, the hopes of the people and of the Emperor have ever turned toward its ultimate re-establishment at Miako, in a machinery all ready at any moment to take up the duties of government.

At the period when the government of Japan was settled, many of the institutions of China seemed to have been copied or transferred by the founders of the empire. This must have occurred at a very early period in its history. While the original model has been followed, modifications have from time to time been introduced to meet the varying exigencies of the country. But perhaps nothing points more strongly to a Chinese origin for the ruling ranks of Japan than the early adoption of this form of government. As in China six boards are found at Pekin, so in Japan eight boards are found at Miako. The names of these boards or departments, the titles of the officials, the ranks of the subordinate officers, are all found under Chinese names.

Klaproth has given in his "Annals of the Emperors" a sketch of these eight boards, with the offices under each. It is probably taken from the "Shoku gen sho," a little work written in the year 1340 by Kitta Batake Chikafusa, and in use at the present day as a concise account of the government of Japan.

The study of such a subject is rather dry and uninteresting, but it is necessary for any one who wishes to make himself acquainted with Japanese history, either of the past or of the present day, to read and understand this book. What here follows is only a rough sketch with a little further filling in. In what may be called the preface to the "Shoku gen sho"—a slight historical introduction—the author says: "We gather from old records, that in the time of Sui ko (the first Empress), in the twelfth year of her reign, A.D. 605, Sho toku, being prime minister, settled twelve grades of officers. Afterward, the Emperor Kwo toku, in the fifth year of his reign (A.D. 650), divided the country into eight provinces (or divided the government into eight departments), and definitely fixed the offices. Subsequently, in the first year of the Emperor Mun moo (A.D. 697), Fusiwara no tan kaiko Kamatariko (canonized as Kassunga dia mio jin) was appointed great minister, and by him laws were made and the officers and nobles were appointed. At one time the numbers were greatly diminished, and again they were increased, and fresh officers, 'uncommissioned,' got employment. But the ministers, the 'Nai dai jin' and the 'Chiu nagoon,' existed before the first year of Mun moo. But authentic records of that period do not remain in existence at the present time. In old times there was a separate office of religion known as the 'Jin ngi kwang' or 'Kami no tskasa,' answering to the 'Ta chang sz' in China. The two officers who superintended the rites in worship of the gods were above all other officers. This was the pristine custom in the kingdom of spirits (Japan), arising from the reverence paid to the gods of heaven and the spirits of earth.

"In the earliest times the Emperor Zinmu established the capital within the bounds of the province of Yamato, at Kashiwarra. At that time, in the beginning, Ten shio dai shin (the heaven-illuminating spirit) came down and placed three things—a ball or seal, an eight-cubit mirror, and a grass-shaving sword—in the palace, on the throne of the Emperor, which received homage such as was offered in early times. The efficacy of the spirit was great, so that the Emperor dwelling with the spirit was, as it were, equal to a god. Within the palace these three emblems were placed in safety, that it might be said that where these are there is divine power. At this time two high officers, 'Ama no koya ne no mikoto' and 'Ama no tane ko mikoto,' regulated the sacrificial rites and court ceremonies, until the time of the Emperor Soui-zin (97–30 B.C.), who, fearing the majesty of the divinity, took away these three efficacious symbols, the sword and the seal and the mirror, and put them elsewhere (*i.e.*, in a palace he built at Miako); which was the origin of the idea of the Emperor's sitting like a god in the place of a god.

"In the reign of Swee nin (A.D. 29–70) the great spirit Tenshio, or Ten shio dai jin, descended upon the province of Isse (when the Emperor measured and divided that province), and that Emperor built and endowed the temple or yashiro of Isse. This is the most sacred temple in the empire.

"At that time the O nakatomi family were hereditary officers of religion, and of rites of worship.

"After the officers of state had been appointed, the officers of the Jin ngi kwang, or spiritual department, were settled. Originally the Jin ngi kwang was the highest department of all. The temple built by the Emperor at Isse had separate officers of worship, and as to duties, both regulated worship; the offices were similar in their origin and character, but the

department of religion was of the highest importance. Therefore, in the kingdom of spirits (*i.e.*, Japan) these officers of
religion ranked above all other officers. At that time a man
of the fourth rank could be an officer of religion, but now it
is confined to the second and third ranks. Formerly, of old,
any one was considered capable of filling the office, Nakatomi or other; but in the middle ages, since the time of the
Emperor Kwa sann, it became hereditary in the family of
his son, and no other family could fill the office; and it has
since been filled by the members of the royal family.

"Originally the name Nakatomi designated an office.
When one of the holders was made Oodai jin, he added O
(great) to his title; but his descendants did not use the title,
therefore they are simply called Nakatomi."

Such is the introduction to the "Book of the Government
of the Empire." What follows is the names of the different
offices, and ranks of officers, whether civil or military, stating what rank is eligible to hold each office, what offices can
be held in conjunction by the same person, together with the
Chinese equivalent of each title wherever it can be given.

Every office in Japan is divided into four—a head and
three subordinates. The head is called by various titles,
Kio, Kami, Tayu, Daiboo, etc. The highest subordinate is
called Skay or Ske—in Chinese, Tsu—to assist or help; or
Kai, to attend upon; also Tso, to assist: all three characters
are used. The next is Jo—Chinese, Shing, to assist—deputy.
The clerks are called Sakkan—Chinese, Shuh—attached to
as a tail, dependent on. Each of these may be subdivided
into great and small, Dai and Sho; and further, frequently
into sa and oo—*i.e.*, right and left. Besides these official
grades, the title of Gong, or Gonno, is found. This seems
to be an honorific title, and is generally conferred by the
Emperor upon Koongays and persons about his own court.
It seems to mean honorary substitute or deputy, and is added
or prefixed to another title. This is the word K'ün in Chinese, with the meaning of power, balance, temporary substitute.

With these explanations it may be possible to understand the titles and descriptions of offices and officers given in the Shoku gen sho.

The first or highest office was that of religion, or board of rites, the Jin ngi kwang (shin k'i kwan), the office of the worship of spirits. This office, at first entirely for regulation of the Sinto religion, was rendered unnecessary by the introduction of Buddhism, and has been practically done away with—the higher titles and larger emoluments being absorbed by the younger sons of royal families, while the working part of the board has been joined with the highest board, Dai jo gwang.

The Dai jo gwang, or Matsuri koto tskasa, is the great office of government. This is the "cabinet," and is over and superintends the eight boards and the affairs of the whole empire. The chief of the department is the Dai jo dai jin—the great minister of the whole government. He is also called Sho koku. This office is not always filled up. The holder is in settled times nearly invariably one of the "five families." This is the highest office in the state, and was commenced by the Emperor Ten shi, who conferred it on his son. When this office is vacant, the next in rank, the Sa dai jin (left great minister) is highest official in point of rank. The highest subject generally receives at the Emperor's hands the title of Kwanbakku, first given A.D. 880. The Kwanbakku is always near the Emperor's person, and not engaged so much as others on public business. If the sovereign be a minor or a female, a regent is appointed, who is naturally the most powerful subject in the empire. He is named Sessio, or Setz jio, helper of the government. When such a regent is appointed for a young Empress, it is generally intended that he is to marry her, and become Emperor. The Kwanbakku was, in old times, called Omurazi. He is frequently spoken of as Denga sama. The Dai jo dai jin is commonly known as Sho koku, the Sa dai jin as Sa foo sama, Oo dai jin as Eoo foo sama, Nai dai dai jin as Nai or Dai foo sama. There may be only one of the three titles,

Dai jio dai jin, Kwanbakku, or Sessio, conferred at a time; but whoever holds it is known to be the highest official, and he may have all three titles at the same time. The office of Dai jio dai jin has frequently remained vacant for length-ened periods.

In the Dai jio gwang there are four ministers. Dai jin means great minister, and the prefix of Sa is left, of Oo is right. In Japan the left generally takes precedence. And these four stand in this relation to one another. The three first are known as the "Sanko," or three exalted ones. There is another officer, that of Nai dai jin, inner or mid-dle great minister. This office is filled up if there be no Dai jio dai jin; but if otherwise it remains in abeyance.

Since 1780 the Shiogoon has generally been elevated to be Oodai jin or Sadai jin.

The next officer below the Oodai jin is the Dai na goon. There are ten of them. They act with the Sanko in the Dai jo gwang office. They seem to be the mouthpieces to and from the board, and in consultation with the board. They are generally Koongays. But some of the highest Daimios are competent for the office, Owarri, Kishiu, and Mito.

The Chiu (or middle) na goon—ten officers of much lower rank than the last—never deliberate with the board, but are consulted after or before. They are generally Koongays.

The Sangi (Ts'an i), also called Sei sho and Gisso (I tsau), is a very important office—eight officers. They are of high rank (above the last), and are chosen for their talent for the office. This seems to be to report upon the proceedings and conclusions of the other officers of the board; to watch and also advise, and sometimes to act as judges. They are both civil and military. If a man has shown himself qualified for this office he may rise to it, though not originally of high rank.

The Sho (or lesser) nagoon are much below the above officers in rank. They are said to help the memories of the principal officers, to put seals to deeds, and carry communi-cations to other boards: they are both military and civil.

Gayki or Kwanmu—five officers who act as secretaries to one of the three officers of the Dai jo ngwang. Divided into great and small, Dai and Sho, gayki; the head man is called Kioo ku mu. The duties consist in writing out the patents and titles conferred by the Mikado. In cases of dispute between high officers, they seem to write out a statement of the case on both sides for the decision of the board. They look after any newly-introduced business, such as introduction of foreigners to the country.

Ben-gwang, seven officers, all Koongay—a higher office than the preceding. Two head men, left and right, Sa and Oo dai ben. This is a very responsible office; all the business of the board passes through the hands of the officers. They superintend and set apart to each of the minor offices their business.

Sa chiu ben and Oo chiu ben, two men.

Sa sho ben and Oo sho ben, two men.

These are subordinates in the office, but men of rank.

Gonno ben. This is an honorific title, giving high rank, but having no business or duties to perform.

The Ben-gwang officers are always in their handsome official dress, and are at once recognizable on the street.

Shi, eight men. Their business is to act as bookkeepers or registrars of the transactions of the board; they take charge of the books, and are referred to for information of past transactions.

Sa and Oo dai shi, four men.

Si sho, twenty men, attendants of the three high officers.

Kwa jo, four men, attendants of the Ben-gwang. Though low, the office is an important one.

HATCH SHIO, THE EIGHT BOARDS

The eight boards under the Dai jo gwang are:

1. Nakatskasa no sho.
2. Siki bu sho (Ch., Li po).
3. Ji bu sho (Ch., Li po).
4. Min bu sho (Ch., U po).
5. Hio bu sho (Ch., Ping po).
6. Gio bu sho (Ch., Ying po).
7. Okura no sho (Ch., Ta fu sz).
8. Koo nai sho (Ch., Kung po).

I. Nakatskasa no sho, or Naka no matsuri koto suru tskasa (equivalent office in China, Chang shu shang).—The Board of the Interior Government, superintends the palace and the affairs of the Emperor, and regulates the imperial household.

The head man, Nakatskasa no kio, is always of very high rank—generally a son of the Emperor, or of one of the royal families.

Nakatskasa no ta yu, chamberlain of the household.

Nakatskasa no gonno tayu is always a Mayka no tenjio bito koongay.

Nakatskasa no shoyu.

Nakatskasa no gonno shoyu.

Nakatskasa no dai and sho jio, subordinates of the above.

Nakatskasa no dai and sho sakkan, secretaries.

Dji jiu, eight men of high rank.

Wo do neri, ninety men of low rank; clean rooms, etc.

Neiki, writers to the Emperor's dictation, or for his perusal on government business; correspond about conferring rank, and write out documents connected with this. They are always able men, and any man may rise to fill this office if he shows talent.

Dai neiki, one man; sho neiki, two men; the latter subordinates and successors of the former.

Kemmootz, Dai and Sho, two men.

These are the reporters or spies (ometskys) upon the officers of the whole board—literally, lookers into things (kien wuh).

Sho den, one man of low rank to superintend the servants and to see that rooms are cleaned, etc.

Kangee no tskasa, keepers of the keys, now done away with.

Included under this department are the establishments of the Emperor's grandmother, mother, and wife. These are called the Shi ngoo—four offices.

The office of the Emperor's grandmother is Tai kwo tai kowu goo siki, the great Emperor's great Empress's office.

That of the mother, Kwo tai kowu goo siki.

That of the wife having a child, Kwo tai kowu goo siki.

That of the wife before she has a child, Chiu ngoo siki.

The ladies rank as Dai nagoon.

Under the Nakatskasa no shio there are several minor boards or rio.

O do neri no rio.—In this office there were formerly 800 men about the court, as messengers, servants, etc.

Odoneri no kami, Ske, etc.

Dsu sho rio, surveying office for plans of houses, maps of towns, country, harbors, seas, etc.

Dsu sho no kami, Ske, etc.

Koora rio, storehouse officer, has charge of the valuables belonging to the palace—a responsible office.

Officers—Koora no kami, K. no gonno kami, K. no ske, etc.

Noo ee rio superintends the making the clothes and sewing generally of the palace.

Noo ee no kami, N. no ske, N. no gonno ske, etc.

Ong yo rio (literally, clear obscure office), department of astrology—composer of the almanac—observers of the heavens.

Ong yo no kami, O. no ske, etc. Ong yo no haka se and Gonno haka se, teacher of astrology.

Rayki haka se, composer of the almanac and teacher.

Ten mong haka se, astronomer-royal.

Ro koku haka se, keeper of time by the clepsydra; teacher of time-keeping.

Taku mi rio, office of the carpenters, woodworkers. Taku mi no kami, etc.

Palaces, temples, houses and bridges in Japan being, for fear of earthquakes, nearly entirely built of wood, the trade of carpenter rises to a science, and, including architecture and engineering, is a business or profession which is held in high respect.

In the official list mention is not made of the head man of the tanner class, or that which deals in skins of dead animals, which occupation is an abomination to the pure

Buddhist. The name of the class is Yayta. They live in Yayta mura or village of skinners, often called Yakunin mura. The head man is Kobowozi. His duty is to go every day to the palace and clear away all dead animals—rats, mice, birds. He wears two swords, and is generally handsomely dressed. The class belongs to the Ikkoshiu sect of Buddhists. Some of the men following this trade are very rich. Teikoya in Osaka and Siroyama in Yedo are both wealthy. The head skinner of the "eight provinces," Danza yay mong, claims to be descended from Yoritomo. He also is reputed to be very wealthy, exercising great power over his own trade, which is governed by its own laws. Living in a fine house near the Yosiwara in Yedo, he is a despotic ruler, and can punish with death those under him. His private chapel or Bootzu dang is said to be the finest in Yedo.

II. Siki bu shio (Chinese, Shik po shang; Chinese equivalent office, Li po), the Board of Civil Office. Has legislative functions, and under this board is the department of public instruction and the college. The head man of the board is the Siki bu kio. He is generally a Sinwo, or a member of the imperial family. If the Kio be an able, energetic man, his position enables him to obtain great power, and he may become the first man in the empire. Formerly, men known by the name Si sho were sent by the board to all the provinces to report on the government of each. They were changed every four years, but the custom has become obsolete.

Siki bu no Tayu.

Siki bu no Gonno Tayu, both men of high rank, who practically carry on the business of the board.

Siki bu no Sho yu and Gonno sho yu, etc.

Under this board is the Dai gaku rio (Ch. equivalent, Kwoh tsz kien), office of instruction or education. The head man is Dai gaku no kami. This office is divided into four sub-classes, which have to do with the instruction conveyed in books and literature to the people.

1. Ray ki shi, history, including the history of China and

Japan and a little of India and Ceylon, as Buddhist countries.

2. Migio, religion—originally Sinto religion only.

3. Mio bo, laws and jurisprudence.

4. Santo, mathematics, arithmetic.

These are called the four paths, Shi do.

Besides these officers there are teachers or professors
named Haka se (pok sz).

1. Munjo haka se, two men; teachers of history, otherwise called Shiu sai.

2. Mio gio haka se, teacher of religion and the works of
Confucius.

   Jokio, two men.   Chokko ko, two men.

   On no haka se, two men, teachers of music.

   Sho haka se, two men, teachers of writing.

3. Mio bo haka se, two men, professors of jurisprudence.

4. Sang no haka se—teachers of mathematics, arithmetic
—two men. Is always in two families, Mio shi and Otsu
ngi. The former teaches arithmetic and the abacus; the
latter teaches the science of taxation.

III. Ji bu shio (Chinese office, Lai po). This board deals
with the forms of society, manners, etiquette, worship, ceremonies for the living and the dead, etc.

Ji bu kio, the head officer of the board, of very high rank.

Ji bu no tayu, two men; Ji bu no gonno tayu, two men, etc.

Oota rio (Ch., Ya yoh), a department of the board—
superintends music and poetry in all its branches.

Oota no kami, etc.

Gengba rio is another department, called also O shi maro
wo dono: takes charge of embassies from outer countries—
Corea, China, and India; looks after Buddhism. All business connected with foreign countries comes within the scope
of this office.

Genba no kami, head officer, Ske, etc.

Misasaki rio, an officer to look after the tombs of the
Emperors.

Misasaki no kami is head officer.

IV. Min bu sho (Chinese, Min po shang)—Chin. office, Upo, board of population and revenue. Tame no tskasa, board of the population—states, provinces, land, houses, census. In this office is kept a book or register for the registration of all deeds connected with land and landed property, surveys, and statistics of the empire. The book is called "Min bu shio no dzu sho."

Min bu kio, head officer, of high rank.

Min bu no Tayu.* M. Gonno Tayu.

Min bu no sho, etc.

Kadzuye rio, the office for taxes paid in money. Officers —Kami, Ske, jo, and sakkan.

San shi, office for money taken in country places only.

Chikara rio, somewhat similar to the above; taxes paid in kind, rice, etc. The office is now merged in the Kadzuye rio.

V. Hio bu sho (Chinese office, Ping po), Board of War— war-office. This is the most important department.

Hio bu kioh, the head officer, is sometimes of the imperial blood.

Hio bu no tayu. H. no Gonno tayu, sho, etc.

Hyato no tskasa, seems to be a sort of police in case of war. Hyato no kami, ske, and sakkan.

VI. Gio bu shio (Chinese office, Ying po), board of punishments. The name is changed to Ke be ishi, which includes the criminal courts, with the machinery necessary to their working, but the titles remain.

Gio bu Kioh, head of the office.

Gio bu Tayu, Gonno tayu, sho, etc.

Dai han ji, the first judge.

This officer is the judge of civil and criminal cases. There are no barristers or advocates used in the law courts of Japan. Each man states his own case.

Shiu goku ji—prison department.

---

* This was the title of the young man living in Paris in 1867. Commonly called brother of the Tycoon.

Shiu goku no kami, ske, etc.

As this title is supposed to convey some disgrace with it, no one considers it an honor, and therefore it is generally combined with some other.

VII. Okura no shio (Chinese office, Tafu sz), officer over the imperial storehouses and granaries.

O kura kio is an officer of high rank.

O kura no tayu, O kura no Gonno tayu, etc.

Ori be no tskasa, weavers of the imperial silks.

Ori be no kami, etc.

VIII. Koo nai shio, the board of the interior of the palace; was formerly a department of the Naka tskasa shio. Superintends the furniture, food, pathways, etc.

Koo nai kio, first officer, of high rank.

Koo nai no tayu, and Gonno tayu.

Koo nai no sho and Gonno sho, all of high rank.

Koo no dai jo and sho jo, etc.

Dai zen siki, purveyor to the Emperor's guests.

Dai zen no daibu, first officer.   The Prince of Nagato, Matzdaira Daizen no daibu, holds this office.

Dai zen no Gonno daibu, of high rank.

Dai zen no ske and Gonno ske.

This was formerly the highest ske at court.

Mokoo rio, officer of carpenter and woodwork about the palace.

Mokoo no kami, high rank.

Mokoo no Gonno kami, etc.

San shi, book-keepers.

Oee rio, purveyor of food for the gods of the palace.

Oee no kami, one man.   This is said to be a lucrative office; probably much is provided and little consumed.

Oee no ske and Gonno ske, etc.

Tonomo rio, department for superintending the cleaning of the palace.

T. no kami, etc.

Ten yaku rio—medical department—two apothecaries, medical attendants upon the Emperor, etc.

Ten yaku no kami, etc.

Ee no haka se, teachers of medicine.

Nio yee haka se, teachers of diseases of women.

Shin no haka se, teachers of acupuncture.

Jee yee, one man—Emperor's personal medical attendant.

Ee shi, similar, but of lower rank.

Kammon rio (Ch., Si sau shü), scavenger department in the palace.

Kammon no kami—the Daimio Ee holds this title. In 1859 this Daimio was regent under the Shiogoon's government, and was assassinated in the streets of Yedo.

Kammon no ske, etc.

O Kimi tskasa, chamberlains to the Sinwo or royal families.

O Kimi no kami is hereditary in the family of Owo.

Nai zen shi, purveyor of provisions for the imperial household.

Nei zen no kami, obsolete.

Bu zen no kami fills the office above.

Ten zen, of low rank.

Miki tskasa, office for presenting wine to the gods in the palace. Upon every household altar in Japan is seen a small bottle of wine.

Miki no kami, etc.

Ooneme tskasa, overseer of the female officers of the palace, O. no kami and O. no sakkan.

Mondo no tskasa, superintends the water supplied to the palace, M. no kami, M. no sakkan.

These (the Ooneme and the Mondo) are the two lowest offices in the eight boards. In the offices about the court the subordinate officers under the rank of kami are known by the general name of Shi kwang.

The second part of the Shoku gen sho relates to the Boo kang, executive and military departments.

Dan jo dai (Ch., Yu shi t'ai), was formerly at Miako, is now at Yedo. The Kebe ishi at Miako seems to be what remains of the office at that place. The office has very great power, acting apparently as police of the empire, the business being to arrest criminals of all descriptions. The office is within the inclosure of the castle at Yedo.

The head officer is the Dan jo in. He is of very high rank—sometimes of one of the royal families, or one of the three highest ministers.

The second is Dan jo no dai hitz; below him, D. sho hitz, etc.

Sa kio siki, office of the left half of Miako.

Sa kio no daibu, mayor or governor of high rank—now has but little power, as the business is transferred to the Kebe ishi office.

Under the Sa kio siki is To itchi tskasa, superintendent of the east market.

To itchi no Kami.

Oo kio siki, office of the right half of Miako; similar to the above. Oo kio no kami, and the office of Sei itchi tskasa, superintendent of the west market.

To ngoo, office of the heir-apparent, son of Emperor.

To ngoo no fu, head of the office.

To ngoo no yaku shi, two men, teachers of the prince—are always either Munjo haka se, or Mio gio haka se, and of the families of Sungawara or Owe. To ngoo no bo keeps the prince's accounts. To ngoo no daibu is always Dai jo dai jin, or Kwanbakku, or son of one of the highest ministers.

To ngoo no gonno daibu, etc.

Shuzen Kang, purveyor for the prince. He is always Nei zen no kami to the Emperor.

To no mo sho, keeper of the chambers of the prince.

To ngoo no shunen sho, keeper of the horses of the prince.

Isse no sei goo rio, or Sei ki no mia no tskasa. This was an old office in connection with the Emperor's daughters, who officiated as priestesses at Isse. It is now obsolete. In the year 5 B.C. the Emperor Sei Nin established his daughter at Isse as priestess of the temple he had built in honor of Ten shio dai jin. He gave her the title of Seigoo or Sai koo.

Shuri siki (Ch., siu li chih), carpenters of the Buddhist temples.

Shuri no daibu.   This office is filled by the Daimio of Satsuma, "Shimadzu shuri no daibu."

Sh. no gonno daibu, etc.

Kangay yushi.   This seems to be a military board of deliberation.   Kangay yu no cho gwang of high rank.

Kangay yu no ji kwang, one man of high rank, generally a Ben gwang.   This is a very high office; the officers are always known from their fine dress.

K. no hang gwang, military secretaries in the office.

Shuzen shi, the Mint.

The Mint is not now at Miako, but at Yedo, where the Shiogoon's officers keep it in their own hands.

Shuri goo jo shi, superintendent of Sintoo temples or mias. Head officer is always a Ben gwang.

Dzo ji shi, superintendents of Buddhist temples.

Bo wo ngashi, military man, superintends the banks of the Kamongawa, a river at Miako.   Is at the same time Ta yee no ske.

Se yaku in, doctors for the poor in Miako.

Ke bi ishi, Police and Executive.   The Kangay yu no cho, the Gio bu shio, and the Kebi ishi, are now merged in one department, to which all the Kokushiu Daimios, the Dai jo gwang, Giobushio, the Ometski, and city governors belong, and is very important.

The head officer is Kebi ishi no bettowo, a military man of higher rank than the Sanghi.   There is a saying that a Kebi ishi no bettowo should have seven virtues.   These seven virtues, the book remarks, it is very difficult to find in one man.   K. no bettowo is one of the men with most power over the natives in the empire.

K. no ske, two men.   They are commonly known as Ta yee no ske, and every one in Miako can recognize them at once by their dress.

Then follow the titles of men as heads of some of the large families or clans of Japan.

Fusi wara ooji no choja (chang shang), the head of the clan Fusiwara. By men of this clan all high civil offices are filled. The offices of Sessio and Kwanbakku are filled by members of this family. When the country is torn by civil war, then he who gets the power may take the title, as in the case of Taiko sma and his son.

Genji no Choja, the head of the family of Gen. Gen and Minnamoto are the same name (Ch., un, a spring of water). It is supposed to be pre-eminently military, and having gained the upper hand in the long civil wars with the He family, it has advanced in honor, especially under the present dynasty of Shiogoons, who call themselves Minnamoto.

The Shiogoon is Minnamoto no choja, and as holding this title he now is also Shiungaku in no bettowo, or principal of the college of Shiungaku in, formerly in Miako, now in Yedo. He is also head of the college Joone wa in.

Then follow some of the officers more immediately about the Emperor's person.

Nai keoo bo no bettowo, office of music for the ladies, generally held by a man of high rank, with some knowledge of music.

Nai zen no bettowo, examiner or presenter of the Emperor's food, of high rank.

Mi dzu shi dokoro no bettowo, superintendent of the kitchen in the palace, is always Kura no kami.

O oota dokoro no bettowo, superintendent of singing and poetry, an officer of very high rank, sometimes one of the royal family.

Ki roku dokoro no bettowo. Every day there meet in the Emperor's study, or Ki roku, this officer, who is of Koongio rank, one of the Ben gwang, one Kaiko, and one Yori oodo, who come to write for the Emperor.

Kaku sho no bettowo, superintendent of a certain kind of music (Yoh).

Kuro wu do or Kurodo dokoro, an important department in the palace. The Emperor Saga, A.D. 810, commenced the office. The officers seem to be noble attendants on the Emperor's person, and to appear about him when in public.

Kurodo no Bettowo is an office held by one of the highest ministers—Kwanbakku or Sadaijin.

Kurodo no To (or Tono kurodo dokoro), two officers, one Ben gwang, one military.

Go-i (fifth rank) kuro do dokoro, three officers, civilians, always rise from this to higher rank: first, to Hatch shio no ske, then to Kangay yu no jikang, to Kebe ishi no ske, to Tono Kurodo, and to Sanghi.   Therefore this place is sought after by the Kindatchi (sons of Go sekkay), as it brings them prominently forward; but it is an office requiring great energy and exactness, and mistakes are apt to bring the officer to trouble.   The dress of the K. no To is somewhat similar in color to the Emperor's.

Roko-i (sixth rank) no kurodo, four officers.   Must be sons of Shodaibu (fifth rank); must be able and of good courage, and steady men.   The first officer gets as his per- quisite the kikuji no ho, the used outer clothes of the Em- peror, of yellow and green colors mixed.   One of the lower officers gets the inner white silk dress, which is changed every day.   The Emperor never wears linen or cotton.

Hi kurodo, many, all of low rank, and are the men- servants of the palace.

Ko do neri, lower servants.

Dzo siki, military officers, young men, guards of the kurodo.

Tokoro no shiu, attendants.

Take ngootchi, private soldiers.

Then follows another short historical notice of the Sho koku, all the provinces of Japan, to the effect that formerly all Japan belonged to the Emperor Zin mu, who was, before becoming Emperor, a (kami yoh) god.   He came from Miazaki in Fiuga, and at the time Japan was wild and bar- barous.   He fought his way to Yamato, and made his capital Kashiwara.

At the time of the tenth Emperor, Shiu jin, Kashiwara

existed.   He sent embassies to all the separate princes of
Japan.   He appointed four generals of the north, south, east
and west, Si dono shiogoon, and, war ensuing, he conquered
all Japan.

Emperor Say mu, A.D. 150, the thirteenth after Zin mu,
appointed rulers over the country.   These were then called
"Kooni no miatsko," and he subsequently divided the empire
into provinces.   These lords were afterward called "Koku
shiu," and again were known as "Kami to you."

The provinces were divided into—

Gay koku, inferior provinces.

Dai koku, large provinces.

Jo koku, superior provinces.

Chiu koku, central provinces.

Ki nai koku, the five provinces round Miako.

To each of these there were appointed officers—kami, jo,
ske, and sakkan.

The provinces were classed together as To kai do (eastern
sea-road), fifteen provinces—1, Iga; 2, Isse; 3, Sima; 4,
Owarri; 5, Mikawa; 6, Tootomi; 7, Suruga; 8, Idzu; 9,
Kahi; 10, Segami; 11, Musasi; 12, Awa; 13, Kadsusa; 14,
Simosa; 15, Hitatsi.

To sando (eastern Highland), eight provinces—1, Oomi;
2, Mino; 3, Hida; 4, Sinano; 5, Kowodsuki; 6, Simodsuki;
7, Mootz; 8, Dewa.

Dewa and Mootz are large outlying provinces, and one
Kami is not sufficient, therefore another office is established
there, "Azetshi no foo."   Originally Mootz and Dewa were
one.   About A.D. 713, in the time of the Empress Gen mei,
Mootz was divided; and the Empress Gen Sio, who succeeded, created the office of Azetshi shi; and the Emperor
Sio mu added Chinji foo and Fooku shio goong, and Goon
king and Goon so.   Azetshi shi is the chief officer of Mootz,
and is of high rank.

Azetshi shi no keji, his secretary.

Chin ji foo is another officer in these provinces, of which
the head officer is named Chin no shiogoong.   The Daimio

4

known as "Sendai" is the head man of these provinces, and, as Kami of Mootz, is known also as Fooku shiogoong.

In these provinces are the two officers Akita no jo and Ske. The Emperor Sio mu built a fortress at Akita, and appointed an officer in charge. Dewa no ske and Akita no ske are different titles of the same officer.

Hoku roku do, north-country provinces route. Seven provinces—1, Wakasa; 2, Etsizen; 3, Kanga; 4, Noto; 5, Etjiu; 6, Etsingo; 7, Sado.

San in do. The back or north Highland route. Eight provinces—1, Tamba; 2, Tango; 3, Tajima; 4, Inaba; 5, Hoki; 6, Idzumo; 7, Iwami; 8, Oki.

San yo do. The fore or south Highland route. Eight provinces—1, Harima; 2, Mimmesaka; 3, Bizen; 4, Bitsjiu; 5, Bingo; 6, Aki; 7, Suwo; 8, Nagato.

Nankai do. Southern sea route. Six provinces—1, Kii; 2, Awadsi; 3, Awa; 4, Sanuki; 5, Iyo; 6, Tosa.

Sei kai do. Western sea route in Kiusiu. Eleven provinces—1, Tsikuzen; 2, Tsikugo; 3, Hizen; 4, Higo; 5, Buzen; 6, Bungo; 7, Fiuga; 8, Osumi; 9, Satsuma; 10, Iki; 11, Tsusima.

The Emperor Siomu created an office in the island of Kiusiu, Da zai fu, but it is now done away with. All the lords of that island were formerly required to come to Miako once every four years.

Military department. The imperial guards are called Sho ye (Ch., Chu wei), "all keep."

Sa kon ye fu, and Oo k., office of the left and right guards. A military office is Jing, or Goong, or Oo rin goong, or Ye fu no jing.

Tai sho, generally commander-in-chief of the army, is sometimes called Shiogoon and Baku foo, is always of the highest rank, his office making him of equal rank with the Sadaijin.

Besides the Tai sho there are two officers, the Sa and Oo daisho; sometimes called Sakonye no taisho. The Sadaisho is the superior officer.

Chiujo, lieutenant-generals of the guards, four, or at times six, officers.

Sa kon ye no Chiujo and Oo kon ye, men of high rank.

Shojo (small general), major-general. Of these there are eight or ten. Are also of high rank, especially if appointed while young.

Shogeng. Military offices of inferior rank to the above.

Shoso. Secretaries; adjutants.

Banjiu. Also called Konye no to neri—servants. All the officers above are near the Emperor as guards.

Gay ye. Outer guards.

The office is Sa (and Oo) ye mon no foo. The Emperor Sanga changed the name from Ye ji no foo.

Sa ye mon no Kami.

Sa ye mon no ske, etc.

Sa (or Oo) hio ye no foo is another office.

Sa (or Oo) hio ye no Kami is head officer of high rank. This officer is frequently mentioned by the Jesuits.

Sa hio ye no ske.

Oo hio ye no ske, etc.

Soma rio or Sa-oo ma rio. The office of right or left superintendent of the cavalry.

Sa ma no Kami.; Oo ma no Kami. Both of high rank.

Sa ma no gonno Kami; Oo ma no gonno Kami.

Ske and Gonno Ske. These take rank above all other ske.

Sa and Oo ma no dai jo and shojo. This is the first rank attained by a commissioned officer in the army.

Hio ngo rio. Ordnance storehouse.

Hio no Kami. One officer.

Gay boo no Kwang. The outer military department. The army in distinction from the guards.

The annals of the army are very ancient. In Tenshio dai jin's time, the title of the commander-in-chief was Fu dzu nushino kami, known by his posthumous honors and title as Kashima Mio jin in Hitatsi province. The title of Shio-goon (tsiang kiun) was first used by the Emperor Shiu jin 50 B.C. In the Emperor Kei ko's time, his son, Yamato taki no mikoto, **was dai** shiogoon, and there were two others, Sa and Oo shiogoon. This Yamato overran all Japan and the island of Yezo, also the three countries of Sinra, Corea, and Haxai or Hiakusai, provinces of what is now known as Corea, and put into them Japanese offices and officers; and after that commenced Goonfoo or military offices, or, in short, a standing army.

Chinjiu foo. Office for northern provinces. C. no Shiogoon, an officer who is general and commander-in-chief in the provinces of Mootz and Dewa. Mootz no Kami (Sendai) is generally the hereditary Shiogoon of these provinces. He is bound to keep, in the two provinces, an army of 5,000 men.

Chinji foo no fooku shiogoon is an officer called out only during war.

Chinji foo no goon kan, etc.

Se i dai Shiogoon (Ch., Tsing i ta tsiang kiun), tranquilizer of barbarians; great army general. Yamato take no mikoto was the first called Tai shiogoon. Se i was a title first given to Bunya no wata maro for bringing all the wild northern part of Japan under rule. This is the officer known to foreigners as Tycoon.

Se i shi. The office of the tranquilizer of barbarians.

Sei fu is one name by which the Shiogoon's castle in Yedo is known. This title—and it is now only a title—has for long been in the Minnamoto family. Yoritomo was Sei Shiogoon (not Kubosama, as Kæmpfer says).

Sinwo. Imperial families; previously explained.

Koongio. This class includes all of the three first ranks, and Sanghi, though of fourth rank. Only three men have been of the first rank and first class while alive, Tatchibanna moroye, A.D. 749; Fusiwara no Oshikatz, 762, a great tyrant; and Nangatte, so bad a man that the book will not say when he lived, A.D. 770, 780. These three men all lived and rose to power one after the other during the reign of Koken the Empress. This woman is notorious in Japanese history for her outrage of morality in her conduct with Dokio, a priest. She seems to have shown talent and capacity in her public position, and reascended the throne as Shio toku after one abdication.

Daijodaijin, Kwanbakku, Sessio, Sa and Oo daijin, previously explained.

Sho shin, all beneath the third rank, including Tenjio bito and Jeengay, being so called, includes some Koongays and all the Daimios.

Kindatchi, sons of the Gosekkay.

Sho dai bu, officers of the fifth rank and below.

Samurai are all military men and civilians who are independent of trade or farming.

The Emperor's wife has the title of Ko-ngoo.

The Emperor's widow has the title of Nioying.

The Emperor's daughter has the title of Nei shin wo.

The female attendants are called Jo wo ro.

The female inferiors are called Ko jowo ro and Chiu ro.

The female lowest class are called Gay ro.

Then follow the titles of Buddhist officials in temples, such as—1, Dai so jo, equal in rank to Shanghi; 2, Ho yin; 3, Ho-moo; 4, Sowodz and Gonno Sowodz; 5, Ho-ngong; 6, Ris shi.

There are different titles of inferior orders of priests who have to do with ritual, worship, funerals, etc.

The above gives an imperfect sketch of the offices, with the titles, ranks, and degrees, of the officers connected with the government of Japan. Such information is at the best uninteresting; but when it is conveyed in names which have no meaning, it becomes, without some practical acquaintance with the country, as difficult as it is useless to attempt to master the subject. But to one living in the country this knowledge is indispensable, and even for reading the letters of the old Jesuits, who seem to have been thoroughly acquainted with the names in common use by the people, some such information is very needful. Thus we find, among many others, they speak of Toronosqui as Cauzuye dono, and of Don Austin as Chikara dono, titles which are rendered in the above list as Kadznyay no Kami and Chikara no Kami. These titles, as has been said, are in use at the present day, but they refer more to the old form of government of Miako, which has been supplanted by the more recent imitation of it at Yedo. The latter having retained the whole executive in its hands, the mere form has been left to Miako. Now, when the country has begun to have relations with foreign countries, the difficulty of the double government is hanging over the rulers, who have not yet seen that one must be swept away as a thing no longer required. The two parts of the double government come into collision in presence of third powers. The Government of Yedo is still to be explained, and the reader will then be able to see how far the opposing interests of the two capitals throw difficulties in the way of smooth progress.

CHAPTER III

HISTORY OF THE EMPIRE TO THE DEATH OF NOBU NANGA

THE period of the history of Japan which has most interest to a European is that during which intercourse was carried on with Europe. But, independently of this new and interesting element introduced into the country, this is, even to a Japanese, the period of the history of his country which has most interest. It was the termination of a long succession of bloody civil wars, during which the whole empire was deluged with blood, lasting long enough to make the country a desert, the inhabitants savages, when agriculture was totally neglected, and the knowledge of letters nearly forgotten. Family ties were broken; young men were all soldiers; young women were common property. The Japanese may well look upon the man raised up, and who proved himself able to put an end to such a state of things, as a hero, and think his family worthy of the highest honors. To reduce order out of chaos, to insure his country 250 years of peace, during which time every one has been able to sit under his own vine, and to rear his family in happiness, and gather in the fruits of his labor in peace, may well rank Iyeyas as among the illustrious of men.

It is necessary, in order to understand the working of the government as it exists at present, to have some knowledge of the events which preceded and gradually led up to the period when this change began.

In the works of Klaproth and Kæmpfer will be found notes of the earlier historical events occurring in Japan. What follows here is derived from these and other sources, and is an attempt to notice some of the more prominent important events, and to give some interest to the subject by bringing it down to the present time. It is unnecessary in such a sketch to go back to the time of remote antiquity, or to try to get glimmerings of light out of fables, such as the different generations of heavenly and earthly emperors. To notice shortly the more prominent characters and events may be deemed sufficient.

Among the first of these prominent characters was Yamato Daki no Mikoto, prince of warriors, commander-in-chief, and of the imperial family. He is supposed to have lived during the second century. He overran the eastern and northern parts of Japan as far as the island of Yezo. A story is told of his wife having thrown herself into the sea to appease a storm, and from his lamentations over her, as Atsuma or Adzuma, the eastern provinces are spoken of as Adzuma, now sometimes applied to the east generally, and more specially to the inhabitants, who are spoken of as Adzuma Yebis, or "boors of the east," by way of contempt.

Another of these early events in the history of Japan, which bears an interest even to the present day, is the invasion and conquest of the southern part of Corea by the Empress Jingu kogu, known by her husband's name as Chiu ai tenwo, in the third century. The Emperor, her husband, was the son of the above-mentioned Yamato. She accompanied him to the island of Kiusiu, whither he went to put down a rebellion among some tributary states; but before the operation was accomplished he died, and she assumed the reins of power. Her prime minister was an old man, Take ootsi no Sukonne. After raising troops, and collecting ships to transport them across the sea, she found herself pregnant, but she was fortunate enough to find a stone which delayed her accouchement till her return to Japan. Having subdued the three countries of Sinra, Korai, and Hakusai, and compelled them to give up their treasures and to promise to pay annual tribute to Japan, she returned to bury her deceased husband, and was soon after delivered of a son, who was afterward the Emperor Osin, known better by his posthumous title of Hatchimang. Two older sons of her husband by a concubine, asserting their rights of primogeniture, and probably doubting the virtues of the stone, raised an army to oppose the Empress. Take ootsi was sent to defend her rights, and he put them to flight.

There is no incident more frequently taken for a subject by painters in Japan than the Empress Jingu and her infant in the arms of the aged Take ootsi. She is worshiped under the name of Kashi no dai mio jin; but though her victories threw more luster over the arms of Japan, in foreign warfare, than any previous reign, or, it may be added, any subsequent one, she does not seem to rank so high in the estimation of her subjects, or in the company of the gods, as her son. During his reign, Wonin—descended from one of the Emperors of China of the Han dynasty—is said to have introduced for the first time Chinese letters from Corea. His tomb stands in the neighborhood of Osaka, and divine honors have been accorded to him. As has been remarked, it may be doubted how far the Japanese, with their previous use of Chinese titles and names of gods, officers and men, could have been ignorant up to this time of the art of writing. To the Emperor Osin, though unborn, appears to have been given the credit of the conquest of Corea. After his death, in A.D. 313, divine honors were paid to him. He was styled and worshiped as the god of war, and under the title Hatchimang-dai Bosats he is represented as an incarnation of the Buddha of the eight banners. The largest temples have been raised in his honor, and every village, almost every hill, has its Hatchimang goo or shrine in honor of Hatchimang, the god of war.

The introduction of Buddhism was the next event of importance in the history of Japan. This is said to have taken place toward the middle of the sixth century. But it may be presumed, when the Emperor receives the posthumous honor of a Bosat, or Bodhisattwa, in the fourth century, either that the title was given long after his decease, or that the religion was beginning to be introduced at an earlier epoch. In all probability Wonin, who had access to the imperial family, and must have had great influence, had sown the seeds of the new doctrine, and had given the title to his patron. These seeds may not have borne fruit for 200 years; but considering the communication in past times with China, it is difficult to conceive total ignorance of these doctrine. To Corea, therefore, Japan was again indebted for a religion. In the year 552, during the reign of the Emperor Kin mei, the King of Hakkusai, a district of Corea, sent an embassy with a present of an image of Buddha Sakya mooni, with Buddhist books to the Emperor. The priests of the old Sinto religion were roused, but the new made its way. The Sinto religion seems to be all prayers, without any idea of a being to whom to pray beyond white paper, or a mirror, as an emblem of purity. The Buddhist religion supplied this, and presented what is required by many minds, the idea of a pure life through self-denial—self-denial giving a man power over himself, and enabling him to be the servant or the master as his church may require. During the succeeding reign, in consequence of an epidemic, some persecution of the new doctrines was attempted; but Moumaya do no wosi, son of the Emperor, being a convert, was very zealous in the propagation of the faith; while Nakatomi, then in power, and of

the family who superintended the Sinto rites, opposed him.
But the son of the Emperor (known by his Buddhist name
Ziou go taisi, or Sho to ku tai si) prevailed. He was appointed regent during the reign of the Empress Sui ko. He
was a very gentle character, strictly acting up to the injunc-
tions of the new faith. At his death, in the beginning of the
seventh century, there were, according to the Annales, 46
Buddhist temples, 810 priests, and 569 "religieuses" in the
empire.

The introduction of Buddhism through China and Corea
brought with it, as might have been expected, some of the
customs of these countries. The use of the Nengo (Nien
hau; i.e., year name) for marking events and dates was one
of the customs introduced in the year 646 A.D. A woman
ruling as Empress was another of the changes, and was probably used as a means for the consolidation of the new religion. Under the Empress Sui ko the degrees of rank among
the officers of government, similar to those used in China,
were introduced about 604 A.D. Six ranks, of two grades
each, were settled in place of the nine ranks, of two grades
each, as in China. These were distinguished, as in China,
by their head-dress, and by the color of the dress. They
were called by the allegorical names of Virtue, Humanity,
Manners, Faith, Justice, Wit. The first Empress was followed in no long time by a second, Kwo kogoo, and during
her reign she had the good fortune to have as a minister and
counselor Nakatomi-kamatar iko. He was not a Buddhist,
but had no doubt felt the influence which the spread of this
doctrine had exercised over Japan, and is reputed to this day
one of Japan's greatest men, and looked up to as the founder
of her law. During a long life he seems to have steered
safely through the difficulties of politics—acting as counselor
to his mistress, Kwo kogoo, her brother who succeeded her,
Kwotoku, and again when his former mistress reascended
the throne as Zai mei, and subsequently her son Ten si—
gaining over those who might have been his opponents by
suavity and gentleness of demeanor. The last-named Em-

peror deplored his loss, and gave him the hereditary name of Fusi wara, a family of which he was the founder. He was canonized after death, and worshiped as Kassunga dai mio jin, his temple being near Narra. During his life, and the reign of Kwotoku, the eight boards were completed after the model of the Lok po, or six boards of China.

Another change, which commenced after the introduction of Buddhism, was the abdication of the Emperors after very short reigns. This led again to the successive appointments of mere children as Emperors. The ages at which several of the Emperors, over a lengthened period, ascended the throne, tended to reduce the position of Emperor to a name, and to throw the entire power into the hands of the ministers. The system began shortly after the introduction of Buddhism at court, and the minds of the boys and women who successively were nominal sovereigns of Japan were directed to the study of books of the religion, to the erection of magnificent temples, and to the manufacture of enormous idols and bells. Such as the enormous copper figures of Buddha at Narra, Kamakura, and Miako. The latter has been melted down and a wooden figure substituted. Such were the Empress Sei wa, who began her reign at the age of nine; Yozei, who commenced his at the age of eight; Daigo, at thirteen; Reizan, a weakly lad of eighteen; Yenwou, at eleven; Go itsi, at nine; Konye, at three; and Rokusio, at two. But at intervals when a man ascended the throne, as the Emperor Ten si, it is a relief to see that some energy remained in the members of the royal family; and at times the national vigor was shown, and the military spirit, which the people are always proud of asserting, was fanned, by wars with Dattang (or Tartary) and Corea in 658 and 661. About the same time Yezo was once more overrun by Japanese arms and brought into subjection, military stations and officers being appointed in the island and in the hitherto barbarous provinces of Mootz and Dewa, in the north of Nippon. Revolts in the island of Kiusiu about 740 demanded fresh action from the center, and tend to show what a loose hold this central power had at that time over the extremities of the country. Not till the year 794 was this central power finally fixed at Miako. About this year the Emperor Kwan mu built a large palace there, finding that the magnitude of the business transacted by the eight boards of the empire demanded some settled place at which the court and the heads of departments might be permanently located. To the introduction of Buddhism and Chinese literature we may ascribe the completion, by Fusiwara (Tankai ko), who died in 720, of the "Ritz Rio," a code of laws which are in force and use at the present day. The introduction of an alphabet or syllabary (the Hira Kana and Kata Kana) to facilitate the reading and understanding of Chinese was the work of the famous priest Ko bo, born in the province of Sanuki 774, and who died in 835. He was canonized as Kobo dai si, and is venerated as one of the holiest saints of the Japanese calendar, and consequently was very much abused by the Jesuits. He spent some part of his life in China studying under the Buddhists of the time, and brought with him, as many others did, large numbers of Buddhist books. The enduring property of Japanese paper and the absence of white ants have preserved these, and doubtless in some of the libraries of the country and Corea there may be found works of great interest to the student of early Buddhist history in China and India. The Issyekio or catalogue of all Buddhist canonical books has been lately republished.

The custom grew gradually into use of the Emperor, after his abdication, adopting the garb of a priest, shaving his head, and retiring to a religious life. This seems to have been in many cases merely nominal, as some retained not only an interest, but took an active part, in the affairs of the world; while to others the retirement was a relief and an opening to license. The power, numbers, and wealth of the Buddhist monasteries had vastly increased. They threatened to monopolize the land of the empire; and the head of a monastery was equal or superior to one of the most powerful princes. Not only were the priests themselves living off these lands, but each of these establishments had a number of retainers and soldiers sufficient to change the tide of success in any engagement.

For three or four centuries the history of the empire may be written in the successive rise to power of individuals of the great families of the peerage—Fusiwara, Sungawara, Minnamoto, Tatchibanna, and others. Names which are regarded as illustrious in history, and held in veneration to the present day, occasionally shine out, such as Kan sio jo, better known by his posthumous title, Ten mang, the son of Sungawar zay zen kio. He has the character of having been a very able man, and was Kwan bakku and Nai dai jin. Fusiwara no toki hira, ancestor of Koozio dono of the present day, became very jealous of him, and Ten mang being of a quiet disposition, Toka hira obtained an order for his banishment to Dazai fu, in the island of Kiusiu. Here he retired to the hill Ten pai zan, in Tsikuzen, and endeavored to get a letter conveyed to the Emperor, but failed in doing so, and was found starved to death on the 25th day of the second month. A fable is told of letters having passed between him and Haku raku teng, a Chinese poet, both letters being so similar that only one word out of fourteen differed. The repetition of the story in connection with the greatest literary character of the country may show what admiration Chinese literature was held in by the Japanese, and how it was considered the standard of excellence. Ten mang occupies in Japanese schools a somewhat similar position to that held by Confucius in the Chinese. He is worshiped on the 25th of each month, a day which is marked as a holiday. On the anniversary a matsuri or festival is held—"Natane no goku." His posthumous title is Ten mang dai ji sei ten jin. His descendants are known as Ten jin sang. Of temples to his memory there is in Miako a fine one at Kitano, called also Say bio, and in Yedo at Kame ido, and at Yooshima and Shibba. In that at Miako the gilding and lacker are renewed every fifty years. There is in it a large library, with many old pieces of armor and spoils taken during the wars with Corea. These are exhibited annually on the mooshi boshi day, "insect-brushing-away day," when the temple is cleaned.

Among others who made a name to themselves by their bravery and other qualifications was Yoshi iye (son of Yori yoshi, Prince of Mootz), one of the Minnamoto family, born 1057, and known in history by the appellation given him by his enemies of Hatchi mang taro, or eldest son of the god of war. His third son was Yoshi kooni, who settled at Ashikanga, in the province of Simotsuki, and is the common ancestor of the celebrated families of Ashikanga and Nitta.

In 1008 the Empress was one of the great clan of Minnamoto, which was rising to power. The distant parts of the empire were being consolidated by operations against rebels, and the repeated transmission of large bodies of troops to the different parts of the islands to put them down. This war began to create an excitement or rivalry among some of the leaders, who, when the rebellions were put down, had the wish for more enemies to conquer, and could only turn round in jealousy upon their equals. Yoshi iye was sent to the province of Mootz as commander-in-chief, and, after many years' fighting, subdued the rebels, and brought this province, as well as all the Kwanto (the provinces "east of the barrier of Hakonay"), into submission. His son Tame yoshi desired the same post. To Taira tada mori, descended from the Emperor Kwan mu, was given the island of Tsussima, and in 1153 his son Kio mori succeeded him as President of the Criminal Tribunal. This name calls up, to any one acquainted with Japanese history, the recollection of the most stirring events, and the greatest struggle which has ever convulsed the empire of Japan. This struggle was between the Gen or Minnamoto and the He or Taira families. He and Taira are the same word in Japanese writing, meaning "peace," the former being the pronunciation of the Chinese word ping. The Minnamoto family, or Gen ji, stood on the broadest basis, and had risen to the greatest fame, and had recently occupied the highest positions in the state.

The Empress had been of the family, and the memoirs of the family had been written for her edification, or to gratify her own or her family's pride. On the other side, members of the Taira family, or He ji, had occasionally risen up to high rank in the state; and recently the family had been honored for its prowess and its activity in the imperial service.

Yoshi tomo and Kio mori were rising step by step to higher rank and power, when the abdication of Toba no, 1123, and the question as to his successor, threw everything into confusion. His immediate successor was his son Sho toku, in 1124, who after reigning seventeen years retired (mainly on account of the intrigues of his stepmother) at the age of thirty-nine. He left a son, Sighe shto, but was succeeded by his half-brother, Kon ye no in, who, after reigning fourteen years, died at the age of seventeen. The latter had been elevated to the throne by the intrigues of Bi fouk mon, his mother, and she suspected the late Emperor of having caused his death in order that his own son Sighe shto might ascend the throne. But in order to defeat these projects, she induced her son on his deathbed to adopt his half-brother Go ziro kawa. A younger son was thus in actual possession, while his nephew and the eldest son of the elder brother were displaced. The lineal heir endeavored to regain his rights. He raised an army, and on his side were ranged as leaders many of the higher members of the Minnamoto family. On the other side was Kio mori, of the Taira family, and, of the Minnamoto family, Yoshi tomo and Tada mitsi. A battle was fought only eleven days after the death of the old Emperor Toba no in. Notwithstanding the bravery and prowess of the leaders of their opponents, the He ji, the party in power, gained the day. Among the leaders of the Gen ji was Tame tomo, famous for his power in drawing a bow (owing, perhaps, to the one arm being shorter than the other), and, in his subsequent life, as a rover over the Southern seas. He was the first historical occupier of the islands to the south of Japan, Hatchi jo and its chain, linked on to the southeastern promontory, and the Liookioo

Islands, with the chain joined by links to the southwestern promontory of the mainland. He was the brother of Yoshi tomo, who fought on the opposite side. As a reward for their success on behalf of the Emperor *de facto*, Go ziro kawa, Minnamoto Yoshi tomo and Taira Kio mori were both raised to higher rank and power, and to each was given a province as a more substantial acknowledgment of their assistance. From this time mutual jealousy seems to have grown up between these two. But the ability of the reigning Emperor, who thenceforward took the reins into his own hands, seems to have kept down their smoldering jealousy. As to the prince who was endeavoring to resume his lawful rights, he and his father, the Emperor Sho toku, were banished to the province of Sanuki, where the latter died in the year 1164. He died of starvation, having written a letter to the Emperor with his blood, upon a piece of his shirt; but Kio mori would not let the Emperor see it.

The banished Emperor Sho toku was devoted to his worship, and since his death he has to many worshipers taken the place of Compera. This is a name much worshiped in Japan as a god. As a hideous idol with a long nose he has temples erected to his worship in every village. Immediately after the death of Sho toku, in 1163, a violent storm or earthquake took place, and as he was known to have a great reverence for Compera, this convulsion of nature was attributed to the anger of this supposed being, and a magnificent temple was raised by his son and grandson on Dzo dzu Hill (Elephant's Head Hill), at Matzuyama, near Marungame, in the province of Sanuki. Sho toku (known by the adopted name of Seengeen) is by many looked upon as Compera gongen. Compera, from the Chinese characters composing the name, seems to be Kapila, of Indian mythology. Kapila was known as the founder of the Sankya school of philosophy in India, which, in reference to the sacred Vedas, held the authority of revelation as paramount to reason and experience, to which Buddha, either for his philosophical or his moral or religious doctrines, would not submit. Some have thought Kapila and Buddha to be the same person. His anniversary day is the tenth day of the tenth month. He is revered for his great strength, which he exerted in favor of Sakya mooni. In Buddhist history, Daibadatta wished to destroy Say son—*i.e.*, Sakya mooni. He took up a large stone, twenty-four yards long and four arms'-length broad, and threw it down on him. Compera saw the action, and instantly stretched out his hand and caught the stone as it fell. Another name of Compera is He-ira. He is called also Kapira, and "Goo pira," and "Goo he ira." The name of Ee ngio wo—power equal to emperor—is also given to him for his strength. Fudowo mio is according to some the same as Compera. Many persons worship him because his name begins with "gold."

Kio mori turned out to be the ablest and most unscrupulous minister of the time, but the Emperor, who had abdicated, still took the principal management of affairs during the reigns of his son and two grandsons. Kio mori at the age of fifty-one shaved his head, and nominally retired into priest's orders in 1169.

Yoshi tomo in 1159 had conspired to destroy Kio mori. He failed, and was killed while in the bath by his own servant, Osada. His eldest son went to Miako with the view of killing Kio mori, but was discovered and put to death. His second son died. His third son, Yoritomo, born 1147, fled with his mother (Tokiwa go zen, a woman of low origin) and two brothers. Overtaken by snow and hunger, they were arrested and brought back, when Kio mori forced her to become his concubine. His friends demanded that the children should be put to death, but, at the intercession of his own aunt, he saved their lives, but banished Yoritomo to Hiruga ko jima, or one of the islands to the south of Idzu. The other two boys, Yoshitzune and Nori yori, were kept in Miako and educated for priests. The former of them was afterward a well-known hero. His nickname when a boy was Ushi waka, or young ox or calf. Yoritomo, while a boy, was known as Sama no kami, or captain of the left cavalry.

At this time, 1170, Tame tomo above mentioned, who had been roving about the South Sea for years past, landed on the mountainous province and peninsula of Idzu, and attempted to raise a rebellion; but his men were overcome, and he himself committed suicide. A temple was raised to his memory, and he is worshiped both in Hatchi jo and in the Liookioo Islands.

In 1171 the Emperor Taka kura no in, at the age of eleven years, married the daughter of Kio mori, aged fifteen years. This rendered Kio mori still more powerful, and at the same time more imperious in his conduct. He emerged from his seclusion, and placed his two sons in the office of Tai sho or first generals, over the heads of others who had hoped for the places. This raised a community of feeling against him, and again a conspiracy was made to attack and kill him and the whole of his family, but it failed through the treachery of some of the conspirators. The Empress, Kio mori's daughter, 1178, had a son, and in the following year his own son, Sighe mori, died. This son had proved some obstacle to the working out of his father's schemes of ambition, and when he was removed by death Kio mori imperiously ruled according to his own pleasure. His grandson, Antoku, in 1181, became Emperor. Kio mori became very tyrannical before his death, and he not only kept the old Emperor confined, but tried to change the residence of the court from Miako to Fu ku wara, and determined to extirpate the family of Minnamoto. Once more a conspiracy was set on foot to destroy the family of He, by one of the royal princes, who had suffered from the arrogant insolence of Kio mori. Letters were obtained from the old Emperor and secretly dispatched to Yoritomo, then in banishment on the coast of Idzu, and who was looked upon as the head of the Minnamoto family, and the chief enemy of Kio mori and the He kay. His brother Yoshitzune had escaped from Miako, in the retinue of some gold merchants, to the province of Dewa, and was residing in that province with Hide hira, Mootz no kami. Yoritomo had married the daughter of Hojio Toki massa, in whose charge he was during his banishment. Through her father she was descended from Kwan mu, Emperor, and was afterward known as Ama Shiogoon, or female Shiogoon, her name being Taira no Massa go. When the letters were given to him from the Emperor and his son, calling upon him to raise troops to rid the country of Kio mori, and release them from the durance in which they were kept, he immediately wrote to his brother Yoshitzune, calling upon him to assist him. Under such surveillance were these royal parties kept that it was only under the guise of paying a visit to the great temple of Miajima, on the beautiful island Itsuku jima, in the inland sea, in the province of Aki, then belonging to Kio mori, that the conspirators were able to get the letters dispatched. Yoritomo, with Hojio, collected what men he could, and raised the flag at Ishi bashi yama. When he first started only seven men joined him, and he fought his first battle with only three hundred under him, against ten times their number. He was defeated, and with his seven friends ran away, and the story goes that they all hid in the hollow trunk of a large tree near Ishi bashi hatto. While remaining concealed there, the soldiers, having examined every other place, came to the conclusion they must be there. A Kashi warra man (secretly a partisan of the Gen party) volunteered to go and look, and, though suspected, he was allowed to do so. He went up, looked in, and saw the party hiding, and told them to lie still, and taking his spear showed his commander that he could turn it all round the hollow. When he did so, two bats or birds flew out, and he told his commander that the mouth of the hollow was covered over with spiders' webs. The party of soldiers went away. Yoritomo and his friends left immediately, and went to a temple, where they were secreted in the wardrobe for storing the dresses of the priests. Meantime the soldiers returned, looked into the tree, and found that they had been there. They then went to the temple, demanded of the priest where they were secreted, and, on his refusing to tell, they killed him.

Meanwhile Yoshitzune collected what forces he could, and with them went down to Kamakura, at the head of the Odawara division of the Bay of Yedo.

Yoritomo was forced to take refuge in the remote peninsula of Awa, southeast of Yedo, whence he dispatched missives calling on all the Gen family to collect, sending Hojio, his father-in-law, to the province of Kahi, and joining Hiro tsune with a large body of men on the banks of the river Sumida gawa, that division of the Tonay gawa which runs past the eastern side of Yedo. In the province of Musasi he was joined by Hatake yama; while his relation, Yoshi naka of Kisso, raised an army in Sinano. Yoritomo fixed upon Kamakura, in the province of Segami, at a very early date, for his residence. This beautiful classic spot is within two hours' ride of Yokohama, and shows now little trace of having once been the residence of a court. Trivial circumstances probably led him to this conclusion, as it does not seem to be a place suited in any way for a large city or for the capital of a country. He was a man of great ability, and of strong will, but had received no education; and having been brought up in the province of Idzu, had acquired the dialect of the district. The mountain-pass of Hakkone is considered the key to the eastern provinces, and if it were sufficiently guarded, his position would be one of comparative safety, at a distance of a day's march from the pass. His relation, Yori Yoshi, had formerly resided there, and he had probably looked upon it, when a boy, as the family property. From his residence here he was called, by the people of Kwanto, Kam kura dono, a name by which he is spoken of to this day. Kwanto literally means east of the barrier— i.e., of Hakkone—and is synonymous with Ban do, east of the hill. It is a name by which are understood all the eight provinces to the east of the range of hills running down the promontory of Idzu; viz., Segami, Musasi, Simotsuki, Ko- wotsuki, Simosa, Kadsusa, Awa, and Fitatsi. It is called also Kwang hasshiu.

Forces were sent from Miako by Kio mori to oppose

Yoritomo, but at this time his relative Hojio met him with a large re-enforcement, and the He party retired without fighting. Yoritomo overran the province of Fitatsi and put to death Satake Hide Yoshi. The whole empire was now desolated by war. The tide began, before Kio mori died, at the age of sixty-four, in 1181, to turn in favor of the Gen party. But so long as Kio mori lived the cause of his opponents did not seem to hold out much prospect of success, and the relatives of Yoritomo are still found fighting against him, and on the side of the ruling party. Among these were his own uncle Yoshi hiro, and Yoshi naka, another relative. The latter was afterward reconciled to Yoritomo, and rendered him great assistance, being everywhere victorious in the northern provinces of Etsjiu and Kanga. Thence he rapidly pushed on to the capital, and seized the extensive monastery of Hiyaysan. The Emperor An toku fled westward with his wife, Kio mori's daughter. His grandfather, the old Emperor Go Zirakawa, received his deliverers in Miako, and still retaining his interest in the regulation of affairs, saw another grandson, brother of Antoku, proclaimed as Emperor. The possessions of the He party were confiscated and divided among the members of the Gen family. Antoku remained about Da zai foo, the station from which military superintendence of the island of Kiusiu was regulated, but from this island the He party was driven out and crossed over to Sikok. Still they were able in different parts of the country to make a stand, and even to defeat their adversaries in more than one battle. Several of the party had been left in Miako in posts of consequence, the son of Kio mori being regent, and they did what they could to support their cause in the capital. Yoshi naka, who had seized Miako on the part of the Genji, became in his turn overbearing, and roused the impatience of the old Emperor, who stirred up the priests of the monasteries of Hiyaysan and Midera to oppose him. But Yoshi naka suddenly came upon them, seized and imprisoned the Emperor, and beheaded the abbots of the religious houses. He caused himself to be created Sei dai Shiogoon, and finally set himself up in opposition to Yoritomo. Yoshitzune and Nori Yori, brothers of Yoritomo, were immediately dispatched from the Kwanto to Miako to attack him, and set free the Emperor and his grandfather, and he was defeated by them and killed. Meantime, 1184, the He ji had been gathering their strength in the western provinces, and had assembled an army of 100,000 men and fortified themselves. Nori Yori and Yoshitzune attacked them, and after a very severe engagement took the fort by assault and completely routed the army, killing many of the leaders of the party. After this Yoritomo ordered his son-in-law, son of Yoshi naka, to be put to death, and Yoshitzune was appointed governor of Miako. He attacked the enemy in the island of Sikok, and also in the western provinces of Nagato, and at the fort of Aka Magaseki routed them; the mother of the Emperor escaping with the two insignia of rule—the sacred sword and the seal or ball. But in crossing over from Simonoseki the Emperor threw himself into the sea and was drowned. Of the two sacred emblems, the sword was said to have been lost; the seal was saved. At this narrowest part of the passage between Kiusiu and Nippon runs a ledge of rocks, and upon these stands a small column, or tombstone, to the memory of the Emperor. On the Kiusiu side is the village of Dairi, called so from the imperial family having rested there. Moone mori, one of the party, is said to have fled to the island of Tsussima, where his descendants to this day rule as (the Chinese sound of the name) Sso. When the men of the party were all destroyed, the females crowded the port of Simonoseki, and were obliged to live by prostitution; and hence the females of this class in Simonoseki are accorded to this day the first rank of the class, and privileges—in the way of dress, such as wearing stockings, and wearing the knot of the obi or belt behind, like other women, and not before, as prostitutes—which are denied to others. In the center of the island of Kiusiu, between Fiuga and Higo, is a high tableland, partly marsh, extending from twenty to thirty miles in length. According to native accounts, this place was a hundred years ago quite a *terra incognita.* About that time it was discovered that there were people living in three villages within the marsh. The principal village was called Mayra. Further investigation being made, it was discovered that these were remnants of the He ji, who had fled there at this period, and had isolated themselves through fear. They had conveyed their fears to their children, who, when visited, had a dread of being punished for the crimes of their forefathers. The three villages are now under charge of a Hattamoto.

The power of the He family was thus completely broken, and that of the Gen or Minnamoto firmly established, mainly through the prowess and generalship of Yoshitzune. Yoritomo began to be jealous of his brother on account of the credit and reputation he had gained by his success. He picked a quarrel with him on the ground of his having married a daughter of the enemy of the house, Kio mori, and sent forces against him, demanding of the Emperor that his father-in-law, Hojio, should be appointed generalissimo, by this means filling the places of command with his own creatures. Yoshitzune left the capital and retired to Oshiu to his old friend Hide Hira, governor of the province. Yoritomo was enraged at an asylum being given to his brother in the north, and sent orders to have him put to death. Yasu hira, the son of his old friend, attacked him, and Yoshitzune, being unprepared and seeing no way of escape, destroyed himself, after first killing his wife and children. Yoritomo, angry with the man for doing what he himself had ordered, marched against Yasu hira with a large army, and finally destroyed him. Yoritomo built a palace for himself in Miako, but appears generally to have lived at Kamakura. At this latter place are to be seen to this day the remains of his work in the roads cut through rocks which confined the space of ground set apart for his residence.

In 1190 he went to Miako, where he had built a palace, and in great state visited the Emperor; but after a month's residence in the capital he returned to Kamakura. In 1192 the old Emperor Go zira kawa died at the age of sixty-seven. He had lived, after his abdication, during parts of the reigns of five emperors, his sons and grandsons. He had during forty years taken a very active part in the working of the government, and had passed through the most exciting time in the history of his country, and his last years were spent in tranquillity.

Yoritomo was appointed Sei dai Shiogoon. Suspecting his brother Nori Yori of plotting against him, he banished him to Idzu, where he was soon after put to death. He again visited the capital for four months in 1195, but returned to Kamakura, from which place he virtually ruled the empire. He fell from his horse toward the end of 1198, and died shortly after, in 1199, at the age of fifty-three. He is generally regarded as the greatest hero in Japanese history. But his treatment of his brother has been a great blot upon his character, and lowered him very much in the regard of his countrymen. Yoshitzune is looked upon as the mirror of chivalry, and his conduct is held up to the youth of the country for imitation, rather than the calculating, bloody, though brilliant career of Yoritomo.

Kamakura seems to have occupied under Yoritomo very nearly the same situation, in a political point of view, that Yedo does in the present day. The absence of external foes having created a necessity for internal division, two courts arose, the one with forms without power, the other wielding all the power and dispensing with the forms, except when it suited him to demand them. Yoritomo seems to have been the first to establish his court in the eastern part of the empire, a retreat which he chose probably on account of its retired and defensible situation. Standing upon the sea, the place is inclosed by hills, and in order to obtain access to the town a road was cut on either side through the hills. That to the east, toward Kanesawa, is a fine perpendicular cutting through sandstone. The houses occupied by Yoritomo, and after him by Ashikanga, or the sites where they stood, are pointed out.   Here stands a fine temple to Hatchimang, erected since the days of Yoritomo, and upon the spot where his son was assassinated.   It is known as Suruga oka Hatchimang.   An avenue with three fine stone archways leads straight to the sea from the door of the temple.   Upon the platform on which the temple stands is a small shrine to Inari, the god of rice, worshiped everywhere in Japan; another to the spirit of Yoritomo; another to stones in which some divine power is supposed to reside.   Two stones below show that the Phallic worship lingers in Japan, female (so to speak) as well as male, while a temple on the shore, near Ooraga, is entirely devoted to this infatuation.   The tomb of Yoritomo, an unpretending slab, is in the neighborhood. A small hill opposite has the name of Kinoo hari yama, taking this name from Yoritomo having ordered it to be covered with white silk to show some of his lady friends how it looked in winter.   The story may be doubted, if it were only on account of the scarcity of silk at that time.   At Kanesawa are the tombs of the servants of Yoshitzune.   About half a mile from the temple of Hatchimang, on the road to Fusisawa, is the fine old temple called Kenchoji, built by order of Moone taka Sinwo, son of the Emperor Sanga.   Further on is a nunnery or convent for ladies, the Matzunga oka. Looking toward the sea, the little island or peninsula of Eeno sima is visible.   On the road in this direction is a temple built by a daughter of Mito; a little beyond is a place famous for the manufacture of swords; and beyond this is a village with a temple to Kunon, the goddess of mercy (Kwan yin of China).

Turning to the right from the village is a large copper figure of Buddha sitting in the open air, in a position and with an air of great repose.   It is between forty and fifty feet high.   Around this colossal figure are seen in the grass large flat stones.   These are the bases of the pillars of a temple which once covered the figure.   But during a severe earthquake a rush of the sea over a temporary subsidence of the land swept away everything but the massive figure and

5

foundation-stones of the temple. It looks at present far out of reach of the renewal of any such devastation.

The glory of Kamakura has removed to Yedo, and what is said by the Jesuit fathers to have been at one time a town of 200,000 houses is now a village of not 200 cottages.

The son of Yoritomo, Yori ye, succeeded him in all his employments; but proving unequal to the task of governing, he retired, and his son, Sanne tomo, at twelve years of age, was appointed Sei dai Shiogoon, Tokimasa, father-in-law of Yoritomo, being regent; and from this date the power of the Hojio family began. The following year they put to death Yori ye. Tokimasa assassinated Hatake yama, and afterward had designs upon Sanne tomo's life at the instigation of his wife; but they were discovered by Sanne tomo's grandmother, Yoritomo's widow, and Tokimasa was banished. Sanne tomo was assassinated by his brother Kokio (who had become a priest, and officiated in the temple) while descending the stairs of the large temple of Hatchimang goo, at Kamakura, after worshiping there at night. He was the last Shiogoon of the family of Yoritomo. The power fell to the hands of Hojio no Yoshi toki, who ruled with Masa go, widow of Yoritomo, known as "Ama shiogoon," or the Nun commander-in-chief. Hojio Yasu toki was Sikken, a title which was afterward changed to Kwan rei, or minister to the Shiogoon at Kamakura, and began to assume a similar position toward the Shiogoon that the latter held toward the Emperor. Hojio and Hasago raised to the office of Shiogoon Yoritsone, son of Fusiwara no Mitsi ye. Yoritsone resigned the post of Shiogoon at the age of twenty-seven to his son, aged six, who the following year married a daughter of Hojio. The father and son, being in 1251 discovered to be concerned in a plot against the Emperor, were seized; and the office was now given to one of the royal family from Miako, Moone taka, "Sin wo." In his time Hojio Toki yori, then Kwanrei, built the large temple of Kenchoji at Kamakura. The Hojio family (Fosio of Klaproth) at this time absorbed the chief authority in the empire.

The historical notes which follow are taken from a native almanac with the assistance of a native, and are in themselves uninteresting; but they give some short notice of the wars between the Emperors of the North and South, of the rise to power of different families—such as Hojio, Ashikanga, Nitta, Hossokawa, and others — who occupied prominent places in Japanese history down to the time of Nobunanga, when a military genius arose to extract order out of confusion, and system out of a chaos of anarchy. But even the confused and uninteresting mass of names entangled in facts may give an impression of what the state of the country was during a period when nothing but turmoil and boiling brought one after another to the surface, to make way in turn for others from the abyss below. That some information is contained in these notes, may be an excuse for placing them here in such a meager and unentertaining form. But the names of individuals, of places, of temples, become interesting as more is known of the history of the country and the religion of Japan.

In 1260 the Nitsi ren sect of Buddhists was introduced at Kamakura, a sect which has become of more prominence lately, since foreigners arrived in Japan, owing to a saint of the sect, Saysho gosama, having been a great persecutor of Christians.

Hojio Toki yori, minister of the Shiogoon, one of the great men of Japan, died in 1263, aged thirty-seven; and the Shiogoon Moone taka was forced to resign, and his son, Kore Yassu, a child, raised to the office.

In China, the Mokoo (or Mongol), about 1276, had overthrown the Sung dynasty. Corea was compelled to become tributary, and embassies from China were sent to Japan, calling upon the Emperor to send his tribute. At different times several large naval expeditions were fitted out by the Chinese emperor, the Kublai of Marco Polo. One of these, in 1281, reached the coast of Tsussima; but in consequence of severe storms, said to have been raised by the opportune assistance of the god at Isse (whence he is called Kase mo mia, or god of the wind), the vessels were knocked to pieces, and 30,000 men taken prisoners and killed. One of the embassadors was beheaded at Kamakura. The power of the Hojio family had become so great at Kamakura that they retained in their own hands the appointment of Emperor.

In 1282, the Sikken, or Kwanrei, died, and was succeeded by his son, aged fourteen years; so that at this time it would appear that the country was governed by a deputy or assistant of a boy, the deputy or minister of the commander-in-chief under the reigning Emperor, with the advice and assistance of one, and perhaps two, abdicated Emperors.

This state of things could not be expected to continue, and could only exist in a country with no external relations and with no neighbors. The divided government made up to some extent for this want, but it left so many opportuni-ties for individuals plotting to seize the power that it is no wonder that the Emperors and the Shiogoons chafed under it. This was met by a constant accession to these high posts of children, who, when they began to be troublesome, were forced to resign, the Hojio family continuing to hold the real power at Kamakura and Miako, and also in Kiusiu, and deposing the Emperors and Shiogoons when they pleased, and electing whomsoever suited them.

So early as 1284 the laws of the country seem to have followed a policy of exclusion. In that year an officer came over from China in the quality of embassador, accompanied by a priest, but he was taken and executed on the pretext that he was come to spy out the land. Some years after, another priest, Na yissang, came from China, and he also was treated at Kamakura as a spy, and imprisoned, but was afterward liberated, and built the temple of Nan jenji, still standing in Miako.

In 1308, Hana zo no, then twelve years of age, was chosen by the officers of the Hojio family at Kamakura as Emperor.

In 1312 the Kwanrei Hojio Sada toki died, much respected, and the place of minister was kept for his son, Sada toki, for five years by two relations, till he was fourteen years of age, when he became Kwanrei.

The executive at Kamakura had named Go daigo as successor to the Emperor, and he came to the throne when he was thirty-one years of age. He very soon began to be irritated with the position he held, ruled over by subordinates at Kamakura. He married the daughter of Chiooso Kane Kado, a high officer of Chinese extraction.

In 1321 the office known as the Ki rokusho was established in the palace at Miako.

Taka toki, the young Kwanrei, was very dissipated, passing his time between wine and women, and in consequence was hated; and in 1325 Yori Kazoo and Kooni nanga, by secret orders from the Emperor, set out on an attempt to take his life; but he was previously informed of it, and seized them, and put them to death. Taka toki being ill, shaved his head and took orders when he was twenty-four years of age, and his relative, Taka Ske, at Nagasaki, assumed the chief power. The arrogance of the Hojio family at Kamakura excited intense ill-will at Miako, and the attempt to overthrow this power gave rise to the troubles known as the war between the North and South Emperors, which desolated Japan for many years, and which ended in the downfall of both the Emperor and the Hojio faction.

In 1327, Oto no mia, one of the Emperor's sons, determined to break down the power of the Hojio family at Kamakura; but his intrigues were divulged, and he was compelled to shave his head and become a priest, as Tendai no Zass, or head of the Buddhists. But this did not prevent him putting on his armor again when occasion offered. He afterward, under the name of Mori Yoshi, was Shiogoon.

1330. The Emperor still longed to destroy the influence of the Hojio party. He consulted with the Buddhist priests, then a very powerful body in the realm. He built the fortress of Kassangi in Yamato, to be seen to this day; but his design was discovered, and he was obliged to fly to this fort, whence he sent for Koosinoki massa Singhi, then a small officer in Kawadsi, but considered a very able soldier.

In 1331 the forces of Taka toki attacked and took the castle of Kassangi, and taking Godaigo prisoner, sent him to the island of Oki, and for some years there was no Emperor. Ko gen was called "Tenwo" by the Kamakura party, but he was called the False Emperor by his opponents.

In 1332, Otonomia, Nitta, and Koosinoki met at Chi wa ya, a castle near Miako. While the Kamakura army of Hojio overcame the other detachments, they were repulsed by that under Koosinoki. Nitta Yoshi assembled an army in the province of Kowotski. Troops were sent against him from Kamakura, but after several engagements he marched upon and sacked and burned that town. Among the officers of the Hojio party some were killed in battle, others were beheaded, and many killed themselves. Among the last was Taka toki. His son had his throat cut. In Kiusiu the Hojio party was defeated by Owotomo, who seized the governor, whose life was saved, but all the other members of the Hojio family, who had been so overbearing during their period of rule, were massacred by the people. Their authority, which had been paramount for years in Kamakura, and thence in the empire, was completely broken down.

Godaigo was restored to the throne. He had not improved by adversity, and was weak in his character. He removed all the officers in place, and, against the advice of his friends and ministers, conferred rank and power on Ashikanga Taka ooji, who had entered into a conspiracy against him, and who afterward became the most powerful man in the empire and founder of a long line of Shiogoons. The Emperor gave to those who had assisted him large landed possessions: to Ashikanga, the provinces of Hitatsi, Musasi, and Simosa; to Nitta Yoshi Sada, Kowotski and Harima; and to his son, Etsingo; to Koosinoki, Setsu and Kawadsi; and to others in proportion. Mori Yosi, the royal priest, had been appointed Shiogoon, but at the instance of Ashikanga was imprisoned and deposed. The Emperor had been warned against Ashikanga by Madenga koji chika foossa, his minister, in vain. This minister was the author, in 1341, of the "Shoku gen sho," the red book of the court of Miako.

The war which was now commencing is known as the war between the Northern and Southern Emperors—the Hokko cho and the Nancho. Each party set up one Emperor after another, while the war raged under generals who were fighting for the office of commander-in-chief rather than for the empire. Ashikanga and Nitta, Koosinoki and Hossokawa, Kikootchi and Owotomo, were the prominent leaders; while Godaigo, as Emperor of the South, was succeeded by Go mura Kami, retaining possession of, during a series of misfortunes, the three insignia of imperial power. On the other hand, Ko gen, called False Emperor, was succeeded as Emperor of the North by his brother Ko mio, who abdicated in favor of Sh'ko, who was taken prisoner, and Ko ngong took his place, but he and both his predecessors fell into the hands of their opponent. After the destruction of Kamakura and the downfall of the Hojio family in 1332, the theater of war changed to the neighborhood of Miako. Yoshi mitz, afterward the great Ashikanga, was appointed Shiogoon in 1367, when he was ten years of age. On both sides treachery on the part of the generals seems to have been a trivial and common occurrence; and this is not surprising, inasmuch as there was no principle involved, and no party-cry to rally under. Each general was fighting for himself and for his own advancement, while the opposing Emperors looked on apparently without much feeling or interest in the question at issue. By this war in the island of Kiusiu the family of Satsuma largely increased its power and possessions at the expense of Kikootchi.

In the year 1392, by the mediation of O-ooji, lord of the provinces in the west part of Nippon, peace was brought about. He induced the Emperor of the South to bring to Miako the three emblems, and to give them up to his rival, accepting the title of Dai jio ten wo. Thenceforward both Emperors lived in Miako, Go ko matz reigning. During the first troublous times Ashikanga had been strengthening his position, enriching himself and rising in rank and favor to the highest position to which a subject could attain. He built a splendid house for himself in Muro Matchi Street, called the Palace of Flowers, and two others called respectively the Gold and Silver Houses, which were large enough to be taken away in pieces (after his death) and form parts of different temples, of which these parts are still looked upon as the chief ornaments. Such is the temple of Tchikuboo shima in the Great Lake. The titles given him were the head of the Gen family; Joone san goo—*i.e.*, as the Emperor's second son—and Dai Shiogoon. He was at length, before he was forty, raised to be Dai jo dai jin, and during the following year he gave up his titles and place, and, shaving his head, retired under the Buddhist name of Zensan, or Heavenly Mountain. He moved about with a style and equipage similar to that used by the Emperor. He sent an embassy to China, and received an answer, in which he was styled Nippon wo or King of Japan. The Emperor visited him, and conferred on him the title of Kubosama—Kubo being the title of the father or predecessor of the Emperor after abdication, sama implying that he is equal to or "the same as." He was the first to whom the title was given, and it is still a title which is conferred by the Emperor, and is not inherent in any office. He died in 1408. The office of Shiogoon became hereditary in the family of Ashikanga, and henceforth the position of Kwanrei or Minister to the Shiogoon was aspired to as conveying the chief power in the empire. Kamakura was still the usual residence of this officer. Eight families were set apart, from among whom it was eligible to name the Kwanrei, chief among whom were Hossokawa, Hatake yama, and Ooyay soongi—the family of Hossokawa being at this time the most powerful. After the death of the great Ashikanga, his descendants were unable to wield the power which he had transmitted to them. He does not seem to have established any powerful government throughout the empire, but would appear to have held

what he had seized rather from the country being tired of
civil war than from any great administrative talent in himself. During the century which followed, civil war seems
to have been the normal state of Japan—one man after another rising to seize the reins—at one time at Miako, at another at Kamakura. No one chief was able to reduce the
whole empire to a settled state of tranquillity. If one rose
a little above his compeers, they combined against him;
while the monasteries and religious sects were so powerful as to be able to insure success to whatever side they
gave their influence and assistance to. This state of
things continued till Nobu nanga gradually rose out of
the crowd, and struck down the power of these Buddhist
sects.

1410. While the appointment of a Dai or great Shiogoon
was kept up at Miako, an inferior officer, with the title of
Shiogoon only, was placed in Kamakura, with a minister
under him. The men who filled both offices were still of the
Ashikanga family. When so many high offices were held
by powerful chiefs, jealously was excited, and this kept up
a state of constant civil war in some parts of the country.
The three rich provinces of Bizen, Mimesaka, and Harima
were taken from the owner, Akamatz, who to revenge himself invited the Dai Shiogoon to a banquet and assassinated
him. He in turn committed suicide, and his territory was
divided.

In 1414 the three emblems were stolen, but were after
ward recovered. The family of Hossokawa was rising to
power and wealth at Kamakura, while that of Ashikanga
was in the wane.

In 1415, for the first time, an act was passed by the ruling
powers known as a Tokusayay. This is a law suddenly
passed, by which all mercantile engagements are at an end
and all debts cancelled. This act of arbitrary, high-handed
injustice has been carried out over and over again in Japan,
and is generally the act of some high officer who has borrowed money largely. Whether it was carried to the full

extent stated may be doubted, but it has been the cause of much trouble and anxiety.

In 1452 Ashikanga nari ooji, son of the former Shiogoon of Kamakura, was obliged to fly to Ko nga in the province of Simotsuki.

In 1466 the war known in history as the "Onin" commenced, and lasted during the following eleven years. The dispute arose between two sons of the chief Shibba, in which the late Shiogoon and his successor took opposite sides. This was the breeze which fanned the smoldering flame arising in the desire on the part of the wife of the abdicated Shiogoon that her son should be nominated to succeed, otherwise he would be compelled to shave his head and become a priest. The whole country around Miako was desolated by war and slaughter, great excesses being committed, during which houses, temples, libraries, and documents of value were destroyed, and, as might have been expected, a famine occurred in 1472. This, together with the death of the generals commanding on both sides—Yamana Sozeng and Hossokawa—led to a cessation of hostilities in 1474, when some years of quiet and peace followed.

1487. The famous Ota do Kwang was assassinated by Sadamasa. An anecdote related of him is often taken as a subject by Japanese artists. He was out hawking when a heavy rain came on. Seeing a little cottage, he with his attendants went to ask for a grass rain-coat. A beautiful young woman came out, and upon his asking for what he wanted, she went to the garden, pulled a branch of a flower, and kneeling down presented it to the gentleman. Looking at the plant, he at once perceived that she was modestly making a play upon the word rain-coat, the plant being known by the name of "no seed," which implied also by a turn of words that she had no rain-coat to give him.

1487. War again broke out between the Shiogoon and Sasaki in the province of Oomi, which lasted for three or four years, when the Shiogoon fled to the territories of O-ooji, then chief of the western provinces of Nippon.

About 1494 the family of Hojio of Odawara took its rise in the person of Zinkio, who had been a merchant in Isse, but whose genius seems to have been military, and who was known afterward as Hojio so woon. He seized whatever territory in the Kwanto and around the castle of Odawara he could lay his hands upon. During these periods this unfortunate country was not only desolated by civil war and all its horrors, but it suffered severely in addition from convulsions of nature. In 1472 a famine arose as the concomitant of war. In 1475 a very extensive earthquake occurred on the sixth day of the eighth month, when a wave from the sea, during a temporary subsidence of the earth, carried away at one sweep a large part of the lower quarter of the city of Osaka. In 1496 there was a drought all over the empire, which was followed by a famine in 1497. And the next year was marked by severe earthquakes all over Japan; while in 1506 all the old fir-trees on the hill Kassunga yama near Narra died to the number of above 7,000. A similar disease had visited Japan in 1406, exactly a hundred years before. In 1514 severe drought and dreadful thunderstorms were followed in 1515 by earthquakes over the whole country.

The new century brought no cessation from war and assassination. Hossokawa, then prime minister, was assassinated by his servant Kassai. O-ooji, from the western provinces, marched upon Miako, bringing his protégé, the late Shiogoon, with him, and, seizing the capital, caused the Emperor to install him as prime minister or Kwanrei, an office which had for many years been in the hold of the three families, Shibba, Hossokawa, and Hatake yama. An attempt was made in Miako to assassinate the Shiogoon during the night, but he killed the assassins with his own sword.

In 1510 Nangao, a servant, and relative of Ooyay Soong1, minister at Kamakura, rebelled against his master, defeated him, and entered into possession of his castle and territory in the province of Etsingo, where he afterward became very powerful as Ooyay Soongi Kengshing. Hossokawa and O-ooji drove one another alternately out of Miako, but ulti-

mately the latter retired to his own western province of
Suwo; and during the same time Hojio of Odawara was
fighting in the Kwanto with Miura.

1486.   Hossokawa massa moto was made Kwanrei.

In 1521, for the first time for many years, the Emperor
made a public appearance.   The officers and court were both
impoverished.   The land was barely and sparsely cultivated.
The young were growing up in perfect ignorance.   Hossokawa brought Yoshi haru to Miako, and made him Shiogoon,
and put the Shiogoon, Yoshitanne, into confinement in the
island of Awadsi.   The following year the latter died in
the province of Awa, where his descendants still live, and
the head of the family is still known as "Awa kubo."

In the year 1523 an attempt was made to commence a
trade with China at Ningpo.   O-ooji, the lord of the western
provinces, sent over ships.   But at this time the coasts of
China were infested by Japanese pirates, and the attempt
to trade does not seem to have been successful: it shows,
however, that a commerce was beginning before the Portuguese visited Japan.

1528.   Mioshi kaï woong, from the province of Awa in
Sikok, attacked Miako; the Kwanrei, Takakooni, on the
part of the Shiogoon, met him at the Katsura gawa, the
river running into the sea at Osaka, but was defeated, and
the Shiogoon fled to Oomi, where the head of the Sasaki
family gave him shelter.

1530.   The following year the Kwanrei and Mioshi were
again at war in the neighborhood of Osaka, when the former
was defeated, taken prisoner, and put to death.

1532.   Haru moto, whom Mioshi had placed as Kwanrei
in Miako, took offense at some of the proceedings of the
latter, and ordered him to be killed.

1536.   At this period the Emperor was very poor and his
expenses were defrayed by O-ooji, the lord of the western
provinces, to whom the Emperor gave the title of Da zai no
dai ni.   The Emperor Go Tsutchi died in such poverty that
his body lay unburied for some days for want of money.

To this date the annals of the Emperors are brought down. Since the accession of the present dynasty of Shiogoons, the printing of every work relative to government is prohibited. There are slight notices of remarkable occurrences during each year published in an almanac form; as, for instance, it is noted that in 1533, on the tenth month, eighth day—*i.e.*, November—there were observed an extraordinary number of falling stars, and in 1534 a very fatal epidemic passed over the country.

1537. During this year disturbances arose between the Buddhist priests of the Tendai sect of the Hiyaysan monastery, and those of the Hokkay or Nitchi ren sect. The former burned down the temple of the latter, and with it nearly the half of Miako was consumed.

1538. In Kwanto the chiefs were again at war. Hojio attacked Yamano ootchi in his castle of Kawa goi near Yedo and routed him by a night attack. Takeda Singeng, now a lad, turned his father out of his possessions in Kahi.

In 1539, muskets were first known—brought over to Tanegasima by the Portuguese, pistols being known to this day by the name of "tanegasima." According to the "History of the Church in Japan," "The islands of Japan were first discovered in the last century, but at what time is very uncertain—some say in the year 1534; St. Francis Xavier believed it was rather five or six years after. Be it as it will, Father Maffius and others tell us that three Portuguese merchants, Antony Mora, Francis Zaimor, and Anthony Pexot, in their voyage from Dodra, in Siam, to China, were thrown by tempests upon the islands of Japan in 1541, and put in at the kingdom of Cangoxima." This is the southern part of the island of Kiusiu, off which lies the island of Tanega or Tanesima. Mendez Pinto, who appears to have been wrecked in this vessel, gives no date, but, from his account, the sensation caused by the pistols and muskets brought to this warlike nation seems to have been much greater than that caused by the apparition of strangers. It is not wonderful that the year should have been noted in the Japanese

calendars as that in which firearms were introduced.   They
did not anticipate that the arrival of these foreigners was to
be to the empire the source of much trouble.   At this time
the Lioo Kioo Islands seem to have been well known to the
buccaneers on the Chinese coast, and with the strong southerly monsoons, so frequently broken up by typhoons, it was
not likely that Japan could remain long undiscovered; and
the Japanese must have known of Europeans and their customs from their own sailors trading to China and Singapore.

1540.   Mowori Moto nari, ancestor of Choshiu of the present day, and founder of the family, was embroiled with his
feudal superior, Amako of Idzumo, and gave in his allegiance
to O-ooji.   This state of disturbances is noted in the earliest
letters of the Jesuits, written from Amangutchi, the capital
of these provinces, which was afterward visited by Francis
Xavier.

1542.   This year was born (26th day of twelfth month)
To sho Shingku—better known as Iyeyas—at Oka saki in
Mikawa; and during the year Ima ngawa and Nobu hide,
father of Nobu nanga, fought a battle at Atsuka Saka in
Mikawa.   The Portuguese came to Boongo to trade, and
received a warm reception in the territories of Owotomo.

In 1543 the Portuguese came back again; Owotomo,
Boongo no kami, was then lord of this province, and of a
great part of the island of Kiusiu.   An officer, by name
Seito, was sent by him with the Portuguese to Miako.
Hitherto the history of Japan has been made up entirely
from native sources; but after this time the letters of the
Jesuits, and the accounts published from time to time by
Europeans, become of interest.   Kagosima, the port of Satsuma at which these Portuguese merchants first touched, is
not a place adapted for carrying on a large trade.   It is too
far out to sea, and cut off from the interior (which is not
fertile) by high ranges of hills.   The port offered by Owotomo was much better suited to their views.   It is in the
heart of the inland sea, well sheltered, and, at the same
time, having water-communication with the extensive fringe

of coast bordering that sea. The island of Sikok, the most fertile part of Japan, was within easy access. The whole of the western part of Nippon and the island of Kiusiu could bring their products to this port by water, while intercourse with Osaka and the capital was comparatively easy. The objection to Kagosima applies equally to Nagasaki, which is cut off from trading communication with the interior of the country by the difficulty both of its water and land approaches. The family of Owotomo had gradually risen to wealth and power in the island of Kiusiu, and at the time the Jesuits arrived, the Lord or Tono, called by them Francis, was the greatest of the feudal chiefs then ruling in the island.

1545. Miako was reduced by war and fires to such a state that it became impossible to live in it; whoever did attempt to live there ran the risk of being burned, killed, or starved. The Koongays left, and generally settled under the protection of some feudal chief in the provinces.

1548. The Shiogoon, who had fled to Sakamoto, returned to Miako, and Hossokawa was appointed Kwanrei.

1549. Mioshi tchokay, called Mioxindo no in the "History of the Church" (or Naga Yoshi), took up arms against Haru moto and the Shiogoon party, and the latter fled again to Sakamoto, about twelve miles from Miako. Nobu hide, father of Nobu nanga, died, leaving him, his son, heir of all the possessions he had acquired. Francis Xavier, then at Malacca, whither he had gone with the fondness for change and excitement which seemed to have characterized his career, met with some of those who were returning to Japan. He immediately determined to visit it. He arrived in the year 1549, and left it again in 1551, disappointed and disheartened with the realities of missionary work. In the "History of the Church" it is said, in 1549 (p. 72): "On the way from Amangutchi (Yama ootchi) to Miako the ways were infested with soldiers, by reason of troubles between the Dairi and Cubo. Miako inspired Xavier with the desire of planting there the standard of Christ, but the effect did not at all answer his expectations. Miako, which signifies a thing worth seeing, was no more than the shadow of what it formerly had been, such terrible fires and wars had laid it waste, and the present condition of affairs threatened it with total destruction. All the neighboring princes were combined against the Cubosama, and nothing was to be heard but the noise of armies. However, he endeavored to gain an audience from the Cubosama and Dairi; but his poverty made him contemptible. It required 10,000 caixes to gain an audience. To comfort himself he preached in the streets; but the town being full of confusion, and the thoughts of every man taken up with reports of war, none listened to him. After a fortnight's stay, hearing that the Dairi bore only the name of a monarch, and that the Cubo was absolute only in the Tensa and Gokinai, he saw it was nothing but lost labor and expense to have his leave to preach over all Japan when he was not master."

1550. Yoshi haru, late Shiogoon, died. Mioshi tchokay burned Hingashi yama, or Hiyay san, a collection of monasteries and temples near Miako.

1551. O-ooji was attacked by the forces of one of his own officers, Suyay haru kata, who obliged him to fly, and he committed suicide with several high Koongays who were residing under his protection. This Suyay had promised Owotomo, chief of Boongo, to give back to his younger brother, Yoshi Naga, the command in the province of Suwo. At the death of O-ooji the seal under which trade with China had been carried on was lost, and the trade suspended.

1552. At this time the religion of Christ was brought, according to native accounts, by "Nan bang," foreigners from the south, to Boongo. The period at which this event took place was worthy of note. Japan had been for years torn by rival factions, and by the contests of men intriguing for power. The Emperor was powerless, and reduced by poverty and neglect to a position bordering on contempt. The eastern court at Kamakura retained some portions of its former power, and was at least a hotbed where schemes might be hatched for overthrowing either the power of the court of Miako, or that of some of the neighboring princes. Yedo was almost unknown, except as a village dependency of the castle. The western provinces were under the sway of independent chiefs, while the island of Kiusiu hardly acknowledged the authority of the Mikado. A small beginning of commerce with China had been going on for some years past, and was conducted with Ningpo. It was not likely, therefore, that at the first landing upon Tanegasima the country and people of Japan were unknown to the Portuguese buccaneers upon the coast of China. Not many years had elasped since China had been first visited by the Portuguese, and Liampo or Ningpo was their northern port. If Mendez Pinto is to be credited, there were 800 Portuguese then living near that city under their own laws; but if his account of the doings of his countrymen in China be correct —and it is in many things corroborated by concurrent testimony—the men who sailed about these seas were not exactly the men best suited to spread a healthy commerce, or to propagate correct notions of the Christian religion. They were the buccaneers of that day, and mixed up their business of piracy and murder with trade and religion in a strange medley. The vast opening consequent upon the doubling of the Cape induced these men to push their discoveries further and further. Europe had just been convulsed by the throes of delivery of the Church of Rome. Twin children had been born by the Reformation to the Church, and the schismatic operations of Luther without gave rise to the crafty strengthening process of Loyola within the Church. The propagandist zeal of Jesuitism at this period put forth her strength to reap the harvest in Japan; but the bane of the Church of Rome pursued her here, and her desire to make the kingdom of Christ of this world brought to naught all her schemes. The Inquisition was in full operation in Portugal and Spain, where John III. and Philip II. directed the missions of the Church; and the same zeal was carried into India and all their foreign possessions. The whole power, political and ecclesiastical, in the East, was allowed by other nations to be in the hands of the King of Portugal: without his permission no bishop could be appointed; no episcopal see created without his consent; and he retained the right of filling up vacancies in every see. No European missionary could go to the East without his sanction, and with that only in a Portuguese vessel; and no bull or brief from the Holy See was of any effect in the East until it had received the approbation of the King, who in return was supposed to protect and support the Church of Rome. This was known as the Protectorate of the Crown of Portugal, and was annually confirmed by Papal bulls, in which was inserted a clause whereby the Pope annuled beforehand every bull which any one of his successors might issue to the contrary. Such was the epoch at which the Portuguese arrived in Japan.

1553. Mioshi attacked and killed Hossokawa, the minister of the Shiogoon, and the following year attacked Miako, whence the Shiogoon fled to Tanba.

1555. Fighting was going on between Mowori moto nari (ancestor of Mowori Daizen no daiboo) and Suyay haru taka, who had killed his lord O-ooji. Mowori was victorious, and gained possession of all the "middle or central provinces" west of Miako—laying the foundation of the wealth and power which remain to the family to the present time. An embassy was sent this year to Japan from China, to complain of pirates from the island of Kiusiu who were ravaging the coasts of China.

1557. The Emperor Gonara died. Nobu nanga put to death his own younger brother Nobu yuki.

1558. Oki matchi ascended the throne at forty-two years of age. At this time Hideyoshi, better known as Taiko sama, as a young man became an officer in the service of Nobu nanga.

1559. Etsingo Nangao Kage tora, a large feudal chief, went to Miako from his province of Etsingo to pay his respects to the Emperor, and to claim his installation into the office of Kwanrei, when his name and designation was changed to Ooyay Soongi teru tora.

1560. Ima ngawa, lord of Suruga, was one of the chiefs who were competing for power. He had raised a large force and met Nobu nanga, who was not inclined to face him with a small number such as he then had with him; but Hideyoshi persuaded him to join issue, and by skill and stratagem they defeated and killed Ima ngawa, and Nobu nanga took possession of all his territory.

1561. Iyeyas was infeft by Nobu nanga in the province of Mikawa, and made the castle of Okasaki his residence.

1562. Mowori moto nari and Owotomo Boongo no kami, or Zo rin (the great patron of the foreigners in Kiusiu), were at war, which was terminated by the interference of the Shiogoon, who sent down a messenger to restore peace, through a matrimonial alliance and enlargement of Owotomo's territories.

1563. Fighting was going on in the neighborhood of Yedo between Sattomi, who possessed large territories in Awa and Owota, on the one side, and Hojio of Odawarra on the other. A great battle took place between these chiefs at Kowunodai, near Yedo, in which Sattomi was defeated. The defeat took place upon the 9th of the ninth month, a festival-day all over Japan. Since the defeat, Kanagawa and Kawasaki, then belonging to Sattomi, have held the festival on the 19th. Mowori Motonari this year completely defeated Amako, the lord Idzumo, and absorbed his territories, thus becoming lord of ten provinces.

1564. Nobu nanga killed his father-in-law Seito Do Sang, the lord of Mino, and seized all his territory, and changed his own residence, which had been hitherto in Nagoya in Owarri, to Gifoo in Mino.

In 1565 Matza naga hissa hide (Daxandono, or properly Danshio, in "History of the Church") and Mioshi attacked Yoshi teru, Shiogoon, who was surprised, and committed suicide. His younger brother Yoshi aki fled to Oomi, shaved his head, and became a priest. The grandson of Yoshi dzumi aimed at the position of Shiogoon. To oppose the designs of Mioshi, who was attempting to assassinate him, Yoshi aki

joined Nobu nanga, who put him into the post of Shiogoon
in 1568, and they together attacked and defeated Mioshi.

1569.　Nobu nanga found it necessary to begin a crusade
against the Buddhist priests, and their wealthy and powerful
establishments.　He attacked and routed and killed Kita
batake, the lord of Isse.　He built a palace for the Emperor,
but it was so small and shabby that the Emperor would not
inhabit it, but lived in the temple of Kammo, near Miako.
This year the palace and castle of Nijio was built in Miako,
and has since been occupied by the Shiogoons as their metro-
politan residence.

1570.　Nobu nanga was fighting with the lord of the
province of Etsizen, Asakura, who was defeated, and his
territories seized by Nobu nanga.

At this time Nobu nanga, Hideyoshi, and Iyeyas found it
their interest to be friends.　Hideyoshi had grown up as an
officer in Nobu nanga's army, and both are said to have been
jealous of Iyeyas (known as a young man as "Sing Koong"),
probably discerning at this early time superior administrative
talents, as well as a reticence which may have displeased
them.　He is said to have been put forward by them into
difficult positions to get rid of him, but the vigor of his character increased by overcoming the obstacles in his path.　He
went to the province of Oomi at the time Nobu nanga was
fighting with the troops of Asayee and Asakura at Anegawa,
and by his timely assistance turned the fortune of the day.

1571.　The Buddhist priesthood had at this time arrived
at the height of their power.　The arrival of the Roman
Catholics, and the spread of their doctrines, was probably
hailed by many as a relief from the extravagant pretensions
and power of the monasteries, and it was hoped that they
might in some measure balance the power of the Buddhist
priesthood.　All over the country these monasteries had become very wealthy.　The monks, bonzes, or bozans, were
very numerous, and their retainers and dependents formed
an army sufficiently powerful to cope with any single chief.
The policy of the Roman Catholics seems to have been from

the first of an aggressive character, attacking vehemently
the native priests, abusing their characters, and getting up
discussions in public, and thus unnecessarily irritating a very
powerful body in the kingdom. Nobu nanga was very jealous of the power of these Buddhist monasteries, and hated
the priests. He therefore gave his countenance to these
new-comers, who were delighted, as thinking it showed a
zeal for their mission, while, in truth, it was only to gratify
his hatred of the native bozans. He suddenly fell upon the
largest of the monasteries, the Hiyaysan, also called by the
early writers Freno yama, and Hiyay no yama. The grounds
are said to have been of great beauty, near the lake of Oomi,
and inclosing thirteen valleys; and at the time the Jesuits
arrived in the country there were said to be 500 temples
within the area of the monastery. Nobu nanga burned all
the temples and massacred the priests. These latter had
been joined by some of Nobu nanga's late opponents, but he
defeated them all.

1572. Takeda Singeng, at Mikatta nga harra in Tootomi, was fighting with Iyeyas. A great mortality had taken
place in the force of the latter, and he was nearly overcome,
and in great danger, but finally conquered.

The same year the Shiogoon Yoshi aki became embroiled
with Nobu nanga, who arrested him and put him in prison,
thus bringing to a termination the real power of the Ashikanga family.

During the year Iyeyas was beaten by Takeda near
Mitske; he was obliged to fly, and was pursued across
the Tenrio River to a village, Hamamatchi. During the
night he heard music, and creeping up with some of his
men to listen, they saw Takeda himself sitting enjoying the
music, when one of Iyeyas's men fired at him with a musket.
He was wounded and gave up the pursuit. He lingered a
while, but at length died of the injury.

1574. All over the country Roman Catholic temples were
being built, exciting the Buddhist priesthood to wrath.

1575. At Nanga shino, in Tootomi, there was some smart

fighting between Katzu yori, son of Takeda Singeng, and Iyeyas, as officer of Nobu nanga. Katzu yori was very powerful, and had a large army with him of well-trained soldiers, and Nobu nanga was afraid to fight; but Iyeyas declared that if he would not fight he himself would join Katzu yori.

1576. Hideyoshi was sent by Nobu nanga to Kiusiu and the west provinces. As a whim, he this year made a new name for himself out of the half of the names of two of Nobu nanga's officers, Shibata and Niwa, and calling himself Hashiba, a name by which he is frequently spoken of by the Jesuits.

1576. Nobu nanga built the castle of Azutchi (called Anzuquiama in "History of the Church") in the province of Oomi; a castle which now belongs to Ee kamong no Kami.

1577. Matz nanga hissa hide, known in the "History of the Church" as Daxandono, was killed by Nobu nanga.

1578. Hashiba hide yoshi was this year fighting with Mowori teru moto, known to the Jesuits as the King of Amanguchi, and the island of Kiusiu was devastated by war between Owotomo, son of the Jesuits' friend, and Shimadzu of Satsuma, the result being that Owotomo was defeated, and his territory much diminished.

1579. The two Buddhist sects, Jodo shiu and Nitchi ren shiu, held a great discussion upon religion before Nobu nanga at Azutchi, known as the "Azutchi rong."

Akitchi mitzu hide, one of Nobu nanga's best officers, seized the province of Tanba. The Ikko shiu, a Buddhist sect, was very powerful at this time, and had possession of the castle of Osaka, then known as the temple of Hoonganji. Nobu nanga, by one of his generals, had been long besieging it, and had failed in taking it. In 1580 he called in the persuasive interference of the Emperor, and a compact was finally made, under which the priests consented to give up this strong fortress, which has ever since remained in the hands of the executive power.

1581. Hideyoshi this year overran the province of Harima, destroying the castle of Miki, and began to build the chateau of Himeji for himself in that province; while Nobu nanga, assisted by Iyeyas and Hojio of Odawarra, completely demolished the power of the Takeda family in Kahi. The war is known as the "Ten moku san" war, from the place where Takeda concealed and destroyed himself. The tie between Nobu nanga and his generals seemed to have been very slight, and he does not appear at any time to have been considered ruler of the country. On more than one occasion Iyeyas threatened to leave him and throw his weight into the opposite scale. In a portrait drawn of Nobu nanga in the "History of the Church," he is described as "a prince of large stature, but of a weak and delicate complexion, with a heart and soul that supplied all other wants; ambitious above all mankind; brave, generous and bold, and not without many excellent moral virtues; inclined to justice, and an enemy to treason. With a quick and penetrating wit, he seemed cut out for business; excelling in military discipline, he was esteemed the fittest to command an army, manage a siege, fortify a town, or mark out a camp, of any general in Japan, never using any heads but his own: if he asked advice, it was more to know their hearts than to profit by their advice. He sought to see into others and to conceal his own counsel, being very secret in his designs; he laughed at the worship of the gods, convinced that the bonzes were impostors, abusing the simplicity of the people, and screening their own debauches under the name of religion."

This is the character given of him by the Jesuits, who considered him a friend to their cause, and had some hopes of him as a convert. It agrees in the main with the pictures drawn of him by the Japanese. Hating the Buddhist priests, he patronized the Jesuits as a counterpoise, encouraging them to build even in the neighborhood of his own palace at Azutchi. Under the encouragement thus given, the Jesuit priests rose to favor and power at court. The efforts of the fathers to extend their influence were crowned

with success, and at this date the position of the church is
described as follows: "Father A. Valignan, superior of
Japan, for convenience of government, divided Japan into
three parts. The first and principal is that island where
Miako stands. They had there three residences of the Society—Meaco, Anzuquiama (Azutchi-yama in Oomi) and
Takacu qui. In the residence of Miako were two brothers
and two fathers, who preached and celebrated the divine
mysteries daily in a very fair church. In Anzuquiama they
had two fathers and two brothers; the first of these took
care of the church, and of all the Christians round about;
the other instructed the young gentlemen in the seminary,
teaching them their Catechism, and to read and write in
Latin, Portuguese and the language of the country. In
Tacucuqui (Itami in Setzu) there was only one father and
one brother. Justo Ucondono (Takayama), governor of the
place, built in it a very handsome church and house for
the fathers, and furnished them with all the necessaries for
their families. About three leagues off were the churches
of Vocayama, Fort Imori in Kawadsi, and Sanga—all de-
pendencies of this residence. Two leagues from Sanga, Don
Simon Tagandono (Tango no Kami), lord of Yao, had eight
hundred subjects, all Christians. There were also great
numbers of them in Amangutchi, but without any church,
it being expressly against the king's pleasure.

"The second part of Japan is that which they commonly
call Ximo (Kiusiu). There the Christians had most churches,
and the Jesuits most houses. In the city of Funay, the metropolis of Bungo, there was both a college and a university,
where they took degrees of masters of arts and doctors of
divinity. There were twenty Jesuits in the college. The
noviceship stood at Vosuqui, where King Francis (*i.e.*,
Owotomo Boongo no Kami) resided. Besides, they had
two residences—one at the valley of Ju, some seven leagues
from Funay, and another at Nocen—and these four houses
furnished the whole country with evangelical missionaries.
Moreover, they had a house at Facata, in the kingdom of

Chicuzen, that was tributary to Bungo; but Aquizuqui, having made himself master of that country, soon beat them out of those quarters. The kingdom of Chicungo, bordering upon Chicuzen, had only one church, which was governed since Riozogi's conquest by a devout Christian, that prince being unwilling to entertain any Jesuits in his states. In the kingdom of Fingo, which Aquizuqui and Riozogi parted betwixt them, there were two houses of the Society—one in Amacusa and the other at Fort Fundo; and these two residences took charge of above twenty other churches in that country. As for the island of Xequi (Ko Siki), which stands upon the confines of Amacusa, they had only one church, with near 5,000 Christians, who were governed by one of the inhabitants; for the lord of the place, though he was to permit the fathers to visit them, would not hear of fixing a residence; which obliged the Christians, on the more solemn days, to come over to the church of Amacusa.

"In the kingdom of Goto (the five small islands to the west of Japan), since Don Lewis's death, there was neither church nor house, the uncle and tutor to the young prince being, as was said, a most professed enemy to all religion. The King of Firando, indeed, though a heathen, was content to receive two priests and two others for the benefit of the Christians, and chiefly his uncle and son, Don John and Don Anthony.

"As for the kingdoms of Omura and Arima, religion flourished there above all other parts, Bungo only excepted. The fathers had three houses in Omura, one in Omura itself, where the King kept his court, another at Nangasak, and a third at Curi, and out of these three churches they visited forty several churches, and had charge of some 50,000 Christians that were in that kingdom. In Arima they had three residences: one in the city of Arima, with five Jesuits, whereof two had care of the seminary for educating young nobles, among whom was the King of Fiungas' son, cousin-german to the King of Arima, and the rest, all of them sons to the chief lords in the country; the second at Arie;

6

and the third at Cochinozi, a most celebrated port for commerce.

"In the kingdom of Saxuma, where St. F. Xaverius landed at his first entrance into Japan, there were some few Christians whom the fathers visited by times, being all banished by the bonzes, who acted by the King's authority. They reckoned in the kingdom of Ximo upward of 30,000 Christians.

"The third part of Japan (Sikok) contains only four kingdoms, and of these only the King of Tosa received the faith. So Father Alex. Valignan, at the end of his visit, upon his return to the Indies, left 150,000 Christians in Japan, 200 churches and 39 religious of his own order, besides several able, young and virtuous Japonians who helped to instruct the new Christians."

In 1582 Nobu nanga was gradually overruning all Japan. He had given the revenues of the island of Sikok to his son, Nobu taka. "This year he built at Azutchi a splendid temple. In this temple he collected idols of all the gods of Japan, and placed in the midst a statue of himself, calling it Xanthi; *i.e.*, supreme ruler. He then, like Nebuchadnezzar, issued an edict prohibiting any one from worshiping any other idol, and ordered all to resort to this place on his birthday to worship this representation of himself. The first that adored was his eldest son. The nobility followed, and then the gentry and people in their course." This idol is said to be in existence at the present day. Nobu nanga, after this public adoration of his statue, returned to Miako. Akitchi mitzu hide had been one of his most prominent and successful generals, and was at this time in the neighborhood of the capital. Nobu nanga had dispatched a large body of troops to assist Hashiba Hideyoshi in his operations in the west. Whether Akitchi aspired to the position occupied by Nobu nanga, or was really jealous and hated him, in common with others, as a tyrant, or, as some relate, smarted under the insult of being struck by Nobu nanga over the head with a fan, is doubtful. But "when he saw that the

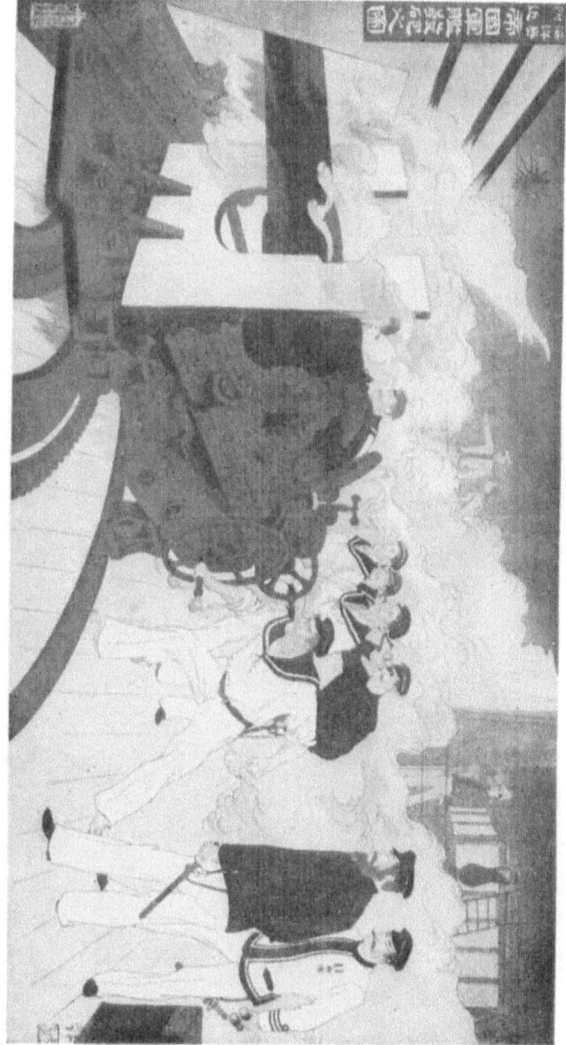

SCENE ON JAPANESE MAN-OF-WAR

Japan.

guards and forces under the immediate command of Nobu
nanga were so diminished in number that he was left nearly
unprotected, he took advantage of what seemed to him an
opportunity. He had been ordered by Nobu nanga to take
a large body of troops under his command to join Hideyoshi.
Accordingly, he marched, but instead of taking the route in-
dicated, he took aside some of the captains whom he knew
to be dissatisfied with the government and discussed to them
his design, and gained them over by declaiming against the
violence, oppression, and tyranny of Nobu nanga, accusing
him of destroying the gods and murdering the priests, and
concluding by promises of wealth stored up in the castle of
Adzutchi yama. He then suddenly wheeled round upon Miako, surrounding Honnoji, where Nobu nanga was residing,
before he was aware of any danger. All the avenues were
closed—no escape was left for him. He was washing his
face when the news came that the troops had invested the
place, and opening a window to see what was the matter,
they poured in a shower of darts and wounded him between
the shoulders. The place was soon in flames, and his body
was consumed with the building. Thus died Nobu nanga,
at forty-nine years of age, a little after he took upon himself the title of god, and had made himself be adored by his
subjects.''

Nobu nanga was by birth of higher origin than his successor, Taikosama, and, as the son of a feudal prince, had,
at a time when might gave right, some pretension to rule.
Descended from Kio mori, he was of the Taira family, that
clan which had contested so long with the Minnamoto for
the executive power in the empire. No question of family
origin entered into his rise or brought about his fall. As
an individual, he rose to power through his military talents;
and probably from want of administrative ability failed to
strengthen himself, or insure the succession of the position
to which he had risen to his sons. The period of his rule
was signalized by the rise and success of the Jesuits, whom
he countenanced, according to their own showing, rather

from hatred to the Buddhist priests than from love for the doctrines of Christianity, or respect for the Roman Catholic priesthood. When he died, the tide of prosperity turned and ebbed till it gradually swept the whole doctrines, priests, and proselytes from the shores of Japan.

Akitchi mitsu hide, who had thus removed the master-spirit of Japan, was not the man to take the vacant seat. Apparently an able second, a successful lieutenant, he was wanting in every quality for command. He had gained over the troops placed in his charge by the promise of plunder. He marched them upon the city of Azutchi yama, where Nobu nanga had stored up the treasures he had accumulated during many years, and in three days squandered the whole in largesses to those under his command.

CHAPTER IV

GOVERNMENT OF TAIKOSAMA

By the sudden and unexpected removal of the keystone of the arch, there was left a blank to be filled up. It may be said that on either side was a stone ready for the purpose. On the one side, Hideyoshi, in command of a powerful army, and he himself with a great reputation as a leader, and engaged, on the part of Nobu nanga, in a war with Mori, prince of the ten western provinces; on the other, Iyeyas, firmly seated as ruler over eight provinces, and hardly acknowledging any submission to the executive at Miako, also in command of an army and fighting on the side of Nobu nanga against Hojo, lord of Odawarra. Had the succession been left to the son or sons of Nobu nanga, there was every prospect of a continuance of the same state of anarchy and war. No one of the three was competent for the post. The eldest, indeed, had perished with his father, leaving a son, a child,

San hoshi.   The third, Nobu taka, was lord of the island of
Sikok and its four provinces.   Nobu wo, lord of Owarri, the
second son, took part with Hideyoshi.

Iyeyas Mikawa no kami seems, during his career, to have
occupied a position apart in the empire.   This is attributed
by his countrymen to a recognition by Nobu nanga and
Hideyoshi of his great talents as a general in command
during war, they being always either jealous or afraid of
him.   He had been nearly uniformly successful in war, even
when fighting against great odds.   They had put him into
dangerous positions in the hope of getting rid of him, but
he had always come out of them with additional credit and
invariable success.   He was ready to obey and equal to command.   Unwilling to thrust himself forward, he could bide
his time, and was prepared for any emergency.   He was
born of a good family, but had cut out for himself a position; and, in the general scramble for landed possessions at
this period, had laid a solid foundation in the province of
Suruga and Mikawa and some portions of other provinces.
He had already been advanced to high rank by the Emperor.
He resided at Hamamatz, in Towotomi, where he held over
the Kwanto supreme sway, with which Taikosama did not
think it wise to interfere.

Hideyoshi, as has been related, was of low origin, and
his birth and lineage a matter of obscurity; but in such estimation is some sorts of pedigree held in Japan (as in other
places) that he contrived to make it appear that his mother
was pregnant with him before she married his reputed father,
Kinoshta mago yaymong.   According to his own accounts,
his mother was daughter of Motchihagee, a Koongay, and
during the troubles she was obliged to fly, and, falling into
great distress, married Kinoshta.   She married a second
husband, Tchikoo ami.   Before her second marriage, she
one night dreamed that she had conceived by the sun, and
thence her child was called Hi yoshi maro.   He was commonly called Ko chikoo (small boy).   His face was small,
and he was like a monkey, whence he got the nickname of

Saru matz; and, even long afterward, when he was Kwan-bakku, he was called Saru Kwanja, or monkey with a crown. When a child, he was very cunning and reckless, and lived on the streets. A story is told of him lying asleep on a bridge in Okasaka. Among others who passed was Hiko yay mong, a noted robber from Owarri. He gave the boy a kick, and asked him his name. He said, "Sarumatz. This is the public road, and is as much mine as yours. Who are you?" He said, "I am Hiko yay mong." "Well," says the boy, "Hiko is a thief and a robber, and I have as good a right to be here as he." He long afterward made Hiko a Daimio— the family as Hatchiska existing to the present time. He went, when ten years of age, to Hama matz, where his master, observing the talent in the boy, recommended him to turn a soldier. He afterward entered the service of Nobu nanga, and called himself Kinoshta Tokitchiro. When he rose in military rank, he took the name of Hashiba Hide-yoshi Tchikuzen no kami. In 1583, upon the death of Nobu nanga, he rose rapidly in imperial rank from lieutenant-general to be Naidaijin and Kwanbakku. As it was unheard-of presumption in any one not of the Fusiwarra family being Kwanbakku, he asked, extorted, or adopted this family name from the Emperor. But he seems never to have used it, and is known by that of Toyo tomi, given him by the Emperor. In no long time after, he rose to be Dai jo dai jin. He was Kwanbakku during seven years, when he retired under the usual title of Taiko, given to that officer on retiring, and was known by the name of Taiko sama, or the Taikosama. After the destruction of Azutchi, the city of Nobu nanga, Hideyoshi fixed upon Fusimi and Osaka as his places of residence, taking possession of the castle of Osaka, which commands the town, adding to its strength by immense fortifications, and building in the center a palace of great magnificence. This castle had formerly belonged to one of the powerful Buddhist sects, and had been wrested from them by Nobu nanga. By command of Taikosama, immense canals were dug, and, by artificial means, smaller rivers were led into that flowing past Osaka, by which the importance of the town as a commercial capital, as well as its strength as a fort, was materially increased. In Miako he built another magnificent palace, known as Jui raku; and had another at Fusimi, between Miako and Osaka. He had married, during his youth, a woman of his own rank. He afterward married the daughter of Fusi yee; and, thirdly, the daughter of Gamo Hida no kami. His fourth wife was the daughter of Kio goku; and the fifth, the daughter of Mayedda of Kanga; and, lastly, Yodo hime dono, daughter of Azai Bizen no kami, of whom the Jesuit letters speak as Kita Mandocoro "quæ est primaria Taici conjunx carissima erat et conjunctissima." But notwithstanding this plurality of wives, it was never pretended that he had a son till his old age. He had a stepbrother, Hide nanga, and a stepsister, who married Musasi no kami, and had two sons, Hidetsoongu (who was adopted by Hideyoshi) and Gifoo sho sho. Another stepsister had a son, Hide toshi, who was adopted by Hidenanga. Hidetsoongu (nephew of Taiko by his stepsister), who was afterward Kwanbakku, was first adopted by Miyoshi Yamashiro no kami, and afterward by Taikosama. Taikosama also adopted Hideyuki kingo, son of Kinoshta, the brother of his wife.

The following account of Taikosama is taken from the letters of the Jesuits: "This man (Faxiba, or Hashiba), who was most certainly immoderately ambitious, seeing his master dead, and with him his eldest son, who had left only one child not full three years old; moreover, finding the second son to be but a weak man, and the third destitute both of fortune and strength to make head against him, he believed it would be easy to content him by a donation of some government, and so the way was fairly open for himself to step into the throne. To carry on his design, he first sounded all the officers of his army, and finding them tight to his interest, for a color of his ambition he took upon him the title of tutor and governor to the young prince and heir to the empire, and put him into a fortress with a train answerable to his birth. Nobu nanga's third son soon smelled out his design, and not able to brook one of his father's subjects in the government of his kingdoms, he leagued with several of the lords who were grown jealous of Faxiba's power, and resolved to make it a trial of skill; but Faxiba, who was an old experienced captain, and had good troops under him, easily defeated them, and put all to death that durst oppose his designs." This is hardly correct, inasmuch as, though he marched into the province of Mino in pursuit of Nobu taka, third son of Nobu nanga, and defeated him, he was not so successful in his action against Nobu wo, the second son, in the year 1584. This latter, without much talent, had wit enough to ask Iyeyas to assist him. He came to his assistance, and in the battles of Komaki and Nangakute, with greatly inferior forces numerically, defeated, first, Hidetsoongu, Taikosama's nephew, and afterward Taikosama himself. Taiko thought it more prudent to make a compact, and having done so, retired to Miako, which Iyeyas permitted him to do without further action.

"Among the confederates of Nobutaka was one Shibata dono, brother-in-law to Nobu nanga. He was besieged in the fortress of Shibatta, and seeing no way of escape, he, having dined with his friends, wife, and children, and retainers, set fire to the castle, first killing his wife, his children, and the female servants; and his friends, following his example, afterward committed suicide, 'and lay there wallowing in their blood till the fire kindled and burned them to ashes.'" Some of the arms and clothes which were found unburned are said to be all kept to the present day as they were found after this catastrope.

"Faxiba, being now in peaceable possession of the Tense (or imperial provinces), and all Nobu nanga's other kingdoms, to give color to his usurpation, affected an affable sweetness, which charmed all that ever saw or heard him. None, besides the Christians, could in the least suspect the sincerity of his intentions; and not long after they, too, were quieted of all their fears; for, knowing very well how respectful they had been to Nobu nanga, either out of real affection, or for that he had no mind to make himself new enemies, he began to caress them, and gave them several particular instances of his favor. He knew the Christians in his service to be famous, both for their piety and their courage; and, above all, he showed a particular respect for Justo Ucondono (properly called Takayama oo konyay no kami), to whom he had been indebted for his good fortune.

"So when the fathers went to visit him, he treated them after the same manner and with the same ceremony as Nobu nanga had done before him; and for instance of his real intentions, he appointed them a place for building a church and seminary (in Osaka), as was done before in Anzuquiama. The Queen, his lady, had also several of the Christians among her maids of honor, whom Faxiba particularly respected for their singular modesty and piety. He permitted them to assist at mass and sermons, and was pleased to show a liking when any of his subjects became Christians, which emboldened them to preach and exercise their other functions with greater liberty than formerly, to the great increase of the faithful. Faxiba, who was advertised of it, far from being displeased, declared he would embrace the Christian religion himself were it but a little more indulgent to flesh and blood."

Taikosama was feeling his way in the novel position in which he found himself after Nobu nanga's death. The Jesuits did not know how their position might be affected. They had basked in the sunshine of court favor for some years past; that might now be clouded over. The bozangs, or native Buddhist priesthood, had been standing in the cold shade for some years; they had everything to hope for in a change. There was not much to be feared from Sanhoshi, the infant grandson of Nobu nanga, as a claimant to the throne. Mowori in the west was quiet. Iyeyas in the east was occupied in attacking Hojio of Odawarra, who was supposed to be in opposition to the government. Hojio was superior in the number of his forces, but inferior in the ability of his commanders. The proverbial saying of an "Odawarra Hio jio"—that is, an Odawarra deliberation—took its origin in the councils of war of Hojio at this time, which, with superior forces, were protracted till Iyeyas attacked, defeated him, and took the Castle of Odawarra.

In the year 1583 the Jesuit fathers prevailed upon the Christian converts Arima and Omura and Owotomo Boongo no kami to send some young lords on a visit to the Pope. Four were sent, two of them being relatives of these lords, and the other two sons of nobles. They were all four boys of the age of from fifteen to sixteen. They took letters with them to Pope Gregory XIII. Leaving Japan on February 22, 1583, they, going by Macao and Goa, reached Lisbon on August 10, 1584, and after an interview with Philip at Madrid, arrived in Rome on March 20, 1585, where they were received by the Pope, and kissed his feet. They reembarked at Lisbon the last day of April, 1586, with seventeen religious of the Society, reaching Goa on May 29, 1587, and finally arrived in Japan in 1590, "eight years from their first setting out," bringing with them an Arabian horse, which had been presented to them by the Viceroy of India.

In 1583 Taikosama finished the fortress of Osaka, a work which consumed a great deal of money and occupied a great number of men, and which, when finished, covered a much larger space of ground than that upon which the castle now stands. During this year the island of Kiusiu was the theater of war. Riozoji held an office, now done away with, as governor of the island. He had formerly been a vassal of the small lordship of Arima, but now had large landed possessions in the island: and being too desirous of extending his own territory at his neighbors' expense, they joined together and rooted him out.

In 1585 Taikosama received from the Emperor the family name of Toyotomi. He called himself Fusiwara, and insisted on the Emperor appointing him Kwanbakku. He had now had sufficient time to feel himself settled in his position; but he thought the native monasteries were still too powerful, notwithstanding the demolition of Hiyayzan, the large monastery near Miako, and the slaughter of great numbers of priests by Nobu nanga, together with the appropriation as a castle of the large monastery in Osaka. The sect of Negoros [Negroes in the Church of Japan] at Kumano, in the province of Kii, occupied a very large monastery, to which the whole of the province belonged in territorial right, the military retainers of the monastery being noted for prowess and skill in fighting. Taikosama having found or made some cause of quarrel moved against them, defeated them, and destroyed the monastery. Most of these retainers were removed to Yedo, where to this day they form part of the guard of the Shiogoon.

This year Taikosama sent Nobuwo to order Iyeyas to come to Miako. He refused to come until it was arranged that Taikosama's mother should come to Yedo as a hostage during his absence, when Iyeyas went to pay his respects to the Emperor. Mowori, lord of the western provinces, was also ordered to come to Miako to acknowledge Taikosama as his superior, an order which he found it prudent to obey. In 1586 Iyeyas married the youngest sister of Taikosama.

A persecuting spirit showed itself among the Jesuits very soon after the departure of Francis Xavier. "Sumitanda," they write, "King of Omura, who had become a Christian in accordance with a promise to that purpose in case his wife should have a child, about the year 1562, or only thirteen years after the first arrival of a missionary in the country, declared open war against the devils. He dispatched some squadrons through his kingdom to ruin all the idols and temples, without any regard to the bonzes' rage." All this, doubtless, was done by the advice and at the instigation of his instructors; and "in 1577 the lord of the island of Amacusa issued his proclamation, by which all his subjects—whether bonzes, gentlemen, merchants or tradesmen—were required either to turn Christians or to leave the country the very next day. They almost all submitted, and received baptism, so that in a short time there were more

than twenty churches in the kingdom. God wrought mira-
cles to confirm the faithful in their belief."

All this time one of the most zealous as well as influential
among the Christian converts was he who was known as
Justo Ucondono, or Takayama oo konyay no kami. His seat
was Takaski, in the province of Setsu, where "he labored
with a zeal truly apostolical to extirpate the idolaters out of
his states, where the number was now fallen to 30,000. He
sent word that they should either receive the faith or be gone
immediately out of his country, for he would acknowledge
none for his subjects but such as adored the true God.
This declaration obliged them all to accept of instruction,
which cut out work enough for all the fathers and missionaries at Meaco." Taikosama still continued his wonted
favors to the Christians, "saying one day, in a familiar
way, that he would willingly become a Christian himself if
they could dispense with him in polygamy." In this way
the Roman Catholics set the example of intolerance, driving
those opposed to them in religious belief out of the country.
True disciples, and breathing the spirit of the Inquisition,
then in full blow in Spain and Portugal, they would not
allow within their own states that freedom under which the
tree planted by them had taken root and was flourishing.

Takayama brought over as a convert, among others, the
young admiral of Taikosama's fleet—Don Austin, as he is
known to the Jesuits; Konishi, Setsu no kami, Yuki Naga,
as his title is in native history. He and his father and
mother were baptized in 1584.

Taikosama, wishing to keep Takaski, gave Takayama in
its stead another estate, Akashi, in Harima; and as "soon
as Justo had taken possession of it, his first thoughts were
to reduce it under the obedience of Christ. The bonzes,
smelling his design, with their idols went to cast themselves at the Queen's feet. The Queen, touched with an
ardent zeal for her religion, spoke to the King in their behalf. But Faxiba, who was no bigot, answered her briskly,
that he had absolutely given Justo that place in change of

Tacacuqui; and for the rest, every one was free to dispose
of his own. Let the bonzes, if the idols be troublesome,
drown them in the sea, or dry them for fuel. Don Justo,
much pleased with Faxiba's answer, took then a resolution
to oblige all his subjects to become Christians,'' and thus
first taught them a lesson which they afterward practiced
upon himself. Justo had the merit, in his religious zeal, of
being unconnected with any seaport town. All the other
lords who had been brought over to the Roman Church were
competing more or less for foreign trade—Boongo, Arima,
Omura, Firando, Gotto; and though some of them seem to
have been sincere converts, others wavered with the rise
and fall of exports and imports. Such, for example, may
the King of Boongo be called, when he returned the following answer to the bozangs: "These good fathers have been
thirteen or fourteen years in my kingdom. At their arrival
I had only three kingdoms; they are now swelled to five.
My treasury was exhausted; it now exceeds any other prince
in all Japan. I had no male issue to succeed me, but now
Heaven has blessed me with heirs. Everything has succeeded and prospered since they came among us. What
blessing did I ever receive from your gods since I began to
serve them? Begone! and never speak ill of those I love
and respect.'' This Boongo no kami on one occasion during war destroyed a most prodigious and magnificent temple
with a colossal statue, burning 3,000 monasteries to ashes.
"This ardent zeal of the prince is an evident instance of his
faith and charity,'' says the Jesuit writer.

This year, upon the occasion of the arrival of the Father
Provincial of Japan at Osaka, Justo and Austin demanded
an audience for him with Taikosama. "To make the way
more easy, he exposed, according to the custom of the country, his presents for the King and Queen. He was introduced (his majesty accepting the presents) to Taikosama
seated on a magnificent throne, and was received by him
with the most marked kindness and condescension. He
commended them for taking so long a voyage to publish

in those parts the law of their God. He gave them sup-
per. After the collation he entertained them with a long
discourse about his government, told them he intended to
make one-half of Japan embrace the Christian religion, and
that he had thoughts of passing into China, not to pillage
and plunder the country, but to reduce it under the sweet
yoke of his obedience. To this end he intended to put to sea
with a fleet of 200 men-of-war. Moreover (and this is the
gist of the conversation), he desired to hire upon any terms
two stout ships of Portugal, well armed and manned, and
by means of the fathers made himself sure of gaining this
point. After the conquest of China, he would build temples
to the true God in all the cities and towns through his empire, and withal oblige his subjects universally by public
edict to become Christians.

"He afterward conducted them through his palace to
the ninth story of a pyramidal building, whence they had
a beautiful view of the country around Osaka. He then
alluded to the famous discussion between F. Froes and the
Buddhist high-priest, saying that at the time he was so incensed at the brute, the insolent bozang, that if he had been
in power he would have taken off his head."

At this meeting the Provincial put in a petition to Taikosama, which he is said by the Jesuits to have granted; viz.,
"That it should be lawful for them to preach the law of the
true God through all his states, and his subjects free to embrace it. That their houses should be exempt from lodging
soldiers. That, as strangers, they should be exempt from
all cesses and taxes which the lords do usually lay upon their
vassals. And he added to that, that he gave them license
to preach, not only in his kingdoms, but through all Japan,
as lords and sovereigns of the whole empire."

Such being the inclinations and views of Taikosama toward the Jesuits in the outset of his reign, by what means, it
may be asked, was he brought to a change? The statements
of the Jesuits are the sole authority for this part of history;
but they seem to have played their cards badly.

"Religion in Japan within this thirty-eight years past, when St. Francis Xaverius sowed the first seeds in that uncultivated soil, has now grown so fair and flourishing that one might well compare it to an orange tree loaded on all sides with fruits and blossoms. It was a field cultivated by the workmen of the vineyard, and watered with kindly showers from heaven, which gave fair hope of a rich and plentiful harvest. It was a ship under full sail drove by the wind of the Holy Ghost, discovering daily new places and countries.

"In the year 1587 they reckoned above 200,000 Christians in Japan, among whom were several persons of distinguished merit—kings, princes, generals of armies, principal lords of the court, and, in a word, the flower of the Japonian nobility. Moreover, what by Cambacundono's [Taikosama's] esteem of our religion, and kindness to the missioners that preached it, and what by his contempt of the bonzes, whom he persecuted with fire and sword, burning their temples and pulling down their idols wherever he came—what, also, by vesting the Christian lords in the most considerable places of the government, and indulging liberty to all his court to receive baptism, over and above, by erecting so many churches to the true God, and so particularly countenancing the fathers of the Society—the number of them daily increased. For, not content with sending frequently for the fathers to his palace, he went one day himself to visit the Provincial on board of his ship, and discoursed him after a familiar way for several hours together. Not that he had any thoughts of religion, for he was so proud that he pretended equality with Divinity itself, but by this had a mind to gain a reputation among the princes of Europe.

"Nevertheless, these fair appearances put several of the principal lords in a humor of being instructed, and the number of the proselytes was so great that the fathers could not rest neither day nor night. They were taken up continually with preaching, baptizing, and instructing such as earnestly desired this sacrament, among whom was Cambacundono's own nephew, a prince about nineteen years of age, presumptive heir to the crown.

"While the Church was in this profound peace, the devil, foreseeing an entire conversion of the whole empire must follow, raised such a furious tempest as drove the ship of the Japonian Church upon the rocks, and split it all to pieces." So writes one of the Jesuit fathers. He then looks about to find a reason for the foundering of the vessel, and finds it anywhere but in the pilots or officers of the ship. The unlucky merchants, whether the failure be ecclesiastical or political, are sure to be made the first scapegoats. Their lives were so dissolute that the immaculate Taikosama was horrified. This not being completely satisfactory, it was further found that "the scandal was so great that Cambacundono, who had notice of it, began to conceive an ill opinion of the Christian religion, and concluded the fathers only used it for a sconce to some underhand intrigue of reducing the empire of Japan under the obedience of some Christian prince." After these two preliminary reasons, the father goes on to assign other causes. "The first was his pride, which rendered him extremely sensible of the least contradiction." At his interview with the Provincial at Osaka, above narrated, his object was to obtain some large foreign vessels to transport troops to China. Hearing that one had "arrived at Firando, he requested it might be sent round to Facata, in Boongo, that he might see it. The captain said it was impossible, owing to the draught of water of the vessel. Taikosama seemed satisfied, but the same night he sent orders to the fathers to depart from Japan within twenty days, and forbade them to preach the Gospel on pain of death." To justify himself, he gave out that "he did this because the Christian faith was contrary to the received and established religion of Japan, that he had long since designed to abolish it, and only deferred the execution till he had conquered Ximo [Kiusiu], where the Christians, being so numerous, might have formed a party against him.

"Besides," says the father, "the main refusal, we discovered afterward two main reasons that put him upon this edict. The first was a design of ranking himself among the gods, by which he hoped to make himself be adored by all his subjects as one of the chief conquerors of Japan. Now knowing that none but Christians would dare to oppose him, he took a resolution of exterminating them forthwith before they could have time to make a party against him.

"The other cause of his aversion to religion was his own lewd life and conversation. Because some of the Christian ladies of Arima had rejected the proposal made by a bozang of entering his service, he was enraged against the whole religion, and resolved to be revenged on the whole body of Christians." This bozang, Jacunin (or Shiaku), had probably been a resident on the estate of Takayama, or Justo Ucondono, at Takaski, or at Akashi, and had smarted under the severity of the treatment by Justo, in turning out of house and home every one not of his way of thinking. This priest is said to have directed his master's wrath against Takayama. "All the forces in the empire being in his power as general, and he the greatest bigot of the sect, it was well if, under the mask of religion, he did not underhand form a league against the state." The consequence was, that a dispatch was immediately forwarded to Takayama, confiscating his estate, depriving him of his offices, and reducing him at once to beggary. Takayama on the occasion seems to have displayed great magnanimity, and acted from a deep Christian feeling. He might have temporized and dallied till the wrath of Taikosama had cooled down, or he might have committed suicide, as a native noble would have done, and preserved his name as a hero and his estate to his son. After prayer, the whole family—his father and mother, men, women, children, and servants—immediately put themselves on their way, with what little baggage they could carry. They found a retreat in the territory of Setsu no kami, Don Austin.

At this time Taikosama issued the following proclamation: "Being informed by the lords of our Privy Council that certain foreign religious were entered into our states, where they preach a law contrary to the established religion of Japan, and impudently presume to ruin the temples of the Camis and Fotoquis, though this attempt deserve the very utmost severity, yet out of our royal clemency we do only hereby command them upon pain of death to depart from Japan in twenty days, during which time it shall not be lawful for any one to hurt them; but if afterward any of them shall be found in our states, our will and pleasure is that they be apprehended and punished as in cases of high treason. As for the Portuguese merchants, we give them free leave to traffic and reside in our ports till further order; but withal we do hereby strictly forbid them, on pain of having both their ships and merchandises confiscated, to bring over with them any foreign religious.''

That this change should sooner or later have come is not to be wondered at. That it should have shown itself so suddenly, is in accordance with Japanese ideas of policy, and the character of the Japanese mind. The empire had been for years, almost ages, torn by internal divisions among small chiefs. The object of Nobu nanga had been to bring them all into one under himself. His lieutenant, Taikosama, totally illiterate, though perhaps not more so than those around him, had been imbued with his master's views. The Buddhist monasteries had been hotbeds of sedition and foci of disturbance, being at the same time large political and military powers of perhaps the second rank, and they had made themselves obnoxious on different occasions by marked insolence to the generals, and even to Nobu nanga himself. They had not even the justification of having preserved (as monasteries did of old in Europe) the literature of the country, not one priest being able to read, or teach the rising generation the rudiments of the written character.

When the Jesuits appeared with meek and lowly appearance, Nobu nanga was charmed with the prospect of establishing them as a counterpoise to the haughty and insolent

Buddhists. He nourished them, showering favors upon them, and in every way encouraging them, more especially borne, as they were, on the wings of wealth and trade. They found Japan, so far as religions went, a free country, where all religious were tolerated so long as they did not become aggressive. But they did not come from a free country. Their ideas were not those of religious tolerance. By a decree of Gregory XIII., January 28, 1585, all priests and religious whatever except Jesuits were prohibited from going to preach in Japan. This was confirmed by Clement VIII., March 14, 1597; and Philip II. of Spain wrote soon after to his viceroy in the Indies to see the order punctually obeyed. This monarch was wielding the power as King of Portugal. No priest could come to Japan without his sanction. He had the power of putting his veto on the appointments made by the Pope. The fires of the Inquisition were blazing. The wish of the Jesuits was, that those who differed from them in religious views should be burned as heretics, to be damned; their hope was that they themselves, holding the true faith, might be burned as martyrs, to be beatified. Doubtless the archives of Simancas could unfold many a letter breathing such thoughts written from Japan, possibly noted by Philip's own hand.

They had hitherto sailed with a fair wind. It may be believed, without going to the full length of taking everything in their letters for truth, or, on the other hand, accepting all that is said against them in the work "La Morale pratique des Jesuites," or "L'Esprit de Mons. S. Arnauld," that they had done some good. Many had been won over from a state of brutishness to submission in their daily walk and conversation to the precepts of the Gospel. Some had gone through severe trials and persecutions, and had stood firm to their professions. Each of the lords of Boongo, Arima and Omura had suffered more or less for the faith they professed. Though the fathers themselves give us a weapon to attack their conversions when they at one time assure us that "to win the favor of Taikosama put several

of the principal lords in a humor of being instructed, and
the number of proselytes was so great that the fathers could
not rest day or night preaching, instructing and baptizing
such as earnestly desired this sacrament" (among whom
was Cambacundono's own nephew, Hidetsoongo), it might
be asked, What sort of converts were these? and how could
these fathers abuse this sacrament in baptizing persons to
win the favor of such a master?

But these fathers appear to have looked upon the bozangs
as their personal enemies. They thought that it was their
special mission to root them out. They would not let the
tares and the wheat, as they looked upon the respective parties, grow together. They attacked these priests wherever
they met them. Francis Xavier, at the commencement of
his missionary life in Japan, visited these "bonzes, with the
design, if it were possible, to convert them to Christ, being
persuaded that Christianity would make little progress
among the people if they who were generally looked upon
as oracles of truth opposed the preaching of the Gospel."
He declared himself much astonished that in Japan the
people "have a profound respect for the bonzes; for though
they be conscious of their hyprocrisy and debaucheries, yet
at the same time they worship them like deities, and pay
them all imaginable submission."

One of the first duties of a missionary should be to learn
thoroughly the religion of the people of the country to which
he is sent. An acquaintance with Buddhism, and its tenets
and principles, would have been a very powerful weapon to
convince or to condemn these priests, without trying to hold
them constantly up to the scorn of their own people and followers. From the commencement of the Romish missions
a continued aggressive action appears to have been kept up
against the Buddhist priesthood as individual men. The
lives and the morals, or the want of morals, of these men,
seem to have been the constant theme of the Jesuit ad-
dresses to the people.

It cannot be wondered at that a body which was politically strong enough to cause uneasiness to the monarch of a country like Japan should not sit quietly under such attacks. We have no objection to you making converts, they may have said; but when it came to breaking down temples and destroying the images, a spirit of intense opposition was aroused. But when to this a system of persecution was added—such as that pursued by Don Justo in his territories, when every one not of his religion was driven out, when the property of the temples was taken from them, and perhaps given to their opponents—only one end can be looked for; viz., that one party should be victorious over the other, and that by a war to the knife, a struggle of life and death. The Buddhists were roused. They could live alongside of Confucianism, or of Taouism in the Yamabooshi, or of the different sects among themselves; but with the new sect, this Roman Catholicism, which broke its neighbor's temples down, abused him to his face, and then turned every one out wherever it had the power of doing so—the only method with it was to use its own weapons and turn it out—to root it out of the country.

This Inquisition mode of dealing could have ended in no other way. Japan was not Spain, as the Jesuits found out.

The Buddhists felt that they were worsted on both sides —by the military power on the one side, which had defeated their soldiers, burned their monasteries, confiscated their lands, and appropriated their temples; by the Jesuits, who had seduced their people, abused themselves, robbed them of their tithes and offerings, broken down their gods, and burned the temples, and were now attempting to make converts in the palace itself, being in such favor as to be received by Taikosama as he received no other.

Taikosama was probably a proficient in the Japanese act of dissembling. At first he was doubtful to which party to incline; but when he had once made sure, after his defeat of the Negoros and seizure of their territory in Kii, that the Buddhists were thoroughly subdued, there could be little doubt, knowing the man, but that he would not give it to that which was threatening to be the cause of renewed disturbance in the empire, and whose emissaries thought they had a right to reprove him whenever it pleased them to do so. But it was Japanese policy to flatter them, to amuse them, to dissemble with them till the moment of making the spring. Inflamed by the Buddhist priests around him, he made up his mind that the new sect must be rooted out. In the year 1586 Nagasaki was taken from the Prince of Omura by Taiko, and made a government port and property. At that time, native history tells us, Satsuma and Owotomo were fighting. To this war Taikosama put an end. Some "battereng," or padres, came to Tsikuzen to see Taiko. He did not like Roman Catholics. He found that two of his own servants were of that faith; they were speared at the temple of Hatchimang at Hakazaki. The padres were sent away. Thirteen churches were destroyed. At that time the province of Tsikuzen belonged partly to Owotomo and partly to Satsuma. Taikosama took it from both, and gave all Hizen and Tsikuzen to Nabeshima, formerly a servant of Riozoji, and whose descendants hold it to this day. He now fixed that Nagasaki was to be the only place where foreign trade was to be permitted.

The proclamation of 1587 caused the greatest dismay in the minds of the Christians. The heads of the church determined that they would, at all hazards, keep their posts. They took refuge in the territories of Boongo, Arima, Omura, Firando and Amacusa, alleging that they were waiting until a ship was ready to take them away. When the time arrived, and the ship ready, the captain excused himself from carrying the fathers this year, as his ship was already overladen, sending a letter to Taikosama, which did not reach him for several months. He was very angry, and took down the churches in the neighborhood of Miako. At the same time he ordered Don Austin to exchange his lands near Miako for others in Kiusiu.

A meeting was held in Firando in August, 1587, at which the heads of the church decided that the proclamation of

Taikosama was not to be obeyed, but that prayers were to be offered up, and that Christians were to keep quiet, in the hope that the storm might blow over.

The following character of Taikosama is given by one of the Jesuit writers: "He reigned in profound peace, and to conserve it he observed these rules in his government. First, After subduing his enemies, and an act of pardon, he never put any one to death, as Nobu nanga, his predecessor, had done, who never spared any of the great ones, which rendered his government odious and cruel; but Taikosama not only spared their lives, but further assigned them sufficient pensions to live on, which made them easy and well content.

"Secondly, He forbade all quarrels and private heats, on grievous penalties, and whoever were found transgressing in this kind were punished with death. If any of these fled, they punished the relations in his place; and in default of relations, his domestics; and in default of these his next neighbors, who were all crucified for not preventing the disorder. No doubt great injustice was committed by this means, and several innocent people suffered. But yet the fear of death made all zealous and careful to stifle these animosities and heats in their very birth, and forced them to live quiet.

"Thirdly, Though he was a tyrant, he would have justice done immediately on all criminals, without regard to birth, quality, services or any alliance whatever; and the party, upon the first conviction of his crime, was put to death out of hand, though he was one of his own relations, and of the very blood-royal itself. He was most lewdly addicted to women, nevertheless he pretended that none had a right to use these debauches but himself, and expressly forbade any of his subjects to keep a concubine.

"Another means of preventing troubles was to keep both soldiers and gentry busy employed; for he put them upon building palaces, raising fortresses, etc., knowing very well that the humor of the great ones is always restless and unquiet if their thoughts are not taken up about other business.

As for the soldiers, lest idleness should effeminate them, he kept them always employed about his works.

"Moreover, besides the pensions allowed them for life, he also maintained them in the field, which kept them in submission and dependence. As for kings, lords and governors, he made frequent alterations and changes to break their measures, and hinder them from growing popular. Above all, he studied the humor and genius of his subjects; and if any were found to be of a turbulent nature, he secured them, and by that put them out of the possibility of revolt in his absence.

"In fine, what rendered his government so peaceable, was his immense treasures; for by these riches he bound all his subjects tight to his interest, keeping all in hopes, though he never intended them any favors. These were his principal ways and means of maintaining peace in his governments."

A very little consideration of the position in which Taikosama, as ruler of Japan, was standing to these foreigners, must lead to the conclusion that he could take no other step than that which he had taken. They had come to the country uninvited. They had found the country in the possession, so to speak, of a religion which had never shown a persecuting spirit. They had come in their own vessels. From the very outset they had displayed a hard, persecuting spirit, with a tendency to re-embroil the country in war, out of which it was only now emerging. They had insisted on every one coming into subjection to them, with the alternative of leaving house and home in case of refusal. They were, as usual, now calling in the assistance of the temporal power to force the yoke of their priestly supremacy on the people of Japan. Had Taikosama been able to send them away in vessels of the country, he would no doubt have done so. But having no vessels, he gave them the alternative of living peaceably in the country, or of leaving it. They forced the ruling powers of Japan, by their encroachments and persecuting system, to retaliate upon themselves, and then gloried in considering themselves martyrs. They were, in short, constituting themselves and their flocks, over whom they, as priests, had no political authority, an *imperium in imperio*. They were teaching them to be rebels to their own government, and the priests themselves were obliged to end in the spirit in which they ought to have commenced —a spirit of meekness among their enemies. It would seem, from old as well as from recent experience, that, for Christians to live among heathens, it is necessary to have an "exterritoriality" power; but that is equivalent to saying simply that the Christian power is the strongest, and it means to enforce what it thinks right.

According to the resolutions of the meeting at Firando, the Roman Catholics kept quiet and in retirement in the several provinces in which they were settled.

The first of the line of Owotomo began as personal servant of Yoritomo; and a portion of Satsuma's territory was given to him, after which the family rose to greatness during the wars between the Emperors of the North and South. About 1374 they acquired a large territory in the northeast of the island of Kiusiu, covering the whole of Boongo and parts of Boozen and the adjoining provinces—Tsikugo and Tsikuzen. In the middle of the sixteenth century this territory included nearly one-half of the island. The family was ruined in the persecution of the Roman Catholics. The principality of Arima covered, at one time, the greater part of the province of Fizen. The territory, as was often the case with small proprietors in feudal times, was at different times enlarged and contracted. Latterly, it seems to have included only the peninsula on which the town of Simabarra stands, and but little more.

Omura is the name of a town which stands on the landlocked bay of the same name, in the province of Fizen, about twenty miles from Nagasaki; and the territory held by the lord of that name included a strip of ground round the city, and the greater part of the peninsula on which Nagasaki stands. The family seems to have been an offshoot from Arna, and never to have been of any great

7

power until the rise of Nagasaki, which no sooner became of any value than it was taken from the lord by Taikosama, and has ever since remained government property.

The lord of Boongo, who had patronized the Jesuit priests ("our Mæcenas," as they call him), and afterward had been converted and baptized, had died in the year 1587. He had abdicated in favor of his son, but at one time resumed the reins; but before his death had the pain of witnessing the diminution of the family estates by powerful and rapacious neighbors. His son, after losing part of his estates and the favor of Taikosama, thought to regain both by showing some activity in acting up to the recent proclamation. He was the first to commence the persecution of his father's friends. Meantime, Taikosama returned to Miako, and seems to have forgotten his edict and the Christians altogether. Probably the truth is, that during all this time, though he was annoyed by the Jesuits and their proceedings, he was working out in his own mind the means of making an attack upon China. He saw in the foreign ships easy means of transport, and, knowing the influence the priests exerted over the merchants, his hopes lay in keeping in with the former to obtain the assistance of the latter in his design. Some time after the promulgation of the edict, he received most graciously Father Valignan, Provincial of Japan and the Indies, as embassador from the Viceroy of India, and as associate with the four young embassadors who had returned from Europe.

The annexation of Nagasaki by government in 1590 was a great blow to the Jesuits, inasmuch as it had been a source of wealth, through the lord of Omura, who was a Christian; and also, inasmuch as hitherto the governor had always been a Christian, and he was now exchanged for two heathens. The place had increased rapidly from the time the Jesuits first went there, probably about 1575, when there were only 500 houses in the place, till 1590, when there were 5,000 families resident, besides merchants and tradesmen who came there in June from all parts on the arrival of the fleets.

In the year 1592, Taikosama carried out the project he had long been thinking on, viz., the invasion of Corea and thence of China, called in the letters "a foolish and temerarious enterprise, infinitely hazardous, if not morally impracticable." It is difficult to see what motive existed for this invasion. Being a man of war from his youth, and knowing nothing else, he perhaps longed for new conquests. The Jesuit writers attribute it to a wish to use up the Christians in the island of Kiusiu, as well as to get rid of—Uriah-like —some of the best generals of his army, who were believers in the new doctrines. Another reason they give was his wish to rival the greatest hero of the empire, now worshiped as the god of war—Hatchimang—who had conquered Corea through his mother. He made great preparations, giving out that he was going to lead the army himself. He handed over the power he held in Japan to his nephew, Hidetsoongu, giving him, through the Emperor, the title of Kwanbakku. He appointed four generals of the army, two of whom were Christians, Don Austin and Kahi no kami, son of Don Simon; the two other generals were Toronosuqui and Aki no kami. Under the two former were several Christian lords, Arima, Omura, Amacusa, Boongo, Tsussima, Don Austin's son-in-law, and others, with an army of 40,000 men. The total number of men collected, including seamen and tradesmen, was said to have been 300,000, a large number to supply with food, and only possible with an army fed nearly wholly upon rice. One-half of the army, after a council of war, set sail from Nangoya in Fizen, and was landed at Fusancay or Fkusan, at the southern extremity of Corea. Don Austin commanded this division. In no long time he repeatedly defeated the Corean army and captured several fortresses. Taikosama ordered Toronosuqui and his half of the army to follow into Corea without delay. He came up to the support of Don Austin, but, according to the Jesuits' account, treacherously held back his men that Don Austin might be defeated before he came to his support. The Coreans seem to have shown no capacity for war, and in no long time nearly the whole fortresses of the kingdom were in possession of the Japanese.

Taikosama, according to the Roman Catholic authorities, still jealous of the body of Christians, especially after Don Austin's success, collected 150,000 men out of Kiusiu, and sent them over to Corea, ordering the commander-in-chief to return the vessels immediately in order that he might follow in the spring. This is said to have been a ruse to shut off their return.

Meantime the large force in Corea was being neglected; they were left without provisions or ammunition. Their men, deserting, were taken and killed, and at length Don Austin was forced to fall back, and, after several engagements, signed an agreement with the Coreans by which the latter were to send two embassadors to Taikosama, and the Japanese were to retire, and only to occupy twelve forts on the sea-coast. The Japanese army was computed to have lost 150,000 men. A truce was concluded, and embassadors accompanied Don Austin to Japan. The following demands were made: 1. That eight provinces of Corea be handed over to Japan; 2. That the Emperor of China give one of his daughters to Taikosama; 3. That there should be a free trade between the two countries, and that China and Corea should pay Japan a yearly tribute.

In 1592, Lupus di Liano, a Spanish envoy, was dispatched from Manila to lay complaints against the Portuguese before Taikosama. He was lost on his return with the vessel in which he sailed.

In 1593 the governor of the Philippines sent over another envoy. He took over with him four religious Recollects of St. Francis. These were the first arrivals in Japan of any other order not of the Jesuit, with the exception of one Dominican, who accompanied the previous Spanish envoy. Among the presents was a Spanish horse richly harnessed. Among the presents brought by Father Valignan had been an Arab horse. The blood of these presents has probably influenced the breed in Japan.

At an interview with Taikosama these Franciscans asked to see his palace. "With all my heart, provided you do not preach in my states." The religious, being resolved not to obey him, gave no promise, but made a low reverence. Shortly after, the governor of Miako sent to the Jesuit fathers to tell them to go on with their work of piety, but with privacy and prudence. In consequence of this they hired a house and met privately, none appearing in public except two. "But the fathers of St. Francis thought not themselves obliged to such condescendence. Their ardent zeal made them believe that such deference to the order of the sovereign was contrary to the liberty of the Gospel, and that they ought to preach the faith despite of all laws to the contrary." They went to Taikosama and asked for some place away from secular people to build a little house for their own private convenience. He did not carry his edict into execution against them, but referred them to the governor of Miako, who assigned "them a very sweet seat without the walls of Miako, commanding that they should neither preach nor hold assemblies of Christians, according to Taikosama's orders. But the fathers, without regard to either the governor's advice or Taikosama's orders, built immediately both a church and a convent with a wall about it. Even the wise and more prudent among the Christians advised them to be seriously careful of what they were doing. The governor, hearing of it, sent and requested them to shut up their church." He was obliged to inform Taikosama, saying, "He feared that these religious, who call themselves embassadors from the Philippines, intend to preach like the rest." "They won't," replied he, in a passion, "if they be wise; for if they do, I'll teach them to laugh at me."

These Franciscans, thinking they were most successful, wrote to Manila for others to come over to assist them. They opened a church at Osaka, and designed to erect a third at Nagasaki. To this end they desired the governor would obtain leave of Taikosama for two sick to change air. The governor said in case of health they were free to go

where they pleased.   Upon this two went to Nagasaki, and
began to say mass and preach publicly without any regard
to the Emperor's mandates.

The Jesuits were much surprised that these Franciscan
fathers should fix a residence in their jurisdiction without
their consent; while the lieutenant-governor, having received strict orders not to permit any service in the town,
was in doubts what to do.   He referred to the governor,
and he, being alarmed for himself, ordered a note to be
taken of every one who disobeyed the law, but said he
would apply for further instructions to Taikosama himself.
Hearing from Miako that these men had asked and received
permission to go to Nagasaki on the plea of sickness only, he
ordered them out of his jurisdiction, which seems to be a
very lenient course of treatment, considering the trouble
that had already arisen out of this preaching.

The success of Konishi (Don Austin) in Corea seems at
first to have operated in his favor.   Taikosama was delighted; but as soon as this first feeling was over, alarm
at thinking he was a Christian, and as such could command the services of a very large body of his countrymen
at a word from the Jesuit priests, seems to have been the
most prominent feeling in his mind.   He knew by experience that the Buddhist priests had been able to keep the
armies of Nobu nanga at bay for several years.   He therefore dissembled, and in the mean time he recalled Justo to
court, and gave him a large pension.

At this time, however, another circumstance occurred
which occupied his mind for a time.   Hidetsoongu, his
nephew, had been acknowledged as heir, and power was
delegated to him as regent while Taiko should be away in
Corea.   Of this young man a somewhat extraordinary account is given in the Jesuit letters.   In 1587, when Taiko
chose to make a great show of favor to the Roman Catholics and the missionaries, the fathers were taken up continually with preaching, baptizing and instructing such of the
principal lords as desired earnestly this sacrament, among

whom was Taiko's own nephew, and presumptive heir to the crown.

"Hidetsoongu was a young man of three-and-thirty years of age, endowed with all the qualifications that can be desired in a young prince. He had a quick and penetrating wit, and excellent judgment, and withal a most courteous and obliging behavior. He was wise, prudent and discreet. He abhorred the vices of his country and loved learning, and took pleasure in it. For this reason he was delighted in the company of the fathers, and knowing that our religion set value on virtue and good manners, he took a particular affection to it.

"But all these good qualities were quite obscured by a strange and most inhuman vice. He took a strange kind of pleasure and diversion in killing men, insomuch that when any one was condemned to die, he chose to be executioner himself. He walled in a place near his palace, and set in the middle a sort of table for the criminal to lie on till he hewed him to pieces. Sometimes, also, he took them standing, and split them in two. But his greatest satisfaction was to cut them off limb by limb, which he did as exactly as one can take off the leg or wing of a fowl. Sometimes, also, he set them up for a mark, and shot at them with pistols and arrows. But what is most horrid of all, he used to rip up women with child to see how the infants lay in their mother's womb. Father Froes, who had seen and conversed with him, describes him as you have seen." This account is corroborated by native history.

For many years Hidetsoongu had been looked upon as his uncle's heir. He had three children; but about this time one of Taiko's wives had a son, who was thought by many to be supposititious. "Be it as it will," write the fathers, "he made great rejoicing for it all over Japan, and insisted on his nephew adopting the child as his son."

The consequence was that uncle and nephew became jealous and distrustful each of the other. In the "History of the Church" a full account is given of their meetings in

Miako. "Taikosama sent to his nephew to say he would invest him with full power. Hidetsoongu prepared a magnificent feast. The day was settled, but the uncle was afraid to trust himself within the palace of Juraku, where the nephew was waiting for him. At last he was persuaded to go, and went with great magnificence in a triumphal chariot (a closed box) all laid with gold, drawn by two large oxen with gilt horns. The procession lasted from morning till two in the afternoon. All this time Taiko minded more the security of his own person than all the entertainments. He placed guards all about his apartments, and advised his nephew to lodge in another palace. The nobility generally believed that Hidetsoongu would never let slip so fair an opportunity of avenging the injuries he had received, and therefore every one took care of himself. But no attempt was made on Taiko's life. Appearances were kept up for some days; but the nephew, disgusted with his uncle's treatment, secretly began to make the preparations which had been expected of him long before." But he was betrayed by the first of the nobles to whom he applied—probably Mowori (known as Choshiu), who gave Taiko information. In no long time Taiko brought the matter to a point by asking explicit answers to plain questions, and in the meantime collected troops about Miako. When he thought he was safe, he sent to his nephew and ordered him off instanter to his father's territory. He was then ordered to enter the monastery of Koga, used as a retreat by exiled nobles. He marched, accordingly, all night. The prisoner was treated as badly as possible; and in August, 1795, an order came from his uncle that he and his servants should rip themselves up. Hidetsoongu paid the last attention one friend can pay to another in Japan, and cut their heads off after they had stabbed themselves. He himself repeatedly stabbed himself, and one of his esquires took his master's saber and cut off his head, and then stabbing himself, fell on his body. Father Froes seems to have been on the spot at the time.

Taikosama, in the whole of this affair, showed a spirit of extreme cruelty and vindictiveness. He, not satisfied with the life of his nephew, put to death all his friends, and then, collecting his family, sent his wives and children, the eldest five years of age, his own grand-nephews and nieces, to execution; with savage atrocity sending for his nephew's head that it might be shown to them at the scaffold. They were all beheaded to the number of thirty-one ladies and three children, and their bodies thrown into a hole in Sanjio Street, over which a sort of erection or tomb was built, and on it the inscription, Tchikushozuka, "The tomb of bitches," which remains to this day. A temple has been built close by, and is named Tchikushozuka no dera.

Taikosama had long set his heart upon the hope of prevailing upon the Emperor of China to send an embassy to Japan, and, to his own surprise, his ambition was gratified. Don Austin, according to Jesuit accounts, by working upon the fears of the officers of the Celestial court, induced them to send two men to Corea, who were ordered to pass over into China. Taikosama made preparations to receive this embassy with great magnificence, but in the end treated the envoy with marked insolence and rudeness.

In August of 1596 a comet was visible for fifteen days in Japan, and on the 30th of the same month a frightful earthquake is recorded to have occurred. By this the greater part of the buildings recently erected at great expense at Osaka and Fusimi were completely demolished. Recurring at midnight of the 1st of September with awful violence, all the magnificent buildings raised by the Taiko were in a moment thrown down—two lofty eight-storied buildings, visited by the fathers, being destroyed. Stones, each of which had required the united efforts of 1,500 men to put in their places, were hurled out. The heavy roofs of temples and buildings, subsiding *en masse*, buried many under them, and, as usual in Japan, the fires which arose carried death to those buried under the wood. The occasion is used by one of the fathers, in his letter, to indulge in a sneer against the Buddhist priest-

hood.   In doing so, he gives some insight into the tenets inculcated in their sermons by these Buddhist priests.   ''He
was preaching on the evening prior to the earthquake with
such a torrent of eloquence as to bear all before him, and
the main drift of his discourse was the mercy and bounty of
his god toward his clients, particularly at the hour of death.
He enlarged upon his charity to mankind, showing that he
would have all men to be saved, without distinction or exception of persons, exhorting them to cast themselves on his
mercy.   So soon as he had made an end of speaking, the
people cried out with a general voice, 'Our god be merciful
to us!'   But Amida was probably asleep, for that very night
the temple fell to the ground, the idol was broken, and the
preacher narrowly escaped with his life.''   By this convulsion the immense copper figure of Buddha at Miako was
broken.   The Jesuit accounts state that seventy women
about the palace at Fusimi were killed, the Taiko himself
narrowly escaping to a mountain top, where he dwelt in a
reed hut, for fear of being swallowed up in the chasms of
the earth.   Saccay, the richest and most voluptuous city of
Japan, suffered, at the same time, greatly from one of those
fearful incursions of the sea consequent upon a temporary
depression or bending downward of the crust of the earth.

In the meanwhile Taikosama's passion began to cool, and
the fathers ''had grounds to hope that religion would be re-
established, as he was rather pleased at their obeying his
edict, and keeping quiet in deference to his wishes.''   He
still took pleasure in occasionally receiving the bishop, and
winked at the fathers remaining in the capital.   But when
everything was again promising of fair wind, another storm
arose, and again the origin is attributed by the Jesuits, not
to the Japanese, but to the same Franciscan fathers who
had recently arrived from Manila.   The Jesuits' letters say,
''The Recollects of the regular observance of St. Francis,
who were lately settled at Miako, being now conversant in
the language of the country, began to preach publicly in the
churches, to hear confessions and baptize the infidels, with-

out any regard to the Emperor's orders. Had religion been on the same footing as heretofore, the zeal and labor of these holy men would have wrought wonders, but the design was so ill-concerted at this juncture, that, instead of reaping any advantage by it, as was expected, it drew a bloody persecution both upon themselves and the other Christians. For being newly established in Japan, little acquainted with the genius of the people, and less with Taikosama's designs, they gave full scope to their zeal without regard to the Emperor's threats, or even to the advice of their friends, who counseled them all along to act in concert with the other religious, who by their prudence and wise conduct had counted so many thousands of souls in this mission. But nothing was able to stop this torrent of zeal. Designing well, they believed themselves obliged to overlook all human respects, and this persuasion made them jealous of friends' advice as savoring of jealousy and envy. The Christians, not at all satisfied with their conduct, begged of them to moderate their zeal; but being men that undervalued their lives, and in a persuasion that the Emperor would never offer any rudeness to persons of their character that bore the name of embassadors from one of the greatest monarchs of the world, they continued their functions with new fervor and zeal. The natives said, 'These men neither regard our counsel nor the Emperor's orders, but one day they'll repent it.' "

But still, notwithstanding these infractions of the recently published edict, there was no ill-will shown to these men. Four new governors of state had been appointed. These governors, hearing of the friars' rashness, sent to them privately to admonish them of their danger, telling them that if it came to Taiko's ears he would certainly put them all to death. This information only added new life and vigor to their zeal, so desirous were they of suffering martyrdom for Christ. The viceroy sent for two of these friars to the palace, and reprimanded them severely for slighting the Emperor's desires. This notwithstanding, they went on with their functions. The superior of the Jesuits, F. Organtin, hearing of those complaints by the governor, as well as the Christians and heathens, sent to Friar Baptist to lay before him the danger himself and his family, as well as the whole Church of Japan, was in if he did not (so far as reason, conscience and zeal of God's glory would permit) study to give the governor satisfaction, and yield a little to the times. "I do not find," says the writer, "what answer was given, but this is certain, they both preached and administered the sacraments after that more publicly than before."

These men, under the quality of embassadors, had come to the country, and under the same name were remaining in Japan to insult the supreme power, and to irritate the government into taking the only means in its power of supporting its own dignity; viz., putting them out of the way. "Guenifoin" (probably Kio no kami, or governor of Miako), "who had all along favored the Christians, foreseeing the ill-consequences of this refractory humor, suspended still the execution of his threats, and did not so much as hint at it either to the court. However, the business was discovered at last, and the friars were betrayed by their friend Faranda, the person who invited them over from the Philippines." They intrigued with this man, who seems to have used his knowledge of the Spanish language and his acquaintance with the Roman fathers of the church for his own advancement. "At first they had some difficulty in accepting his invitation (in the name of Taikosama) to visit Japan, as contrary to the decree of Gregory XIII. forbidding all priests (the Society excepted) to preach in Japan. All the able men whom they consulted agreed that embassadors were not included in this decree; and Sextus Quintus having given leave to the religious of St. Francis to preach the Gospel through the West Indies, the islands of Japan fell in course as part of the whole."

The conduct of these men would in any country have exposed them to the notice of the government. There is little need for drawing into the question of the treatment of these embassadorial fathers the conduct of the captain of a rich Spanish galleon wrecked upon the southern coast of Sikok. This man lost his ship, and the treasures were seized by Taikosama. "Upon being examined, he pointed out on a map the territories belonging to the King of Spain, and added that the way in which he obtained such extensive possessions was by first sending missionaries; and so soon as they had gained a sufficient number of proselytes, the King followed with his troops, and, joining the new converts, made a conquest of the kingdoms."

Upon the conduct of these Franciscan fathers being brought to the notice of Taikosama, he at once ordered them to be executed. At first the Jesuits thought that all Christians were included in this order; but the Giboo no sho wrote to Nagasaki to the governor, in the name of Taikosama, to see that no affront was offered to the Jesuits, whom he was pleased to have reside there on condition that they did not preach, or baptize, or hold assemblies.

The Father Provincial of the Jesuits, considering this condition opposed to the law of God, resolved to take no notice of it, but wrote to those under him to extend the empire of Christ, but still by such ways and means as might not give the Emperor cause of complaint. These five Franciscans were sent down from Miako to Nagasaki to be there executed, under the following sentence:

"Seeing that these men have come from the Philippine Islands in the quality of embassadors, yet have continued residing at Miako to spread the Christian law, which I some years ago prohibited, I command that all of them, together with those Japanese who have enrolled themselves under this law, be arrested, and let the whole twenty-four undergo the punishment of the cross at Nagasaki. And once more I prohibit the foresaid doctrine in time to come. Let all know this, and, further, that it be carried into execution. But if any one will not obey my edict, he, with all his family, shall be punished."

The punishment of the cross is inflicted by tying the criminal to a cross and transfixing the lungs and heart with two sharp spears. The twenty-four were thus executed at Nagasaki on February 5, 1597. The religious of St. Francis, together with the three Jesuits, were all placed in the Catalogue of Saints by Urban VIII., in the year 1627.

These men were punished by the Taiko not on account of their religion, but as contumelious persons, defying his laws. He appreciated the benefits of foreign trade, he valued the presents brought to him, and he admired the learning of the Jesuits; but he now saw a new doctrine being adopted by his subjects which would tolerate no other near it. The followers of this doctrine were becoming a great political power in the state, and more particularly in Simo or Kiusiu. Several of his principal military officers adhered to this new sect. Some of the highest nobles in the land had, according to the accounts of the Jesuits, favored it. The bishop, to whom no doubt extraordinary external reverence would be shown by the Roman Catholics, was an occasional visitor at Taikosama's court. F. Rodriguez was apparently in constant attendance as interpreter. The desire to continue to participate in the advantages of foreign trade was being counterbalanced by the probable dangers of the ascendency of such a power in the state, and Taikosama was becoming alarmed. There was a strong party opposed to the Roman Catholics—those who had been expelled from their lands, or who had been obliged to conform to retain them; those who were envious or jealous of the rise of such men as Konishi from a comparatively low position to a high military command; the priests, whose flocks were being withdrawn, and their incomes thereby diminished; and all that numerous class whose interests are on the side of things remaining as they are—all these were pressing that something should be done to overthrow the political structure which these foreigners were attempting to raise.

During the life of Taikosama these men, with their native associates, were the only sufferers for disobedience to his edict.

While Taikosama seemed every day becoming more timid

and afraid of what steps might be taken by the Christian party, an embassy arrived from Manila, to whose demand he replied that "he put to death the Franciscans because they preached the Christian religion in his empire contrary to his express command." But he did not pursue his harsh measures any further. He wished to get rid of such disturbers of the empire; and "hearing that Spain and Portugal were now under one prince, he became jealous to the last degree that the Jesuits of these two nations concerted together, under the color of religion, to bring Japan under the same yoke." He determined, therefore, while all the Christian princes were in Corea, to send away by ship all the foreign priests. But still he allowed a few to remain in Nagasaki, on condition that they did not stir out of town, nor preach.

He ordered Terasawa, governor of Nagasaki, to assemble all the Jesuits and ship them off by the first convenience to China. This, in truth, seems to have been the only resource left to him if he wished to retain the government of the country, or to preserve it from once more undergoing all the horrors of a civil war. If he had heard of the doings of Philip II. in the Netherlands during the few years since the first arrival of these foreign priests in Japan, he might have learned lessons of more decided measures for refractory subjects, and have carried out his wishes in ridding Japan of them by a more summary method of persecution.

During the summer of 1598 Taikosama was attacked by dysentery, and was so ill that his life was despaired of. His son (real or supposed) was then about six years of age. He saw that, in all probability, the power, after leaving his own hands, would fall into those of Iyeyas, now ruler of the eight provinces around Yedo. He therefore determined to strike up a family alliance between his son and the granddaughter of Iyeyas, thinking he would thereby induce the latter to throw his whole weight into the scale on behalf of his own grandchild and her husband, and that thus the power would descend to his own family. The marriage was immediately celebrated; and Iyeyas swore that he would turn the government over to Taiko's son so soon as he was able to rule by himself. Still further to strengthen the party of his son, he appointed five governors of the country (as Gotairo), and four others, to be about the boy, with instructions to obey Iyeyas, to acknowledge his son as sovereign so soon as he came of age, to continue all the lords in their places as he had appointed, and to oppose all innovations on the laws now established. To strengthen the position of his son still further, he appointed boards of officers, Tchiuro and Goboonyo, or five rulers.

On his deathbed, such little animosity as he may have had toward the foreign priests seems to have been mitigated, as he sent for, or allowed, Father Rodriguez to visit him, when he thanked the father for the trouble he had taken in visiting him in health as well as in sickness.

A temporary amendment enabled him to rouse himself, when his chief thoughts ran upon strengthening the citadel of Osaka, where 17,000 houses were pulled down to build the wall, which was a league in circuit. He only survived a few days, dying upon September 15, 1598; all his nobility, according to the fathers, "being much better pleased to see him on the list of dead gods than in the land of living men."

CHAPTER V

GOVERNMENT OF IYEYAS

WITH the removal of Taikosama, the hopes of the Roman Catholic party revived.

Once more the keystone of the arch was removed, and the ordinary institutions of the country were found unequal to the crisis.

The deceased ruler had foreseen this, and had made such arrangements as he could to strengthen the position of his young son. He foresaw that Iyeyas was the man of the future; the man most fitted by talent, military capacity, and position, to take the reins. He therefore tried to bind him by ties of marriage, as well as by oaths, to support the youthful inheritor of power. He had, as one of his methods of governing, induced or compelled the nobles to lavish large sums of money in presents to himself, in keeping up large retinues, in making expensive journeys between their country residences and the capital, and in building palaces in the two cities of Osaka and Fusimi. By these means the nobles were impoverished. They could not afford to keep many armed followers. Mowori of Nagato had been lately compelled to give up some of his territories, and to pay his respects at the court. Satsuma had suffered during the recent wars in Kiusiu. Iyeyas alone had kept aloof from Taikosama. He had kept his court and established himself at Yedo, where he was allowed to remain undisturbed, an object of jealousy as well as of fear. Still he seems to have been occasionally about the court of Taikosama, as he is mentioned in one of the letters as being present at the meeting of Taiko and his nephew. He perhaps kept Taikosama's mother still as a hostage in Yedo. Each of these potentates, in all probability, knew and read the other's thoughts—each thinking that the territories and the position of both would fall into the hands of the longest liver. The most dissembling are often the most credulous, and Taikosama was catching at a straw when he summoned Iyeyas to his deathbed. Iyeyas had refused to visit him on a former occasion without a hostage in the person of his mother. On this occasion he came, but, no doubt, with sufficient precautions. He saw that a political crisis was impending, and he knew that the fruit he had long waited for was falling into his hands. There was little reason now why he should not seize it.

The only persons who seem not to have descried the change that was at hand were the Roman Catholic fathers. By their own letters they do not appear to have paid any court to the sun rising in the east. No missions are men-

tioned to Yedo, or in the Kwanto; no interpreter is sent to
the court of Iyeyas; no conversions are spoken of there as
in Miako and the west; and no priests were located there,
who might have been acceptable if they had been able to
speak in the dialect of the eastern provinces. The Jesuit
fathers, up to this time, had rarely mentioned any of the
provinces east of Mino or Owarri.

The Taiko had put to death his nephew, who was of an
age fit to have held the reins after his departure. He left,
as successor, Hideyori, a child of six years of age. The general belief was that this child was not the son of Taiko, but
he himself appears to have firmly regarded him as such.
Recollecting his own origin and rise to the pinnacle of power,
and knowing the turbulent spirits among the lords, his countrymen, whom he had all his life long been trying to curb,
it is little wonder that he felt uneasy at the prospect opening
up to this child.

The Jesuits of this time write: "As to religion, there was
all the grounds in the world to believe it in a fair way of
being established in Japan. So many potent kings and general officers being all Christians at the head of a victorious
army, and masters of Simo (Kiusiu), where the inhabitants
had all embraced the faith, it was only prudence in the regents (the Gotairo), who were divided among themselves,
to keep fair with them. Above all, Samburandono (Sanhoshi), grandson and heir of Nobu nanga, having lately
professed himself a Christian, it was probable the Christians
and malcontents would join in these divisions, put him in
possession of his ancient rights, which the late Taikosama
had unjustly usurped. The faithful began to breathe after
the tyrant's death."

Probably the conversion of Sanhoshi (if true) to the Christian side blinded these fathers to the weakness of his claims,
and to the weight, power, and talents of Iyeyas. The claims
of Sanhoshi and Hideyori were equally weak. Both were
the heirs of men who had risen from comparatively low rank
and seized the coveted position, which had been hereditary

in the families of their predecessors, but which, having been held by these men, their fathers, respectively one after the other, could not be said to be in their families hereditary.

The first step taken by the Gotairo, or five governors appointed by Taikosama before his death, and who now assumed the power in the name of Hideyori, was the recall of the army from Corea, showing how much the whole expedition depended upon the will of the one man, and with how little favor it was regarded by the people of Japan. This brought back to the island of Kiusiu a strong re-enforcement of Christians with Don Austin at their head; and his bitter foe, Toronosuqui, the strong opponent of the Roman Catholic party.

In the letters written by the Jesuits at this period, the Taiko had generally been spoken of as the Emperor, and very rarely is any notice taken of the real Emperor, then living at Miako. Still less notice is accorded to the Shiogoon, Yoshitaru, who was then living at Miako, and holding the highest hereditary office that could be held by a subject. He was of the Ashikanga family, and, so long as he lived, neither Nobu nanga nor Taikosama could hold this office. In 1597 he died, and the office, which in the family had become an empty title, was not conferred on any of his relations. The family is still represented by individuals at Miako, who, though receiving some privileges, live in poverty and obscurity. The death of this man, and the cessation of the hereditary claim to the office, opportunely opened to Iyeyas the prospect of combining once more the chief power with the highest hereditary office in the state.

The year 1599 is given, in the native annals, as the first year in which the English and Dutch ships visited Japan (they are said to have come to the town of Saccai, near Osaka). Dutch pilots had been navigating those seas during several years past; some of the accounts given by Linschoten being the results of observations by Dutchmen. William Adams, the English pilot of the Dutch fleet of five sail, which left the Texel on June 24, 1598, did not reach Boongo till April, 1600, with only nine or ten men surviving out of the crew, and these nearly worn out with scurvy and privations. He was taken to Osaka, where he had an interview with Iyeyas, who was much pleased with him; but the jealousy of the Portuguese was roused, and they tried to instill into the ears of those to whom they had access malicious reports against these newcomers.

Meantime, it was impossible that affairs should continue long peaceably on the present critical footing. The Jesuits, however, were elated with the appearance of things. "(Giei-aso) Iyeyas ko,* now called Daifusama" (another name for Nai dai jin), "spoke favorably of religion, giving them leave to exercise their religion at Nagasaki, so that every one thought the Society re-established in the exercise of her functions.

"However, it was not long before the governors fell at variance among themselves—Jiboo no sho and Asano dan jo in the first place. The grudge between them was of an early date, but the office now held by both induced them to come to a kind of agreement. A like dissension happened among the lieutenant-generals in Corea about the late treaty of peace, and the differences ran so high that each took opposite sides on their return home—Don Austin and his followers with Jiboo no sho, and the rest with Asano dan jo. Several of the lords and Daifusama himself labored hard to compose the difference, and at last sentence was given in favor of Jiboo no sho and his party. Asano resolved to right himself by the sword, and in a short time many lords came over to his party. Don Austin, with Arima, Omura, Satsuma, Tchikugo, and Terazawa, stuck close to the interest of Jiboo no sho. But what set the whole kingdom in a flame was a misunderstanding between Jiboo no sho and Daifusama, the regent of the empire. The former charged Iyeyas with assuming an air of authority, and with secret practices, as if he intended to make himself master of the imperial do-

---

* Ko, coming after a name, has the meaning of "a high personage," a title of honor.

main. Iyeyas answered these complaints of the governors with a great deal of modesty and calmness, and, in the main, gave a fair account of his conduct. But finding that his opponents were levying troops, he gathered an army of 30,000 men out of his own states to prevent a surprise.

"The nobility were then all at court, part at Fusimi and part at Osaka, about the young prince. But seeing war declared between Jiboo no sho and the regent, every one armed himself and his followers, until they reckoned in the two towns 200,000 combatants, besides inhabitants. The streets swarmed with soldiers, and nothing was looked for but a grand massacre. But it being enacted that whoever first broke the peace should be declared an enemy to the state, it was each one's business to keep from hostilities. In this manner they continued for some months in the same town, and not a stroke on either side. At last Daifusama being much superior to his adversary (whom most deserted to serve the regent), he sent to him to rip up his belly for the public good.

"Don Austin, who joined interest with Jiboo no sho (otherwise Ishida mitzu nari), knew very well that would not serve Daifusama's turn, unless, at the same time, he could involve the rest of his party in the same ruin. In the meantime, Daifusama seized on the castle of Osaka with the young prince so suddenly that neither the garrison, nor Jiboo no sho, who lived hard by, had time to put themselves in a posture of defense. This was a thunderbolt to the latter, who fled to Fusimi, to the governors, where he was joined by Don Austin. Daifusama pursued them, and a temporary peace was struck up, on condition that Jiboo no sho gave up his commission and retired to his residence in the province of Omi. He took a son of Daifusama's with him as hostage."

After this, Iyeyas was supreme, the governors continuing to retain their empty titles. The Roman Catholics applied to Iyeyas, who received them so kindly that they were generally of a persuasion that he intended to restore the churches and permit the fathers to preach the Gospel, "so very easy are we to believe what we have a mind should happen."

However, at this moment they were annoyed by the lord of Firado showing symptoms of intolerance, for in one night six hundred Christians left the island and came to Nagasaki, contrary to the laws and edicts of Taikosama. The province of Higo, in the island of Kiusiu, was now under the rule of Don Austin, and by his orders the inhabitants were being converted or coerced into Christianity.

At this juncture the Emperor was a mere shadow. The power had fallen nominally into the hands of a boy. The scepter, or seat of power, was at the disposal of the most powerful. The respect for, or fears of, the lately deceased ruler had not died out; and the carrying out of his wishes, and the establishment of this boy in his place, was the alleged intention of each of the contending parties. The one party was made up of those chiefs or lords who had been about Taikosama during his life, and had been appointed to high offices under him, such as the five governors or regents for his son. To these were added those who had been engaged as commanders in the Corean wars, of whom Satsuma and Konishi were the ablest and most powerful, the latter being looked upon as the greatest soldier of his day.

On the other side, Iyeyas had evidently determined that the boy, now his grandson by marriage, should not stand in the way of his own advancement to power and position, and that he should be made the ladder by which he might reach his object.

The empire again resounded with the preparations for war. "Daifusama was grown so absolute since the late troubles at Osaka and Menco that he acted and did all by himself, none daring so much as dispute his commands. This sore perplexed the governors and mortified them to the quick; however, as soon as Jiboo no sho was retired [to his castle of Sawoyama, by orders of Iyeyas], they all returned back to Osaka and Fusimi, Cangerafu only excepted,

who pretended a grant from Taikosama to live three years
in his own states." This was probably Ooyay soongi kange
katzu of Etsingo, one of the wealthiest and most powerful
of the lords, and to him Iyeyas sent orders to repair immediately to the young prince on pain of being prosecuted as
an enemy to the state. The confederates were trying to
divide the forces of their opponent, and to gain by stratagem
what he was beginning to feel himself able to obtain by the
open assertion and display of power. He had possession of
the castle of Osaka and of the town of Fusimi. In the latter
he left his son with a garrison. The confederate lords hoped
to seize those places so soon as Iyeyas left them. Letters
were dispatched to Jiboo no sho and to Konishi, who immediately joined the league, "having no other intention but to
keep their promise with Taikosama, and to preserve the crown
for the young prince." They tried to draw over the head
officers of "Daifusama's army; and all things being in readiness, they wheeled round upon Osaka, and so secured most
of the nobility to their party. The governors, flushed with
their success, sent a manifesto to Daifusama, with heavy
complaints of his conduct. They commanded him to return
to Quanto, and positively forbade him the court."

The governors at the same time ordered all persons in his
army to return to their posts or homes on the penalty of punishment falling on their relatives and property. This order
brought about the death of a Christian lady, Grace, wife of
Itowo Tango no kami, one of the commanders in the army
of Iyeyas, of whom the Jesuits speak as a miracle of beauty
and piety. Her husband having joined the army of Iyeyas,
left command with his servants that, in case of any such
order being issued and put in force, they were to cut off his
wife's head. His orders were obeyed. His chief servant
informed his mistress, with tears in his eyes, of his master's
orders. He, falling on his knees, begged pardon for what
he was about to do, promising to revenge her by his and his
fellow-servants' suicide. With one blow he cut off her head,
and, thinking it indecent to die in the same room as their

mistress, they retired to another, where they cut open their bellies, while one of them set fire to the powder, and blew up the part of the palace in which they were lying.

The army of the league now numbered 100,000 men. The chiefs determined to attack the citadel of Fusimi. They contrived to set it on fire, and in a few hours was consumed "this splendid and last monument of Taikosama's greatness, the richest and noblest palace in all Japan." After this they felt themselves strong enough to take the field, and hazard a battle, if necessary, which should decide the fate of parties. "'There was this difference betwixt the regents' and the governors' troops: The first, being under one supreme head, acted vigorously and with unanimous consent; whereas the other, depending on several masters, and having each separate interests, the whole time was spent in marches and countermarches to no manner of purpose."

Iyeyas laid siege to Gifoo, the fortress of Hide nobu or Saburo dono, the nephew of Nobu nanga, in the province of Mino. By a stratagem and ambuscade he routed the army, completely destroying it, and entered and seized the castle, taking prisoner Hide nobu. He then turned back westward to meet the army of the governors, which was lying on the west of the plain and village of Sekingaharra. The army of his opponents had been re-enforced by the troops of Satsuma and of Konishi. This plain is to the east side of the hills which form the east wall of the Lake of Owomi. One hill of this ridge, Ee buki yama, is still noted for the foreign plants which grow upon its sides, the result or remains of the labors of the Portuguese missionaries who had a residence upon the hill. From this hill flows to the east the waters of the Kisso gawa. One of the main roads of Japan, the Naka sen do, passes through this plain from east to west, and at the village of Sekingaharra another road crosses the former from the northwest. Here on this plain the two armies met; but before the most decisive battle in Japanese history was fought they lay thirty days facing one another, "and durst not strike a stroke."

The army of the league numbered 80,000 men, while that of Iyeyas could only muster 50,000. Each party had been engaged in trying to gain over some of their opponents before trusting to the fate of war. Iyeyas had been delayed by his enemies in the eastern provinces; but hearing of the position of affairs at Sekingaharra, he marched rapidly up, and in October, 1600, joined his army with a considerable re-enforcement of troops. His motions were so rapid and so secret that his opponents were not aware of his being in the province. The following day he commenced an attack upon the army of the governors, commanded by Jiboo no sho and Don Austin. "No sooner had the armies begun to move than several of the general officers, with the troops under their command, marched straight over to the side of Iyeyas, which put the rest of the army in such consternation that, instead of fighting, they turned tail and fled without looking behind them. Daifusama, perceiving them in disorder, gave word for his men to advance; and making his way through the lines, which made very little opposition, gained a complete victory almost without the trouble of striking one stroke for it. None besides the general officers and some of the leading men had the courage to face the enemy at the first onset. These partly dispatched themselves, partly were killed by the enemy, and partly were taken prisoners. Among these latter was the celebrated Don Austin. This great hero, seeing his men in a rout, and no possibility of rallying again, threw himself into the midst of the enemy's troops, slaying on every side, and bearing all down before him, till, wounded from head to foot, and overpowered by numbers, he was forced to yield to fate and surrender himself prisoner, together with Jiboo no sho, who had not the heart (as he confessed himself afterward) to open his belly after the example of the worthies above mentioned.

"As for Don Austin, nothing but conscience could possibly have hindered him from such an attempt; and therefore choosing, as he did, to pass for heartless and a coward, and

8

to expose himself to an ignominious death rather than offend God, was an action of the first rate, worthy to be found upon the roll in the history of his other heroical exploits.'' The native account would make out that Don Austin attempted to escape from the field of battle, taking the road leading to the residence of the Roman Catholic priests on the hill of Ee buki yama, but was taken prisoner before reaching a place of safety.

The immediate result of this very decisive victory was to blow to the winds the rope of sand which his enemies had been endeavoring to coil round Iyeyas. His opponents were scattered and their hands paralyzed. Iyeyas was master of the situation. He lost no time in marching westward to gain possession of Osaka. He seized Sawoyama, a castle then belonging to Jiboo no sho, and now known as Hiko-nay, the residence of Ee kamong no kami. The brother of the proprietor was in command of the place. He put to death all the women and children, and set fire to the house, to take from the enemy the honor of leading him in triumph. Mowori was in command at Osaka, and, as ruler over ten provinces, he was now the only chief who was likely to dispute with Iyeyas the position of regent. But he was panic-struck, and, though at the head of 40,000 men, gave up the place and surrendered to the conqueror, who immediately entered the town in a kind of triumph, and soon after all Japan submitted to his government. He was, in truth, now the monarch of Japan. The Emperor was in existence, but this was only known near Miako by the titles which he occasionally conferred on those about his court.

Hideyori, the boy representative of Taikosama, was only seven years of age, and had no very strong claim to be considered that potentate's successor, a position which he could not hold without the assistance of Iyeyas, his wife's grandfather. Iyeyas had felt that the peace of the state was depending upon him, and that, from the position which the regents had taken up, either he or they must yield, and neither would give way without an appeal to arms. The

Jesuits seem all along to have shown a want of foresight in omitting to see that he was the coming man, and made a mistake in placing their trust in Don Austin, whose position was now to them a source of great anxiety.

Into the late war there does not seem to have entered any religious element of discord, as Christians of rank were found upon both sides. The lords of Arima and Omura and Kahi no kami (who is frequently mentioned by the Jesuit writers) were in the army of Iyeyas, while Don Austin and others took the opposite side.

Ishida, Jiboo no sho, being now a prisoner, was not likely to receive much mercy at the hands of Iyeyas. Letters had passed between them which reduced their position to a personal quarrel. He had already been once spared by his foe, and had retired on parole to his castle of Sawoyama. Thinking that an opportunity for revenge had arrived, he put himself at the head of the army of the confederates. He had again failed, and now found himself a prisoner in an ignominious and dishonorable position. But Konishi Setsu, or Tsu no kami, also a prisoner, ran the risk of losing his life, more probably from jealousy of his military capacity than from any other reason. He was the son of a drug merchant in Sakkai. The eulogiums pronounced upon him by the Christian writers may pass for what each values them at; but he had been trusted in a very responsible position by Taikosama in Corea. He had subsequently been degraded at the instigation of his rivals, and afterward reinstated for the accomplishment of schemes requiring the utmost acuteness in diplomacy, as well as for the execution of plans requiring military skill and prowess. He had shown himself capable of both. As an evidence of the position to which he had raised himself was the marriage of his son to the granddaughter of Iyeyas himself. He had been appointed to the office then known as viceroy of the island of Kiusiu, and was at the same time commander-in-chief both of the naval and military forces in the Corean war. Had Iyeyas acted with his ordinary clemency and judgment, he would after his victory have pardoned such a rival and family connection; but there were hungry wolves who personally hated Don Austin, who gloated over his downfall, and cast longing eyes on his territories, about to be confiscated. Chief of these was Toronosuqui, "Vir ter execrandus," as the Jesuits style him, one of the coarsest men of Japanese history, but since his death canonized as a saint in the Japanese calendar as Say sho go sama of the Nitchi ren sect of Buddhists. Hitherto known by this name of Toronosuqui, he figures in the subsequent letters of the Jesuits as Canzuge dono, or properly, as the title now is, Kazuyay no kami.

After his capture Konishi seems to have been treated with great rigor—not being allowed to see any of his relatives or any foreign priest—and was beheaded, along with the Jiboo no sho, at Awata ngootchi, the common execution ground at Miako. His young son was shortly afterward inveigled and murdered by Mowori, who thought to please Iyeyas and save himself, after his mean surrender of himself and his position, by sending the head of Don Austin's child to his wife's grandfather; but Iyeyas was disgusted, and Mowori in the end was stripped of the greater part of his possessions.

Native writers agree with the Jesuit accounts in giving Iyeyas credit for great moderation and sagacity in the use of the power which had fallen into his hands. Thinking himself firmly seated, he tried to make all know that he wished the past to be forgotten—that he was not angry with those who had been in arms against him, but that he was grieved that it had been necessary that so much blood should have been shed. He granted an amnesty to all who would accept of it; and even some—such as Tatchibanna—who were not very influential, and who would neither accept of it nor submit to him, he left quietly alone to allow time to work. The great secret of his power seems to have been, that when he once made a promise he never broke it, and the most perfect reliance was placed upon his word. "In effect, Daifusama, being naturally of a meek and easy tem-

per, took quite different methods from Taikosama, who had
rendered himself extremely odious by his cruel and severe
oppressions. He proposed to himself to govern more by
love than fear; and therefore, contrary to the maxims of his
predecessor, pardoned several of the lords that bore arms
against him. Moreover, he sent a pardon to Don Austin's
lady and daughter (who expected, according to law, to have
shared his fate), as also to his brethren and their children;
and, what is more, he did not show any resentment to the
fathers for being constant to the interests of Don Austin, or
for harboring his lady at the time of her retreat at Nanga
saki.'' The only unsettled portion of the empire was the
island of Kiusiu. The territory of Don Austin in the province of Higo was handed over to Katto Kiomassa, or Toronosuqui, who, as has been said, was a virulent opponent of
the Christian religion. While Don Austin held this territory, by the advice of his spiritual superiors, every one had
been compelled to be baptized and turn Christian, or to leave
the territory. It was now the turn of the opposite party to
use the same tactics, and most mercilessly they followed the
example set by these Spanish priests both in Japan and in
Europe.

Satsuma, who had escaped from the field of Sekingaharra, expected that the weight of the victor's wrath would
shortly fall upon him, and he prepared for it. The subjection of Kiusiu was intrusted to Kuroda Kahi no kami and
Terasawa Sima no kami, with the lesser lords who had territories in the island. Satsuma was obliged to yield, and
submitted to Iyeyas, receiving back from him the greater
part of the territory then held by him.

The part of the island of Nippon east of the barrier of
Hakonay, in the province of Segami, is commonly called
Kwanto; and the Hasshiu, or eight provinces beyond the
boundary toward the east part of the island, had more or
less for many years been under the entire rule of Iyeyas.
Kamakura, which had at one period been a rival to Miako
as a second capital, had fallen into decay. Odawarra, the

castle of the Hojio family, at the head of the same bay, had never risen to any position as a central city. The Nishi maro, a part of the castle of Yedo, had formerly been built and occupied by Owota do kwang, whose memory is to this day cherished in Japan, and his name and writings are still extant on some parts of his castle or shiro. On a summer house in the garden of the castle is a couplet in poetry which is looked upon as a prophecy of coming events with reference to its accomplishment in the present age:

"From this window I look upon Fusiyama,
With its snow of a thousand years.
To my gate ships will come from the far East
Ten thousand miles."

Considering the associations which hung around Miako and Narra and Osaka as the capitals, imperial, ecclesiastical and commercial of the empire, it might be deemed a great stretch of power and firm confidence in himself and the stability of his system of government, that Iyeyas should think of removing the location of the executive to Yedo. He had doubtless pondered long and deeply over the best system of government for the country. He had seen the anarchy which preceded the rise of Nobu nanga to power; he had seen the want of system by which the structure of government at that time had crumbled down with the fall of the one man upon whose shoulders it had been supported; he had all the experience since that time to be gained from ruling an extensive territory of his own, combined with what observations he might make upon the system of Taikosama. In the settling of that system, doubtless, he had a large share; but he went further than Taikosama, and, disregarding the old associations connected with Miako, he removed the seat of the executive to his own provinces and to his own court in the city of Yedo, in what was considered a remote part of the empire, the inhabitants of which were looked upon as rude and unpolished, and regarded with contempt as savages of the east—"Azuma yebis." The city, when

Iyeyas first took possession of the shiro, consisted only of one street, known then and now as Koji matchi. It had increased very much in size under his care, and through the residence of the court, the Daimios, and their wives and families, and in no long time became a city of commercial importance. Although Yoritomo, and the Shiogoons and Kwanreis who succeeded him, held court at Kamakura and in the Kwanto, no one had ever called upon the great feudal lords, or Daimios, as we may now call them, to reside or keep up establishments there; but Iyeyas seemed to think that in an empire like Japan, without external foes, strength would be gained by a division of the empire. All his plans seem to have had regard to the welfare and peace of the country rather than the gratification of ambition, which he never allowed to master his judgment.

This year (1600) and the following Iyeyas devoted to internal improvements, especially in the highways of the empire. The road between the two capitals, Yedo and Miako, was greatly improved. He arranged the stations (tsoongi, or shooku), to the number of fifty-three, at nearly equal distances along the road, for the accommodation of Daimios and others traveling on official business. The Do chioo, or laws of the roads, were laid down, regulating the traffic, but more especially the movements and service of these lords when traveling.

In the year 1603 to Iyeyas was given the hereditary title and power of Se i dai shiogoon, or tranquilizer of barbarians and commander-in-chief. The last who had held this office was Yoshikanga Yoshiteru, who died in 1597. Hideyori was made Naidaijori.

CHAPTER VI

HISTORY TO THE EXPULSION OF CHRISTIANITY

THIS termination of the sixteenth century was in Japan one of the most notable time-marks in the history of the empire. It was an era at which a long series of intestine broils and of civil war came to an end, and gave way to an unexampled period of peace and happiness. Indirectly, Japan was affected by changes of greater ultimate results which had commenced long before at the opposite side of the world.

Portugal, in the zenith of its maritime glory and power, had hitherto retained in her own hands the navigation and the trade of the East. Bold as these early navigators were, the accounts given of their proceedings show them to have conjoined, in strange recklessness, religion with war, trade with piracy—"the sweet yoke" of their own ideas of government with ferocious cruelty to every one opposed to them. Perhaps this was to some extent necessary, when the health and prowess of a few men, not easily replaced in case of loss, were opposed to the climate and weight of numbers whose losses could easily be recruited by others equally useless and contemptible as foes. Grotius says of Englishmen of that time, that they obey like slaves and govern like tyrants. Toward the latter part of the century, the bigotry of Philip II. was raising powers against him in Europe, before which the then colossal but unwieldy empire under his rule was destined to crumble to pieces. The same intolerant policy which his emissaries in Japan were pursuing was being carried out by the old man, in the conscientious belief that he was furthering and hastening the kingdom of heaven, by fierce persecution and diabolical atrocities. The dreams which led men to undertake long voyages to America in the pursuit of a Utopia, infused a new spirit of boldness and adventure into the navigators of maritime countries. At the same time, the Reformation and the changes in the religious ideas among the people of Europe, and especially in Holland, England, and for a time in France, tended to throw contempt on the concessions and grants and privileges given by the Pope to Portugal, and by which their trade to the East was up to that time hedged in.

In 1577 Sir Francis Drake broke in upon this monopoly; and the Spaniards complained of the English infringing their rights, granted by the Pope, by sailing in the Eastern seas.

The Portuguese vessels which traded with the East had hitherto carried their produce to Lisbon or Cadiz, and thence it was carried to the coasts of Europe by the Dutch and English. But when war broke out between these countries, Philip, thinking to clip the wings of his enemies, interdicted this trade. This compelled them to take a longer flight, and seek Eastern commodities at the fountain-head. The navies of the Dutch and Portuguese came into collision on the Eastern seas, and the former were victorious, and one after another of the large Portuguese carracks fell to the English and Dutch privateers.

In 1599 the East India Company of England was set on foot, and commenced operations, after being nearly arrested by the English government to please the Spaniards, by acknowledging their rights in the Eastern seas; and in 1598 the Dutch fleet sailed, of which William Adams of Gilling-ham was pilot.

According to native accounts, in the sixth year of Kay cho English vessels came to Ike no oora; but one of these was wrecked during a gale in the Sea of Segami. A message was dispatched from Yedo to order the crew to be sent there. Among them was Adams. He remained in Yedo, but the others returned.

The vessels belonging to the East India Company sailed

from England upon the eighth voyage, under the command of Captain Saris, in 1611, with the intention of opening a trade with Japan. There seemed at this time every prospect of the Portuguese monopoly being broken up, and of the trade of this distant country being thrown open to the Western world. Amid the broils and quarrels with which Japan was torn, whether among the lords, or between the Buddhists and Roman Catholics, or the natives and Portuguese merchants, or the Portuguese and Dutch and English, it is curious to see the practical and sound good sense of one man, putting him into a position of eminence and trust, when all around him was deceit and jealousy. Rising, after five years of obscurity and hardship, on the ground of his simple strength of character and practical training, William Adams seems to have become the trusted confidant and referee of Iyeyas on foreign questions. Residing in Yedo, at the southwest corner of the Nihon bashi, or bridge of Japan, the street where he lived retains to this day the distinguishing name of "The Pilot's," or Anjin. He seems to have afterward removed to the street Yaiyossu, in close proximity to the castle moat.—Both Anjin and Yaiyossu may be corruptions of the name Adams. In Cantonese dialect, an cham is a word for a compass, and "Adams" might be written with these characters.—Here his knowledge of geometry, navigation and mathematics, with some acquaintance with shipbuilding, brought him under the notice of Iyeyas, by whom he seems to have been employed as interpreter, shipbuilder, and general confidant on foreign affairs. He was ultimately raised to the position of a small Hattamoto, or lesser baron, with ground equal to the support of eighty or ninety families, besides his own rental. This estate is said, in one of the letters from Japan, to be in Segami, and to have been named Fibi, and situated in the neighborhood of Ooraga, the port of Yedo, and must certainly be known to the Japanese government as having belonged to the English officer.

Doubtless, by all these changes, the position of the Portuguese and of the Roman Catholic priests was changed in Japan. The converts of Nagasaki would see foreigners coming who paid no respect to the priests and bishops whom they had been taught to reverence. The powers in the country would begin to see that the profits of the trade could be enjoyed without winking at the coercion of their own people to a foreign religion, and which placed them at the disposal of a power exterior to the state. The English and Dutch tried to loosen the hold which their rivals had in the good opinion of their customers; and the eyes of the Japanese were thus opened to the evils of admitting foreigners to their shores, who were likely to prove centers of disaffection and to instill ideas of freedom and lawlessness among the subjects of the empire.

The letters of the Jesuits throw their own light upon the state of the Roman Catholic Church in Japan at the different points where churches or seminaries had been erected, and it may thence be gathered in what manner they treated their neighbors, or those over whom they could pretend to assume any power. On the other hand, from the narratives given by Cocks and Saris, some idea of the position of the seafaring communities at Firado and Nagasaki, and other ports, may be obtained. These seaports seem to have been too often the resorts of the lowest class of adventurers. The result was uproars, broils and murders among the foreigners, requiring ever and anon the intervention of the native authorities.

Iyeyas was in all probability ignorant of all these circumstances, which were effecting an indirect change upon those resorting to the country. At the Roman Catholic party he had aimed an effectual blow by putting the leading man of the party, Don Austin, out of the way on grounds totally unconnected with his religion. And the foreign priests do not seem to have given him personally much concern at this time. In the neighborhood of Miako they did not dare of late to make any public displays. In 1604 there were of the Jesuits 120 in Japan. They flattered themselves that "as

for religion, it flourished everywhere, and made vast progress through all the kingdoms under so easy and peaceable
a government. Notwithstanding, two obstacles still existed
—the one Taikosama's edict, and the other the vices of the
people. But what gave our religion most reputation was
the gracious reception the Cubo himself [Iyeyas] was pleased
to give the fathers of the Society." The Jesuits had recently
extended their mission to the extreme north of Japan, and
even into the islands of Yezo and Sado.

During this and the previous year the Jesuits were unfortunate, inasmuch as the vessels bringing the yearly sup-
plies, as well as the large annual carrack from Macao to
Japan, were taken by the Dutch privateers; but Iyeyas,
hearing of their loss, presented a donation to the Society,
by which means they "made a tolerable shift for the rest
of this year."

Terasawa, Sima no kami, who had been governor of
Nagasaki, irritated by the influence brought to bear against
him by the Roman Catholic party at Miako, turned the
weapons they had taught him to use against themselves,
and tried to force his subjects to renounce the new doctrines.
Part of the estates of Don Austin had fallen to his share.
Another part had fallen under the rule of Toronosuqui, who
in the year 1602 "ravaged the vineyard of the Lord like a
wild boar that thirsts after nothing but blood. He began
like a fox and ended like a lion." Thus it was in the part
of the empire in which most intolerance had been shown by
Don Austin (under the instruction of foreign priests) to his
countrymen, and where they were obliged either to adopt
the Roman Catholic doctrines or leave the country, that the
plan was retaliated upon themselves.

Native accounts tell: "In 1608 a Dutch ship came to
Hirado and asked that Adams might be sent down from
Yedo. He was sent. Iyeyas wrote under the red seal that
the English and Dutch might trade in any part of Japan.
Hide tada also allowed them to trade; but the padre sect
were not allowed to come to Japan. But the English traders

said that there was no profit to be made out of the trade as it was obliged to be conducted, and said they could not come back; therefore the Dutch only remained.''

About this time Iyeyas directed his attention to the internal economy of the empire—improving the public roads, placing inns upon them, and strengthening his castles at Yedo, Suraga, Miako, Osaka, and Kofu. He was aided in this by the discovery of valuable gold-deposits in the island of Sado, and the coin the koban was for the first time put into circulation. During the year 1609 Shimadzu yoshi hissa, a relative of the Prince of Satsuma, set out from Satsuma with a force of vessels and troops to bring the King of the Lioo Kioo Islands more completely under the power of Japan, and succeeded in his object, receiving the islands he had conquered as a gift from the hands of Iyeyas.

The designs of Iyeyas against Hideyori began to develop themselves. Upon the occasion of the investiture of his son with the title of Shiogoon, he expressed the thought that Hideyori ought to pay him a visit to compliment him; but his mother refused to allow Hideyori to do so, protesting she would rather cut his belly open with her own hand than allow him to go, thus showing the extreme suspicion she had of the intentions of Iyeyas.

At this time the Christians enjoyed a profound peace, which was attributed in the Jesuit letters rather to the fear of this party joining Hideyori than to any love for the doctrines promulgated. But at the same time there were men in power not unfavorable to them, and they were always able to keep anything obnoxious out of view. Such were Kowotsuki no kami, the favorite of Iyeyas (called by the letters Coxuquendono), and Itakura, governor of Miako.

In the year 1606 the Portuguese bishop, Cerqueria, visited Iyeyas at Miako, and was received by him with the honors given to one of their own bishops of royal blood. However, this favor did not seem to last long. The mother of Hideyori, incensed at some of her ladies having declared themselves Christians, appealed to Iyeyas. This was an opportunity of pleasing her not to be missed, and he issued forthwith the following proclamation:

"The Cubosama hearing that several of his subjects, contrary to the late edict, have embraced the Christian religion, is highly offended. Wherefore let all officers of his court be careful to see his orders observed. Moreover, he thinks it necessary, for the good of the state, that none should embrace that new doctrine; and for such as have already done so, let them change immediately upon notice hereof.—24th of the 4th moon" (1606).

No immediate action appears to have been taken upon this proclamation.

In the year 1607, Iyeyas expressed a desire to see the Father Provincial. He accordingly set out for Kofu, a castle in the province of Kahi, where Iyeyas was residing, and here he was received with much kindness. In their notice of Yedo the fathers say that Iyeyas employed during the previous year above 300,000 hands in the works about the castle of Yedo. The towers of the castle were nine stories high and gilt at the top, together with delicious gardens, terraces, galleries, courts, and magnificent works. By these fathers the mountain Fusiyama is mentioned as an active volcano, "a mountain of fire, famed for its beauty, height, and whirling flames." Even at this time it is to be noticed that all the "kings of Japan" had their palaces there.

In this tour a slight notice is given to Kamakura (Cumamura, as it is called by the fathers), "where the Cubos and Xogoones formerly kept their courts. It is currently reported that there were upward of 200,000 houses in that town alone; but when these fathers went that way they were reduced to near 500."

Notwithstanding these slight appearances of returning favor to the Jesuit fathers, the opposition to conversion increased as the profits from trade decreased. The ruling powers in the island of Kiusiu were now more or less against the Romish priests, who inculcated a line of conduct which was incompatible with living at peace with a neighbor, if holding a different view of religion. Nagasaki was in 1607 said to be entirely converted to the Christian religion. It was divided into five parishes. "There were two confraternities—a house of mercy and a hospital—which diffused a sweet odor of sanctity all over Japan." But this odor did not extend to the Portuguese who frequented the port, and, in consequence of some act of misconduct, Iyeyas ordered Arima (Don Protase, as he is called by the Roman Catholic writers) to burn a large Portuguese vessel then lying in the harbor. The consequence was that the captain left the place. He was pursued by an overwhelming force, and, overtaken during a calm, was forced to blow up his ship.

During the year 1611, Iyeyas seems to have made up his mind that, to settle the country upon a sure basis, some definite understanding must be come to with Hideyori and his mother. Of what his designs really were there are probably no proofs, as he was not generally communicative before action. He marched from Soonpu to Miako at the head of upward of 70,000 men. The general suspicions of his countrymen pointed to Hideyori as the cause of a movement on so large a scale. Arrived at Miako, he insisted upon an interview with the young man, then twenty-three years of age. After much delay and show of suspicion, this was agreed to, and he arrived at the capital with a splendid retinue. Here he was received with the utmost deference and kindness by Iyeyas, who shed tears over the remembrance of his father's kindness. The visit was returned in a few days, presents were interchanged, and the prince returned to his mother at Osaka overjoyed with his reception.

The Jesuit writers notice that during the same year died Canzugedono, King of Fingo (Toronosuqui), the persecutor of the Christians; "and, as Heaven would have it, he was seized with an apoplexy on the very day he was intending to renew the persecution against the faithful." Native accounts attribute his death to poison administered by order of Iyeyas at Fusimi. He had thrown out some seditious and rebellious threats against Iyeyas. Among other things stated against him, he refused, when ordered, to shave off his whiskers at court. He was, as has been stated above, canonized in the Japanese calendar by the title of Say sho go sama—probably on account of his opposition to foreigners, and the zeal with which he tried to root out Christianity. To this day the mark of his hand upon paper is used as a charm placed over the door to drive away evil spirits. Since the admission of foreigners in 1858, his character as a saint worthy of worship has risen in national estimation, and his temples have been rebuilt. One in Yokohama is more largely patronized than any other temple in the place. Processions in his honor are among the most prominent indications of religious feeling, and the sect to which he belonged, the Nitchi ren shioo, has profited largely by excitement and enthusiasm.

During the year, at Nagasaki, notwithstanding the proclamations which had been issued by government against such exhibitions, upon the beatification of St. Ignatius of Loyola, the Society of Jesuits made a solemn procession through the streets, when forty priests assisted in copes, besides religious of St. Francis, St. Dominic, and St. Austin, who then resided in the town. The next day the bishop officiated *in pontificalibus*, and the ceremony concluded with illuminations of joy. The same order was observed at Arima.

During the following year the Shiogoon Hide tada, the son of Iyeyas, married the sister of Kita Mandocoro, wife of Taikosama, mother of Hideyori, and niece of Nobu nanga.

Hideyori had still many adherents, who were attached to him and to his father's memory. Iyeyas had been afraid of acting against the Christians so severely as to compel them to throw their weight into the opposite scale; but he began to see that he could keep all the advantages of trade through the Dutch, and get rid of the political dangers which threatened Japan through the foreign priesthood. The Jesuits allege that the Dutch encouraged him in these views, explaining how the Society had been driven out of their coun-

tries by the princes of Germany and Holland as disturbers
of the public peace.

In 1612 he determined to get rid of these ever-disquieting
agents, the more excited thereto by finding himself in the
meshes of a net out of which he could only break his way
by force. He found that the Prince of Arima, one of the
warmest and most devoted to the cause of Christianity
(whose son had married the granddaughter of Iyeyas), had
been intriguing with the officers at court, to win their good
offices by bribery, in gaining for him large additions to his
territory. He now, for the first time, acted with severity
against some of the native Christians about the court. Fourteen were condemned to death, but the sentence was com-
muted to perpetual banishment and confiscation of their
estates. This action on the part of Iyeyas himself at once
brought out into bolder relief the two parties. Those officers
who had hitherto winked at the Christians, and had permitted them to carry on their worship and preaching undisturbed, now saw which way the wind was blowing, and
acted accordingly. This severity was carried into the heart
of the court—one of the concubines of Iyeyas being confined,
and banished to the island of Oshima, and thence to the
smaller island of Nishima, and thence to a rock, Cozu shima,
upon which seven or eight fishermen lived in straw huts,
subsisting on what they caught; and these men were ordered
to keep this lady.

Shortly after this, Don Protase of Arima suffered. His
son Michael, who had been brought up as a Christian, fearing to lose possession of his father's dominions, informed
against him, accusing him of crimes, and suborning witnesses against him. Upon the proof offered he was beheaded. This Christian's son Michael, who had divorced
a Christian lady to marry the granddaughter of Iyeyas, then
turned apostate, and began a persecution within his territories of all who professed Christianity. He began, in order
to please Iyeyas, by putting to death two boys, his own
nephews. Here again, where the Jesuits. had been most

intolerant, the tables were turned upon them. In the province of Boongo, at one time the stronghold of the Roman Catholics, the same action was being taken; and about this time, in Yedo, the Shiogoon, on the representation of informers, put to death some natives who had built a new church, and banished the father out of the country.

In 1613, Don Michael of Arima was pressed by his wife and others to renew his severities, and eight Christians were burned near his castle by slow fires.

In 1614, Iyeyas was stimulated by the opponents of Christianity to take action against those who professed it. With the advice of his council he issued orders that all religious, European and Japanese, should be sent out of the country, that the churches should be pulled down, and the Christian members be forced to renounce their faith. To carry out these orders, all foreign priests and natives, members of the Jesuit Society, were ordered to leave Miako, Osaka and Fusimi, and retire to Nagasaki. Hojo Segami no kami°was ordered to see that this order was executed; but he was chosen, perhaps, from a desire to remove him out of the way, as well as to take the opportunity of seizing his estate. Accordingly, while he was so engaged, he was accused of some crime, and his estates confiscated. The native Christians were banished to Tsoongaru, at the northern extremity of the island. At Kanesawa, in Kanga, Justo Ookon dono Takayama was ordered to leave with the others. Still further to make sure of the success of his projects, Iyeyas dispatched to the island of Kiusiu upward of 10,000 men, under three leaders, for the purpose of overawing the Christians and putting down any attempts to rise in that quarter. In Kiusiu the new doctrines had first taken root, and had flourished with greater luxuriance than on the main island of Nippon. The lordships were smaller, and therefore the advantages of trade were proportionably greater in the eyes of the proprietors. But as in the outset these lesser lords had favored what seemed to them a source of revenue, when things turned against the religion they distinguished themselves by zeal in putting down what in the end threatened to deprive them of everything. In them the government found the most active and zealous assistants. Many of these lords or their parents had been baptized. The Jesuits had there most sway, and had used it with the most intolerance; and Iyeyas determined, before striking a blow at Hideyori in Osaka, to remove any chance of a diversion being made in his favor on the part of the Christians in this distant part of the empire. But if we believe the letters of the fathers, the fortitude and courage with which martyrdom was endured by professing natives must be looked on with admiration. The better classes lost everything—lands, position, comforts, in many cases their wives and children, and, last of all, their lives—in the cause of their faith. The poorer gave up their lives, all they had to give, with zeal, fortitude, and even joy.

In the other parts of Kiusiu, in Tsikuzen and Figo, and in the remote islands of Xequi or Kossiki, the same spirit was shown toward the Christians; and upon October 25, 1614, three hundred persons—in a word, all the Jesuits, except eighteen fathers and nine brothers, with a few catechists (who lay hid in the country for the help of the faithful)—were shipped off out of the country by a Portuguese vessel. This mode of dealing with persons in the position assumed by these foreigners and their adherents seems to have been at once lenient, yet determined, and mercenary without being severe. The party had assumed a political aspect threatening to the state. The very ladies of his household had been supported by these foreigners in opposition to the Kubosama himself. And as it was intended to be a final political step, and not a religious persecution, any foreigner found thereafter spreading such intolerant doctrines would be treated as a political partisan. Justo was put on board a Chinese vessel with some Spanish priests and some Japonian clerks, and set sail for Manila, where he died shortly after his arrival.

The step of removing from the capital and its neighborhood all the foreign fathers was, in its results, of the utmost importance to the cause of religion.   During the rule of Nobu nanga and Taikosama, Father Rodriguez, the inter-preter, a man evidently well acquainted with the language and with the court, was invited or allowed to remain in the capital.   From the accounts sent thence it is evident that by tact and judgment Father Rodriguez had maintained his place, that he was in communication with the highest offi-cers at court, and exercised an unseen but potent power in behalf of his brethren.   With such a person at court, oppo-sition cannot so easily gain head.   Evil reports are warded off, occasional words in favor can be thrown in; but with the withdrawal of such a power from the court the foreign cause becomes powerless.   Every one is ready to abuse, and to chime in to please his superior.   There is no possibility of warding off the blows aimed.   It is impossible to know whether the highest power knows anything of the edicts put out in his name.   The Buddhists, a powerful body, would be ready to press down upon and thrust out opponents who had borne themselves so proudly in the day of their prosperity.   Their own tactics recoiled upon the fathers; and when they were turned out of court, without friends or advocates, their cause became hopeless, and with their downfall the position of all other foreigners in the country was involved.

It is, perhaps, not a good defense of the policy adopted in Japan, to remember that it was nearly identical with that which England was compelled to adopt at the same time, and under similar circumstances.   In both countries the change was conducted by the government, and in both the spirit of the people rose against the interference of a foreign priesthood with the national concerns.   The truth is, that the doctrine of the Papal supremacy is an "exterritoriality clause" of itself, which, operating in a country professing another faith, creates an *imperium in imperio*, which be-comes very embarrassing to a government, whether it be Japan or England.   The confiscation of abbey-lands in Eng-

land may be compared with, or was analogous to, the confiscation of the lands of the lords of Japan, while informers
in each were rewarded by a gift of the property belonging
to offenders of less note. The difficulty with which Japan
had to cope was, that there was no mode of escape from
persecution by going into exile into other countries until
the storm had blown over.

In 1615, after getting rid of these politically dangerous
persons, Iyeyas seemed to think that he might push things
to extremities with Hideyori and his mother. He ordered
up all the troops in Kiusiu to Osaka, and thither he repaired
with a large force. He had endeavored for some time to
make Hideyori spend his revenues so freely as to impoverish
his exchequer. He had induced him to rebuild the large
temple of Buddha in Miako, and the day was fixed for the
consecration; but the suspicions of the mother were roused,
and the solemnity was postponed. The young man had presented a large bell to the temple, upon which, it is said, that
a wish was engraved that Yedo might be destroyed. This
bell is never struck. This was made a pretext for a quarrel,
and as the deserters from the castle reported that it was unprovided, it was forthwith invested, and war entered upon.
There were many able commanders in the party of Hideyori,
and the castle of Osaka was defended so well that after some
time Iyeyas was obliged to retire and raise the siege, as he
was losing prestige by delay, and men by desertion. An
armistice was agreed upon at the desire of Iyeyas; but it
seems to have been demanded only to give time. The surrounding country was desolated, and before long hostilities
were renewed; and as a part of the army of Hideyori was
encamped outside, a general battle ensued on June 3, 1615.
In the account of the Jesuits, two of whom were present,
the army of Iyeyas was on the point of defeat, when, probably through treachery, the castle was set on fire, the troops
of Hideyori became panicstruck, and a total rout and general slaughter ensued. In the relation by Trigautius it is
stated that in no battle in Japanese history did so much

slaughter take place as in this.   The populous neighborhood,
the density of the city, the lawlessness of the troops, all combined to produce a fearful carnage.   No certain information
was ever got of the death of Hideyori or his mother.   In all
probability they committed suicide, and their bodies were
destroyed in the conflagration.   Reports were circulated of
their having fled—some said to Koya, others to Satsuma;
but as diligent search was made for six months after, and
no trace of them was discovered with certainty either then
or in after years, the common report is likely to be correct.
His natural son was taken and beheaded.   After this decisive battle, Iyeyas, having satisfied himself that he had
made all things sure about Miako and Osaka, returned to
Soonpu, and his son to Yedo.   However, Iyeyas did not
live long to gather the fruits of his sowing, or witness the
success of his schemes in the working of his laws.   He died
on March 8, 1616, at Soonpu, advising his sons to be kind
to the nobles, and, above all, to govern their subjects in the
spirit of tenderness and affection.   He died not without suspicion of his having been poisoned by his second son, Hideyas,
the elder brother of Hidetada, the Shiogoon.   He was buried
in the hills of Nikko, a short distance north of Yedo, with
great splendor.   His posthumous title or name and rank is
To sho, Dai Gongen mia (Tung chau, Ta K'iuen hien kung)
d'zo jo itchi-i, Dai jo dai jin—The Eastern Light, the Illustrious Gem (a Buddhist title for a deified being) of the first
rank, Prime Minister.   He is often spoken of as To sho goo
and Gongen sama, but this latter is a generic term, and not
specially applicable to any individual.

   The East India Company endeavored, shortly before the
death of Iyeyas, to open a trade with Japan, and the letters
of Captain Saris, Cocks, and others, give an interesting account of the country at the time.   In answer to a letter from
the King of Great Britain, Iyeyas granted to his majesty's
subjects certain privileges of trade, and the settling of a factory in Japan, and confirmed these under his broad seal for
the better determining thereof.   This document, a fac-simile

of the original, is to be seen in Purchas.   For sufficient reasons, the factory was in no long time withdrawn, and the trade entirely ceased in 1621.

In 1619 some notice of the persecutions carried on against Christians is given in Mr. Cocks' letter, which corroborates the accounts received through the Roman Catholic channels, and is worthy of note as being written by one who evidently bore no great goodwill to that form of the Christian religion, and will render it unnecessary to allude further to the fearful particulars detailed by Trigautius and others:

"The persecution in this country, which before proceeded no further than banishment and loss of civil and religious liberties, has since (as this letter tells us) run up to all the severities of corporal punishment.   The Christians suffered as many sorts of deaths and torments as those in the primitive persecutions; and such was their constancy that their adversaries were sooner weary of inflicting punishments than they of enduring the effects of their rage.   Very few, if any at all, renounced their profession; the most hideous forms in which death appeared (by the contrivance of their adversaries) would not scare them, nor all the terrors of a solemn execution overpower that strength of mind with which they seemed to go through their sufferings.   They made their very children martyrs with them, and carried them in their arms to the stake, choosing rather to resign them to the flames than leave them to the bonzes to be educated in the pagan religion.   All the churches which the last storm left standing, this had entirely blown down and demolished, and heathen pagodas were erected upon their ruins."

Edict after edict emanated, or at least were said to emanate, from the Shiogoon, ordering more and more severe action to be taken against the Christians.   There remained no power of verifying these edicts, no one to speak a word at court for the unfortunate creatures; while they were surrounded by hungry wolves, who might invent edicts in order to profit by the confiscation of property, whose interest it was that the infant heir should be destroyed with his father,

and who were further incited by the priests, or bozangs, who
gnashed their teeth in the hour of victory over enemies who
had lorded it so proudly over them in the short days of their
prosperity.   By such ferocity, combined with a strict watch
kept up on foreign vessels, the Christian religion was nearly
extirpated; but in the district of Arima, nearly the whole
of the inhabitants, having all their lives professed Christianity, at last in desperation resolved rather to fight than submit to such a system of persecution.

CHAPTER VII

THE LAWS OF IYEYAS

IYEYAS had shown himself an able commander, and an
astute, if a somewhat unscrupulous, diplomatist.   He is
known to this day as a legislator.   Hitherto the country
seems to have been governed by the laws of Tankaiko, and
these are still in force.   But Iyeyas thought it necessary to
lay down rules for those who formed his own court—the
military chiefs (with their two-sworded followers), whom he
intended to act as the executive throughout the empire.   He,
to this end, issued one hundred rules or directions as his testament, to be bequeathed to his descendants in power, as a
guide to them in the office which he hoped would be hereditary in his family.   It is said that Iyeyas was assisted in
drawing up this code by Nijio dono, Kon chi eeng, Tenkai
sojo and Kanga.   The originals are now kept at the temple
of Koo no san, and it is intended that no one but the ministers of state shall ever see them.   These rules are commonly
called "Bookay hiak kadjo"—the hundred lines or rules for
the military class.   The title is Go yu i jowo or Yu i **geng**
or gong—the last testament of Tosho goo, in one **hundred**
sections.

The following translation of these rules is to be looked upon as a mere sketch, or such defective information as a Japanese who understood little English could convey to the author, who understood little Japanese, and the division into 100 sections is difficult to ascertain in the original.

* No one is to act simply for the gratification of his own desires, but he is to strive to do what may be opposed to his desires—*i.e.*, to exercise self-control—in order that every one may be ready for whatever he may be called upon by his superiors to do.

* The aged, whether widowers or widows, and orphans, and persons without relatives, every one should assist with kindness and liberality, for justice to these four is the root of good government.

* Respect the gods, keep the heart pure, and be diligent in business during the whole life.

* If the Kubosama (or Shiogoon) should die childless, then Ee, Honda, Sakakibarra, and Sakai,* together with the older and most able servants of the Kubosama, are to meet together, and, no matter whether he be distantly or nearly related, they are to fix upon the man most worthy, and of most merit, as successor.

* Upon whomsoever the Mikado may confer the title of Se i shio goon, it is ordained that the customs shall continue as in the time of Kamakura dono (Yoritomo).

* All the rice produce (cheegio) of the empire (at my disposal) amounts to 28,900,000 koku. Of this, I arrange that 20,000,000 is to be divided among the Daimios and Shomios or Hattamoto, and the remaining 8,900,000 koku shall belong to the Kubosama.

* It is the duty of the Kubosama to guard from danger the Emperor and his palace, and to preserve peace and tranquillity in the empire in every direction.

---

* These four are the highest of the official or Fudai class of Daimio, and are commonly known as the Si Ten wo, or "four heavenly emperors"—a Buddhist title.

9

* All the Bookay—*i.e.*, military officers—are to take care that the laws of the empire are not lightly changed; but as sometimes necessity may arise for a change, they may yield on special occasions.

* All Daimios and Hattamotos who adhered to me and my cause up to the time of the war at Osaka (with Hideyori) are to be Fudai. Those who since that time have given in their adhesion, and have remained steadfast, are Tozamma (Ch., ngoy yeong), outside lords. Of Tozamma there are eighty-six, of Fudai eight thousand and twenty-three, and of Kammong, or relations of my family, thirteen. Of visitors (lords who visit Iyeyas on equal terms, called Okiak-sama or Hin re-i), five, who are:

1. Kitsure gawa dono, } descendants of Yoritomo.
2. Iwa matz manjiro,   }

3. Matzdarra Tajima no kami, who was the seventh son of Hideyas (elder brother of Hidetada), and so grandson of Iyeyas. He was adopted by Taikosama, but was returned to his father on the birth of Hideyori, and was afterward adopted by Yuki.

4. Tatchibanna hida no kami—of a very old, illustrious family. He was military teacher of Iyaymitz ko, third Kubosama, and would not acknowledge Iyeyas as his superior, but had not much power, and was not disturbed by Iyeyas.

5. Tokungawa Mantokuji was a very old branch of the Tokungawa line.

* Ko fhoo jo nai (a name of the shiro or castle of Yedo; the Chinese characters are different from the Ko fu of the province of Kahi, where the Shiogoon has a castle) presents on the left side the shape of a dragon, on the right, that of an (washi) eagle; to the northwest lies the second, Kuko or Maro; to the north lies the third; to the west, the fourth; to the southwest, the fifth.

The O ban goomi, or large guard of the Kubosama, consisting of twelve companies, may be likened to the twelve gods (the Yakushi riorai). The Sho eeng bang—the lesser guard of ten companies—are like the ten stars. The Dzeng koo or Sakitay (who lead the van in war) are thirty-three companies, like the thirty-three heavens. The Mochizutzu, musqueteers (who fire balls of five momays weight), are seven companies, like the Stchi wo or seven lights—the sun, moon and planets. The Sho ban gashira, numbering twenty-eight, are similar to the twenty-eight stars. The Ro shing —*i.e.*, old servants (acting as the Gorogiu or cabinet)—are as the four heavens. Over them, and higher, is placed the Shiogoon. These are all so arranged to suit well-known and easily remembered arrangements in the Buddhist books of religion.

* There are many Fudai, but of this class the Mikawa, or old Fudai, are to rank the highest. Of these there are fourteen: 1, Tori yee; 2, Itakura; 3, Owokubo; 4, Todda; 5, Honda; 6, Ogassawara; 7, Akimoto; 8, Sakakibarra; 9, Sakkye; 10, Ishikawa; 11, Kooze; 12, Katto; 13, Abbe; 14, ———. Of these families, if able men can be found among them, the Gorogiu or cabinet is to be chosen. Tozamma Daimios, however able they may be, cannot have seats in the Gorogiu, or take any part in government.

* The families and names of all Daimios, large and small, who have acted with me in my wars, shall continue (*i.e.*, shall not be removed from the peerage), however badly they conduct themselves, unless they turn rebels or traitors.

* In regard to the Koku shiu, Rio shiu, Joshu (classes of Daimios—the first, lord of a province; the second, lord of a district; the third, lord of a castle), Tozamma and Fudai, if they break the laws and oppress the people, no matter how old the line or how large their territory, I will use my power and forces to brush them away from both territory and castle. This is the duty of the Shiogoon alone.

* Among officers the different ranks are to be observed, each according to his rank or his official income; but if they are equal in both, the eldest in years shall take precedence.

* The President of the Hio jo sho [a deliberative court in Yedo with judicial powers] must be selected as being a

man of the clearest mind and best disposition; and once every month it shall be the duty of the Shiogoon to go to the meeting, without giving previous notice of the day, when he himself must decide on the questions brought before him.

* Each province is divided into kowori, sho, mura, and sato—districts, parishes, villages, and hamlets. In the mura and sato, should there be any family of old standing among the lower classes, even though the head of it may be very poor, he ought to be appointed officer; and if a rich man settles in the village, he is not to be made an officer. This is to be the law in all territories, whether of a Koku shiu, Rio shiu, Jo shu, or Ji towo (ground-head, *i.e.*, landed proprietor, not eligible to office).

* All Daimios and Hattamotos not in office (*i.e.*, not residing at Yedo), whether Tozamma or Fudai, are commanded not to be unjust toward me. My business is to guard the Emperor and his court and the whole empire of Japan, and I command you to assist me in repairing and keeping up all the imperial castles, roads, rivers, and guards.

* The repairing the Shiogoon's residence, the keeping in repair public roads, keeping up ferries, etc., is Fushin; Daimios are sometimes called shokowo; when they are acting as guards, as in Kanagawa, they are "Katamme"; and in keeping up these guards, the whole expense is borne by the Daimios.

* Irayzumi, the marking a criminal with ink or gunpowder; Go ku mong, putting a decapitated head in a box for exposure; Haritske, spearing on a cross; Ushizaki, tying four oxen's tails to a man's limbs, and starting them off by fire to tear off the limbs; Kumma iri, boiling a criminal in hot water. These are old punishments for criminals. The officers are to try to discover who are worthy men, and they are to be rewarded with territory, titles, and rank. Criminals are to be punished by branding (or marking), or beating, or tying-up, and, in capital cases, by spearing or decapitation; but the old punishments of tearing to pieces and boiling to death are not to be used.

* When I was young I determined to fight and punish all my own and my ancestors' enemies, and I did punish them; but afterward, by deep consideration, I found that the way of heaven was to help the people, and not to punish them. Let my successors follow out this policy, or they are not of my line. In this lies the strength of the nation.

* In regard to filling in new ground, if there are no objections, it may be done according to the laws in force in the time of Yoritomo; but if objections are made (by neighbors or others), it is not to be carried out.

* In case also of wishing to make new canals (hori), or lakes (Ikay), reservoirs of water, old precedents are to guide the officers.

* If there be a lawsuit as to a property or a road, if it is shown to have existed fifty years, the question cannot afterward be reopened.

* Among officers outside and inside there are at times unseemly brawls as to rank, but these are all to be settled now, and I settle them accordingly in the following order:

Tai ro sin, Orussuee, Tai ro jiu (now Gorojiu), Soshi, Osaka jio dai, Soonpu riobang, Waka doshi yori, Soba yo nin, Kokay, Sosha, Jeesha boonyo, Oku toshi yori (obsolete), Nishi maro russui, Owo metske, Kotai yori yaï, Hira toshi yori (obsolete), Kanjo boonyo, Matchi boonyo, Oku ko sho ngashira, Naka oku ko sho, Sho eeng ban gashira, O ban gashira, Shin ban gashira, Onando kashira, Ko nando kashira, Kiri no ma tsu may bang, Gan no ma tsu may bang, Fuyo no ma yakunin, Tskyebang, Ki roku sho yakunin and Hio moku no mono, Ten shoo bang, Hozo bang, Hatta boonyo, Katana ban gashira, Motchi yumi ngashira, Motchi tsudzu gashira, Sakitay gashira, Yari boonyo, Kooshi boonyo, Ma ya betto, Funatay ngashira, Makanai gashira, Jusha, Eeshi, Fushing boonyo, Tan sz boonyo, Do bo ngashira, Zashiki bang, Hi no ban gashira, Katchi metske gashira, Kobito gashira, Iga no kashira, Kurokwa kashira, Tayshi gashira. And below this rank, all the captains or officers of companies will settle the ranks. When the official income is above 10,000 koku, the Roshing or Gorogiu shall settle, below this the Waka toshi yori. The highest of all is the So to rio, the Tai ro shin, or Go tai ro, or Sosai; *i.e.*, the Regent.

* There are men who always say Yes (*i.e.*, agree with me), and there are others who sometimes say No (*i.e.*, express a different opinion from me). Now, the former I wish to put away from me, and the latter I wish to be near me. The elders of the Gorogiu are to examine and see that men do not do such business only as is agreeable to them, and avoid all that is the reverse. I wish to have about me all opinions of men, both those who differ from me and those who agree with me.

* If some man should say such a one deserves to be put to death, the officers must not act upon his wish alone; but if all the people say such a one should be put to death, the officers must examine into the case; and if all the people say such a one should be rewarded, I myself must examine, or the country will be lost.

* As to cormorant-fishing and hawking, some men used to say that these amusements were useless and expensive, and they were in consequence interdicted. But I do not prohibit them. They strengthen the body, and with riding, archery, hunting, and shooting, are not to be forgotten or omitted in time of peace by the military classes in the empire.

* Singing, dancing, and music are not strictly military occupations, and soldiers ought not to devote themselves to these accomplishments; but at times the mind is oppressed, and the heart is heavy, and requires relaxation and mirth, and therefore these are not to be altogether prohibited.

* I am descended from the Emperor Saywa Ten wo,* but

---

* Saywa made the laws as to the Shinwo and royal families. His sixth son was Sadadzumi Sinwo. On Momidji yama (a little hill within the grounds of the Yedo castle) is a small temple. On the altar are tablets with the names of men of six generations: 1, Sadadzumi; 2, of his son Tsune

my family had lost all its property through the power of our
enemies, and had sunk down to Matzdaira [a small village
in Mikawa, from which the family of Iyeyas takes its name];
but through the kindness of the Emperor I have, relying
upon documents and history, changed (or traced) the name
of my family to Seratta, and Nitta, and Tokungawa, and in
all time coming this last is to remain the name of the family.

* I have fought ninety battle, and narrowly escaped with
my life eighteen times. Having so escaped, I therefore out
of gratitude erected eighteen temples, and I wish my sons
and descendants to adhere to the Iodo sect (of Buddhists).

* In Booffoo (the military office; *i.e.*, Yedo) I built the
temple of To yay san, and requested the Mikado to install
as chief-priest a Sinwo —*i.e.*, of the royal family of the first
rank (he is now known as Oo yay no mia, and is the most
illustrious personage in Yedo in point of birth and honors
acceded to him: he lives in To yay zan, a residence formerly
the property of Toda, Idzumi no kami)—to pray that the evil
influences of the devil may be warded off, and that peace
and prosperity may prevail over Japan. And also in order
that if the Mikado should be induced to side with traitors or
foreigners, and these concert with or gain possession of the
person of the Mikado, then the Dai Shiogoon shall instate
the Oo yay no mia as Mikado, and punish the rebels.

* From ancient times there have been different sects of
religion other than the Jashiu (Crooked sect; *i.e.*, Christians). Now any one of the people can adhere to which he
pleases (except the Christian); and there must be no wran-
gling among sects, to the disturbance of the peace of the
empire.

---

moto (who first took the name of Minna moto); 3, of his son
Mitz naka (a soldier of note); 4, of his son Yori nobu; 5, of
his son Yori Yoshi; 6, of his son Yoshiyay (otherwise called
Hatchimang taro), and of his son Yoshi Kooni (whose descendants divided into the Nitta and Ashikanga lines). The
temple was erected for the reception of those tablets, to which
worship is offered every morning.

* The families of Minna moto, Taira, Fusiwara, Tatchibanna, Soongawara, Oway, Ariwara, and Kiowara, are all direct descendants of Mikados. Out of these families the head of the military must be chosen. If there be among these families men of good character, but uneducated, cowardly, and ignorant of the way of holiness, such are not to be selected for this office. Therefore it is necessary that all the members of these families should be diligent in study.

* To insure the empire peace, the foundation must be laid in the ways of holiness and religion; and if men think they can be educated, and will not remember this, it is as if a man were to go to a forest to catch fish, or thought he could draw water out of fire. They must follow the ways of holiness.

* All men are liable to sickness. If doctors become rich they grow indolent, therefore it is improper that they should acquire territory or landed property, but they are to be paid by every one, high and low, according to the visits paid.

* Those who study the stars, and the higher orders of Sinto priests, formerly spread the idea that they were worthy of equal reverence with the gods. If in future they presume to do so, they are to be punished.

* In former times, when high-priests and ministers of the Buddhist religion committed crimes, and were liable to punishment, the people thought that to punish them was the same as punishing the gods. They are to think so no more, but the military officers are to punish such offenders without fear.

* Booffoo, Osaggi, Booggi, Itchiko Meeko, Nobooshi, Yamabooshi, Gozay [these are different kinds of impostors, fortune-tellers, diviners, fox magicians, mesmerizers, clairvoyants, etc.], Maykura, and vagabonds who go about without regular business and breaking the laws, raising quarrels, must all be punished.

* Let every gentleman with the right to wear a long sword remember that his sword is to be as his soul, and that he is not to part from it but with his life.   If he forget his sword he must be punished.

* In the Nengo of Boon ro ku, 1592–96, the two officers Ogochi and Assano surveyed all Japan.   They made a report, which was laid before the Emperor.   A survey of the provinces, counties, districts, and parishes was made, together with the forests, mountains, rivers, and a calculation was made of the value.   If a man possess land yielding 1,000 koku, he is to provide five horsemen.   If 10,000, 50 horsemen.   If 50,000, 250 horsemen.   If 100,000 koku, 1,000 horsemen.   This is one "goon" or regiment.   3,000 horsemen make one battalion, over which is placed one general or Jo sho.   Over 2,000 is placed a Lieutenant-general, or Chiu sho.   Over 1,000 is placed a Kasho, or Major-general [all this is altered now].   But I have a regard for old customs and long service, therefore the house of Ee shall be over all the generals.   Ee man chiu was my general, therefore I presented him with a gold Sai hae [a baton like a fan, used by high military officers]; and I made Honda "Kasho," and gave him a paper Sai hae.   The above arrangement all military officers are to make themselves acquainted with.

* If disputes arise as to the boundaries of the territories (Rioboong of Daimios or of Hattamoto), these are to be referred to an Owometske and the Kanjo boonyo, the head of the Treasury.   But if the disputants refuse to abide by the decision, and fighting ensues, the ground in dispute shall be confiscated by the Shiogoon.

* Byshings (Ch., Peichin)—*i.e.*, large retainers of Daimios—even if they have large landed possessions, and are equal in wealth to Daimios, are not on the same footing with Jiki shing (*i.e.*, retainers of the Shiogoon), and are always inferior to the latter in rank, even though superior in wealth.

* In fights among the common people, even if two or three are killed on one side, both parties are to be looked upon as criminal, and to be punished, but not so severely as if a man out of forethought murders another, and does not act on the heat of the moment.

* If a man employs another to commit a murder, if a man poisons, and wishes to make profit or advantage to himself out of a murder, or if a thief murders to steal, such men must be discovered, even if the grass of all Japan is looked through.

* Of the four employments in Japan—the Samurai, two-sworded gentlemen; the Hyaksho, the farmer; Shokonini, artisan; and the Akindo, merchant—the Samurai is the first in rank. If one of the other three are rude in conduct to a Samurai, he himself can punish him. But among Samurai there are different ranks, some being Jiki shing, others By-shing, retainers of the Shiogoon and retainers of Daimios, and others servants of Byshings, who also are Kimi and Shing, master and servant. If among any of these an inferior is rude or impolite or insolent, then he is to be treated as if he were an Akindo; *i.e.*, a merchant.

* That one man and one woman should live together is a great law of nature, therefore at the age of sixteen all men and women ought to be married. But no man is allowed to marry a woman of the same surname with himself, but examination must be made as to the parentage and line of descent of the betrothed, and thus the way of heaven will be adhered to.

* If a man have no son he may adopt one, but the father must be fifteen years of age before he adopts a son. If a Daimio or Hattamoto have no son or adopted son, the line becomes extinct. But if the last heir of a Daimio's family be very delicate and sickly, he may, even if young, adopt a child to keep up the line of the house. This is the way of Confucius.

* (In old times the Mikado went round the provinces.) Hereafter an officer must go round all the provinces once every five or seven years, and make a report to the Shiogoon. (This is now obsolete.)

* As to the old Kokoshu, I will not interfere with their provinces; but in the case of recently-made Kokoshu and Daimios, if they keep the same territory for a very long time, they become proud, and oppress the people, therefore in the case of these latter it is well to change them occasionally from one territory to another.

* Among Hyaksho, Shokonin, and Akindo—*i.e.*, farmers, artisans, and merchants—if their wives secretly commit adultery, the law of nature is broken; and whether the husband report the matter to the officers or not is of no consequence, both parties must be punished; but if the husband is a proper spirited man, and puts the adulterer to death, he is not to be punished. But if he should wish to pardon both the wife and her paramour, it may be done. The judge is not to be hasty.

* If the same thing take place in the family of a Samurai, the judge must be very severe and strict in punishing.

* In Japan there is an old saying that the same heaven cannot cover a man and the enemy (murderer?) of his father or mother or master or elder brother. Now, if a man seek to put to death such an enemy, he must first inform the Kets dan sho [this is a department which takes cognizance of criminal matters] office at the Hio jo sho, and say in how many days or months he can carry out his intention. This is to be entered in the book of the office. If he kills this enemy without such previous intimation, he is to be considered as a murderer.

* If a servant kills his master, he is to be considered as the same as the Emperor's enemy, and his relations are all likewise to be considered in the same light, and must be extirpated root and branch. If a servant has made the attempt, even if unsuccessful, the family is to be extirpated.—Kando is to take the name of a family out of the book of Japan.

* In regard to wives and concubines, the law and customs are the same as between master and servant. The Mikado is allowed twelve concubines. Daimios and Hattamotos are allowed to have eight. Tei fu—*i.e.*, men with titles—and Sho daibu are allowed five. Officers and Samurai are allowed two concubines. This is to be found in the old holy books of the Rai ki rites and ceremonies (Lei, king of

China). At times very foolish and bad men have made the way of the Rai ki dark, and have addicted themselves to numerous concubines, and so broken the laws of nature. In former times, whenever Daimios or officers have lost their territories and castles, it may in nearly all cases be traced to this cause. Hence the man is not upright who is much given to women.

[It is a common error with writers upon Japan to allege that the Japanese are indifferent to the respectability of their wives; and, indeed, that they rather prefer to take one from among the public courtesans; and, further, to convey the impression that nearly all the women of the country go through some such course before marriage. Such an idea is contrary to common sense as well as to propriety; and the common belief that the spirits take a warm interest and perform an important part in the marriage of every pair in Japan, shows that the rite itself is looked upon as a very important institution, requiring Divine sanction and blessing, and not to be lightly entered upon for the gratification of temporary or transient feelings. On the other hand, intercourse between parties not married is looked upon as disreputable, or at least an attempt is made to convey such an impression to young persons. All such connections are called "damass koto"; *i.e.*, a false, a sham affair; and it is said of such persons that the fox—*i.e.*, the devil—has tied the yeng or knot. It is a common saying by youths, "I know that it is damass koto; but the fox always brings us together again, and I cannot cut the thread." As their idea of the yeng is taken from the Chinese, it shows that polygamy is not, with that large portion of the human race, looked on with approval. In China the first wife is the only wife; the others who may be taken afterward are concubines. In these countries the position of a prostitute is different from what it is in Christian communities, as they are forced to the life, and educated to it from childhood; and the education and mixing with the world in conversation gives them often a cleverness and power of pleasing which are often wanting in the ladies brought up in the quiet and seclusion of a Chinese family. Besides, they go to the same churches and worship the same gods, going through their devotions as religiously as the rest of the community.]

* The relations of the husband are with external things, those of the wife with internal. The observance of this leads to the peace or smooth-working of the empire. If these relations are changed, folly ensues, the house is deranged, and it is as if a hen were to crow in the morning. All men are to take care to avoid the beginning of this evil.

* At Iwatski, and at Kawagoi in Musashi, and at Sakura and Seki yado and Koga in Simosa, and at Takasaki and Oossuee in Kowotsuki, and at Ootsu no mia in Shimo tsuki, and at Odawarra in Segami, nine places are to be castles, which are as the guards or outposts of Yedo. The Daimios in possession of these castles are to act in unison with Yedo as a center.

* At the castles of Soonpu and Kunowo there must be placed able commanders, as these places are the keys of Yedo; to Osaka in Setsu and Fushimi in Yamashiro, officers of the fourth rank must be sent, and an able Fudai Daimio, besides twelve captains. If war begins, Osaka and Fusimi are the keys of the country.

* To the Nijio castle of the Kubosama at Miako one of the principal Fudai must be sent, who must be a general, because he is the head of the executive at Miako, and has the direction of the San jiu san koku; *i.e.*, the thirty-three provinces west of Miako.

* In the provinces round Yedo there are sixteen gates where travelers are examined. At each of these gates a Fudai must be stationed, to see that the laws are observed, and that not a spear the size of a needle passes toward Yedo, but pack-horses and carriages may pass.

* The office of Kiusiu Tandai (the Viceroy of the island of Kiusiu) was formerly held by the Owotomo family. Since this family has been destroyed, the office has been in abeyance. I now command Shim adzu and Nabeshima (Satsuma and Fizen) each to act as Viceroy in alternate years, and will not permit any other to fill the office.

* Within the castle of Yedo are twenty-eight places or gates (Bansho or Mitskay), with guards; without there are twenty-eight. Those within the castle are to be kept by Fudai, those outside by Tozamma.

* In regard to San kin [those who are officially on duty in Yedo] officers, care must be taken to note such as are diligent and such as are indolent, and they are to be rewarded or punished accordingly. Those who are rich are to be put into situations entailing expense, and those who are poor into the less expensive.

* All the Daimios on duty in Yedo are not to be employed simultaneously, as some may be suddenly required for extraordinary service.

* Foreign ships are allowed to come to Nagasaki. Old and trustworthy officers are to be sent there. The kimbang or guards are to be four captains, whose official income shall be more than 3,000 kokus each. There are to be both foot and horse soldiers. As the expenses are great there, the Yakunins or officers must receive yaku rio; *i.e.*, additional money according to their business.

* As by convulsions of nature, such as earthquakes, the courses of rivers are changed, lakes are made or dried up, and mountains overthrown, the expense of repairing these ravages and paying the laborers is to be borne by all Daimios in proportion to their revenues.

* In all the empire the main roads are to be six keng wide (or about sixty feet*). Cross-roads are to be three mats wide, or eighteen feet; Yoko mitchi, or bridle-paths, two mats; Katchi mitchi, walking paths, one mat or six feet; Sakuba mitchi or tchika mitchi, less than three feet. On

---

* There are two keng, one used at Miako, known as Miako no keng, or Kioma, or Homma, the longer of the two. The other is the Inaka keng, or Inakama, shorter by three or four inches. Taikosama introduced the second.

either side of a ferry landing, ground is to be left to the
width of sixty mats, or 360 feet, so that when many persons
may collect care may be taken. This is the custom as to
ferries ever since the time of my ancestor, Nitta, Oee no
skay, Yoshi shige, Nioo do, called "Josay dono."

* All the revenues arising from rates levied at ferries,
lakes, hills, etc., are not to be used by the military department, but are reserved for the Mikado's treasury.

* It is not allowed to any one to build a house in the middle of wheat or rice fields, as the shadow of the house and
trees spoils the surrounding ground, and renders it unpro-
ductive. If any dare so to build, all the building is to be
swept away, and he is to be confined for 100 days.

* For the settlement of what is old plantation and what
is new, it is decided that Furui yama, or old trees, are those
which at the level of the eye are three feet or more in cir-
cumference. Atarashi yama, or new plantations, are trees
which are less than three feet at the level of the eye.—At
one time this was a source of great trouble in Japan.

* If a large tree overshadows a neighbor's house or dry-
ing-floor, so that rice, grain or wheat cannot be exposed to
the sun, when necessary the branches may be cut off.

* Every year the Kanjo sho is to send in a report of bad
bridges, roads, etc., in need of repair.

* In the good old-fashioned times the relations of master
and servant were like those of water and fish, but now, in
these times, people are apt to become proud and to dislike
their work; but every one is to do faithfully the work assigned to him, and not to throw his work or duties on another. This is very important to be remembered, and is not
difficult to be learned. The result is like water flowing
down encircling the country, at which all the people rejoice.

* Honcho, or Japan, is the (Shin koku) country of spirits.
Therefore we have among us the Jiu (Confucianism), Shaku
(Buddhist), Sen (Ch., Tseen), Do (Taouist), and other sects.
If we leave our gods (Shin), it is like refusing the wages of
our master and taking them from another. Therefore a

watch is to be kept as to this.   But as to Itchiko (divination) and Buddhistic practices, the workers are not to be driven away, but the people are not to follow them.

* In regard to dancing-women, prostitutes, brothels, night work, and all other improper employments, all these are like caterpillars or locusts in the country.   Good men and writers in all times have written against them.   But as it is a law of nature that man should desire the society of woman, it is enacted that these people and places shall not be tolerated; but as it would, if the laws were rigidly carried out, be a perpetual punishing and nothing else, they are not to be administered severely, but out of a regard for the uneducated and the nature of mankind these offenses are to be lightly passed over.

* It has been the wont of my ancestors ever to follow out the thread of the customs of (Yoritomo) Kamakura dono, and no other customs are to be observed.   But the heart and goodness of Hige mori (Komatzu dono, eldest son of Kio mori) is never to be forgotten.—This refers to the steady opposition made by him to the "mauvais desseins" of his father, Kio mori, against the family of Yoritomo in 1170–80 A.D.   He is called in the "Annales des Empereurs" "homme habile, vertueux, et juste."   He was extremely distressed at hearing of the treachery of his father in inviting the regent to a conference, and then ordering him to be cut to pieces. After his death, Kio mori, seeing no one to oppose him, regardless of everything, acted according to his own pleasure.

* When a master dies, his servants think it their duty to commit suicide.   This is an old custom, but it is quite unreasonable, and nothing can justify a man in so acting. Sometimes, instead of committing suicide, there is a custom of putting into the grave figures representing servants. This is more unreasonable than the other.   Such persons are not upright, and those who in future do these things must be severely punished.

* If war arise, the (Taisho) commander-in-chief has no other business but to mold men to his use.   The master of

men must know what each is useful for. Men are like in-
struments—one cannot do the work of a chisel with a ham-
mer; one cannot make a small hole with a saw, but a gimlet
must be used. The principle is the same as to men. Men
with brains are to be used for work requiring brains; men
of strong frame for work requiring strength; men of strong
heart for work requiring courage. Weak men are to be put
into poor places. Every man in his proper place. There are
places for weak men and places for fools. All this must be
regulated by the head and brains of the Taisho. Soldiers
are to be chosen on these principles, so that with a thousand
men in one body, the whole may act together, and the empire have peace. This is always to be kept in memory.

* If one man rises to be full of, or puffed up with, military power (Boo i ippai), he will try to make himself equal
with or superior to the highest, the Mikado. This is a very
serious error; there is always a tendency to it. But when it
happens, it is natural that he should become proud, and not
respect the Mikado. The land of spirits—*i.e.*, Japan—will
be lost. The judgment of Heaven will assuredly fall upon
him.—This is intended for his successors, the Shiogoons, who
might be puffed up with their position.

* The Sinwo kay and Mia gata—*i.e.*, the families of
those of the royal blood—are the supporters of the Mikado.
All the high ranks of the Mikado's court, the Koongyo and
the Koongays, are not to alter the old laws of the empire,
but are to pay the highest respect to the Mikado, and are
not to be rude or insolent.

* As to the Hinrei Skiaku [the descendants of old Shiogoons, such as Ashikanga, Hojio and others, to whom rank
and territory have been assigned], their history and pedigree
are to be inscribed in a book. What their customs may be
is of no consequence to me, but if they interfere with the
laws or the government established by me, or even if they
become very proud and oppress the people, I will punish
them.

* As to Nagoya, Wakayama and Mito [known now as

Owarri, Kii and Mito, the San kay, or "three families," sons of Iyeyas], and the fifteen Kammong, the heir must always be the eldest son, and the territory of each cannot be divided among two or three sons.

* Diamios with incomes of 100,000 koku, and the Roshin or Gorojiu, and officers upon outside business, and all captains of the guards, are to be of the same rank as Kokushu.

* In regard to Fudai and Tozamma, and wealthy retainers of Daimios (Byshings and Karo), in going from and returning to Yedo they must observe the laws of the road, and they are not to make their trains very splendid or very poor —*i.e.*, a man of large income is not to go with a very splendid train, neither is a man with small income to go with a very meager retinue; and they are not, as if they were puffed up, and to show their military power, to give trouble to the hotels, or oppress the coolies and porters on the road. This is to be notified to Daimios each time they come to Yedo.

* As to ships, the sea, rivers, roads, porters, horses, the rates are now all settled for greater or shorter distances, and also as to weights to be carried; but all government carriage is to be done with the greatest expedition, regardless of expense.

* All San kin (those Daimios officially resident in Yedo) are to make a present (or rather pay a tax) to the Gorogiu, and to the under officers of state. Those whose incomes exceed 10,000 koku are to give gold, or kin badai—*i.e.*, gold instead of a horse; if below 10,000 koku, they give silver (gin ba dai) to each of the high officers. Wealthy Daimios, with large official incomes, are to give much, those with small incomes are to give little. This money the Gorogiu is to appropriate to the expenses of the office.

* Among the servants of the Shiogoon are those who have much ability and influence, and those who have little of either; they are to act together, and mutually to assist one another. By this means the government will work smoothly. Men must be divided according to their abil-

ities and dispositions, but they must be rewarded or punished according to their actions.

 * When I built the Danring (eighteen temples) before mentioned, I put, *or* I made them, San mong (hill-doors). [The San mong temple of Hiyay san near Miako is a copy of the Tien Tai shan of China.] The Ten dai no zass (head of the Buddhists) asked me why I had built these San mong or hill-doors, saying that he was the same as the center of heaven, and had his seat upon the three stars (San tai say, three sets of stars). I returned no answer. Now it is my wish that long life may be given to the Mikado (10,000 years); therefore in the sixty-six provinces I built seventy-three. I have written in a book the names and numbers of these temples, and have sent this to the temple of Ten dai san (in Miako), therefore be it known that no other San mong temple is to be built.—This San mong must allude to some kind of Buddhist temples of that name.

 * All oo rin kay (military) officers and others under the Shiogoon have since the time of Kamakura dono (Yoritomo) received a commission from the Mikado. All these are under the commands of the Shiogoon. The business is the same as that of the Jin nee kang, office of the gods in old time. Therefore, when a death occurs in my palace, or among those who come to my residence (*i.e.*, Yedo), the customs of the Jin nee kang are to be observed.—The custom is to consider, when a death takes place in a house, all connected with it as temporarily unclean. In the Emperor's family women at certain times move to another house; when a child is born, the father and mother are considered unclean for a time, and cannot go to office or to a temple; when a death takes place, persons entering a house either do not take off their shoes, or put on others for the purpose, and there should be neither smoking, eating, nor drinking in the house for three days.

 * If a man neglects his duties and gives himself up to gambling and drinking, and thinks that because he is of rank he may do so, and so seduce others beneath him to the

same practices; if such a one has not been taught that such conduct is wrong by his teacher, it shall be considered the teacher's crime; but if he has been taught, he himself shall be considered the offender, and dealt with accordingly; but in these offenses there are great differences in degree, and some are to be punished severely, others lightly.

* Men are prone to become indolent and lazy at work, and in consequence become thieves, breaking the laws and occasioning trouble: all these must be severely punished by death; and if any one sets houses on fire, forges seals or signatures, poisons, coins false money—such shall be either burned alive or be speared on a cross.

* A government can easily gather information as to what men do in their business, but as to what they think in their hearts it is more difficult. Kamakura dono, in reference to this, followed the customs of the Tong dynasty of China, and had recourse to informers, offering rewards to such as should give information as to evil-disposed persons.

* In regard to the Go koku, or five grains—i.e., grain of every kind—if these are not abundant, the way of the government of the Emperor is obscure. If crime abounds, the Shiogoon shows himself destitute of executive energy. He himself must be active and diligent in his own duties.

* The higher men (? nobility) make the laws, and the lower classes follow and obey; but it is sometimes difficult to act up to the rules laid down, therefore men of rank are not to order one thing and do another themselves, but are to take care that they carry out what they profess, and observe the laws which they lay down.

* In regard to Kokushu (territorial princes, or lords of a province) and Joshiu (larger Daimios), if they act in such a way as if not to amount to crime, still may be deserving of censure, they cannot be punished personally, but they are to be ordered to carry out some expensive undertaking for the benefit of the country.—Such as making a fort; that at Kanagawa was thus made by Oki no kami.

* Upon the death of the Kinri (the Emperor), or Sento

(retired Emperor), or the Emperor's wife or near relative, all music and shows of pleasure are to cease for a time. If one of the San ko (either the Oo- or Sa- or Nai-daijin) dies, or the Dai shiogoon, notice shall be given of how many days this cessation shall be.—Mourning for the Emperor lasts for thirteen months.

* When a new Emperor ascends the throne, the expenses are all to be undertaken by me, the Shiogoon, and in these I must be liberal.

* If any representative of a foreign nation comes to the country, the officers must take care that everything is in good order—that horses and horse-furniture be good, the houses and roads clean. If they are dirty, it can be seen at a glance whether the nation is prosperous or the reverse.

* If a foreign vessel should be wrecked on the shore of Japan, the officers of government are to be immediately informed, and an interpreter is to be sent to ask what they require. Sometimes the officers may require to be strict and severe, at other times hospitable and kind. The vessel is to be watched, and no trading allowed.

* It is said that the Mikado, looking down on his people, loves them as a mother does her children. The same may be said of me and of my government. This benevolence of mind is called Jin. This Jin may be said to consist of five parts; these are humanity, integrity, courtesy, wisdom and truth. Therefore I have divided the government into Tozamma, Fudai, Shing and Sso. This mode of government is according to the way of heaven. This I have done to show that I am impartial, and am not assisting my own relations and friends only. Between the Shing and Sso it is improper that there should be any communications, and therefore they are not to be in correspondence with each other.

* If punishments and rewards are distributed unjustly, upright men will disappear. The people will become timid and niggardly. Therefore it is of the utmost importance that there be not the smallest act of injustice committed by government officers.

These laws have not been made recently by me, but have existed from generation to generation in the Minnamoto family. What I have written is like a reflection in a mirror. The arrow, if it does not pierce the bull's-eye, will perhaps strike the target.

Old customs must, when found good on examination, be retained.

The principles and sentiments, and at times the very words of these laws, seem to be taken from the writings of the old sages of China, Confucius and Mencius. Confucius, in the Chung yung, seems to have been the model after which the code was drawn up. It is founded upon the five duties of universal obligation—that of a sovereign and minister, of a father and son, of husband and wife, of elder and younger brothers, and between friends; and upon the principle that the administration of government lies in getting proper men, and that such are to be obtained by means of the ruler's own character.

The idea of turning to look inward and examine one's self is prominent in the writings of Mencius.

Mencius said people have this common saying—"The empire, the state, the family. The root of the empire is the state—the root of the state is in the family—the root of the family is in the person of its head." And Iyeyas seems to have recognized these principles as the foundation of his rule, believing that when too much weight is given to the state, despotism ensues; when the family preponderates, oligarchy of an aristocracy prevails; and where the interests of the individual man become paramount, democracy rears its head.

Those who framed the code were in all probability acquainted with the writings of the Chinese sages and their commentators, and perhaps they refer, in the allusions to Kamakura dono or Yoritomo, to some laws laid down by him or his officers, who had more opportunity of studying the Chinese writings than could fall to the lot of men who had been brought up in the troublous times when Iyeyas was a youth.

The consideration of such laws laid down by Iyeyas, and which are more or less still in force, leads to a comparison with the condition of Europe during the time when feudal institutions were in force, the genius of these laws being in many respects the counterpart of that which was in force in Europe in feudal times. The constitution of all warlike nations in early times has tended to this condition. The discoveries of gunpowder and printing have been the great means of breaking down this system; and in our day steam is rapidly breaking up what these had left.

The man to whom had been given the most capacity for dealing with men and for conducting war, was selected to take the command of those who saw these qualities in him, and confided in his ability to prosecute any undertaking to a successful termination. Of necessity such a man must be a soldier. He must have the capacity to govern as well as to fight; to make laws as well as to lead in battle; to conciliate men as well as to control them. He divides the spoils among his followers, allowing to each a proportion according to his merit.

A larger portion was retained by the chief, because, independently of being able to appropriate it, he was to rule over all, and to incur expenses on behalf of all in the general control of the acquired territory.

This chief generally retained in his own hand certain privileges, such as a more or less controlling voice in the legislature, power of life and death, and of making peace or war and treaties of commerce, coinage of money, right of property in mines of gold and silver, and other rights. He had the power of conferring some of these on the barons holding land from him and under him as superior. By subdivision a feudal kingdom was cut up into many small but semi-independent baronies. The execution of legal decisions became difficult, offenders escaping to other jurisdictions.

Through the greater expenses falling upon the king, his

power often waned, while that of the barons waxed greater; and to render their independence perpetual, and at the same time to assure a support to the chief, the system of entail was fallen upon.

The barons were ever and again adding to their property and power by marriages, by successions, by purchase, or by force and might. Honors and even offices became hereditary.

So long as weapons of war were in each man's possession, and every one was in proportion to his personal strength and activity a soldier, no great expense fell upon the chief. His followers could be summoned at an hour's notice.

But when the introduction of gunpowder rendered personal strength and activity of comparatively small value, it increased the expense falling upon the leader. Trained skill required time, and education was necessary. Large guns, requiring expensive ammunition, called for a more expensive system of fortification. The lesser barons could not undertake these. The expenses of war fell entirely upon the king. Trained soldiers required a standing army. When there is any coast to defend, a navy is required.

In the practical working of the system of Iyeyas, there was the difference between Japan and European countries, that, until the use of steam, she had no neighbors to dread as foes or to covet as vassals. There was always an attempt to compensate for the want of this external pressure in the duality or separation of interests between the Mikado, the fountain of honors, and the executive, by whatever name the head officer might be called, whether Kwanrei or Shiogoon.

Security was sought for by the laws of Iyeyas, not against external foes, but against the decadence of the dynasty from internal weakness, or from the power of those who ought to be supporters becoming overwhelming. There was in Japan no call for great expenses, either in keeping up fortifications, armaments, or a standing army or navy. No embassadors were dispatched to foreign courts, to consume the revenues of the empire. Against the tendency to the aggrandizement of the barons, and their increase in wealth and power by marriage and other means, Iyeyas fixed the amount of territory which each lord was to possess. Land which produced of rice annually a certain quantity was allotted to each baron, according to his rank or rights. But one great difference between this system and that of entails in Europe lay in this, that the estate granted to each baron could not be added to or diminished, either by marriage or by purchase or by might, except by express permission and grant from the Shiogoon, the superior of all. This law tended to prevent the enormous accumulation of land in a few hands. This land they might lease or grant to their retainers, some of whom were very wealthy; but so long as such a one was a retainer of a Daimio, whatever his wealth might be, there was little chance of his rising to honors in the state.

The barons in Japan are bound to bring a certain number of men to assist the lord superior in war. Each of these followers is paid by the baron by so much land producing a certain quantity of rice.

Succession to these lands is hereditary, but not strictly to the eldest son, while the custom so common over the East of adoption is allowed, and all the rights of a son are conferred upon the adopted one. Many of the present Daimios are adopted children—frequently no relative whatever of the person who so adopts. But while Iyeyas declared that these fiefs should be hereditary, he at the same time laid it down as a principle that it was good that these lesser lords should not remain too long in one place, but that, when occasion seemed to require it, it was well to change them from one barony to another. He would no doubt have gladly laid down a similar principle as to the Kokushu, or lords of provinces, but their power and influence were too great to be lightly interfered with. This power has been frequently put forth down to the present time. A Daimio with an income of 10,000 koku is ordered to remove to the territory of another with the same revenue; or perhaps, if there be some cause for reproof, a Daimio will be transferred to a territory in the far north, such as Tanagura, and the baron then living there, who may be the son of one who had been similarly deported, is removed to the better locality.

Iyeyas provided for the payment of stated presents on arrival at Yedo. At other times gifts are made to the Shiogoon; and, as under the feudal system, presents are to be offered on other occasions, such as marriage or becoming of age.

The civil authority of the Shiogoon was liable to much limitation, and this Iyeyas seems to have expected. At first an officer was deputed by the Shiogoon to reside in the territories of the greater barons, and to report to Yedo when he saw anything taking place worthy of animadversion. But this has been done away with, and the Kokushu are virtually in full possession of power, each in his own provincial territory.

Under the laws above recited the men of the country are divided into four classes—the gentry, agriculturists, artisans, and merchants. The gentry are separated from the other classes by the distinctive badge of wearing a long sword, which they are warned never to forget. By this sword the class is distinguished over the whole empire. But the class is again subdivided by the respective badges, shields or coats-of-arms of the chiefs, worn prominently on some part of the dress—generally on the back and on each breast.

The right of wearing two swords brings with it privileges which may be looked upon as means of paying the class— somewhat as purveyance under the feudal laws of England conveyed privileges, which were gained generally at the expense of the agricultural class along the highroads. Under these laws all two-sworded men are allowed to demand carriage for themselves and goods along the highway at a much lower rate than others, and this naturally ends in paying nothing. Their goods are permitted to enter towns free of customs, or at much-reduced rates. Such privileges become in time very irksome to the class which has to pay for them.

While a Daimio is not permitted to add to his territories

by purchase or marriage, these may be increased at the will
and by the favor of the Shiogoon, or they may be diminished
by his fiat. While, if any officer has been thought deserving
of a little punishment, he may be desired to build a fort or a
bridge, or make a road, or do something which shall benefit
the country, and at the same time act as a pecuniary fine
upon the person upon whom the honor is conferred.—The
fort at Kanagawa was built in this way.

One of the strongest measures of control used by the
Shiogoon toward the barons is put forward when they have
been known to be intriguing against their superiors. This
is sometimes carried out without trial or previous step of any
kind, and consists in the intimation to the lord that he is to
divest himself of the insignia of rank, hand over the power
which he holds as a Daimio to some other individual (generally a near relative and a minor), and confine himself to
one room until further orders. Such an intimation would
probably not be given unless the government were sure of its
ground. But the power consists in the position in which his
own retainers stand toward their lord. If he, upon receiving
such a notice, obeys it at once, no other changes take place;
the individual is simply removed out of the way, and the
offices are transferred to his successor. The wealthy and
powerful vassals remain, with their property, unaffected by
the step. But should he presume to offer resistance, and
rise in rebellion, all the retainers suffer with him. They
will all be, in case of the failure of the rebellion, deprived
of their territories, which will be taken from them and given
to others. It is therefore the interest of all those about a
Daimio that he should obey a sentence which they all have
an idea he more or less deserved. All those about him,
therefore, insist upon his abdication; and he, feeling himself alone and forsaken, is obliged quietly to yield, and thus
trouble to the whole province is averted. But in the case
where the retainers believe that the cause of their master is
a right one, and that he has the power as well as the ability
to defend himself, they will rally round him, and defy even

the highest government. This took place in the case of Choshiu against the Shiogoon; while the cases of Satsuma, Owarri, and others, who were deposed by the regent in 1858, show how the power is at times exercised.

As a further means of warding off intrigue and plotting among these powerful and wealthy barons, the plan was adopted by which all were brought to the court of the Shiogoon, as inferiors or vassals, to pay homage. The custom among these vassals of paying their respects once a year had been long in use in an unsettled and desultory way at Miako, but henceforth Iyeyas insisted upon each Daimio visiting his capital of Yedo at certain periods, fixed in proportion to the distance of his territory. And he further insisted that his court should be looked upon as the natural residence of these lords, by their having their wives and families always resident in Yedo. And it was this law which rendered such stringent measures to be taken at Hakonay and other gates to prevent the passage outward of females. By this constant moving of the Daimios to and fro between Yedo and the provinces, money was circulated; large sums were spent in Yedo on the establishments they kept up there, and large sums were spent on the way and at the residence of each in his own province.

Iyeyas seems further to have been jealous of any intercourse being carried on between these Daimios one with another, and in these laws measures are taken to prevent this as much as possible. The different classes of Daimios met in different rooms in his castle, and one of one class is not allowed to go into the meeting-room of another.

All these compulsory measures of vassalage in Yedo have tended to keep up in the Daimios a feeling of inferiority to the family in power, and are liable, when the influence of this family wanes, to become very irksome.

The general features of the country help with these aids to keep the power in the hands of one man or family. The number of islands, and the length and narrowness of the island of Nippon, divided as it is by a mountainous ridge, prevent intercommunication being kept up or leagues being formed between contiguous proprietors.

It is the duty of one set of officers at the court of Yedo to inform each Daimio when he is to come to the capital, and it is probably their care to see that the owners of contiguous properties shall not be at the same time at their respective country-seats.

Many of these customs had been in use in the empire during the rule of those who had preceded Iyeyas; but he seems to have gathered what he thought good, and strengthened what seemed weak, so as to provide a firm basis on which to place his dynasty, and inclose it with safeguards that should resist attacks from the restless and warlike men upon whose shoulders his seat had been raised.

With the wish natural to a great administrator, Iyeyas settled all the offices about his court for the good government of the empire. These are mentioned above; but as these offices require a more minute mention, they are given more in detail below. These rules run over a large ground in their dealings with or allusions to all ranks and relations.

Except in the cases of high treason or open rebellion, the families of the feudal barons were not to be attainted. Primogeniture and male succession were encouraged as much as possible, and adoption of heirs sanctioned even during early youth, and sons so adopted can be returned.

The higher Daimios were not allowed to take office or to have any part in the government, except by giving their opinion when asked.

The Board or Parliament, where all officers on duty in Yedo met for discussion and consultation on general business (the Hio josho), was settled.

The punishment of crimes was modified, and the old cruel modes of death done away with. Clemency toward enemies was urged as the proper method of gaining them over.

Recreations for all men were allowed and approved of as useful both to body and spirit.

Reverence toward the Emperor was inculcated by the

example of the Shiogoon, and by advice to the high officers about the court.

The high-priest at Yedo was to be appointed from a near relative of the Emperor, in order that, if there should be a party siding with the Emperor, the Shiogoon might have a rival of the family in his own hands and interest.

The exemption from civil and criminal jurisdiction claimed by the priesthood, and in which they were strongly backed up by the Roman Catholic priests, was abolished. A tendency to the idea that the priesthood, and priests as individuals, were hedged in by a divinity, which gave them a license for the committal and an immunity from the punishment of crimes, was pointed out as an evil to be guarded against.

Gentlemen having the right to wear two swords were to consider such an honorable responsibility.

The empire was surveyed and good maps were made of every district.

The power of judging of what was insolence from an inferior to a superior, and the power of punishing it, were given, in a rather unguarded way, to individuals.

Marriage was encouraged, and placed upon the footing of its being the way of heaven that one man should have one wife.

The reverence to be shown toward father, mother, elder brothers, and teachers, is put forth upon the old Chinese views, and the relations of master and servant are in like manner treated of.

The military position of the country, the passes through the hills, and dangers, are all alluded to. The strategical positions about Yedo are noticed.

Roads come under regulation, and the building of farmhouses.

The government is considered as bound to do its best to provide cheap food for the people. Mourning for the Emperor, religious sects, foreigners, prostitution, suicide—all come in for recognition in the Bookay Hiak Kadjo.

CHAPTER VIII

THE POSITION AND COURT OF THE SHIOGOON

In the above code Iyeyas laid down the order of rank in which the officers about him or under him should move. The offices were probably more or less settled and in existence during the rule of Taikosama and of Nobu nanga, and of the ministers who had filled a somewhat analogous office during many generations at Kamakura.

The head of this Yedo system, as it may be called, is the Shiogoon, the commander-in-chief or head of the military department of the empire, under which is included the police and financial departments.

From the account of the court of the Mikado, as given in a previous chapter, it is to be gathered that the Mikado is the chief ruler over the empire. To him the whole empire looks up with reverence; from him flows the stream of honors conferred upon subjects—all equally his servants.

After the royal family (the Shinwo), the highest subject is the Kwanbakku, who is at the head of the five highest families of Koongays. After these follow the other Koongay families in order, down to the lowest and poorest enrolled in the peerage of the empire.

Beneath all this court, and standing upon a lower platform, is the court of the Shiogoon, at the head of which is the Shiogoon, the commander-in-chief of the army, and around him the Kami or Daimio class, who receive and hold their territory from him as viceroy for the Emperor. The words Shio goon were derived in early times from the Chinese. Tsiang kiun is the title of the general commanding one of the divisions of the army in China.—In ancient times in Japan the title of the commander-in-chief was Mono nobe.

The past history of the empire has shown that the Emperor himself was originally the leader or commander-in-chief of his own armies, but that in course of time the office was conferred upon one of the younger members of the imperial family. It was afterward transferred to the man who in a lawless revolutionary period showed himself capable of seizing and holding the command of the army. Thus Yoritomo held it, and so it afterward became hereditary in the Ashikanga family, until the last of these died out a few years before Iyeyas achieved the object of his ambition.

In any consideration of the government of Japan and its relations, it is necessary to have clear ideas of the position in which the Emperor and the Shiogoon stand to one another. A reference to the history of the country, as given above, may in some measure explain these; but it may not be without use to state briefly what is the position of the Shiogoon.

The Japanese generally are imbued with the idea that their land is a real Shin koku, a Kami no kooni; that is, the land of spiritual beings or kingdom of spirits. They are led to think that the Emperor rules over all, and that among other subordinate powers he rules over the spirits of the country. He rules over men, and is to them the fountain of honor; and this is not confined to honors in this world, but is extended to the other, where they are advanced from rank to rank by the orders of the Emperor. The doctrine of the divine right is carried perhaps further than it ever was in England, though, after all, he is probably only regarded as "that sanctified person who, under God, is the author of our true happiness." He confers rank upon the officers of the empire, and from him Nobu nanga, Taikosama and Iyeyas received whatever rank each held in the empire. By the death of the last of the Ashikanga Shiogoons the opportunity presented itself of giving the title to one who had earned it, and it was given to Iyeyas.

The name by which the Shiogoon of the present day is

known to foreigners is that of Tycoon; there is, however, no such title as Tycoon in the language of Japan. The two words Tai kiun are Chinese, signifying "the great prince, sovereign, or exalted ruler," implying that the bearer of the title is the great sovereign or ruler of Japan. Such a title conveys an idea of superiority over all in the empire which is not conveyed by any of the native titles given to or assumed by the Shiogoon. The title is of foreign growth, and the assumption has been looked upon with great jealousy by the Mikado.

By the old Jesuit writers the head of the executive was frequently spoken of as the Emperor, the Kubosama, and the Xogune, etc. There was, indeed, in their case, some difficulty, as of the three Iyeyas alone was Shiogoon, and that toward the end of his life. Kubosama, as has been stated elsewhere, was a title of respect given by the Emperor to the first Ashikanga. It was given to him after he had given up the title of Shiogoon, and it is somewhat inconsistent to use them together.

The title used by the Mikado to the Shiogoon is Tai jiu, "the large tree"; and this is probably the best name that could be used by foreigners in speaking of him, or in addressing him officially. That used by the Daimios in addressing him is Rioo ay, or "the green tent."

The son and heir of the Tai jiu, whether his father be alive or not, till he is fifteen years of age, goes by the name of Takke cheoo, two Chinese words meaning a bamboo shoot of a thousand years. He generally assumes the *toga virilis* (the ceremony known as Gembuku) when he is about fifteen; but if he is called to the succession as a child, this may take place at an earlier period, or about eight or ten, when he has his head shaved as a man and takes his man-name, by which he is thenceforth known.

There is a civil title which the present dynasty has been proud to assume as patrons of learning; namely, the head or rector of the two principal colleges of the empire, June wa and Shoongaku drio in no bettowo, implying that he is the principal patron or rector of the two colleges of June wa and Shoongaku. This title is assumed as his being the "Genji no choja"; *i.e.*, the head of the Gen or Minnamoto family. He may be spoken of as Minnamoto no choja—as such he considers himself as the first of all the military families of the empire. These titles he assumes, and they may be called family and literary honors. So soon as he has passed the ceremony of Gembuku, the Emperor confers rank and title upon him; these are civil and military, and also of rank or position. The lowest civil rank given to him is probably Dai nagoon, from which he is raised to Naidaijin, Oodaijin, and Sadaijin, and may be raised to the highest, Daijodaijin; but this is generally reserved for the Kwanbakku. The military rank given him is Shiogoon, to which the prefix Dai, "great," may or may not be added. The Dai Shiogoon is the commander-in-chief of the army, and, being to a certain extent looked upon as hereditary, is only an honorary title. To this title is sometimes added the two words Se i (Ching i of the Chinese), the chastizer or tranquilizer of the barbarians or of foreigners; *i.e.*, outside people at a distance from court. This title was originally given with reference to the conquest of the Ai nos in the north of Japan and Yezo; but it has lately been applied to foreigners by the Mikado in his dispatches, as when he says, "I have given you the title of Se i; why do you not fulfill the expectations which I had of you?" Se i fhoo, the office of the pacificer of barbarians, is one of the names applied to the castle of Yedo.

Over and above these the Mikado denotes his place in the ranks of the nobility, as that he is of the second grade, first or second class.

The titles of Iyeyas were Jin itchi-i, first of the second grade.—Oodaijin, the great minister of the right.—Se i dai Shiogoon, tranquilizer of foreigners and great commander-in-chief.—June wa, Shoongaku drio in no bettowo, principal of the two colleges of June wa and Shoongaku.—Genji no choja, the head of the Gen clan.—Minnamoto no Iyeyas.

The name of Daifusama, by which the Jesuits spoke of

Iyeyas, is a corruption of Naidaijin, as Nai foo sama, or, according to the subsequent use of sama, lord of the inner office.

The Shiogoon adopts a crest or coat-of-arms differing from that in use by the Mikado. It is called awui, or a representation of three leaves of a species of mallow, "awui," joined at the points and inclosed in a circle. This is used in all official matters issuing from the office. No one is allowed to use it but those who are relatives of the Shiogoon, or upon business emanating from the office.

Iyeyas took up his residence at Yedo, in the castle which had been built at a former period by Owota do kwang, and which was formerly known by the name Tchi oda, and is at times still so called. Large sums of money were expended upon this residence. It was increased greatly in size. A deep trench or moat was dug round it, cutting it off from communication, except by the gates, with the town. This trench or moat was and is kept filled by a canal drawn off from the Rokungo kawa, near the village of Omaro, about nine miles from Yedo. At Miako the castle of Nijio Maro is his residence.

At Osaka, the large castle, formerly the temple of Hoonganji, and the residence of Buddhist priesthood, afterward converted into a castle or fort by Taikosama, is in possession of the Shiogoon.

At Surunga, the castle formerly belonging to Imagawa is kept up at his expense.

In Kahi, the castle of Kofu, formerly the property of Takeda, is another residence, while in different provinces there are minor seats or residences occupied by retainers and officers.

Iyeyas was buried at Nikko san, where a magnificent tem·ple was reared in his honor, to which repair at certain times his descendants and the officers of the dynasty to pay reverence to his names, to commemorate his greatness, or in the way of official duty.

CHAPTER IX

THE DAIMIOS

IN the above laws Iyeyas speaks of Daimios and Shomios, among whom the territories at his disposal were to be divided. The division was made in the ratio of twenty millions to the Daimios to eight millions which he reserved to himself. "Daimio" is compounded of two Chinese words, signifying "great name"; "Shomio" is "little name." The latter title has fallen into disuse, and is generally replaced by Hattamoto, meaning "the root or foundation of the flag." The Daimio class may be considered to include every officer who holds directly of the Shiogoon, and has an official income from land held of the Shiogoon of the annual value of 10,000 koku of rice and upward. The real value of a koku is difficult to ascertain, as it varies much at different times, whether it be looked upon as a measure of rice or as a coin —a kobang, as it is commonly reckoned. Of 4 kobangs assayed by the United States mint the variation was from 3 dollars 57 cents to 5 dollars 95 cents, or from 15s. to 24s. 10,000 koku are considered equal to 25,000 piculs of rice, or nearly 4,000,000 pounds. There are many men whose incomes are upward of 10,000 koku, but who do not hold their land of the Shiogoon, but of some Daimio. Such are not Daimios, but servants or retainers of a Diamio, known sometimes as "By shing."

The offices and officers of the court of the Shiogoon have continued, with but little change, from the time of Iyeyas down to the opening of the country in 1858. The order in which these officers took rank was settled by Iyeyas; but the offices seem to have been more or less in use during the time of his predecessor Taikosama, and had probably existed for many years. Iyeyas in his laws did not for a moment contemplate any interference with the court of the Emperor. That was above him. The lowest Koongay of that court was above him until the Emperor should have conferred upon himself some title of rank.

The nobility of the Emperor's court are all Koongay. Their names are enrolled in the Great Book of the Empire as enjoying patents of nobility, while the names of Daimios as such are not so enrolled. As Daimios they are not nobles of the empire. Daimios (literally Ta meng), or feudal lords (Chu haou), are, in contradistinction to Koongay, called Jee ngay (Ti hia). The former means "noble families," the latter meaning low, on a level with the earth. The Shiogoon himself is Jee ngay until he has been ennobled by the Emperor. Till recently, Daimios, except the few whose presence was required upon duty, were not permitted to visit Miako. Even when they received rank and title from the Emperor, a relative was sent to pay homage.

Iyeyas, as head of the executive, dealt with these Daimios and Hattamoto, or lesser barons, only. Among them there are recognized four classes; viz., Koku shiu, Ka mong, To sama, and Fudai. The highest class—Koku shiu (Kwoh chu)—"province lords," were those whose ancestors had been in possession of large territories, and who in several cases opposed Iyeyas in arms, yet whom he thought it safer to conciliate than to irritate, looking upon them as more on an equality with himself than the others. About the time of Iyeyas there were seventeen of these province lords, to which number four have since been added. The second class—Ka mong (Kia mun), family doors or gates—consisted of relatives of his family who had assisted him in his rise to power, and upon whom he conferred territory. If the "San kay," or three families of his own line, be included, there were ten Ka mong. The third class—To sama (Wai yang)—were those who, being no relatives or connections, were possessed of considerable landed property, and who sided with Iyeyas during his struggle for power. The fourth—the Fudai (P'u tai)—includes the officers, retainers, captains of his army, or those who in civil capacities, but subordinate, assisted him. Of this Daimio class there are about 200. Fudai are the only Daimios who are eligible for office, or who are allowed to take a part in official business. In rare cases To sama have given up their rank and privileges in order to participate and take an active part in official politics.

The being a Daimio or Kooni kami implies that the officer belongs to one of these four classes, and has an annual income from land, as has been said, of 10,000 koku of rice.

The standing of Daimios as a distinct nobility is not recognized at Miako, and it is therefore an object of ambition to them to obtain imperial honors at the hand of the Emperor, such honors being looked upon as much higher than the names by which they are known at the court of the Shiogoon, and which are conferred by him. These latter are invariably the name of a province, of which each is styled "kami." There are three provinces from which titles as kami are never taken by Daimios: Kadsusa, Fitatsi, and Kowotsuki; these provinces as a title being reserved for the relatives of the Emperor. This gives rise, as mentioned before, to the distinction between titles as Kooni kami and those known as Kio kwang. These latter titles are much coveted, and a great deal of money is expended and interest employed in endeavoring to obtain a title from the Emperor. If an officer has both descriptions of titles, the Kio kwang always takes precedence, as in the case of Satsuma: he is a Koku shiu and a Kooni kami, as such he has the title of Ohosumi, or Satsuma no kami; but he is rarely so spoken of. Holding the imperial title of Shuri no dai bu, he is known by this added to his family name, Shimadzu, Shuri no dai bu—i.e., Shimadzu, head of the ecclesiastical carpenters' office. In addition to these designations from provinces by which Daimios are generally known, the Shiogoon has thought to confer higher honor upon some, and to attach them more to his family and its interests, by giving them permission to use his family name. The name of the parent stock is Tokungawa, but the branch to which Iyeyas belonged was known as Matzdaira (a village in Mikawa). When the ruling officer is powerful, these lords are proud to use this name; when he is insignificant, they avoid it. Thus the lord of the western provinces of Nippon uses at times the family name of Mowori, at other times he is Matzdaira, Daizen no dai bu.

The higher class of the lords (the Koku shiu), who generally rule over one or more provinces, are frequently called by the name of one of the provinces as spoken according to the Chinese pronunciation of the character. Thus Mowori is ruler over the province of Nagato; *i.e.*, long gate or entrance—in Chinese, Chang mun, Japanized into Cho mong. The latter word is dropped, and instead of it "shiu," or province, is added—whence Cho shiu, the name by which he is frequently spoken of. Satsuma is thus Sas shiu, Owarri, Bishiu, etc.

One difficulty in completely understanding the use of the various titles in Japan arises from a confusion in the application of the word "kami." As a title, this word is conferred by the Emperor and the Shiogoon. The word, when conferred by the Shiogoon, is the Chinese character "shau," with the meaning of keeper, or to take charge of. Used in this way, the name of a province is invariably prefixed, as Yamato no kami. And as the names of the provinces are known as our counties are with us, the title is at once understood by a native. But this is quite a different word from that found in the title of Ee Kamong no kami. This is an imperial title. The Chinese character representing this word is that of "tau," or head, and implies that he is the head of a department; viz., that which takes charge of the verandas and outside pathways about the palace. Again, the word occurs in military titles, as Sa yay mong no kami. In such a title the Chinese character "tuh," meaning to keep, to lead, or a general, is employed, implying that he is commander of the guards of the left gate. In a fourth instance the Chinese character is "ching"—correct, to govern, or to see that things are correct; and the word is found in such titles as Oone me no kami, Oone me being the department of the female officers about the palace. It is therefore evident that the office must be known before the title can be translated, and that the word prince will not give a correct translation of "kami" when connected with such an office as Gengba, which is the office for foreign affairs.

The term "tono" is still frequently applied to Daimios by the common people, and is often conjoined with "sama," as Tonosama. It is the Chinese word "tien," a palace or hall, and was originally conferred upon the crown-prince of China, and thence transferred to the son of the Kwanbakku. The Portuguese writers frequently use "dono." "Sama" is the Chinese "yang," and was at first conferred upon Ashikanga yoshi haru when the Emperor for the first time gave him the title of Kubosama. From this it passed as a title of respect to other high officers, but has now become as common as esquire in England. "Tono" in the same way is now used by Hattamoto. "Yakatta" (Ch., kwan), a word sometimes used by the Jesuits for Daimios, is properly restricted to the castle of a Daimio, and is used only for the more or less fortified residences of the more powerful of the class.

The five hereditary orders of peerage used in China are not known in Japan except by name (Ko, Ko, Haku, Shi, and Dan). Of the Daimio class the Shiogoon is the head.

Of the present dynasty, if such it can be called, Iyeyas was the first. He derived his descent, in his officially published pedigree, from the Emperor Say wa, one of whose descendants was Iyo no kami, Yori yoshi. His son was Hatchimang Taro, Mootz no kami, Yoshi Iyay. He was known in history as a great warrior, fighting in the province of Mootz for twelve years. His third son was Siki bu no Ta yu, Yoshi kooni, the founder of the families of Nitta and Ashikanga. His son was Nitta, Oee no ske, Yisho shigay, commonly called Dai ko een (great light). His fourth son was Yoshi Suyay, called Tokungawa shiro (*i.e.*, fourth son), from whom was descended Minnamoto no Hirotada, the father of Iyeyas, who was the eldest son. Iyeyas claimed to be descended from the Nitta family. His grandfather was adopted by Matzdaira Tarozayaymon, then a farmer in Mikawa, at the village Matzdira.

I. Iyeyas had twelve children: 1. A daughter, married Okudaira Mimasaka no kami. 2. A son, Nobu yas. His father suspected him of intriguing against him and was said to have killed him in Mikawa. In one of Mr. Cocks's letters he says, "It is said that the eldest son was disinherited on account of his having lost his nose by disease." 3. Etsizen chiu nangoong, Hideyas. As a boy he was given to Taiko-sama, and was adopted by him. After Taiko had a son, he gave Hideyas in marriage to the heiress of the family of Yuki, in Kadsusa, an old family; and after all the territory was overrun and despoiled, his father gave to him the province of Etsizen. 4. Hidetada ko married a daughter of Taiko, and succeeded his father as Shiogoon. 5. Tada yoshi ko, commonly called Matzdaira Satsuma no kami. He got Kioss, in Owarri, a place formerly belonging to Nobu nanga. 6. Nobu noshi. 7. A daughter, married to Hojo Sagami no kami. 8. A daughter, married first to Gamo Hida no kami and secondly to Assano Tajima no kami. 9. Etsigo, Kadsusa no ske Tadateru. 10. Owarri, Hioyay no kami, Yoshi nawo, the founder of the line of Owarri—one of the "three families." 11. Kii, Dainagoon, Hitatsi no ske, Yori yoshi, was first of the Kii or Kiisiu line—one of the "three families." 12. Mito, Chiunagoon, Sayaymong no kami, Yori fhoossa, the first of the Mito line—one of the "three families."

II. Hidetada, appointed Shiogoon in 1605, married the daughter of Taikosama. He had nine children: 1. A daughter, married Hideyori, the son of Taikosama. 2. A daughter, married Komatzu. 3. A daughter, married the son of Etsizen, the third son of Iyeyas. 4. A daughter, married Kiogoku. 5. A son, died in infancy. 6. Iyaymitz ko, the third

Shiogoon. 7. Tada naga. He intrigued to kill his brother Iyaymitz, and, being detected, was confined to his room for life. 8. A daughter, who married the Emperor Go midzuno. 9. Hoshima, Higo no kami, Massa yuki, founder of the family now known as "Aidzu."

II. Iyaymitz ko, appointed Shiogoon in 1623. He had five children, of whom: 1. A daughter, married Owarri. 2. Iyaytsuna ko, the fourth Shiogoon of the dynasty. 3. Kofu, Sama no Kami, Szna Shigay.

IV. Iyaytsuna ko, appointed Shiogoon in 1650. He was said to have been killed by his wife, who was the daughter of a vegetable seller, and had been employed as a servant about the palace. Her father was given the wealth and rank of a Daimio, as Matzdaira Hoki no kami. The family crest was (in reference to the father's occupation), and is to this day, two Japanese turnips crossed. He left no family.

V. Tsna yoshi ko, appointed 1680, was son of Kofu Sama no Kami. He had three children of whom: The second, a daughter, married Kii, Tsunatoshi. 3. Iyay nobu ko, succeeded as Shiogoon.

VI. Iyay nobu, appointed in 1710. He had three children: 1st and 2d were sons, who died young. The youngest of the three was Iyay tsoongo ko, who was the seventh Shiogoon.

VII. Iyay tsoongo, 1713. He had no children, and was succeeded by a son of Kii Tsna toshi, who married the daughter of the fifth Shiogoon.

VIII. Yoshi mone, 1716. During ten years of his youth a regent held the reins. He is regarded as one of the most able of the successors of Iyeyas. Is called, from his family, Kiishiu Kubosama. He abdicated in 1745, and died in 1751. He had four children, of whom: 1. Iyay shigay was the ninth Shiogoon. 2. Moone taka was the founder of the Go san kio family of Ta yass. 4. Moone kori kio. He is the first of the Go san kio family of Stots bashi.

IX. Iyay shigay ko, 1745. He had two sons; 1. Iyay

haru ko, the tenth Shiogoon. 2. Shigay yoshi kio. He is the first of the Go san kio family of Saymidzu.

X. Iyay haru ko, 1762. He had six children, of whom: A daughter, died young. Another daughter married Owarri. Iyay motu ko, who was called "half Shiogoon." It is generally believed that he was poisoned by his brother Iyay nari. Iyay nari ko, who married a daughter of Satsuma. And the sixth, a daughter, married Kii.

XI. Iyay nari ko, 1787. He had fifty-one children; but as he was subject to epileptic fits, and weakly in mind and body, he is not generally believed to have been the father of many of them. Of his children: The 2d, a daughter, married Owarri. The 3d was Iyay yoshi ko, the twelfth Shiogoon of his line. The 11th, a daughter, married Mito. The 13th, a son, became Kii, Dainagoong. His son, Iyay muschi ko, was Shiogoon in 1858 to 1866. The 17th, Asahime, married Maizdaira, Etsizen no kami. The 26th, Ta yass, afterward became Daimio of Owarri. The 28th, a daughter, married to Matzdaira, Hizen no kami (Nabeshima). The 32d, a daughter, married to Kanga. The 34th, a son, Mikawa no kami, known afterward as Kakudo sama. He was adopted by Matzdaira Etsigo no kami, and was considered a very able and judicious man, much respected. A party wished, in 1858, to make him Shiogoon, but he declined. He republished, for Japanese use, Kanghi's "Dictionary of the Chinese Language." The 39th, a daughter, married to Matzdaira, Aki no kami. The 41st, a daughter, married Sakai, Oota no kami. The 42d, a daughter, married Tokungawa, Mimboo kio. The 43d, a son, adopted by Owarri. The 45th, a son adopted by Kiishiu, and afterward became Kii, Dainagoong. The 46th, a son, adopted by Etsizen no kami. The 47th, a son, adopted by Awa no kami. The 49th, Okura no tayu, adopted by Yamato no kami. The 50th, Hiogo no tayu, adopted by Sahio yay no kami. The other thirty-four children died in infancy or childhood.

XII. Iyay yoshi ko, 1837. He had twenty-five children,

of whom: The first six died in infancy. The 7th, Iyay sada ko, succeeded him. The 9th, Tokungawa, Mimboo kio, was adopted by Stots bashi, one of the Go san kio, and he himself afterward adopted a son of Mito, which son was, until his abdication in 1867, the last Shiogoon of the dynasty. The 21st, a daughter, married Arima, Naka tskasa no tayu. The 25th married Mito. The rest all died in infancy.

XIII. Iyay sada ko, appointed in 1853. He had no sons.

XIV. Iyay mutchi ko, 1858, formerly Haru taka, son of Kii, thirteenth child of the eleventh Shiogoon, succeeded to the office. The death of Iyay sada without an heir was the origin of much intrigue and trouble in the empire during the year 1858. There were two claimants to the succession; the one was the son of Mito, who had been adopted by Tokungawa, Mimboo kio, the ninth son of the twelfth Shiogoon; the other was the eldest surviving son of the eleventh Shiogoon, and who had been adopted by Kiishiu. It became, therefore, a struggle between the two houses of Mito and Kiishiu, and the regent sided with the latter. It was a question between a son adopted out of the line and a youth who had been adopted into the line. Iyay mutchi died in 1867, and was succeeded by Stots bashi as Yoshi hissa, who in his turn abdicated in 1868, and so the dynasty of Tokungawa terminated.

It has been stated above that the offices about the court of Yedo were all settled by Iyeyas. In his testamentary rules he laid down the rank and order in which they were to stand in the court. These may be here more particularly described.

In the family of the Shiogoon, as given above, mention is made of the San kay and of the San kio. The former name means the three families, the latter the three princes of the blood.

The "three families" referred to are the descendants of the three youngest sons of Iyeyas—to the one of whom was given the lordship of Owarri, to the other that of Kii, and to the third that of Mito, a town and district in the province of

Hitatsi. The heirs of these nobles stand at the top of the list of Daimios, and from out of these families is chosen, in case of vacancy, a successor to fill the seat of Shiogoon.

The San kio (three princes of the blood) were sons of the eighth and ninth Shiogoons, and having in view the possible extinction of the direct line of Iyeyas at the time, these young men and their families seem to have been set apart, in imitation of the Sin wo, or imperial families at Miako. They were assigned residences within the palace *enceinte* at Yedo, but take no regular part in public business. They are paid a yearly income by the Shiogoon, each having a separate little court. The three princes are respectively called Ta yass, Stots bashi, and Say midzu. The last, the house of Say midzu, is, so to speak, at present extinct, and the residence unoccupied, and though it is in the power of the Shiogoon to reappoint a member of his family, it is not likely soon to be filled up. The Go San kio are not styled Daimios.

The Go tai ro, or Regent.—In a hereditary jurisdiction, such as that of the Shiogoon, provision must be made for the contingency of the youth or incapacity of the heir upon his succession. Under this name, which means the great or illustrious elder, a regency—an office similar to that of the Sessio at Miako—is provided. It is an office which is only filled when necessity calls for such an appointment; and there are only certain men eligible for the office. He must be a Fudai Daimio, and, if possible, one of the four known as the Si Ten wo. These are Eeyee or Ee, Sakakibarra, Sakkai, and Honda. Of these the first, Ee Kamong no kami, is called the Do dai, or foundation-stone of the power of the dynasty. the ancestor of the family, Ee nawo massa, having been lieutenant-general and right-hand man to Iyeyas.

So long as things go smoothly, and the wheels of government revolve, such rules may be carried out; but when any country begins to ferment, the ablest or the least scrupulous man comes to the surface. Previous to the accession of the thirteenth Shiogoon, Iyay sada, Ee had gradually crept into a position of power (to which he may have been more or less entitled) through the mental infirmity of the reigning Shiogoon. He assumed or was voted into the office of regent. Intrigues were rife in Yedo and Miako, and in consequence of his leaning toward foreigners, or for other reasons, he was assassinated.

It seems to have been the custom that the Fudai and Kammong Daimios settled who was to be regent without any reference to the Emperor; but since the opening up of the country the Emperor has risen in importance, and at present he or his officers settle who is to be the highest officer when necessary. A common or vulgar name for the Gotairo is Koken, or Oshiru me—*i.e.*, looker back or behind. They have seldom held office long, and have too often come to an untimely end.

The Go ro chiu, or Toshi yori (the senior central officers, or the "Cabinet," as they may be called), consists generally of four or five Fudai Daimios appointed to the office by the Shiogoon. All Fudai aspire to the office, but the members are in quiet times chosen from the thirteen families mentioned in the laws of Iyeyas as head Fudai. Among the members of the Cabinet one is generally looked upon as Prime Minister; but they all take duty in monthly rotation. It is considered a great honor to have been ten years in office, and the Shiogoon in such a case raises the territorial income of such officer. This is the most responsible office, and too often in times past has entailed upon its possessors the mistaken duty of retrieving an error by the cowardly retreat of suicide. They are responsible for the whole acts of government, which are supposed either to have originated with them or to have been carried out with their cognizance. The Go ro chiu meets daily at 10 A.M. in the Go yo shta be ya, a room in the palace. They preside in the Hio jo sho, or deliberative assembly of acting officers, when the Shiogoon is not present. But it is natural to suppose that when great international questions come before the country, as the opening up of trade with foreigners, the larger Daimios and Koku shiu should have a voice, and should take a share in changes of such magnitude. Consequently of late the Go ro chiu has been rather set aside as things move toward Miako, where before long the power and responsibility will fall to the corresponding office at the imperial court.

The Japanese have a saying, that a wealthy man should have little power in the state, but that comparatively poor men should have the power. This seems to be one of their principles of government.

Soba yo min is an office which is only occasionally filled, as when the Shiogoon is young. He seems to be an officer of communication between the Go ro chiu and the other departments. This is the highest office filled by Hattamoto.

Waka toshi yori—literally, the younger elders or senators. They are generally five in number, a second Cabinet, or Under-Secretaries of State. They are Fudai Daimios, or Hattamato. They are frequently promoted to vacancies in the Go ro chiu.

Sosha are generally Fudai, in number about thirty. Their duty seems to be attending to officers arriving at the palace. It is an office of little power and considerable expense. They rise in ordinary times to be Jee sha, temple lords, and other offices of authority.

The Kokay, or Kowokay, can hardly be called officers of state. The name means high families (Ch., Kau kia), and includes the male representative lines of some of the families of distinction in ancient times, such as Nobu nanga, Ashikango, Yoritomo, Arima, etc. It seems a matter of policy to keep them under the eye of the court, giving each an allowance from the state of territory from 500 to 1,000 koku per annum. They are looked upon as men of high rank but little power, being neither Daimios nor Koongays, but between the two. They are occasionally employed to act as proxies for the Shiogoon in state visits to the temples of Nikko or Isse, and have attempted of late to assert their right to act as embassadors to foreign countries. There are about eighteen Kowokay at present.

O Tsu may shiu are Fudai Daimios who act as guards to the apartments of the Shiogoon. From the room in which they meet in the palace they are spoken of as Gan no ma Daimios.—The room being painted with representations of wild geese.

Jee sha (Ch., Sz shie) boonio, temple governors. These are described by Kæmpfer as "imperial commissioners, inspectors, protectors and judges of all the temples and the monks belonging thereunto. This employment is, after the Emperor's Council of State (*i.e.*, the Go ro chiu), one of the best in the empire, and the persons invested with it are very much considered at court. They hold their court at Yedo. All civil affairs relating to the clergy—such as lawsuits, disputes arising about the limits or revenues of their lands, prosecutions for wrongs or damages received, and the like—are brought daily in great number to be decided in this court. Again, all criminal cases—as rebellion, disregard of the imperial proclamations and commands, and in general all capital crimes committed by the ecclesiastics —are tried before them, and, in case of conviction, punished with death, though these criminals are much more indulged than other people and cannot be executed without the consent of and a warrant signed by the general at Miako. Another branch of the business of these Dsisia Bugjo is to take care of the maintenance of the clergy, to keep the temples in repair, and otherwise, in all cases where the secular power and authority is wanted, to assist them."

Every Japanese is registered (or is supposed to be registered) in some temple, and whenever he removes his residence, the Nanushi, or head man of the temple, gives a certificate. The books of each temple are sent to Yedo, to the office of the Jee sha, where they are copied. These officers act as judges in disputes between priests of one temple with those of another; between Daimios in disputes about boundaries; between Samurai and Hattamoto, but not between merchants or farmers. The prison under their charge is better kept and under milder restrictions than other prisons. They have under them numerous Do sin, or runners of a higher class, to seize criminals. As they have to keep up the prisons under their charge, the office is looked upon as one of expenditure and not of profit. The numerous interests with graduated degrees of ruling power in Japan render great tact necessary in disputes between these interests. The monasteries and priesthood are still very power-ful, the Daimios become jealous of interference, and the interests of those holding of the Shiogoon, as well as of those holding land of the Emperor in the Go ki nai, must be considered; so that it is absolutely necessary, not only that distinct laws should be laid down, but also that it should be established who are to be the judges between rival claimants.

One temple lord sits on the bench in the Hio jo sho every month in rotation, and he is thence spoken of as Tski ban.

O Russui are Hattamoto officers, but rank as Daimios, who have charge of the apartments of the Shiogoon, and of the women of the palace when he is absent. They are all old men. All young persons entering or leaving the private quarter of the palace are examined as to sex. In the office there is a female examiner. These officers give passes to females on visits of business or ceremony. There are generally eight officers, who have each under them ten Yoriki and fifty Do sin. The income of each is 15,000 koku.

Owo ban kashira.—These are the captains of the great guards of the castle of Yedo. There are twelve, seven Daimios and five Hattamoto. Their duties are entirely military. Under these twelve are one hundred Owo ban, who are all Hattamoto.

Sho eeng ban kashira is also a military office, apparently the bodyguard of the Shiogoon. There are ten commanding officers.

Okosho ban kashira.—These seem to be lords-in-waiting upon the Shiogoon, of whom there are ten. They are Hattamoto, each having thirty men under him.

Owo metsuki—literally, great or senior attached eye.—

Of these there are five head men. Beneath these are the Metsuki, and an inferior body of men called Katchi metsuki.

This is a very important department of the government of Japan. The title is frequently translated "spy," and the duties seem in some cases to corroborate this view. But the idea of espionage by no means conveys an accurate understanding of the subjects under the care or control of these officers.

One of the principal objects of the superintendence of this department is the eight roads of Japan, and the regulations of the laws of these roads. Another is the manners and customs of officers in reference to state dress, their intended marriages, going and coming to Yedo, and visiting else·where; death and mourning of officers; receiving reports sent in by the branches of the office in the provinces as to the military equipment of Daimios, the uniforms, devices, flags, which they use; in regard to religion, and especially the Roman Catholic; as to the Yakunins, or inferior officers of the Shiogoon's government, their number and duties, and the census of Japan. Such are some of the different kinds of business which come before this office.

The laws of the roads are regulated in a separate branch of the office, under the Do chiu boonio. The book of laws or orders is the Do chiu boonio kokoroee, and, in its present form, seems to have been published about 1840.

There were formerly five highways, afterward two were added, and by the addition of the road to the temple of Nikko, there are now eight. The office issues rules for Daimios and Hattamoto passing along these roads, and for merchants and farmers when traveling. In every village or town along the road these rules are affixed in the To iya or government office, for all the villages upon these highroads are to a certain extent under the control of the government, even when the road passes through the territories of Daimios. The following are headings of these regulations:

As to providing two-sworded men with lodgings on the road, and cangos or chairs to travel in.

YOKOHAMA AND HARBOR

Japan.

As to children traveling, two in one cango, or mother and child.

As to members of the Gorochiu when traveling.

As to different customs, if such officer be traveling on private or public account.

As to giving a passport to a traveler (Saki buray); as to where he is to sleep, and at what hotels he is to stop on the road.

As to traveling during the night, if it be necessary.

Rules as to sleeping at towns.

Rules as to (tcha tatte onna) servant-women, and other descriptions of women, in inns.

To keep accounts in each town of the number of coolies and horses used on the road each day.

As to Buddhist priests when traveling on the road.

As to affixing in six public places in Yedo the (Kosatsu) laws of roads.

As to the rates for carrying goods.

As to the officers who examine the weights of goods.

Laws as to the porters on the road.

Rules as to going into and leaving hotels on the road.

Rules as to government goods carried upon the roads.

As to officers who travel at government expense—as the Tenso, Emperor's messengers, etc.

As to how many porters each Daimio is entitled to, and the rate of payment. If he wants more, he must pay at a higher rate.

If one of his servants travels by himself, he is not to be provided for.

Rules as to tenants of government lands when they come to Yedo.

Rules as to the dress and payment of meshi mori onna— that is, servant-women who occasionally act in both capacities—in inns.—By law two women only are allowed in each inn, but more are kept, and fines paid for keeping them. The strictness and minute care with which the Japanese government watches over its people is shown in the regulations laid down for public women, known as Joro. This name is only applied to those who are kept in government establishments in the larger towns, as Yedo, Osaka, Miako, Nagasaki, where a place in the town is set apart for their residence. The laws for the regulation of the morals are very different in different parts of the empire. In the territories of some Daimios, as Tosa and Kanga, public prostitutes are not permitted, indecent songs are interdicted, and the inns and bathing-houses regulated; but the government of the Shiogoon considers these things to be necessary evils, and takes them under its own charge. The finest women in Japan are said to be in Etsizen and Idzumo, where they are famed for the fineness of their complexions and smoothness of skin, with higher noses and little or no smallpox. It is said that men cannot leave Neegata, where the public women are called Hak piak ya gokay, or 808 widows. This name arose after one of the desolating battles in old times, in which that number of husbands was slain and the widows obliged to seek for wherewithal to live. In one night in 1860 the officers in Yokohama seized 108 young women who were suspected of leading immoral lives without a license from government. The most beautiful public women of Yedo annually take a prominent part in the processions, or matsuri, and their portraits are sold and hung up about the large temples and places of resort.

Laws as to thieves and robbers on the highway.

As to fires breaking out in villages on the road.

As to the duties of Daimios on such occasions.

As to rivers, and crossing them. Crossing rivers is often very dangerous, and the porters are made responsible for knowing where the path of safety lies, and when it is unsafe to attempt passage.

As to giving public notice at a hotel before a Daimio arrives.

As to harai kata (sweeping and cleaning the road before a Daimio arrives).

As to things lost on the road.

When a Daimio's servants are lodged in a separate inn from their master.

If a man become insane upon the road.

As to fighting among gentlemen's servants.

As to deaths by killing in such quarrels.

As to Daimios falling sick on the road.

As to Daimios returning to Yedo on account of sickness.

As to rivers when impassable from high floods, what Daimios are to do.

As to obstructions from unexpected convulsions of nature, such as an earthquake, flood, etc.

As to servants of Daimios who have died upon the road.

As to behavior of Daimios when meeting the Tenso or Koongays upon the road.

As to the rates for carrying Daimios' luggage.

As to occasionally examining goods contained in boxes.

As to government packages having the go shu een, or red seal, upon them.

As to government packages passing through Yedo.

As to the porters of Yedo.

As to persons wishing to travel very quickly.

As to Owo ban kashira, captains of the guard of Yedo, when traveling.

As to porters who have become sick, or who may have run away.

When sometimes a passport has not been previously given on the road, the Daimio to give to the keeper of the government inn his seal and a paper to this effect.

Some officers travel free on the road, and their expenses become a tax upon the people living in villages along the road, and who are supposed to benefit by the travelers. Of such are Daimios coming to pay respects to a new Shiogoon upon his accession. In 1861 the Ooyay no mia, or High-priest of Yedo, traveled with 250 followers. He was about nineteen years of age. The walls of the inns at which he stopped were newly papered, and new clean mats put on the floors. For this the villages paid, he paying one boo—*i.e.*,

1s. 6d.; and on leaving, his servants tore the paper off and cut the mats, that they might not be used again.

As to the Shoshidai, or envoy of the Shiogoon, when traveling.

As to the governors of the castles of Osaka, Soonpu, or Miako, or the guards of these castles. Governors of places held of the Shiogoon, but at great distances from Yedo, as Nagasaki and Hakodadi.

As to Koongays and such high officers when traveling.

As to Ray kayshi, or messengers sent annually to Nikko by the Emperor.

As to carriage of ingredients for making gunpowder.

The Daikwangs, who look after the government farms and woods. All of their men and goods are carried along the public roads at the expense of the villages.

By this office the ceremonial due to high officers upon the road is arranged.

If a Daimio in his norimono meet a high Koongay—one of the Sekkay or Monzekke—his porters must not walk on, but must stop till the high officer has passed, but he need not get out.

The same respect is to be paid to the otchatsubo, or jars containing the tea for the use of the Shiogoon.

A Byshing—*i.e.*, one of the higher retinue of a Daimio —must leave his norimono and kneel down, taking off his hat.

The same respect is to be shown by these Daimios and Byshings to anything bearing the red seal of the Shiogoon, to the great guards bringing up muskets, to the governors of the castles at Miako, Soonpu, and Osaka, and to the Shoshidai.

When a Daimio meets the Tenso, his norimono is to be carried slowly, and on one side of the road.

A Byshing must kneel and take off his hat.

Porters can be obtained from 4 A.M. to 8 P.M., but not at any later hour.

Koongay and Monzekke are to be provided at the public

expense with 35 horses and 50 porters. If they require more, they must defray the expense themselves.

The "three families," and higher Daimios and Emperor's messengers, are allowed 100 horses and 100 porters; lower Daimios, 50 horses and men. Some Daimios are not allowed to travel on the tokaido.

It is enjoined that members of the Gorochiu, the envoy and governors of Osaka castle, when they meet a Daimio upon the highway, ought to speak to him; but if they do not wish to speak, they may say that they are not well.

If they meet in the same hotel at night, the Daimio is to ask them if the Shiogoon requires his assistance in any way.

When they meet on the road, the Daimio must open the door of his norimono and act as if he were going to get out, but the other must request him not to do so.

Otchatsubo, or jars containing tea for the use of the Shiogoon, are treated with great respect. If a captain of a guard meets these jars carried by porters, he makes his bearers go to one side, and his followers kneel and take off their hats. The porters call out as they go along the roads, and all the common people kneel down. This custom was begun by Iyeyas. Recently there have been slights and insults offered to these jars, to show personal feeling on the part of some of those opposed to the present state of things, as Satsuma.

Byshing entitled to carry a spear, upon meeting a member of the Gorochiu, or the Shoshidai, or tea-jars, etc., must wait till such dignitary is past. Byshing not entitled to a spear are under the same customs as common people.

Two-sworded men singly meeting the tea-jars, Gorochiu, etc., stop and take off the hat only, but do not kneel down.

All common people must kneel down and take off their hats to Koongays, Shoshidai, Gorochiu, Oban kashira; and, though there be no law for it, a Daimio often takes it into his own hands and punishes or kills a man or woman who does not kneel down while he is passing. Such was the case with Shimadzu Saburo and Mr. Richardson in 1862; but

Shimadzu was not even a Daimio, but the father of the young Daimio. On one occasion a Byshing of Kiogoku, Nagato no kami, killed a man of Matzdaira, Sanuki no kami, for turning aside upon the road and making water while his norimono was passing; while another ordered a woman to be cut down for standing and looking at him.

A Daimio with an income of 200,000 koku, witn 20 horsemen and 120 footmen in his retinue, is allowed 300 porters. One of 100,000 koku, with 10 horsemen and 80 footmen, is allowed 150 porters. One with 50,000 koku, with 7 horsemen and 60 footmen, is allowed 100 porters; and so downward in proportion.

When a Daimio meets a Gomiodai, or envoy from the Shiogoon, he is to give him half the road, and to stop his norimono while the envoy is passing.

The same respect is to be shown to envoys from the Emperor (Chokoo shi), the royal family, the Tenso, and other high officers.

In the case where one Daimio has taken possession of an inn on the road, and another comes from an opposite direction and wishes accommodation, this is sometimes the cause of serious fighting.

If a Byshing be in the retinue of his superior lord, and a government official with the red seal be met, he must not get out of his norimono or off his horse; but if alone, he must do so.

If a Daimio meet an imperial envoy (Chokoo shi) or Eenshi, or a member of the royal family, a relative of the Emperor, or a high Koongay, he may, if he wishes, turn off the road up a by-road till the great man shall have passed, to save himself from getting out of his norimono and kneeling down, or, if he be riding on horseback, from dismounting.

To lower Koongays the Daimio must give half the road.

If a Byshing or Hattamoto is on government business with the red seal, he is to be treated as a Daimio.

To one of the "three families" a Daimio is to get out of

his norimono and propose to kneel, but is to be requested not to do so. As a general rule, to men of the third rank and above, Daimios must kneel; to men of the fourth rank and below, no ceremonial is required.

These headings may give some idea of what the duties of the road department of the Owo metski office are.

It is further the duty of the office to see that the roads and bridges are kept in repair.

From these rules it is evident that great exactness must be insisted upon in traveling along the highroads as to the days when officers are to leave each place, and the houses at which they are to stop, in order that there may be no confusion in official arrangements, and to avoid unpleasant collisions which might happen on the road. The office must even at times take into consideration the private feelings of individuals. At one time the young Eeyee Kamong no kami was coming up to Yedo with a large retinue, and Shimadzu Saburo of Satsuma was going down to Miako. In two days they were to meet on the tokaido, when the whole country expected to see a fight, for which both parties were prepared. But the office hearing of it, sent peremptory orders to Eeyee to go round by another road.

The Owo metski office must be consulted previous to the betrothal or marriage of a Daimio or his eldest son, and also previous to the adoption of a son by a Daimio. Marriages and adoptions are generally made in their own class, and frequently among relatives; but some of the Daimios are married to the daughters of the highest Koongays.

The members of this office appear to act as reporters in all government meetings. Indeed, whenever two or three persons meet together in Japan, there seems to be some member of this silently observant office present. Reports of everything that goes on throughout the empire are sent in to this office for the information of government, and these reports are recorded for reference. Men acting nominally as horseboys and servants in the foreign consulates have been emissaries from this department.

By law every innkeeper is obliged to keep a book (Yado cho), in which every traveler is noted down, and what he may do or say that may be thought worth reporting. Similar books (Gio koo cho) are kept in public brothels, in which are noted the names of men frequenting them (if the names can be got), or marks upon their bodies; how much money they spend, the saki they drink, etc. These are all for the use of this office.

The prevention of the spread of the Roman Catholic or Jashiu mong sect is one of the cares of Dai Kwang department of the Owo metski office. The names, with the genealogy, of all the families among which there were known to be Roman Catholic converts, are carefully kept. Boards, called Christang hatto kaki, on which are printed a prohibition of the Christian religion, are put up in every large temple. Individuals belonging to the families under observation are not allowed to move their place of residence without permission of this office. If one dies, intimation must be given to the office, when an officer is sent to view the body, and all the relatives sign a certificate. Or if at a distance, it must be preserved in salt. The Dai Kwang office superintended the Yay boomi, or trampling on the cross, once a year at Nagasaki. It is the duty of the office to examine for Christians all over the western provinces once in three years. Whenever a child is born in a family formerly Christian, notice must be given to the office. Marriages must be reported; and also the intended adoption of a son. Adopted sons are sometimes thrown back again by the adopting parents, but Christians are not allowed to do this. A register for the same purpose is kept by the governor of Miako. These forms are kept up to the great-grandchildren of the original Roman Catholics, but have of late fallen into desuetude; but it may hereafter prove the means of stirring up dying embers of faith among the descendants in the recollections of their ancestors. The members of this department, while sitting with others, report, but have neither a voice nor a vote.

Matchi boonio.—The street governors, or, as they may be called, governors or mayors of Yedo. (The Shiogoon himself is considered governor of Yedo, and Mito is hereditary Fuko Shiogoon or Vice-Shiogoon, and ought as such to reside constantly in Yedo.) Of these there are two; the one over the east, the other over the west part. The authority of these officers is chiefly over the mercantile class. They have little or no power over the Samurai, or two-sworded gentry. Their duties are with the streets and police of Yedo. They sit as judges alternately, and take cognizance of all questions and quarrels among the mercantile class. Upon a Daimio coming to stay at Yedo each alternate year, he is to call on and pay his respects to the Gorochiu, Wakatoshiyori, Owo metski, and Matchi boonio, before he goes to his own house.

Go Kanjo boonio may be called the head of the exchequer. These are two officers who keep the accounts of the empire; they also act as judges in all cases between persons of the agricultural class. They have great power. Of the Do chiu boonio, or governors of the roads, one is always Kanjo boonio, and one is Owo metski. The mint and coinage of money come under this department. Under them they have five men as seconds or assistants, Kanjo gim maku, besides two men who upon alternate days keep the accounts of the expenses in the Shiogoon's palace.

Sakushi boonio are two Hattamoto officers, superintendents of the carpenters of the Shiogoon, and under them are four men, Daiko kashira. As mentioned before, the trade of a carpenter is looked upon in Japan as a very honorable occupation.

Besides these, there are Shta boonio and Fusim boonio, who superintend the carpenters of the offices and women's apartments, the wells in the castle, providing tables, boxes, mats, etc.

Goong Kan.—The naval department has two governors —Goong Kan boonio. These may be called Lords of the Admiralty, but until recently the office was one of com-

paratively minor consideration.   There were four naval instructors under these governors who had picked up some
little knowledge from the Dutch and from Dutch works on
naval affairs.   Latterly, the office has become one of much
greater importance.   Great attention is being paid to naval
matters and to steam, and the office has consequently been
remodeled.   The government has invested largely in steam
vessels, and has erected steam works for making and repairing all sorts of machinery, and is making every attempt to
obtain a well-educated set of men, who shall be thoroughly
instructed in all the branches requisite for naval officers.
At Nagasaki the Japanese government has one large set of
works, and another in the vicinity of Yedo.   A dry dock has
been excavated for the cleaning and repair of the vessels of
government.   Until lately the Japanese government seems
to have paid no attention to keeping any vessels of war.
Fast-rowing boats were kept near Nagasaki, and one at
Uraga, in the bay of Yedo, and at other stations ordinary
boats were kept.   These, however, were generally noted
for speed rather than strength, and rarely put to sea, but
watched vessels coming to land and overhauled them on
the part of the custom house.

Ko bo shin shi hai.—This seems to be an office for young
unemployed Hattamoto officers, where records are kept of
what each excels in, for the information of government.

Shin ban kashira.—School for teaching young officers
about the court riding, rifle-shooting, etc.

Okosho is a general name for officers waiting on the
person of the Shiogoon.

Naka oku go ban shiu.—Some of the private guards of
the Shiogoon.

Hoko nando.—Men who look after the dresses and clothes
of the Shiogoon; and others are in the flag office or the spear
office.

Hiaku nin Kumi no kashira.—These are guards.   They
were originally Yamabooshi priests, called Negoro and Nen-
goro, or, as the translator of the letters writes it, Negroes, in

the large monastery of Kumano, in the province of Kii; and after their buildings were burned down by Taikosama, and their lands confiscated, they joined the army in a body, and Iyeyas attached them to himself as guards.

There are departments for superintending the manufacture of bows and arrows, and muskets, rifles and cannon.

Another office has the charge of balls, shells, powder, etc.; and another has the charge of the armory, containing bows and arrows, rifles and coats of mail.

Hon maro russui ban.—The Hon maro is the name of that part of the castle or shiro of Yedo occupied by the Shiogoon. Six officers keep it when he leaves it temporarily.

Ni no maro russui ban.—Keepers of the part assigned to the son or concubines of the Shiogoon.

Hikeshi.—These are fire-brigades in the service of the Shiogoon in Yedo, of which there are twelve, one to a district; each under the charge of a Daimio.

These guard against fires in the castle, the government godowns in the town, and the large temples where the tombs of the Shiogoons are. Each brigade has a leader, who holds on the end of a long pole a mattoyay, or white solid device, easily seen at night. The duty of this leader seems to be to stand as near the fire, and as long as he possibly can; and in fulfilling this duty they appear to rival the fabulous salamander. Each brigade has overcoats with distinguishing marks, and masks the better to stand the heat. However, in wooden buildings their organization seems of little use. The fires generally wear out of themselves, the inhabitants carrying off their money, clothes, mats and windows to places of safety. There are other fire-engines and fire-brigades in Yedo under the Matchi boonio. The town is divided into forty-eight districts, corresponding to the letters of the alphabet I, Ro, Ha, to each district, and there is a brigade. If a fire breaks out in the Ro district, all the men of the Ro brigade go to it. The rest of the town unburned pays each man of the brigade employed four tenpos, or about 6d., after the fire.

Daimios keep men of their own as firemen, generally men in some small disgrace, whose names have been erased from the town books or dismissed from employment.

At one time fires occurred so frequently in Yedo that a notification was issued that the proprietor of the first house in which a fire should thereafter originate should be transported to the islands. The first offender was Mito. It would not do to transport him, so he fell upon the plan of borrowing, through the priesthood, on payment of a large sum, 30,000 days from eternity, beyond which time he had little prospect of living. This has frequently since been found to be an ingenious plan for men of wealth escaping punishments.

Metski are lower officers of the Owo metski department, and seem to act as judges in civil cases. There are fourteen Metski.

Tskybang are messengers, attendants in war or during fires to the Shiogoon.

Taka jo.—Keepers of the Shiogoon's hawks.

Katchi ngashira.—The officer who superintends the men lining the streets when the Shiogoon goes out—a ceremony, however, which has been done away with.

Jiu ri si ho—meaning "ten miles in four directions."—Men whose duty it is to take care that no one shoots within ten ri—i.e., twenty-five miles—of the castle. Even within this distance there are places in which native sportsmen are allowed to shoot, for which permission is given upon application. An infraction of this law was the reason given for the seizure of an Englishman in 1859—one of the *causes célèbres* in the early history of Great Britain's relations with Japan. This is a sub-branch of the Owo metski office.

Shiu mong aratame is the branch of the same office which examines into the religion of individuals, especially with the object of restraining the spread of Christianity.

Do chiu boonio is the officer who has charge of the highroads, bridges, etc., under the Owo metski.

To zoku (Tau tsih—catch thief) Hi tske is the same as

Kai yaku—*i.e.*, reforming officers. This is, in its subordinate offices, a very wide department—aiming at thorough espionage, secrecy in detection, and surveillance, as well as overpowering strength in carrying out the wishes of government. The whole of society in Japan is permeated by officers of this department. All public places are full of them. Inns are kept by them; they reside as priests in temples, or wherever the general public resorts. The keepers of these inns and farmers in the country are frequently in the employ of the police. There is a saying in Japan, "Dorobo oi zen" —implying that it is better to put money on a thief's back than to apply to the police. The police runners have means at the stations for constantly strengthening themselves by gymnastic exercises, and are taught to tie up criminals in a variety of ways, from so lightly as to lie like a net, to so tightly that before long the victim is strangled. They are always provided with a short iron baton, with which, in case of resistance, they strike their man over the head to stun him.

Ko boo shio boonio.—The military school where drill exercise, the use of weapons of war, fortification and military tactics generally, are taught to young officers. There are three officers over the establishment, but many teachers of the different branches. The school is in Owo ngawa matchi or street in Yedo. Artillery is taught near the garden of the Shiogoon at Hama go teng. Sword-practice with sticks (kenjits) is a favorite amusement with young officers. They have sticks with basket guards, with which they practice. Before beginning, each puts on an iron wire grating over the head, a bamboo-and-leather belt around the chest, and bamboo guards for the arms with gloves. Yet with all this one is sometimes severely handled. The sword is long, two-handed, sharp on one edge and at the point, and for about two inches from the point on the back; so that they either cut or thrust, and aim at cutting the neck with a back cut. They are very dexterous at the use of this weapon, whether against a sword or a bayonet or spear. Practice with the rifle is also very common in the government schools, and in the grounds of Daimios about Yedo. There is a large parade ground or open country to the back of Yedo for the use of the military, called Hiro.

Naka kawa bansho.—An office for the examination of boats coming from and passing to the interior by the communicating branch of the river—the Naka gawa. Upon this stream boats can go to the provinces on the northwest, north and east of Yedo. Besides these there are officers who have charge of the Shiogoon's barges and boats.

There are officials whose duty is to examine into alleged encroachments by Daimios in Yedo upon the roads, streets, rivers, or sea. The superficial quantity of land as gardens that an officer may hold in Yedo is regulated by his official income. (One tsubo equals thirty-six square feet.) An income of from 300 to 900 koku may have 500 tsubo, 18,000 square feet; 1,000 to 1,900 koku may have 700 tsubo, 25,200 square feet; 2,900 koku may have 1,000 tsubo, 36,000 square feet; 4,000 koku may have 1,500 tsubo, 54,000 square feet. And so on up to 150,000, whose allotment is 7,000 tsubo, or about 500 feet square.

There are sword-keepers of the Shiogoon, and also keepers of the books or library, and a keeper of the presents, gifts, or tribute paid by each Daimio. Gifts as tribute are being received daily, and are regulated by order. But frequently handsome presents are voluntarily made by Daimios, perhaps in some cases for favors to come. For instance, Owarri is ordered to present to the Shiogoon upon the first month, third day, congratulatory cakes.

Upon the third and seventh months a large noshi—symbol of a present with a piece of dried fish—with paper and two tubs of wine.

On the 18th of the fourth month, fish; and again in the same month, A-ï, a fresh-water fish, considered a delicacy.

On the fourth and eighth months, the same fish preserved in vinegar.

On the sixth month, the first day, ice. It is a custom in Japan to use ice upon that day.

On the sixth and seventh months, muskmelon.

In hot weather, in summer, anything he thinks may please.

On the sixth day of the ninth month, one obang (a large gold coin, worth above £6) or more.

During the ninth and tenth months, persimmons—the best come from Mino.

During the eleventh month, tea, cakes, fish, saki and Owarri radishes, which are very large and fine.

During the twelfth month, fish, persimmons, storks, which are supposed to be a royal bird, and only for the table of the Shiogoon; but many people eat them.

A present from an inferior to a superior, as from a Daimio to the Shiogoon, is "Kenjio"; the reverse is "Hyrio." The Shiogoon is said to have called in proclamation the steamer "Emperor," presented to him by her majesty the Queen of England, "Kenjio."

The Shiogoon has also four secretaries for private business, and others for government business.

There are professors or teachers of the works and writings of Confucius. There is a school or college for the study of foreign books; but the school was lately entirely remodeled, and greater encouragement given to the study of foreign languages, books and arts and sciences.

There is an observatory, with astronomers, compilers of the almanac, etc.

Nineteen physicians attend upon the Shiogoon, five of whom practice after the European system, and fourteen after the Chinese. There are five surgeons, of whom one practices according to the European system, and medical officers for treatment by acupuncture—*i.e.*, by insertion of fine needles. These are fine flexible wires, not so strong as those used in imitation of them in Europe, but requiring a tube to be used for their insertion to prevent the needles bending. There are also dentists and oculists and medical

men for attending officers on duty at the castle, and others
for attending officers who are outside the castle. There is
one medical man for vaccination, together with consulting
physicians; and also doctors to look after the sick poor and
destitute. There is or was a public hospital at Koishikawa.

There is an officer who may be called poet-laureate.

There are musicians to the court, and teachers of the
Sinto religion; also teachers of a game, a kind of chess, as
well as chess itself.

After these are the keepers of the wicket-gate by which
females go out or come in, and men to look out from a lofty
platform. Such are always raised in Daimio's houses, to
enable the watchmen to look down upon the surrounding
streets by day, and to look out for fires by night.

There are keepers of the jewels belonging to the Shiogoon.

There is one officer who looks after the food for the Shiogoon, and keeps the accounts of the expenditure of the table,
as well as inspectors of rice for the use of the Shiogoon
himself.

The head-cook superintends the kitchen, and there are
also cooks for guests.

Hama goteng boonio.—The governor of the Hama goteng,
a garden on the seaside beneath the castle in Yedo. This is
a large piece of ground cut off by a canal, and formerly kept
as a private garden for the recreation of the Shiogoon on the
seaside. It is one of the places offered to the foreign ministers for residences in Yedo, and refused by them upon, possibly, good grounds. It has since that time been converted
into a ground for artillery practice. There were three head
gardeners.

There are men to look after the garden for medicinal
herbs, and officers who have charge of the curtains used for
concealment or privacy. These "macu" have been sometimes thought by foreigners to be intended to represent forts;
but they are constantly used in Japan by pleasure parties
and others wishing to be in the open air, and yet to enjoy
a little privacy; and it is considered rude to look over the

edge of one at the party inclosed. They may be used also in war to conceal the numbers of a host. The "mong," or crest of the owner, is generally stamped upon the curtain, which has at a distance, perhaps, given the idea of loop-holes.

Kane boonio.—Four officers who pay out and receive payments on account of the Shiogoon. Payments are made on the 6th, 14th and 26th days of the month. Money is received on the 1st, 10th, 18th and 24th.

There is an office for the exchange of notes or orders for officers. Banks and Daimios issue paper money, called tayngata, and also gin sats (silver card), kin satz (golden card). They are much used by the merchants in Osaka in business transactions.

Koora boonio.—Officers in charge of the rice storehouses belonging to government. These storehouses of rice are very large, as a great part of the pay of officers is given in rice. It is considered degrading to speak of paying money in sal-ary. Even presents of money among the lower classes are always wrapped up in red paper neatly folded. A man is hired as servant for so much rice, known as footchi—*i.e.,* rice given on hire; footchi is always given in addition to money, and it is proper to speak of footchi, not of money-hire. In Taikosama's time one footchi was 10 ngo of rice; now it is only 5 ngo, or about 2 pounds. In speaking of a man's income, if pioh (or piculs) are mentioned, rice is meant; but if koku, ground to the valued extent of pro-duction. Retainers are paid 30 piculs a year, and half a sho (1½ pounds of rice) per diem. In government pay-ments the rice is measured in boxes, not weighed. The Chinese picul is equal to 133 pounds, but the Japanese was generally larger, and ranged from about 150 to 160 pounds. The koku, therefore, would be 450 to 500 pounds. Accord-ing to Williams, it contains 5.13 bushels.

There are officers in charge of the oil and lacquer, and others over the working carpenters and masons. Others are over the government forests and trees, for superintending planting, cutting, etc. Special officers have charge of the Shiogoon's pleasure barges on the river. A tax or license is imposed upon all boats plying on the river at Yedo, collected by another officer.

Tattame boonio.—Officer to look after the mats about the palace. The whole floor of the rooms of the palace is exactly covered by mats, each six feet long by three broad. These mats are two inches in thickness, and are made of straw tightly tied together by string. This is covered by a woven web of fine, long, strong, dried grass from the seacoast. In the houses of all classes in Japan these mats are used, but in those of the wealthier classes they are very beautifully made, soft and pleasant to walk on for persons wearing stockings only, as is the custom. The reception room in the palace is called the Hall of a Thousand Mats. If there be such a room it would be 150 feet long by 120 wide; but as the partition walls in Japanese houses are, between many of the apartments, only light sliding screens, movable at pleasure, it may be easy to throw open a very large room in an extensive building such as the palace is.

There is a jeweler to the court, and auditors of accounts, who are also assayers or examiners of gold and silver.

There are teachers of riding to the Shiogoon, and veterinary surgeons and horsebreakers.

Katchi me tski.—A low class of spies. These are kept secretly by government, and are employed in nominal employments, in houses, shops, or wherever information is likely to be obtained. They are frequently grooms, as in this capacity they accompany their masters wherever they go. They write down whatever they hear or see that is suspicious: the thin paper partitions of the rooms give facility for this, as they have only to put the tongue against the paper and then push the finger through, when a hole sufficiently large is made, through which both to see and hear. If these men allow themselves to be detected by Samurais, or officers, no mercy is shown to them. If they have, as is generally the case, a sort of written commission, and this is

found upon them, they are put to death and the paper is sent
to the government. No notice is afterward taken of such a
deed. It is looked upon as a dangerous profession, and they
know the risk, but they are generally well paid. Daimios
use them also. Mito had a man in 1862 in the employ of
Ikeda, then governor of Yedo. He watched his master
intriguing against his lord, and assassinated him. An officer was long in the employ of the British consulate at
Yokohama who was in constant communication with the
government.

There are officers, keepers of the stairs of the castle, and
others who look after the fires and fireplaces.

Bowozu are young men who act as servants to guests or
officers residing in the castle. It is not permitted to Daimios
to bring their servants into the palace. They are waited on
by the Bowozu. These men are said to be open to giving up
to any one copies of any or all documents passing through
the government offices on payment of a small sum—30 to
50 itzaboos per annum.

Officers are appointed for keeping the time by striking a
large drum, and there are men who give signals by blowing
a shell, such as is used generally for directing movements in
warlike operations.

Yoshiba boonio.—Yoshiba is the name of a penal establishment on the island of Tsukudajima, at the mouth of the
Yedo River, to which certain criminals are sent, to prepare
oil and charcoal.

The above list comprises all the officers engaged in the
service of the Shiogoon, and who may be considered government officials conducting the business of their departments in
offices in Yedo. But as the office of Shiogoon is in abeyance
it remains to be seen in what manner the government is to be
hereafter carried on; and whether the court of Miako, which
is now temporarily removed to Yedo, will return to the older
titles and offices as known at Miako, or will adopt the forms
and offices which have been in use at the court of the Shiogoon in Yedo.

The Hio jo shio—The Board of Deliberation.—This is a large place of meeting for deliberation in Yedo, outside of the palace-moat, and close to the residences of the Gorochiu. On fixed days of every month certain officers sit here for the discharge of their duties. These seem to be to receive complaints against officers, and to decide cases brought before them for judgment. Upon other fixed days, all Daimios or Hattamoto upon duty in Yedo seem to have the right, or are called upon as a duty, to meet for the discussion of political matters laid before them. Hio jo means to deliberate or hold a consultation; and at these times the Gorochiu, Wakadoshi yori, Owo me tski, and other officers, meet here for deliberation upon affairs affecting the government.

Within the palace Daimios meet in rooms according to their rank, and the class of Daimios is often spoken of by the name of the room in the palace in which it meets—as the Obee ro ma, the Tomari no ma, the Yanangi no ma, the Gan no ma, the Kiri no ma, the Tay kan no ma, the Fuyo no ma, or the Goyobeya, or the Siro jo in (or Kuro jo in), in which last all classes seem on occasions to meet. But it is only in rare cases that all are called together; such an occasion was the proposal brought before them by Commodore Perry to overturn the old laws and throw open the country. It has been seen that Iyeyas in his laws thought the meeting of this assembly, the Hio jo sho, very important, and he said that the president must be a man of the clearest intellect and best disposition, and that once in every month it should be the duty of the Shiogoon to go to the assembly without previous intimation, and there act as judge.

Immediately in front of the building stands a box, known as the Mayassu hako. Into this box any one may put a paper of complaint upon any subject which he wishes to bring before the assembly. These papers, "Mayassu," are taken out and examined, and those which are signed are discussed, those which have no signature are burned. There are similar boxes at Miako and Osaka.

The following may be taken as a sketch, or very im·

perfect translation, of the matters which come under the cognizance of the assembly as instructions to officers:

1. When a complaint is made with reference to ground in a street in front of, and generally belonging to, a temple, and which is frequently let as shops, etc.; or in reference to Go rio, ground belonging to the Shiogoon; or Shi rio, ground belonging to Daimios—these complaints are not to be taken up by the board, but are to be referred to the Tskiban (the temple lord who is sitting for the month).

2. All quarrels and complaints between and against Yedo street people, citizens of Yedo, are to be referred to the governor of Yedo.

3. In the Kwang hasshiu, or eight provinces immediately around Yedo—Awa, Kadsusa, Simosa, Hitatse, Simotsuki, Kowotsuki, Segami and Musasi—disputes between the tenants of the Shiogoon and those of Daimios or Dai kangs are to be referred to the treasury governor. These three governors are known as the "San boonio."

4. Proceedings as to disputes between Daimios as to ground.

5. Between brothers as to succession to the father's property.

6. In the case of a demand for a new trial after a decision has been given.

7. In regard to petitions from friends to let a prisoner out of confinement on the ground of his innocence, must have good reasons shown.

8. If the people want an alteration or change of a law.

9. What is to be done with papers, Hakko so, put into the box.

10. If people complain of officers.

11. In a complaint of an improper judgment in a case (perhaps in another court).

12. Business in the Hio jo shio. The 2d, 11th and 21st days of the month are "Siki jits," or days when public political business is discussed. The 4th, 13th and 25th, "Tatchi yeibi," the officers meet as judges to decide cases. On the

6th, 18th and 27th, "Uchi yori yeibi," secret meeting days, the officers meet to examine and discuss secret political matters among themselves.

13. The form to be followed when a case has been for a long time before the Hio jo shio and is referred to another judge, as the street governor; and what is to be done in reference to complaints against the Gorochiu, Wakatoshiyori, or Owometski.

14. Complaints against Yakunins, or officers on duty outside of Yedo, are to be referred to the Shiogoon.

15. Disputes as to water for irrigation, and embankments of rice fields, which are sources of frequent quarrels, are to be taken up by the Hio jo shio.

16. In disputes as to boundaries of property, the old titles in the hands of the disputants are to be examined, and compared with the "Midzu cho" (water book, or register), kept in the Daikang office for the registration of boundaries and property.

17. In disputes as to land, to apply to the proper office to have surveys made.

18. What is to be done in cases of forgery of title-deeds of lands, or of maps of villages, islands, etc., which is a common offense.

19. As to disputes between Kanushi, heads of temples and of government temples.

20. In cases where application is made by the friends of a criminal to have him pardoned, such is not to be entertained in cases of arson, theft, murder, either as principal or accomplice, striker of father or mother or master, gamblers, head men of villages convicted of extorting money, mikassa (literally three hats),* and men who have bought young girls secretly. These crimes are not to be pardoned.

---

* A gambling game analogous to the "white-pigeon card" of China (Pak kop piu), at which much money is lost by families. A head office issues papers upon which the eighty first characters of the "Thousand Characters Classic" are

21. As to arbitrations ordered by officers, only a certain number of days to be allowed to make such arbitration—the office to settle how many.

22. When a petition has been presented by one party and the other does not appear, what is to be the proceeding.

23. Accusations of theft and fire-raising are not to be brought before the Hio jo shio, but before the officer in whose jurisdiction the offense is committed.

24. In cases of discovery of a long antecedently committed murder.

25. If a man destroys a summons issued by the office, and refuses to obey it.

26. Cases of persons trying to pass the barriers at Hakonay and Arai, without the knowledge of the officers stationed at the barriers.

27. In a case of firing a pistol or gun at another without killing, the punishment is "chiu tsui ho"—*i.e.*, the culprit is not allowed to enter a town or village. If a man wishes to shoot or sport near Yedo, he must get a license from the Yakunins to do so within the ten ri between Hatch ogee and Kanagawa upon the Tama River. Native sportsmen frequently shoot.

28. How persons are to be dealt with for snaring birds, or *feræ naturæ*, on the hunting-lands of the Shiogoon.

29. In towns, if a man have committed a small offense, the Yakunins may order his door to be shut upon him, and him to be confined in his own house.

30. Cases of embezzlement of money by village head men.

31. Punishment for a man who has failed to enroll his name in the official register.

32. If a man offer a bribe to an officer he is to be se-

---

printed in rows. These may be purchased for any price the purchaser chooses to lay upon them. During the night ten characters are marked by the office. The purchaser marks ten, and speculates upon his hitting some or all of the same as were marked at the office.

verely punished; the officer, if he accepts it, is lightly dealt with.

33. All the property of a person convicted of theft or robbery is to be confiscated.

34. If the people on a Daimio's territory send a remonstrance against his oppression to the Hio ko shio, what is to be done with it.

35. All the goods belonging to a debtor may be sold to pay his debts, except his wearing apparel.

36. If persons try to bring wild ground into cultivation, and call it their own without informing the officers, what proceedings are to be taken.

37. Cases of litigation as to rented ground.

38. When persons are unable, from poverty, to pay government taxes upon ground occupied by them.

39. In regard to loans of money, of which twenty different kinds are alluded to—to a friend, to a temple, etc.

40. If the whole of a loan cannot be repaid, and it is referred to the officers, they are to settle the interest to be paid. Upon large amounts the interest is placed low, upon small amounts it is high. Upon 10,000 cobangs the rate will be 80 cobangs per month, or nearly 10 per cent per annum. Upon one boo it may be one tenpo a month, or 75 per cent per annum.

41. In borrowing money, the interest is to vary with the security. If the security is land, the interest is to be low; with any other securities the interest should be high.

42. In disputes as to money: If no witnesses are brought forward; if partners in business quarrel; if persons in theaters quarrel; if a collector uses subscriptions to temples for his own purposes; if the evidence depends upon a paper without a date; if no rate of interest is mentioned—then these cases are not to be taken up.

43. If it is alleged that a Daimio has borrowed money from some town or body of people, and they do not bring forward a receipt, such is to be dismissed.

44. If one creditor refuses to have a composition.

45. The officers may settle the time to be allowed to pay off a debt, after which the securities may be taken. For 1,000 cobangs, 12 months to be allowed; for 30 cobangs, 40 days.

46. When property already mortgaged is given in security.

47. In cases where the cargo of a ship is secretly sold upon her passage, and a story of bad weather is told.

48. When a father has sealed a draft of his intended will, and has not written it out, what is the position of the heirs.

49. When false witnesses are suborned.

50. Houses or ground are sometimes sold by relatives when the heir is young. It is therefore criminal to buy ground without giving intimation to the proper officer.

51. It is the custom to have guarantees for servants, to whom wages are generally paid in advance. If the servant runs away with his wages, his surety must pay for him.

52. Half-yearly engagements with servants at the third and ninth month are usual. If a servant runs away before his time is out, his surety is responsible.

53. If it is another servant that is surety, he is responsible.

54. When a Daimio's servant runs away, what is to be done.

55. It is usual to have ten sureties—how this is to be settled. Not more than ten to be allowed.

56. If a runaway servant steals from his master.

57. If a man stays away from his wife for ten months she may marry again. When he returns he is to be punished.

58. If a poor man secretly marries and has a child, and exposes it on the street, or if another man buys it and exposes it, either shall be speared or beheaded. The head man of the street is to be fined and deported from Yedo, and the Gonin gumi or police guard of the street are to be punished.

The headman of a village or block of streets is Nanushi; under him is Iyaynushi. The Go nin gumi are five police in every street, who are appointed and paid by the streets.

Nanushi often have much power and become wealthy. Iyeyas in his laws tried to prevent this, as it is in too many cases the result of oppression and bribery. In Yedo and Osaka the government appoints the Nanushi; in Miako the people appoint them. The Nanushi of a village is generally a hereditary office.

59. If a man shall have adopted a daughter and then sells her to the government stews (Yosiwara), he is to be punished. The punishment is to vary according to the wealth and the ability of the offender to support the child.

60. If any one secretly sells girls for prostitution to any one but the Yosiwara, he is liable to punishment.

61. If a man sells his wife to the Yosiwara without reason, he is to be beheaded. But if the wife agrees to be so sold, and they are very poor, they may make such an arrangement. It was formerly the custom to kill a wife if she was unfaithful, but of late the custom has been to dispose of her to the Yosiwara.

62. The crime of adultery is to be punished with death (? in the case of the wife only).

63. Men and women who commit suicide together are not to receive burial like men, but like dogs. If they attempt and do not succeed, they are to be exposed on the Nihon bas (bridge) for three days, and then made beggars.

64. If a bozan or priest commit adultery, he shall be beheaded. In cases of fornication, if it be the head priest, he shall be transported to the islands; if a young priest, he shall be exposed on the Nihon bas for three days. (Some years ago one hundred and seventy young priests were thus exposed on the bridge at one time by Midzu no Idzumi no kami.)

65. In cases of persons professing San cho ha (three birds) Foosjiu (not take), Foossay (not give), they are to be transported. What these may mean it is difficult to find out; but possibly they are names for some form of religion, either Christianity or Mohammedanism.

66. No one is allowed to introduce new forms of religion

or new gods into the country. If they do so, they are to be banished from villages.

67. In cases of suicide the officers must be informed. If they are privately buried with Buddhist burial, both priests and friends shall be punished.

68. Mikassa, Bakuji and Mujing, different kinds of gambling, are to be severely punished.

69. Slight cases of theft are to be punished by flogging and banishment from towns and villages. In more serious cases of theft, the criminals are first to be carried through Yedo publicly, and then are to be beheaded.

70. In reference to buyers and receivers of stolen goods.

71. As to those who engage in a trade without belonging to one of the guilds.

72. As to informers.

73. What steps are to be taken as to persons falling down dead in the streets.

74. As to things lost.

75. As to accomplices, or persons who indirectly assist criminals to escape.

76. Forgers are to be beheaded.

77. As to putters-up of seditious placards on the walls.

78. What is to be done with a man who (as is sometimes done in Yedo), on meeting a respectable man, suddenly accuses him of striking him, or says he is married to his daughter, or gets up some story to extort money from him.

79. In cases when a man is the indirect cause of loss to another—as by coming too late, and so loss is sustained. This is a crime, though the loss may be small.

80. Men who give false statements to officers.

81. As to false money, poison, false medicines, and false weights.

82. As to setting a house on fire by mistake.

83. An incendiary is to be burned to death.

84. A reward to be given to the man who detects him.

85. As to murder of different kinds. In cases of acci-

dental death, a fine is to be levied on the homicide. It is said to be a common custom in Japan to compound for crime by paying relatives and bribing officers.

86. When a man kills another in self-defense.

87. If a man kill another by accident, as by a rifle-ball, he is to be transported; but if it is done in a military school, he is not punished. If a working man kills another by accident, he is banished from towns and villages.

88. If a man is angry with another for marrying a girl he is in love with, and breaks in the door and causes a disturbance.

89. If a man is drunk and angry, and breaks some article of value, the punishment is to be light; but if several are together, they are to be punished severely.

90. If, when drunk, he kills a man by accident, he is not to be severely punished.

91. If a man recovers from sickness and refuses to pay his doctor.

92. As to offenses committed by mad persons.

93. If a person under fifteen years of age commit murder, transportation is the punishment.

94. As to concealing criminals.

95. As to proclamations about offenders.

96. The officers cannot command a son to inform on or to give up his father or mother, or a servant his master, or a younger brother his elder.

97. In some cases the relatives of a criminal may be arrested and confined, but this Chinese plan is not commonly used in Japan.

98. Gowo mong—examination by torture, as striking, or pouring water down the throat.

99. As to escaping from banishment on the islands, or crimes committed during banishment.

100. As to escaping from prison.

101. As to men who free themselves from their irons.

102. The higher rank a man is of, the more serious is his crime.

103. And, *vice versa*, a crime is to be considered lighter in a man of low degree.

104. As to criminals who have been banished from towns and villages, if they try to return.

105. If he is ejected a second time he is marked, and if he returns a third time he is beheaded. These marks are broad black bands across the arm. The different towns (Yedo, Miako, Osaka, and Nagasaki) have different ways of marking.

106. If any one shall secretly make weights. All the weights are made and issued by government in Japan.

107. In regard to the keepers of the street gates in Yedo, if one shall find any money or article of value and keep it.

108. In Yedo it is the custom to take out a drunken man, or a man that has died on the street, and lay him in another. This is to be punished.

109. If a man accused of a serious crime should die, his body is to be preserved in salt.

110. In reference to criminals and prisoners in bad health. There are four hospitals for criminals in Yedo.

111. A criminal whose time is expired, and who has neither home nor friends, is to be put to work in Tsukuda-jima for one thousand days, and at the end of that time the profits of his labor are to be given him, and he may get a street gate to keep.

112. If a man forces a girl to marry him, he shall be beheaded.

113. Rules as to pawning and pawn-shops. Pawn-shops charge very high interest—about ten per cent a month.

114. If a man be taken ill upon the Tokaido, he is not to be sent from one village to another, but is to be kept, and a doctor sent for to attend him.

115. If a man who has no right to do so shall wear two swords.

116. What is to be done to squatters upon wild ground, who have not given notice to the officers of their having done so.

117. If a man tries to conceal or prevent the confiscation of his ground.

118. When the son of a criminal of high rank wishes to shave his head and become a priest, in some measure to save the reputation of his family, he is to inform the officers, and make arrangements with them.

119. In reference to the children of a criminal, a difference is made between the children of an officer and a common person.

120. All villages have registers and plans of the ground belonging to each, and to the families of the villagers. These are sealed and kept by the head man of the village (nanushi), and he is bound to let any one inspect the registers. If he refuse, and complaint is made, he is to be punished.

121. What is to be done upon their liberation with criminals who have been confined for slight offenses.

122. Different kinds of punishment for different offenses. Of these there are specified forty-six.

In case of disputes between persons belonging to the four provinces round Miako, Yamashiro, Yamato, Tanba, and Owomi, they are brought before the street governor of Miako; but if a dispute arises between a person living in one of these provinces and an outsider, the case is brought to Yedo. Litigation arising in the provinces of Idzumi, Kawatchi, Setsu, and Harima, is brought before the governor of Osaka.

No taxes are paid in Miako.

If a murder or arson be committed within the territory of a Daimio, it is not necessary to bring the case to Yedo.

If the servants of a Daimio kill the servant of another Daimio the case must be brought before the Gorochiu.

If a Daimio has no island or place fit for transportation, the criminal's relatives are bound to keep him in confinement.

The above is a sketch of the cases which may come before the criminal department of the Hio jo sho.

Hio jio shio russui are four officers who have charge of the building when not used.

Ro ban.—Keeper of the prison (roya). The execution-ground is at the southeast corner of the prison, under a willow-tree in front of the back gate. The office of executioner seems to be hereditary. Kubikiri Asayaymon is at present the executioner, and it is said that his son at fourteen could cut off a head at a blow. The prison is surrounded by a high embankment, to prevent fires reaching it. If a fire occurs within the building the prisoners are all liberated, and those who return have their punishment mitigated.

Jowo ro sama.—These are female officers. They are twelve daughters of Koongays in Miako, who reside in the palace at Yedo to superintend all the females, servants, etc., and to look after their manners and morals. They are always unmarried while in office, but sometimes marry Daimios. They generally come to the palace young, and are instructed there in their duties. They have the opportunity of having great power, being at liberty to write to Miako about anything they may deem improper either in the conduct of the ladies, women, or men of the court of Yedo, or of the Shiogoon himself.

Officers employed in situations at a distance from Yedo. —There are six main roads or entrances to Miako; over each of these the Shiogoon places a guard under a Daimio, maintaining in addition a guard in the city itself. With the Sho shi dai there are nine Daimios resident in Miako.

Shoshidai.—This is the representative of the Shiogoon at the court of Miako. It is an office requiring much tact and independence of character. Formerly it was held by one of the more powerful Daimios, but it was found that the tendency to be won over to the party of the Emperor was great, and it is now generally intrusted to a Fudai. His duty is to act as a go-between or embassador to the imperial court, and at the same time report to Yedo all changes. He does not address himself personally to the Emperor, or even to the Kwanbakku, but to the Tenso, the officer deputed for that purpose, and who in turn is at times sent to Yedo as envoy from the Emperor. The office is one which entails great expenditure, but it is one in which personal influence may be largely used for the furtherance of intrigue and the acquisition of power. When Sakai was made Shoshidai, the Shiogoon gave him an addition to his income of 10,000 koku per annum. He fell into disgrace with the Emperor, and committed suicide in 1862. The Emperor accused him of telling him falsehoods, while Sakai did not know that the accounts furnished him were not true. Had he not committed suicide, his property would have been taken from his son. His father committed suicide also as Shoshidai at Miako in the time of Kokaku, grandfather of the present Emperor.

Miako matchi boonio.—Two officers, governors of Miako, under the Shiogoon, whose duties are similar to those of the governor of Yedo.

Kinri tsuki.—Two officers who act as messengers between the imperial officers and the Shoshidai.

Nijio dzei ban.—The castle of the Shiogoon in Miako is called Nijio. Two Daimios, and men under them, are appointed guards or governors of the castle.

There is a keeper of the storehouses in Miako belonging to the Shiogoon; also a keeper of the weapons of war, guns, great and small, and an officer who superintends the boats on the Yodongawa, the river running past Miako, to give out licenses and receive the payment.

Fushimi boonio.—A Daimio, governor of the town of Fushimi, near Miako. Here Taikosama resided, and built the costly palace which was destroyed by an earthquake. All Daimios have or had residences at Fushimi.

Osaka jiodai.—Governor of the town of Osaka.

Jiobang.—Keeper or warden of the castle of Osaka, built by Taikosama.

Dzeibang.—Captains of the guards in that castle. Two Daimios take this duty.

Kabang.—Four Daimios. These three last officers are all together keepers of the castle of Osaka.

Osaka matchi boonio is street governor of Osaka.

Funate is head officer over the boats and boatmen.

Kohoo, or Kofu.—The capital town of Kahi province, or Koshiu, where the Shiogoon has a large castle, built by Takeda Singeng. Hattamoto that have fallen into the black books of the government for vicious conduct, or immorality, drinking, etc., are sent to this castle. Sometimes as many as 500 Hattamoto are there in a sort of arrest, under surveillance before being again employed.

Nagasaki boonio.—Governors of Nagasaki, of whom there are two, and two Daikangs to look after the lands belonging to the Shiogoon. Nagasaki and the land in the vicinity and the island of Amakusa belong to the Shiogoon.

Narra boonio.—Governor of Narra, the ancient and ecclesiastical capital of Japan, a short distance from Miako.

Soonpu (Suruga no fu) is the castle of Suruga, built by Imangawa, and occupied by Iyeyas some years before his death, and afterward occupied by the ex-Shiogoon, Yoshi hissa. There is a governor of the town and castle. At one time the treasury of the Shiogoon was kept at Soonpu.

Suruga kabang.—One military Daimio. One of the Shiogoon's physic gardens for medicinal herbs is at Soonpu, in charge of an officer.

Kowo no san.—Tombs of some of the early predecessors of the Shiogoon. Iyeyas was buried at Nikko, in Simotsuki, a day's journey north of Yedo. There is an officer in charge of the tombs at both places; where there are also, as officers, a keeper of accounts and a gatekeeper. In the province of Isse, at the great temple there, the Shiogoon is represented by an officer, Yamada boonio. Over the town of Sakkai, near Osaka, is a governor.

Ooraga boonio.—The "gate" or seaport of Yedo below Kanagawa, in the bay of Yedo, has two governors. At Ooraga all junks and boats are examined by custom-house officials.

Sado boonio.—Two governors of the island of Sado, where are the gold mines.

Neegata boonio.—One governor of the town. This port

formerly belonged to a Daimio, Makino Bizen no kami, but about the year 1840 the Shiogoon displaced him, and gave him Nangaoka, in Etsingo, in place of Neegata. It was alleged that an illicit trade was being carried on between Corea and this port, and also with the Dutch. It is said to be a fine harbor, and was one of the ports opened to foreign trade by treaty; but the harbor was found, or supposed to be, too shallow for large ships. It has fallen off considerably in trade and wealth since government took possession of it.

Nikko boonio.—At Nikko Hill is buried To sho goo, or Iyeyas, the first of the dynasty, and a fine temple (Chiu senji) is erected near the tomb. The actual tombs of heroes and great men in Japan, as has been said, seem to be generally very modest and unassuming memorials. From the roof of the temple at Nikko is hung a large chandelier presented by the Dutch. The Shiogoons after Iyeyas are buried, some at the Shibba, a temple in Yedo, some at Ooyayno or Toyay san, another large temple in Yedo; others at Kowono san; and at Zozoji, in Yedo.

Gai koku boonio.—Ministers for foreign nations. These officers were appointed in consequence of the opening of the country, and their duty is to communicate with the consuls or ministers of foreign nations on international questions, or matters connected with trade. They are Hattamoto of rental varying from 150 to 3,000 koku per annum.

Kanagawa boonio.—There are two Hattamoto, governors of this village, now risen into importance. The one is a man of 5,000 koku, the other of 1,200.

Seki sho.—In the different provinces of Japan there are passes upon the roads, where, by reason of the surrounding hills, the road may be easily defended by a small force. These are considered the keys of the country, and at each place barriers (seki) are erected and guards appointed. These are important from a military point of view.

In the province of Segami there are six seki or barriers. Okubo kanga no kami, Daimio at Odawarra, has charge of them. They are—Hakonay upon the Tokaido, Neboo kawa, Yangura sawa, Sengo ku bara, Kawa mura, Tanega mura.

In the province of Towotomi there are three gates— Imangiri, Arai and Kenga.

In Kowotsuki are fourteen barriers—Fkushima, Go shina, Owo watari and another, Oossui, Yoko-ngawa, Koori, Ka- wa mata, Sarunga harra, Owo sassa, Dai-ito, Kari jigu, Minami maki, Tokura.

In Etsingo province are five barriers—Itchi foori, Hatchi dzaki, Seki ngawa, Mooshi kawa, Yama ngootchi.

In the province of Sinano six—Kiu oochi ji, Nami ai, Obi kawa, Ono ngawa, Fkushima, Ni engawa.

In the province of Simosa four—Seki yado, Matsudo, Fusa kawa, Nakatta.

In the province of Musashi four—Kobo toki, Ko iwa, Itchi kawa, Kana matchi.

In the province of Owomi three—Yama naka, Yana ngassay, and another.

At these barriers no woman is allowed to pass without a passport from the governor of Yedo. No Daimio is allowed to bring cannon or muskets past a barrier without permis- sion. Guards are stationed at each, to examine every young person as to their sex. This is done in order to keep the wives and families of Daimios at Yedo.

In Sinano province there are large forests, the property of government, on the Kisso hills, under charge of a Hatta- moto.

Koondai (Kiun tai) is an officer who has the superintend- ence of all the Shiogoon's land in the different provinces in which it lies. One officer has generally the lands in two or more provinces under his care.

Dai kwan are smaller and lower offices, with duties simi- lar to and under the Koondai. They look after the ground and crops on the ground belonging to government. They calculate the amount payable by rice-fields. To ascertain this they frequently cut a tsubo (six feet square) dry, and thrash it, and calculate the product of the whole field therefrom. They receive the rents, make leases, and act as factors on government lands. There are thirty-seven Dai kwan.

The Officers of the Mint.—The mint in Yedo is in Drio ngai tcho. It is under the superintendence of the treasury governor. There is the Kinsa, or the department where gold is coined; and the ginsa, the mint for silver coins. Deposits of silver and gold are found in several parts of Japan, but the most of the gold used by government comes from the island of Sado; the silver is brought from Ikoo no gin sa in Tajima, and from Iwami province. In some of the territories of Daimios there are large quantities extracted, as in the lands of Satsuma and Sendai. The latter has the right of coining money, but the coin seems to circulate only within his own territory. Silver and gold, as bullion, are much cheaper relatively to coin than in almost any other country: this arises probably from that peculiarity in the laws and customs of Japan—the Tokusayay, previously mentioned—which prevents the natives using either metal as ornaments, or in any useful way. A good deal of gold must be used in the manufacture and ornamentation of the lacquer-ware, which is sometimes profusely covered with gold; but, except for this purpose, there is little or none used, as the ladies do not wear jewelry of any kind—neither earrings, nor rings, nor brooches. No plate is used at their dinners. Owing to this, no one can put the precious metals, if they have any in their possession, to any use, and the owner, in order to realize their value, must take them to the only market, which is government. The government thus has the power of declaring what value it will put upon these precious metals, and pays accordingly for silver bullion thirty per cent below the value which is afterward put upon the coin.

Lastly, among the establishments kept up by the Shiogoon is the Nishi maro, literally the west round, the oldest part of the shiro of Yedo. It was built by Owota do Kwang, as mentioned before. The castle is surrounded by a broad moat filled with water. On the inner side a fine steep bank of grass slopes up from the water's edge to such a height as entirely to conceal the interior. The water is brought from a considerable distance—from the Tama ngawa River—being led in a canal known as Tama ngawa jo sui. This was made by Iyay Mitzko, the second after Iyeyas, and is under the care of the Owometski and Kanjo office. The Nishi maro is intended for the occupation of the child or children of the Shiogoon, or for his father if he have abdicated. It is therefore frequently empty, and in that case officers have charge of the building, who are known as Nishi maro russui.

Within the circuit of the castle grounds are the residences of the Gosankioh—the three princes, Stotsbashi, Tayass, and Saymidzu.

CHAPTER X

THE DAIMIO CLASS

IN the official list of Daimios published at Yedo the pedigree of each is given; the family name and descent; the period when the title commenced; the sons and daughters, with the names of their wives and husbands; where his residence in Yedo is situated, and likewise his houses in Miako, Osaka and Fusimi; the date of his accession to the title; who his wife is; his coats of arms, of which each Daimio has two or more; the presents he is to make to the Shiogoon both during the year when he resides in Yedo and during that when he resides at his provincial residence; the presents the Shiogoon makes to him on his coming to Yedo; how his communications are to be carried on with the Shiogoon and Gorochiu; the shape and color of the leather covering of his official spears carried before him, as the spearpoints are always carried covered with leather; the uniform or livery of his retainers; the title of his eldest son; the names and titles of his large retainers, or Byshing; the mattoyay or solid ensign carried in his train, the flag he carries on his ships, and the large mark upon his sails; the amount of his territorial income; the provinces in which his property lies; the distance of his residence from Yedo; the room in the palace of the Shiogoon to which he goes; the temple in which he is buried.

In the official list the Daimios are classed by families (Kay), from many of which families there are cadets or offshoots.

At the head of the Daimios stand the San Kay, "three families," Owarri, Kii, and Mito. Iyeyas in his laws calls the two first from their cities, Nagoya and Wakayama. There are four provinces from which two Daimios at one time are not permitted to take a title—Mootz, Mikawa, Musashi and Etsigo. No Daimio is allowed to take his title of Kami from any of the three provinces, Kadsusa, Hitatsi, or Kowotsuki—they are reserved for the imperial family.

Of these Daimios, three are generally known as greater Kokushu; viz., 1, Kanga; 2, Satsuma; and, 3, Sendai. Fourteen are called lesser Kokushu: 4, Hosokawa; 5, Kuroda; 6, Aki; 7, Nagato Mowori; 8, Hizen Nabeshima; 9, Inaba Ikeda; 10, Bizen Ikeda; 11, Isse no Tzu, Towodo; 12, Awa, Hatchiska; 13, Tosa Yamano ootchi; 14, Sataki; 15, Arima in Tsikugo; 16, Nambu; 17, Ooyay Soongi. Four are new Kokushu: 18, Etsizen; 19, Tsuyama; 20, Idzumo; 21, Aidzu.

This list comprehends all those who are supposed to be capable of taking an active share in the government of Yedo, or in ruling their own districts in the interest of the present dynasty of Shiogoons.* When from any cause, such as age or infirmity, a Daimio is incapacitated from attending to his duties at Yedo, or when he becomes tired of the trammels of State to which he is subjected, he may abdicate, and hand over the dignities or the more irksome part of the duties

---

* The dynasty having been recently set aside, the country is in a transition state, and the position of these Daimios in the future remains to be worked out.

of office to his son. If he be suspected of intriguing against the powers of the State, he may be displaced, and the title taken from him and given to some relative, or any one to whom the Shiogoon may be pleased to give it. It seems but rarely that any steps are taken against the person of a Daimio, further than ordering him into arrest in his own house, which his successor is often too glad to carry into effect. In the case of a Daimio being accused or convicted of any great crime, he may offer to shave his head and become a Buddhist priest, and so avoid any further consequences. The difficulty of seizing a man of rank in his own territory has probably led to these compromises. Therefore the government tries to act through the interest of the retainers to obtain submission to its decrees. And it is only when a man is powerful enough and wealthy enough (with personal ability to boot, as in the case of Choshiu in 1866) to carry on war, that it becomes necessary to take up arms, and then nothing short of civil war can be the result.

As a consequence of this state of things, there is a large number of persons in Japan who have been Daimios, but who are in a position, real or nominal, of retirement from the world and its cares. These are the fathers or brothers or relatives of those who now hold the title, and who have probably been put in to fill the position on account of their tender age. Many no doubt thus retire of their own free will; but the disturbances consequent upon Ee Kamong no kami's vigorous action in 1857 forced others to give up the title and place in order to save them for their family. Others have, for the same object, committed suicide.

Daimios who have thus retired into private life are called Inkio (Chin., "Yin ku")—*i.e.*, retired into privacy. He is thenceforth known generally by the name of his castle or province, with the word for "late" or "formerly," saki no, prefixed to the highest title which he bore.

In 1862 there were 104 of these Inkio Daimios, whose names are given at the end of the peerage, and of whom the following are most prominent:

1. Owarri, saki no Chiunagoong.—This is the Daimio who was degraded by the regent.

2. Mimasaka, saki no Chiujo.—This is the thirty-fourth child of the eleventh Shiogoon, and known as Kakudo.

3. Akashi, saki no Shosho, is also a son of the Shiogoon, and was adopted by Matzdaira Hiobu no tayu.

4. Ooajima, saki no Shosho. His son is also on the re-tired list.

5. Etsizen, saki no Chiujo Shoongaku.—He was degraded by the regent, but was restored, and afterward became re-gent or Sosai.

A Buddhist name is at times adopted when he does not wish to continue to bear a title.

When he has shaved his head and becomes a priest, he is called Niudo; *i.e.*, entered the path of Buddha.

Keng, Sei, Ang, and Eeng are Buddhist titles taken by those who have retired from the world.

The Hattamoto—literally, "the root or foundation of the flag or army."—This rank was formerly called Shiomio, "small names," in contradistinction to Daimio, "great names." The Hattamoto are officers of the Shiogoon's government, who in rank and emoluments come next to the Daimios. Hattamoto are eligible to fill all the offices in the different departments of the Yedo government under the Gorochiu (to which Daimios alone are appointed). When it is wished to put a Hattamoto into the Cabinet, he is first given by the Shiogoon territory equivalent to 10,000 koku per annum. A Hattamoto may be described as an officer of the government in the possession of land valued from 500 to 9,999 koku. Officers with less than 500 koku are below Hattamoto, and known as Go kennin; and beneath them are Ko jiu nin. Lower still are the account-keepers; Oto torimi, bird-keepers; Okatchi, spies and men about the kitchen; and Yoriki and Do sin. Hattamoto are generally of the fifth rank, or Shodaibu, and never of the fourth. Some Hattamoto have titles from the Emperor, others have titles of provinces, as Daimios have, but those who have any titles are a small minority of the whole number. Some Hattamoto receive titles for one generation only, known as Itchi dai Yoriai. The class is divided into large and small—the former having from 3,000 to under 10,000 koku of land; the latter from 500 to 3,000. They are divided into—

1. Kotai Hattamoto, or those who go to Yedo on alternate years.

2. Yoriaï.

3. Ogo bang.—These live in or have charge of a castle, such as Kofu, Soonpu, etc.

4. Shingo bang.—These act as guards to the Shiogoon in Yedo.

5. O niwa bang.—These are keepers of the gardens, and are generally spies, and consequently avoided by other officers.

Some of the principal families of Hattamoto are the following:

Soonga numa, with 7,000 koku, at Shinshiro, in Mikawa province. An old family, proud of the family name.

Matzdaira Hissamatz is a relative of Matzdaira Oki no kami, related to the Shiogoon's family, and uses the Awoee or crest of the Shiogoon, with 6,000 koku; lives at Izassa in Shimosa.

Takanoya Matzdaira is the lineal descendant of the Nitta family, with 4,500 koku; lives at Nishingori in Mikawa.

Ikoma Tokutaro was, in the time of Taikosama, a powerful Daimio, is now a Hattamoto with 8,000 koku, living at Yajima in Dewa.

Yamano Mondo no ske, also a descendant of the Nitta family; was, in the time of Ashikanga, powerful, with 6,700 koku; resides at Mura oka in Tajima, is considered a good family, and, as related to the Shiogoon, has special privileges.

Hirano.—His ancestor, H. Gonpe, was a noted warrior in Taikosama's time. The family is much respected, has 5,000 koku, and lives at Sawara moto in Yamato.

Kinoshta.—Calls himself of the line of Taikosama, with 5,000 koku. His castle is Tateishi in Boongo.

Yamazaki.—Formerly a powerful family, now with 5,000

koku, resides at Nariwoo in Bitsjiu; is descended from the third brother of Hatchimang taro.

Mongami, lineally descended from Ashikanga, is looked upon as a Kokushiu; resides at Owomori in Owomi, with a revenue of 5,000 koku.

Kowotsuki, at Kowotsuki in Owomi, with 4,700 koku, is the lineal male descendant of the Ooda Genji line.

Besides these Hattamoto, there are Kotai Yoriaï, who are landed proprietors of very old families, but who are as Tozama, and take no part in affairs, such as—

Nassu, a very old family in Shimotsuki.

Mikawa shiu, the line of Iyeyas's family.

Nakajima Mayra was found in the Mayra district in Kiusiu.

There are, besides these, Hattamoto, styled Hira Yoriaï, with revenues from below 10,000 koku downward, such as—

Minagawa, with 9,000 koku.

Seigo, and others.

Kondo nobori no ske, with 5,400 koku, who is looked upon as first Hattamoto, not by rank, but because he refused to take the rank of Daimio from Iyeyas when offered to him.

Koozai, Foonayoshi.—These two are very wealthy. They were formerly engaged in trade with the Portuguese in the sixteenth century.—And many others, with incomes gradually decreasing to 500 koku per annum.

Hattamoto officers have generally been employed on interviews with foreign embassadors, or as embassadors to foreign courts on the conclusion of treaties.

Those who negotiated the treaty with Lord Elgin in 1858 were—Midzuno Tsikugo no kami, a low Hattamoto. He was afterward disgraced, but in 1862 was appointed governor of Hakodadi, and looked upon as a shrewd, wily man. —Nagai Genba no kami was also a low Hattamoto. He was also disgraced in the changes which followed, but in September, 1862, was appointed Sa kio, or street governor of Miako.—Inooyay Sinano no kami was the minister for naval affairs—was of low origin, the son of a Gokennin. He negotiated the treaty with Mr. Harris, United States Minister. He was in 1862 made a governor for foreign affairs.— Hori Oribay no kami was considered an upright man and just in his dealings. After the part he took in signing the treaty, he got into difficulties with Ando and Koozay in the Gorochiu, and committed suicide.—Iwase Higo no kami, a low Hattamoto, a very cunning man, since dead.—Isuda Hanzaburo was an obscure Gokennin.

The Dutch treaty was signed by Nagai Genba no kami; Okabay Suruga no kami, a low Hattamoto; and Iwase Higo no kami.

The Portuguese treaty was signed in 1860 by Misonogootchi Sanuki no kami, a high Hattamoto—he was appointed in 1862 general in command of the castle of Osaka; Sakkai oki no kami, a Hattamoto with 2,000 koku—he is now governor of the exchequer in Yedo; and Matzdaira Djirobe—had office in 1862 in the castle Kofu.

The embassadors who visited Europe were of the rank of Hattamoto: Take no ootchi, Simotski no kami, and others. The embassies were accompanied by agents from the more powerful Daimios, such as Satsuma, Choshiu, and others, who reported their observations to their own masters.

The Kokay, or Kowokay, as has been before stated, is a class which is looked upon as intermediate in rank between Daimios and Koongays. They are not permitted to take part in the affairs of government. They are the representatives of old families, and receive pay from government. The class is divided into Kimo iri kokay and Omotte Kokay.

Among the former are Hatake yama. His ancestor was a partisan of Yoritomo; his tomb is at Kamakura.—Toki, a general of Ashikanga's time.—Yura, a powerful family in the time of Ashikanga.—Otta, the lineal descendant of Nobu nanga.—Rokaku; in the time of Yoritomo known as Sassaki.—Arima, related to Arima, the Roman Catholic.— Imagawa, formerly lord of Surunga, and builder of Soonpu castle; defeated by Iyeyas.—Takeda, of the family of T. Singeng, who fought against Iyeyas. And others.

Of the Omotte Kokay—There are Owotomo, of the family of Owotomo Boongo no kami, the great patron of the Jesuits in the sixteenth century. At one time a very pow· erful family, possessing the greater portion of the island of Kiusiu, before the power of Satsuma rose to a height. The fortunes of the family fell with those of the Jesuits; and to the league formed against these foreigners, the confiscation of the extensive property of Owotomo was the stimulus to energy and the reward of victory.—Ooyay sungi was very powerful in the province of Etsingo, and the family for long held the office of Kwanrei at Kamakura. The direct descendant of the Nitta line was Jera matz manjiro. He was naturally a proud man, and refused to come to Yedo when Iyeyas invited him, and, in consequence, he lost his position; but the other Daimios, who trace their origin to the same source—the Nitta family—support him in a position equal to themselves.

The class of officers next below the Hattamoto is the Gokennin. The highest income they receive from government is less than 500 koku per annum.

Beneath the Gokennin, officers come under the general classification of Yakunins or officials—literally, "business men." This name is applied to the lower officers employed by the Shiogoon—such as Kumi gashira, Shirabbe yaku, Jo yaku, and Shtabang. There are no Yakunins in Miako; there the Emperor's sub-officials are called Kwannin.

Every Yakunin is supposed to swear that he will do whatever, right or wrong, he is ordered to do by his government.

It is not permitted to Gokennin, or to officials of lower rank, to ride in Yedo or upon the highroads; they must walk.

Such being the details of the officers under the Shiogoon, the government is so well regulated as to have worked with comparative smoothness for 250 years. The safeguards and checks which were devised by Iyeyas have been in operation up to recent times. The setting apart of three families from

the members of which the Shiogoon might be chosen, gives
a powerful support to the reigning family. The designation
of four families, from out of which a regent might be appointed, and the further naming of thirteen families from
out of which the Cabinet was advised to be formed, out of
the broader basis of 135 Fudai or working Daimios, who
were generally comparatively poor, gave to all the higher
classes a consistency of interest in the existing state of things.
Power over the person of the individual, and over his personal power of mischief, in regard to the more powerful
princes, was sought to be obtained by the detention of the
wives and families in Yedo, and by visiting the sins of an
intriguing prince, not upon his family or retainers, but upon
himself alone. It would appear that when the Shiogoon is
of age, and of sufficient capacity, he will appoint his own
ministers out of the different families named by Iyeyas to
this end. It is to the interest of the State as well as of the
Kokushiu that they should continue unmolested in the possession of their extensive territories and jurisdiction; and
intrigues are prevented as far as possible by no one being
allowed to visit another within his territories. While the
power which the government held over the persons and
property of these powerful princes, by having the wives
and families as hostages at Yedo, was promoted by the
wish for their welfare on the part of the husbands or parents, it was kept in force by the strange custom of these
powerful lords coming up to the court at Yedo every alternate year, or, in some cases, every six months. Perhaps
this was aided by the dullness of their country quarters compared with the gayety of the capital. If the Shiogoon be
a minor, or incapable of holding the reins of power, the
ablest or the least scrupulous of those who have any claim
to the situation becomes regent, and he rules the empire for
the time being. A regency, however, has not been frequently necessary during the rule of the present family,
but the appointment has never been' held by one man for
more than three years, and the tenure, it is said, has gen-

erally been terminated by assassination. The regent removes his political foes, and appoints in their place men holding his own views. He carries himself as a ruler over men who are his superiors in wealth and rank—the Kokushiu. These men are still obliged to repair to Yedo, where they find, in place of an acknowledged superior, a haughty inferior, to whom they must pay court. This is one weak point of the system, and that upon which it threatened to break up. This forms the last chapter of the history of the empire.

The above is a sketch of the court of the Shiogoon, with which one must be acquainted before the past history or the current events in the empire can be thoroughly understood.

CHAPTER XI

THE HISTORY OF THE EMPIRE CONTINUED

THE history of Japan, during the two and a half centuries after the death of Iyeyas, presents a continuous narrative of tranquillity and peace when contrasted with the stormy times which preceded that era. The laws which Iyeyas made, and the steps which he took, seem to have brought about the end which he had in view; namely, establishing his own family as *de facto* rulers of the empire, and placing them upon a seat which should be too strong for any rival to overthrow.

The peace which was so happily granted to the empire was so perfect and of such duration that in the year 1806 a great national festival was held, when the nobles and people congratulated the Emperor upon what was an unprecedented fact in the history of Japan, and indeed it may be said of any nation, an unbroken peace of nearly two hundred years.

The only subject of discord left behind him by Iyeyas at his death was the question of the treatment of the foreigner in his twofold capacity of trader and missionary. The foreigner as a trader Iyeyas wished to retain at his ports, in order that he himself might enjoy the benefits of trade, and keep himself acquainted with what was going on in the world around him. The foreigners as proselytizing missionaries bringing professions of peace and goodwill, but who seemed to be in reality preachers of sedition and organizers of rebellion, were not to be tolerated; and he came to the conclusion that if any real peace was to be obtained for the country, it must be at the expense of the former. "Perish trade," he said, "that my country may have the greater blessing of peace." With the view of carrying out his plans, another edict was, in the year 1616, promulgated against the Roman Catholic religion, about which time the evidence of these fathers would lead to the belief that, "from Taikosama's death, 1598, to the year 1614, the fathers of the Society baptized upward of 104,000; and what is more, in the three first years of the persecution, when the very pillars themselves began to shake, they converted 15,000 more. By this time the Jesuits had traversed the whole empire, and claimed converts, not only in Yedo, but in Oshiu (or Mootz) and Dewa to the extreme north. The province of Oshiu is separated from Dewa by a long chain of high mountains all covered with snow, and here it was that the poor exiled Christians lived, destitute of all human assistance. One of the Jesuits, moved with compassion at their misfortune, took a journey into that country, climbing up the hills over hideous precipices in deep snow. He visited privately the Christians that wrought in the mines, and confessed and communicated them. The same he did at the hospital of lepers, which happened to be at that time full of Christians." This was, as we are told, done quietly, and by the assistance of converts; but, as heretofore, while some of the different orders of the Roman Church were disposed to keep quiet till better times should dawn, and carry on their ministrations in secret, as it were, others were still inclined to show a zeal without knowledge, and thus kept up the ardor of

13

their enemies about the court.　During the year 1626 Midzu no and Take naka were sent down to Nagasaki to examine into and report upon the state of the Christian religion; and the government, knowing that the Cross was the symbol of the faith, and an object of the highest reverence among the Christians, resolved to make the question of such reverence the shibboleth or test of the individual strength of faith.　In 1636 orders were issued by government that every one in Nagasaki was to assemble each month for the purpose of standing upon, with the object of desecrating, a copper "ita," or plate, with an engraven representation of the Christian criminal God—*i.e.*, of our Saviour.　This order was strictly carried out at Nagasaki, while another such plate was (and is) kept at Osaka for the purpose of testing suspected persons.　This act of desecration is known as "Yayboomi," and was carried out till the recent conclusion of treaties with Christian nations.

This last device of the government appears to have been successful in separating the Christian element from the heathen; but it terminated in a way which was, perhaps, not expected by the authorities; namely, in driving the poor Christians of the island of Kiusiu to band together, and ultimately in desperation to take up arms in their own defense. Had the Christians resorted to this *ultima ratio* at first, instead of leaving it as the last card they had to play, the result of the game might have been different from what it turned out to be.　Refusing to perform such an act of irreverence and desecration, they were obliged to fly to the hills and band together for the common object of protection.　The numbers increased until they amounted to upward of 40,000 men.　The most prominent leader among them appears to have been Massida shiro, fourth son of Jimbe, in Kobemura, in Hizen province; and he was assisted by two brothers, Oyano Kozayaymon and O. Kemmootz.　These are probably the two brothers to whom Tavernier, the great Eastern traveler, alludes in an appendix to his work, when he mentions, on the authority of one Father Barr, who seems to have been in Japan at the time, that "none were more zealous or faithful to the Christians than the two lords of Ximo, Francis and Charles, sons of the lord of Buzen."

The Roman Catholics who had been recently forced out of the city of Nagasaki and the town adjacent gathered themselves together under the command of Massida, and resolved to make a final stand in the island of Amacusa, at that time belonging to Terasawa, formerly governor of Nagasaki, and under the charge of his retainer Miako tobe. The first move of this Christian army was to seize the castle of Tomioka. This put them in possession of the island, after which the army crossed over to occupy the castle of Simabara, situated about twenty miles from Nagasaki, and meditated an attack upon that town. The movements of both parties seem to have been slow, as, after a delay of twelve months, the government issued orders to the Daimios of the island of Kiusiu to collect, equip and send forward an army under the command of Itakura Suwo no kami to besiege the castle and town of Simabara. Itakura, probably acting upon the advice of his augurs, the Buddhist priesthood, attacked the city upon the first day of the year, and was killed in the attempt, when the command devolved upon Matzdaira Idzu no kami, with Toda san mong and Matzdaira Sin saburo. After sustaining a siege of two months, and repelling several attacks, the Christians were at last overcome and the castle was taken. The whole of the persons found in the city— men, women, and children—were massacred, to the number of 31,000. The three leaders were taken, together with a woman, beheaded, and the heads put up on the gate of the Dutch factor's house at Hirado. After the affair was over, the native accounts say that "the guns from Nagasaki were of great use, therefore he presented money." The factor at the time appears to have been named Koekkebekker, and the statement that money was presented implies in the native account that it was given to the Dutch for the assistance derived from their cannon, which are said to have fired from a ship and a battery on shore 426 balls. A great deal has been made of this against the Dutch, as using their influence to extirpate Christianity from the empire; but when the guns were demanded by the Japanese, the Dutch factor was powerless to refuse.

A few native vessels were at this time permitted to trade with China, Hainan, Formosa, and Tonquin; and there must have been a considerable number of Japanese collected in Macao and its neighborhood, some probably traders or runaway sailors, others as refugees on account of religion, or as being educated for the priesthood. Up to a recent period the remains of a large building with a garden-wall were visible on the Lappa, opposite Macao, which was known to the Chinese as the "Yut pone lao," or Japanese hall, now better known as the "Fan kwei lao," or hall of the outer devils.

According to native history, in the year 1640 some of the "Jashiu mong" (one of the names by which the Roman Catholic sect was known in Japan) came to Kagosima in Satsuma. Orders were given to the inhabitants not to speak to and not to listen to these foreigners. Two officers, Kangatsume from Miako and Baba saburo from Nagasaki, were ordered to investigate and communicate the result. They found that "there were in one ship seventy-three men of this sect; of this number sixty were beheaded, and the remainder were sent to the islands." This is the way in which native authors put the arrival and treatment of four Portuguese gentlemen who were sent as embassadors to Japan from Macao in order to endeavor if possible by a last stroke to reopen the trade which had been lost. The four gentlemen, with their suite and the crews of the vessels to the number of sixty men, were beheaded at Nagasaki, while the remaining thirteen were sent back to Macao to inform the authorities there of the treatment they had received. In the Cathedral of Macao may be seen a painting of the execution of these embassadors.

Deeply regretting the loss of the trade of Japan, and nothing daunted by the fate of these envoys, King John,

upon ascending the throne of Portugal after the separation
of the kingdom from the dominion of Spain, thought it a
good opportunity to attempt to reopen negotiations; and
with this view Don Gonzalo de Sequeyra was dispatched
with two vessels and numerous presents to pave the way.
He was, though more fortunate, not more successful than
those envoys sent from Macao. By the accounts of native
historians, "two black ships came to the island of Iwoga
sima, south of Satsuma. They said they were all Nanbang
men, and that there was not one Roman Catholic [priest?]
among them. The captain said, 'My country's king is now
changed. I have a dispatch from the new king, and I wish
it to be forwarded as soon as convenient to Yedo.'" Inooyay and Yamagaki were sent from Yedo to make inquiries.
They demanded that the powder and guns should first of all
be given up, and then they would hear what the envoys had
to say. The captain replied, " 'Trading is a matter which
concerns all countries. If Japan does not choose to trade
with us, that is her affair, but the guns and powder cannot
be given up.' Thereupon all the Daimios in the island of
Kiusiu were ordered to hold themselves in readiness with
men and boats. The name of the envoy was Koni sa aru,"
etc., in which an attempt was made to write his name in
Japanese sounds. He said he was a relative of the King of
Portugal. Answer was sent down from Yedo to the effect
that these ships had committed a serious offense, but that
they should be dealt leniently with, and were to be ordered
to leave the shores and not to return. After staying in all
forty-three days, the two vessels departed. They had two
captains and 400 men. The one was 156 feet long by 42
broad; the other was 144 feet long by 36 broad. Each vessel had 20 large guns. After this visit orders were given to
the Kiusiu Daimios to have always in readiness a force of
55,000 men and 997 guard-boats for the protection of the
coasts. In the year 1666 another edict was issued against
the Roman Catholics, so that it would appear that some
sparks of the faith were still lingering here and there,

which the government feared might at a moment be fanned into flame.

In the year 1709, Abbe Sidotti, an Italian priest of good family, determined to devote himself to the cause, and to make another attempt to regain Japan to the Church of Rome. With difficulty he found a captain of a vessel trading at Manila, who agreed to put him ashore on some point of the coast, and there to leave him to his own resources. When off the coast of Satsuma a boat was lowered, and the abbe, with a few small coins in his pocket, was put on shore. The boat returned, and the ship sailed away. After a long interval, a report reached the Dutch factory, through Chinese, that the abbe had been taken and immured between two walls, and allowed to perish of hunger. But this has lately been disproved by the discovery of a full account of his arrest and examination, and detention about Yedo until his death, which does not appear to have taken place for many years. This was the last effort made by the Church of Rome to regain the footing she had lost.

Hidetada, the son and successor of Iyeyas, would seem not to have possessed the talents or firmness of his father, but he had the advantage of his father's advice and assistance during the greater part of his rule. His son, Iyaymitz, when he was capable of ruling, and had come to the office of Shiogoon, found that the spirit of the Daimios had been softened by the long peace. The yoke of the Tokungawa family did not gall their necks, and they preferred peace and ease in the assured possession of their estates, to the risk and violence of wars and constant disturbance in the empire. Iyaymitz on more than one occasion visited the Emperor in Miako with great pomp, but a real or suspected attempt to assassinate him seems to have put a stop to these visits.

The year 1634 is given as the date at which the custom of the Daimios visiting Yedo on alternate years commenced. The Daimios coming to Yedo and returning from it are spoken of as Sankin and Kotai. The custom seems to have been long in use in Miako, but in a more temporary way, and simply as being a duty of each lord to visit and pay his respects at the imperial court once a year when they offered presents. This visit was by Iyeyas transferred to his court at Yedo and Soonpu; but it appears to have fallen into desuetude and irregularity during the life of Hidetada. But Iyaymitz, who was an able, proud, and precise ruler, found that his father had not been much respected by the Daimios, who still retained the recollection of the wars and prowess of Iyeyas; but in course of time these men were succeeded by their sons, who were of a more effeminate spirit, and had no such associations. Iyaymitz, taking advantage of this change, invited all the Daimios to visit him in Yedo, when he proposed rules for their visiting and residing at his court, to which they all agreed, swearing fealty, and signing the deed each with his own blood drawn from above the nail of the finger. A hall had been built on the Goteng yama, a rising-ground near Yedo, in which the Shiogoon was to meet the Daimios on their arrival; but under Iyaymitz the custom was discontinued and the ground made public.

During the same year, the "Court of Deliberation," the Hio jo sho, was established in Yedo, with the view at the outset of investigating charges brought against Daimios. The Mayassu hako, or box for complaints, now standing in front of the Hio jo sho, was not placed there till the year 1721.

One Shiogoon after another succeeded to the throne, not always without suspicion of unfair means being used to hasten the conclusion of the reign. It is generally believed that Tsuna yoshi was killed by his wife when he was on the eve of proclaiming the son of Yanangi sawa, one of his ministers, his successor. The heir was Iyay nobuko, the son of the eldest son of Iyaymitz, the father, when a young man, having been sent to the castle of Kofoo under arrest on account of irregularity of conduct. In the year 1716, on the death of the infant Shiogoon, Iyay tsoongu, a difficulty occurred as to the succession, when Yoshi mone, who was of the royal house of Kii shiu, was selected by the Kokushu, on the recommendation of Eeyee kamong no kami, then Regent. Having abdicated in 1745, he died in 1751, and is reputed as one of the ablest and wisest of the Shiogoons of the dynasty. The next Shiogoon was Iyay hige; and during the rule of his successor, Iyay haru, about 1765, a common foot-soldier, Tanuma, rose to be chief minister, a position and power which he used not only to gratify his own evil propensities, but to disseminate the same corruption over the empire. Preventing all communications with the Shiogoon, he did what was right in his own eyes; forbade all persons to study; changed the laws; and devoted himself and the empire to debauchery. He was made a Daimio, and placed at the head of the Cabinet. A conspiracy formed against him failed, and the principal conspirators were beheaded; but he was at length put down by Matzdaira Etsjiu no kami, who published at this time the "Tenka hatto, mikka hatto," or three days' proclamation over the empire.

The Japanese are proud of and delight in the beautiful scenery of their country; and every one who has opportunity, including nearly all the inhabitants, male and female, makes a walking tour at some period of his life over the country, visiting the more remarkable temples, which are generally placed in favorable sites amid woods, and surrounded by fine forest-trees, the immediate precincts being kept with the most scrupulous care and nicety of gardening. Nowhere are the temples more magnificent or the scenery finer than about Miako; and it had been for long the custom for the Emperor to go out and visit some one of the temples in the neighborhood of Miako, and offer worship. In the year 1722 a day was set apart in spring, and again in autumn, on which the whole court should annually go out on a sort of gigantic picnic—the Emperor drawn in a car by oxen, and accompanied by all the Koongays—when they visit some of the temples most renowned for their sanctity or for the beauty of the grounds. This procession is called Miyuki or Gokowo. There are two gardens adjoining the

palace in Miako, Shoongakuji and Katsura, which are said
to be most exquisitely laid out and kept in beautiful order.
The gardeners who have the charge of these gardens belong
to a class or sect known as Gayra, a people who live apart
by themselves in a few villages in the neighborhood of the
capital. They are said to have kept themselves apart in
customs and religion for many generations. In religion,
they say there is but one God, and that all men below the
Emperor are equal. They, as Quakers with us, will not use
terms of respect to other men, such as "kudasare," or call
men by titles, as "sama," similar to "esquire"; saying that
they only adhere to old customs in so doing. They are
themselves respected as being of old and pure descent, and
their children are often selected by Koongays for adoption.
They principally follow the occupation of gardeners, or that
of breeders of horses.

In the year 1639, the Portuguese and Spaniards having
been expelled, and the Dutch factory alone left at Hirado,
the commissioner was ordered to remove his people and
offices to the small factory on Desima, "the Outer Island,"
at the head of the inlet of Nagasaki, and trade was prohibited at all other places in Japan, and to any other nation,
with the exception of the Chinese.

In connection with the Dutch and their position on these
seas, the pirate commonly known as Coxinga is worthy of
notice. Koku seng ya, as he is known in Japanese history,
was the son of a Chinese, Ching tsing lung (Tayshi rio in
Japanese), by a Japanese woman. The father was for many
years, as pirate and admiral, the terror of the Chinese seas.
His son succeeded him in his former capacity, and reduced
the coasts of China to such a state of terror and devastation, that an order was given, as a desperate remedy, that
every person should remove into the interior to a distance of
twelve miles from the shore, leaving the cities to decay and
the fields to waste. In 1647 Coxinga went over to Japan,
and offered his services to, or asked the assistance of, the
government in an attack he meditated upon China; but his

application was refused.   He seems to have again applied to the government in 1658, when he turned his attention to the island of Formosa.   A large number of Japanese converts had fled to this island, and the Dutch had built one or two forts with the view of protecting a trade which they hoped might grow up with China.   In 1662 Coxinga attacked and captured the fort Zelandia, putting to death nearly all the Dutch soldiers, missionaries, and their wives and families. Only a few men and some of the young women were not killed.   A curious but melancholy sigh is wafted over from this long-forgotten remnant of Dutch Christianity and civilization in a letter which was brought to Japan about the year 1711 by the captain of an English vessel who had touched at Formosa on his way out; and as the letter comes through a Japanese channel, there is no reason to doubt its authenticity.   The captain, in answer to interrogations, says, "There is no war in Tonay [Formosa] now, and we have no trade there.   The Dutch head man asked me to give the following letter to the Dutch commissioners in Nagasaki: 'Please ask Japan to help us; we are now shut up as in a prison, and every day we weep.   The names of the Dutch in Tonay are [here the names are given in Japanese].   I hear that this English vessel is going hence to Japan; therefore we take the opportunity of sending this letter to you.   The Tonay country was seized many years ago; but we are still alive, but we are in a most miserable state.   Please help us to return to our country.   We pray you to speak to the Kogee [Kubosama].

" 'Signed by the head man Yohang Hoorohooro, and two others.

" 'There are ten women and several children here.' "

Nicolas Verburgh seems to have been the name of the officer in command of the fort at the time of its capture in 1662, and the signature, as written by a Japanese, closely corresponds to the pronunciation of the name, and Yohang may have been his son John.   From the tenor of the letter it seems hardly possible to doubt but that these were some of the survivors of the Dutch captured in 1662, and if so, it is curious to have such a fact coming to light through Japanese informants, and melancholy to think of such a tedious captivity lightened up after fifty years by the hope of once more revisiting their home, and being redeemed from their never-ending misery.

The name of this English ship is not given, but native history tells us that the captain brought with him an exact copy of the treaty or letter signed by Iyeyas, traced upon paper, and expressed a wish to communicate with the Shiogoon at Yedo. A Dutch interpreter was sent to see if there were any Portuguese on board. The guns and muskets were taken ashore. There were eighty-four of a crew on board. The captain's name was Sayemon Terohoo (Simon Drew?). The ship was 114 feet long by 27 broad. Then follows a list of articles on board—ammunition, which was taken charge of by the Japanese: Gunpowder, 35 tubs; balls, 660; leaden bullets, 2 tubs; iron bullets, 1 tub; small stone bullets, 8 tubs; matchlocks, 47; flint muskets, 23; spears, 24; swords, 339.

There were on board, as presents for the Shiogoon, "one fine English musket, double-barreled, 3 feet 3 inches in length; four muskets with very intricate and finely-made locks, besides eight others which cannot be used, but are very well made; and four molds for making balls."

The cargo consisted of cotton, woolen and cotton cloth, furs, fragrant wood, chintz, scented water, quicksilver, looking glasses, tin, silk, crape, etc. The captain was interrogated as to his religion, as to the Portuguese, and as to a change he had made in the national flag which he sailed under, which he explained by saying that he was told the Japanese did not like the cross.

The Dutch had carried on their trade at the island of Hirado, where an extensive land-locked bay is pointed out as the harbor. They were ordered in 1639 to leave that port, and in future to resort to Nagasaki, where a small island, which was afterward connected by a bridge with the

town, was appointed them as a place of residence and for
trade, being about the same size as the factories at Canton
occupied by foreigners till 1856.

Several attempts were made by other nations, at long
intervals, to reopen a trade with the country; but it was
thought by the Dutch to be their interest to oppose any
such competition, and the Japanese themselves dreaded,
with good cause, any renewal of the former state of things.

The national annals during the period which elapsed between the era of Iyeyas and the reopening of the country
advert to a number of occurrences of temporary and local
importance only.   The comparatively trivial nature of these
tends to bring out into relief the continued quiet and rest
which the country has enjoyed under the form of government established by Iyeyas, and after all complications arising from dealings with other nations were forcibly put an
end to by the expulsion of foreigners.

The Daimio Fkushima Massanori was banished in 1619
to the island of Hatchi jo for a series of cruelties practiced
upon his family, his servants, and his people, which show
that he was deranged; and his extensive territories, occupying three provinces, were confiscated.

In 1621 the Emperor married the daughter of the Shiogoon.

The temple of To yay zan was built in Yedo for the occupation of the high-priest, who is alluded to in the laws of
Iyeyas as being appointed to fill that position as a near relative of the Emperor, and one whom the Shiogoon may place
on the throne in case of rebels siding with the Emperor in
opposition to the Shiogoon.   He is the most illustrious personage in Yedo.   The grounds are very beautiful, and
formerly belonged to the family of Todo.

In the year 1631, about the month of November, it is
curious to observe that the annals take notice of a prodigious number of ironstones having fallen from heaven, showing that the meteoric orbit has been crossing that of the
earth as visibly two hundred years ago as it does now.

This occurrence probably took place during the day, as at other times these meteors are spoken of as falling stars.

The aqueduct by which water is led from the Tamangawa to Yedo, and thence discharged into the castle and town by wooden pipes, was constructed in 1653. Proposals have been made at different times to substitute iron pipes, but the wooden ones still remain—a cause of constant expense to the government.

The burning of the palace at Miako, or of that at Yedo, is one of the most common occurrences in these annals. Titsingh gives a vivid description of a conflagration which occurred in 1788 in Miako, during which the attendants of the Emperor killed more than a thousand persons before he could be carried out of danger.

The government in Japan reserves the privilege of selling weights and scales guaranteed by mark and certified as correct. The weights as now used were settled in 1662.

In 1666 a new edict was issued against the Roman Catholic religion; and in 1668 an order was promulgated prohibiting any new Buddhist temples being erected. In all probability the Buddhist priesthood had been exalted by their victory over the Roman priesthood, and had again acquired so much power as to be once more threatening to disturb the equilibrium of the state. The zeal of individuals had perhaps been again endowing new and enriching old establishments, actuated by feelings with which the state powers did not wish to sympathize. Only four years before this edict, the enormous copper idol of Buddha at Miako had been melted down and coined into copper "cash," and a wooden figure was substituted. If it be true, as is asserted, that it was three or four times the size of the figure of Dai boods, near Kamakura (at present existing in copper, and upward of forty-five feet in height), it must have been of considerable value in coin.

This edict against the erection of new temples is still in force in Japan, and while it is aided by a growing want of zeal in the hearts of the people with a contempt for the priesthood, it may be broken through by the permission given to repair, or restore, or enlarge any temple already existing, however small it may be; and as a temple or shrine is standing upon nearly every knoll or eminence in Japan, there can be no difficulty, were the funds forthcoming, of raising such edifices as were raised of old by the zeal of fervent worshipers.

The Buddhist priesthood in 1720, by a great religious festival all over the empire, commemorated the eleventh centenary of the establishment of Buddhism.

The Japanese claim the discovery and settlement of the Bonin or Monin Islands in the year 1683. The name means "no men," or uninhabited. Attempts were made to colonize the islands, but they seem to have failed; and some English and Americans, with Sandwich Islanders, male and female, succeeded them. But in 1862 the Japanese government fitted out a vessel and carried away all these adventurers, bringing them to Yokohama, and it seems to find the islands a convenient distance to which they can send vessels to train officers and men.

A work was commenced in 1786 which was expected to have proved of great advantage to Yedo. This was the cutting of a canal, and thereby joining several already existing channels, by which a through communication would have been opened up between Yedo, or the Bay of Yedo, and the Pacific Ocean on the east coast. The part of the province of Simosa between Yedo and the east coast is very low land, and it is generally believed that at one time the sea cut off the three provinces of Simosa, Kadsusa, and Awa, which then constituted a separate island; and that the detritus brought down, after a course of nearly two hundred miles, by the largest river in Japan, the Tonay, has filled up with alluvium the sea channel, leaving now only the passage for the fresh water of the river. In the course of the filling up, however, a large lake was left, the Een bang numa. About twenty miles above Yedo, the Tonay, coming down as one river from the Tonay district, divides into two. The one branch, receiving affluents from Hitatsi and the northern provinces, runs due east as the Bando taro, or "eldest son of Bando," and enters the sea between Choshi and Itaku on the east coast. The other branch, running south, enters the sea to the east of the city of Yedo. The Okawa, or Great River, runs parallel with the Tonay, and passes through Yedo spanned by five bridges. Between the Okawa and Tonay, and running parallel to, and communicating by canals with both, is the Nakagawa or Middle River. By these cross canal communications the passage may be made from Yedo to the Pacific on the east, or to the northern provinces by running up to Seki Yado, where the bifurcation takes place. It was proposed to deepen the lake, and cut through a passage from it into the Bay of Yedo.—The lower part of Yedo is so low that it is liable to be overflowed should the Tonay rise above its banks. To avert this danger, a large and important embankment, the Gongen do, has been made at Koori hashi. Should this give way, the whole of the lower parts of Yedo would be submerged, as happened, it is said, in 1844.

The town of Sakura first started the project, and commenced a canal, but did not finish the work. The Shiogoon, seeing the advantages of the proposed cut, ordered the Daimios to cut the remainder of this canal (of about fourteen miles in length), each cutting as his share about 360 feet. The work, which was immediately commenced, was in six months half completed, when orders were given to cease working at it. In 1843 the work was recommenced by orders of government, but when it was within three thousand yards of being finished it was again stopped, and it continues in that position to this day.

The river and canal communications in Japan are more ramified than the mountainous nature of the country would lead one to expect. It is said that Yedo might, by short canals, be put into water relations with Mito on the east coast and Negata on the north, as boats can go up the Tonay to Shimidzu, within eight miles of the navigable part of the

Negata waters; while Miako might be joined by water to Tsurunga on the north and Owarri on the south. By private enterprise, in the year 1832, the Yodo ngawa between Miako and Osaka was deepened and improved by the removal of some rocks. It is said that the Katsura gawa, or Hozu kawa, now a large affluent of the Yodo gawa, formerly ran to the north through the province of Wakasa; but a private individual, Yodo yo, cut a channel by which this river now flows southward into the Osaka River. His family is permitted to levy tolls upon the new channel.

The occurrence of fearful convulsions of nature is one of the most remarkable circumstances in these annals; and it may be presumed that only the most severe are noticed. But recent observations go to show that almost every day there is an observable motion of the earth at Yokohama from subterranean causes. The native accounts of these, with drawings, give an appalling idea of the suddenness and the severity of earthquakes. In the year 1707 a very severe earthquake shook the whole of the southern part of the island of Nippon, and simultaneously from the side of the mountain Fusiyama [Fusi—literally "not two," or none such] issued an eruption of volcanic matter. This eruption continued for fifteen days; and at Yedo, a distance of seventy miles, dust fell to the depth of two feet. Fusiyama had not given any appearance of volcanic action for centuries. The projection on the smooth outline of the hill on the northwestern side marks the place where this action took place, and is known as Ho yay zan. At the same time the volcano Assama yama, in Sinano, broke out into violent action, by which the two adjacent provinces were laid under lava or dust. The same mountain broke out again in 1783, and of the destruction done at that time Titsingh gives a fearful account. He gives details of an earthquake which occurred in 1793 at Simabara, during which a large portion of the mountain was swallowed up; and the boiling sulphurous springs of Onzen, memorable during the persecutions of the Christians, were dried up. The fear of the inhabitants was quickened by the recollection of the eruption of Assama yama, in Sinano, only ten years before. The inhabitants, with their houses, were engulfed in the openings of the earth; they were carried away by boiling water issuing from the hill; they were killed by falling stones and enormous rocks; they were surrounded and burned by streams of fiery lava; they were drowned by the stoppage of rivers. Some were found suspended from trees, some on their knees, some on their heads in mud, the streets strewed with dead bodies. The falling houses immediately took fire, and the unfortunate inmates were burned, or were confined prisoners. The outline of the coast was completely altered, and the country converted into a desert. A number of vessels were sunk at their anchors, and those which tried to get away could hardly do so from dead bodies and floating wood. Fifty-three thousand are known to have perished in this earthquake in a comparatively thinly populated district.

In 1828 a tremendous earthquake and volcanic eruption took place in the province of Etsingo, during which, at Nadatchi, a large mountain was engulfed and disappeared. This province seems to be entirely undermined by fire. The volcano Taka yama is called the entrance to hell. Oil springs from the ground. Combustible gas issues in such quantity as to be used for cooking and lighting, by simply inserting pipes in the ground. Phosphorescent appearances are seen in many parts. Soda is found in the province in large quantities. Here many flint arrow and spear heads have been found, exactly similar in shape to those found in Europe.

The frequency of these earthquakes is a reason for nearly all the habitations of man being built of wood; and by long experience builders have arrived at certain modes of building, by which the great danger of a house coming down upon the inmates is in many cases obviated. They seem to depend upon the roof for weight; and the piles upon which this heavy roof rests are not fixed firmly into the ground, but some of them are fixed slightly into a square framework of wood, laid on stone, while the others stand simply each upon the surface of a large, round, hard, water-rolled stone, which has been firmly imbedded in broken-down sandstone. By this means the snap of a sudden shock is avoided, and some slight motion is allowed. Whatever be the principle upon which these houses are erected, it is wonderful to see buildings, which seem to be put up in a shape the most ready to topple over upon the least motion, withstand the shocks of earthquakes for ages. There are pagodas in many parts of the country of seven and even nine stories high. At Kamakura is a temple with a narrow circular neck, above which the eaves of a square roof project to about ten feet on every side, resembling the projection of a Chinaman's hat. If it could withstand the wind, it could never be expected to resist an earthquake; and yet it is said to be two hundred years old, and seems as sound as when it was built.

The annals do not disdain to mention the visits of the Emperor to witness theatrical exhibitions, or proceedings of the Shiogoon in quest of sport.

The Japanese appear to be very partial to the theater, and there seems in the nation an innate aptitude for such representation. But while the government regulates this, as it does every other branch of the amusements as well as the education of the people, actors as a class are looked upon as the lowest in the scale of society. The female parts are generally taken by boys.

Some companies go about the country composed entirely of boys or young children, none of whom are apparently upward of ten or twelve years of age. The people enjoy these very much, and will take their meals and sit all day watching the different acts, applauding vigorously at whatever they appreciate in acting, or what may amuse them in the play. Nothing seems to excite their feelings and evoke their applause more than a well-acted suicide by stabbing the abdomen. During the evenings many minor places of amusement are open, such as jugglers, marionettes, and tellers of stories. Wrestling by professionals is another spectacle which always draws a very large concourse of spectators, generally male; but women are on occasions to be seen viewing the maneuvers of the contest with the greatest interest. These spectacles have been well, though perhaps over, described by Commodore Perry. Besides these full-grown wrestlers, companies go about, having under tuition boys of from eight to twelve years of age, who wrestle with all the pomp and circumstance of their full-grown compeers. The same laws regulate the game under the formal umpire. A successful wrestler is hailed with loud applause; and under the influence of the excitement of the moment, money is frequently thrown to the conqueror, or for want of it men will throw their coats or napkins, which they afterward redeem.

The long peace subsequent to the time of Iyeyas, though unbroken by any national disturbance, was not wholly free from local events, which might, had they been fanned, have broken out in serious trouble. In 1837, Osaka and the neighborhood were disturbed by a rising which was instigated by an officer, Oshiwo, who, by the distribution of money and by placards, excited the people of the city against the authorities. During the riot, which may be said to have lasted only one day, nearly all the principal shops in Osaka were pillaged and burned. The ringleader escaped, but was afterward discovered, though he blew the house up in which he was hiding before he could be arrested. Notwithstanding that the government exercises such surveillance over the people, and that one-fourth of the community seem to be spies upon the remainder, risings of the people do occasionally take place. These riots are especially frequent in the provinces of Oomi, Sinano, and Kahi. In the latter, during 1838, a rebellion broke out which threatened to be somewhat more formidable than usual. Several high officers and many men on both sides were killed. In truth, in the province of Kahi (or Koshiu) the people are great politicians and unruly, and at the same time under some sort of volunteer organization. Officers are in general somewhat afraid of an appointment to the province, as the farmers are wealthy, and keep their servants well supplied with arms, which they teach them how to use. A strong force is always kept at Hatch oji, twenty-five miles from Yokohama on the road to Koshiu, as a protection to Yedo.

In the year 1701 an occurrence took place which terminated in a tragedy, and has ever since been one of the national tales of revenge, which, though it was confined to a few individuals, has conferred on them immortality, and the admiration of their countrymen as heroes. Assano, a Daimio from Ako, in the province of Harima, while within the precincts of the Shiogoon's palace, was insulted by a Kokay of the name of Kira, when a quarrel and scuffle took place, during which Assano drew his sword. This was looked upon as such a heinous offense that he was ordered to kill himself, when the government confiscated his property, reducing his family and retainers to poverty. The retainers (known as Geeshi), exasperated by this severity, banded together for revenge, and forty-seven proceeded to the house of Kira, when a fight commenced, which was carried on during the whole night till the morning, by which time they were able to penetrate to his apartment and kill him. The whole forty-seven then proceeded in a regular and methodical manner to commit suicide. They are all buried at the temple of Sengakuji, near the temple first occupied by the British Legation.

In 1672 the powerful Lord of Sendai was put to death by his own servants. He also is memorable in Japanese story, but more on account of his baseness and cruelty, which he showed by a trait of character often chosen as a subject by native artists. Being a man given up to debauchery and the gratification of his passions, he became enamored of Takawo, the most beautiful courtesan of Yedo at the time. He wished her to accompany him to his castle in the north, but she refused. She had an aversion to him, but the offer of her weight in gold probably prevailed with her, or with those in whose possession she was, to give consent. He took her with him, and on the way to his castle, upon asking her if she was not happy, she replied that she was not, when in a rage he drew his sword and cut off her head.

The occasions upon which European vessels communicated with Japan during the seventeenth and eighteenth centuries seem to have been few, and at long intervals. About 1637, Lord Waddell, with some ships, called in at Nagasaki, but was not allowed to communicate with the Dutch.

In 1673, 1768, 1791, 1793, 1796 and 1803, notices occur in the native annals of the visits of foreign vessels.

In 1808, the "Phaeton" frigate, under Captain Pellew, paid a visit to Nagasaki during the time when Holland was at war with England. According to native accounts, the captain wished to carry off the Dutch commissioner. For that purpose he landed his men (in a boat made of leather?), who displayed the usual playful habits of English sailors in a foreign town, "striking everybody, and breaking everything they could." The Prince of Hizen was not on the spot; the governor of Nagasaki was quite unprepared; the Prince's lieutenant proposed to burn the frigate by means of fire-boats, but the frigate sailed before any steps could be taken. The governor of the town, the Prince of Hizen, his lieutenant and the guards, are all said, by native accounts, to have committed suicide.

In 1813, during the time when Holland was absorbed by France, Sir Stamford Raffles sent a vessel from Java with a Dutch officer to take the place of the representative of Holland then at Nagasaki; but the man in possession was able to prevent his opponent landing, and held the place till he was relieved in 1817.

In 1829, the "Cyprus," a vessel containing some convicts who had risen and murdered the crew, touched at Tanega. The "Morrison," which communicated with Japan shortly after, heard of some foreigners who had landed on the island of Tanega and forcibly carried off cattle.

In 1846, American vessels came to Nagasaki to beg permission to trade, and in 1849 some English vessels touched at Uranga.

The native record of events concludes by stating that in 1858 treaties were concluded with five nations—American, English, Dutch, Russian, and Portuguese—and that silver boos were exchanged for dollars. That in 1859 the Regent, Ee Kamong no kami, was assassinated; and the following year was that year in the cycle in which, recurring once in sixty years, it is permitted to women to ascend Fusiyama.

The history of the empire is now brought down to a very important era, when relations with European nations are about to be reopened, but, in comparison with her past experience, at a great disadvantage to Japan, in so far as she had to meet foes greatly in advance of herself in the practical application of scientific investigation to the art of war, and when she allowed herself further to be outwitted in the diplomacy of treaty-making. The wars and animosities of European powers had for a long time drawn them away from the East and concentrated their attention nearer home; and the history of their withdrawal from the Eastern Seas is that of the struggle among European nations for the supremacy of the sea.

The English retired from Japan as a field of trade about the year 1623. The hatred of Holland to Spain and Portugal gave vigor to her efforts, and she drove their ships from the East, and remained in possession of the field, such as it was. By driving away competitors, however, the Dutch undermined their own position, and deprived themselves of support, moral as well as physical, and fell gradually into a position of contemptible dependence for the retention of a worthless trade.

France appears to have made a feeble attempt, at the time when Colbert was Minister, to open up a trade with Japan, under the advice probably of Francis Caron, who had been Dutch commissioner at Nagasaki. In Chardin's Travels may be seen a letter addressed to the envoy, giving most minute instructions as to his conduct and treatment of the Japanese. Some of these might even be read with benefit by envoys of the present day. "You shall keep your finest clothes, and which you have never wore in Japan, as shall likewise those of your retainers, till you are brought to court, and till the day of your audience. As soon as you shall arrive there, you shall cause your retinue to provide themselves with little leather pumps and slippers. The floors of the houses are covered with tapestry in Japan, for which reason you must put off your shoes when you enter them, and have some without quarters that you may quit them with greater ease."

The United States of America came late into the field in Japan, but it may be said that the national action toward Japan has had a wider cosmopolitan influence than any other act since the Declaration of Independence.

The opening up of China, and the enormous trade which followed in opium, silk, and treasure, caused by steam on the one hand and the discovery of gold in California on the other, together with the rapid advance in steam itself, all combined to force a traffic around Japan, and to place these islands on the very highway of commerce. It became every day more obvious that from one side or other, either from the English on the side of China, from the Russians on the north, or from America on the east, some attempt must be made before long to insist at least upon some measures of civil behavior, if not of genuine hospitality, being shown to vessels which required assistance, or which might be wrecked upon the coasts of Japan.

In 1846 an attempt was made by the United States government to endeavor to break down, if possible, the system of exclusion kept up by Japan by the dispatch of two vessels of war, under Commodore Biddle, with the view of feeling the way toward a better acquaintance with the country. The result was not satisfactory, the commodore having been grossly and perhaps intentionally insulted.

Mr. Fillmore, the President of the United States, deter mined to make another effort to break down the barrier, and to make such a display as should show the Japanese that he was to a certain extent in earnest, and at the same time prevent any recurrence of such conduct toward his envoy. It is needless to discuss whether the Dutch or the Russians had any claim to priority of action in the matter. Commodore Perry has endeavored to overthrow any such claims; but such great political steps are seldom the result of a sudden outburst of vigor—it was gradually approached from all sides. It was, as has been said, one of the effects of the great innovator, steam, with other concurring circumstances, such as the opening of China and California, and the conversion of the Pacific Ocean into a highway of commerce. The breaking-up by British troops of the sham of the Chinese as a military nation, no doubt opened the eyes of Western nations. Japan lay in the way. No nation had a better claim to ask it to relax its restrictions upon friendly grounds than America. No nation was, perhaps, better suited to carry out the diplomatic part of such a proposal, whether the character of its officers as individuals, or the generally peaceful professions on the part of the government, be looked at. There can, further, be little doubt but that the United States government was exceedingly fortunate or prudent in its choice of the man for the work. He had some acquaintance with Orientals learned in the school of China, and he brought this to bear practically upon his present work. He says he was convinced that, if he receded from any point which he had once gained, such would be considered as an advantage gained against him—that first-formed impressions among such people carry most weight—that with people of forms it is necessary to out-Herod Herod in assumed personal ostentation and personal consequence—that a diplomatist ought with such persons never to recognize any personal superiority, and ought always to keep aloof from conversation or intercourse with inferiors, and yet cultivate as far as possible a friendly disposition toward the people.

Commodore Perry left the President's letter on July 8, 1853, for the consideration of the Japanese government. He returned in February, 1854, when the Japanese government returned for answer that they had decided to accede to the propositions of the President, and appointed five commissioners to treat with Perry. The treaty was signed at Yokohama, and ratifications were exchanged in February, 1855. Although the treaty was signed and the negotiations brought to a successful termination, this was not accomplished without difficulty and even danger, as, according to native accounts, a large force was collected on the hills overlooking Yokohama, under the command of different Daimios. These forces occupied about fifteen miles of ground between Fusisawa and Kawasaki to the number of a million of men (but numbers are indefinite in the East). They seem to have suffered a good deal from sickness while lying there, and were afterward the subjects of many jokes and caricatures. It was arranged that if any serious hitch took place, or any appearance of force was exhibited on the part of the Americans, a large bell was to sound, and other bells were to take up the signal, and a general combined attack was to be made. Idzu no Daikang volunteered to kill Perry with his own hand, so deeply does personal feeling enter into national questions in Japan; but this he was ordered not to attempt.

In 1854, during the Crimean war, Sir James Stirling, then admiral on the China station, with H.M.S. "Winchester" and a squadron, anchored in Nagasaki with the object of concluding a treaty with Japan. The last article of the treaty was to the effect that "no high officer coming after to Japan should ever have power to alter this treaty." For this treaty the admiral received the thanks of the nation through the House of Commons. It may by some be thought a mistake not to have stood upon the old treaty given to England by Iyeyas in the seventeenth century, which would have been considered more binding upon the government and upon the empire than a treaty made when the position of the Shiogoon was once more being questioned.

These treaties were a step forward, but had this step not been followed up they would soon have become inoperative.

14

Mr. Townsend Harris was appointed consul for America at Simoda, and arrived there in 1856; and being in constant intercourse with the Japanese authorities, he concluded a convention by which further advantages were gained by the Americans. The Japanese government thought that if the further concessions brought no more trouble than what had resulted from the little opening already made, they might, without much danger, open the sluices a little more; and in 1858, Mr. Harris, after much negotiation, arranged the articles of a commercial treaty (based upon the treaties with China), which was signed by him and the Japanese commissioners upon July 29, 1858. After this was settled, Holland, Britain, Russia, and France concluded similar treaties.

The sound of the trumpets which had been blown to herald the approach of the American squadron to the shores of Japan had reached these shores long before the vessels themselves. The government was informed through the Dutch of the coming mission. The American government does not seem to have intended anything further than ostentatious display in the number and size of the vessels sent. They did not propose to follow up a refusal to open their doors, on the part of the Japanese, by any warlike operations. But the Japanese government does not appear to have been aware of this, and at the time they may have felt some doubts as to whether their late treatment of foreigners did not call for some display of power on the part of European nations. Commodore Biddle had been grossly insulted on board a vessel of war. The crew of one vessel had been very unkindly treated, and, according to native report, more than one vessel had recently been wrecked on the coasts of Japan, and the crews treated with severity until they died out. Until the squadron should arrive, the Japanese could take little or no action. But they waited with much anxiety the arrival of the expedition. It was considered as a most important event, fraught with much either of good or evil to the country—which was it to be?

There is a pamphlet, published in Yedo, which professes

JAPANESE SHIPPING PRIOR TO 1865

Japan.

to give some account of the doings in Japan at this time, and which is interesting as showing the internal state of Japan at this most critical time in her history, and the feelings with which the proposed opening of the country was viewed by different political parties. The views of the Emperor are set forth; the daring acts of the Regent in support of his own position; the intrigues set on foot against him, ending in his assassination, and the subsequent train of events which followed thereon, and which have led to the overthrow of the Shiogoon's position and the restoration of the Emperor to the power originally held in the imperial hands. The letters may appear to be tedious, but they show the working of the government more clearly perhaps than a simple description would do. The country was threatened with internal disturbance, and there were two parties divided upon the point of a successor to the Shiogoon, who was weakly in mind and body—worn out and epileptic. As leader of the one party was Ee Kamong no kami, the head of the Fudai Daimios, and having a certain right to be appointed Regent in case of necessity. He seems to have been a clever, bold man, to Western ideas unscrupulous in the means by which he attained his ends. At the head of the other party was Mito, one of the "three families," hereditary vice-Shiogoon in Yedo, and connected by marriage with the families of the Emperor and the highest Koongays in Miako, and with the wealthiest Daimios—a shrewd, clever, scheming old man. What follows must be considered a mere imperfect sketch of what the pamphlet contains.

The name of the pamphlet is a play upon the name Mito, meaning Water-door—Midzu Kara Kori. "Water-machines make," or "A machine made at Mito." The Regent (whose name, Ee, means "a well") wished to take out, as with a bucket, the water in the well and divide it—*i.e.*, to break down the power of Mito.

The pamphlet commences by stating by way of "contents" that the Regent sent Manabay Simosa no kami to Miako to seize Takatskasa, the highest officer of the empire, the Kwanbakku and his son Daifu dono, and Awata, a young relative of the Emperor, and at the time the head of the Buddhists—and that these high officers were all put into confinement, and that all this trouble had its origin at Mito. The source of the Tokungawa—*i.e.*, the line of Iyeyas, or the government by the family of Iyeyas—is very clear, but this work will show how Mito tried to make it impure. The book was published in the spring of 1860. The name of the author is "Every one drunk."

The anticipated arrival of the United States squadron was agitating the rulers of Japan, and parties were divided as to the reception which should be given it. There was probably some political source of discord besides this, connected more or less with the office of Shiogoon, which had fallen into the hands of an epileptic imbecile. It would appear that in 1854 letters were sent to all the Daimios and Ometskis, requiring them to give their opinions as to the reception which should be given to the squadron, and whether the Americans should be repelled by force, or whether a trial should be made of a limited intercourse with foreigners, under the impression that if it was not found to work satisfactorily the ports might again be closed, and the country might return to its old state of seclusion. The answers sent showed that they were divided into a large majority for repelling them, by force of arms if necessary, and a small minority who were for admitting foreigners to trade. All agreed that it was a question of peace or war, but many thought that whether it was to be the one or the other, no answer should be sent until time was obtained to put the shores and batteries into a state of defense. At present, they alleged, the coasts were weak and defenseless, and "if Japan does not conquer it will be a great disgrace, and the country will be defiled. But, high and low, all must be unanimous." In the first place, it must be ascertained how many men each Daimio can muster, and the strength of each in guns, ammunition, etc. In 1854, in the tenth month, the Ometskis sent letters to all the Daimios to obtain information on this head.

In 1855, in the 9th month, the Shiogoon sent a commission to Mito, ordering him to put all the coasts of the country
into a defensible position. The care of the forts along the
shore was to be committed to Mito. The forts and guns
were to be examined. The Shiogoon wrote—"You have
hitherto come to me three times every month, now I wish
you to report to me every second day what is doing."

From published documents, it appears by the Emperor's
own letter, 22d day of the 2d month, 1858, in corroboration
of what is stated in the pamphlet quoted, "that this matter
was discussed before him by the Kwanbakku (Koozio dono),
the Taiko, or previous Kwanbakku (Takatskasa),* and the
Tenso. It appears that the old Taiko pleaded as an excuse
that he was unwell, but as the Mikado sent several times to
command his attendance, he was obliged to come. At the
conference the Taiko expressed an opinion contrary to that
of the others, which had been given in favor of the course
advocated by the Shiogoon. The Mikado was very angry"
(with these others), "and it was with difficulty the Kwanbakku succeeded in pacifying him. On the 23d a document
bearing the refusal of the Mikado to the treaty was written
out. Then three officers went to the residence of Hotta, the
Shiogoon's first Minister of Foreign Affairs and Envoy to
Miako, to obtain the Mikado's consent to the American
treaty, and informed him of the document hereunder. The
messengers sent by (to?) the Mikado were afflicted, and shed
tears because they did not succeed."

The Mikado wrote to the Shiogoon: "23d, 2d mo., 1858.—
It is difficult for us to grant you the approval you ask" (to
the treaties). "For the honor of the name of the first Mikado
it is impossible to agree to it.

"It is our duty to take care to tranquilize the minds of
our people.

"The Shiogoon should gather every one's opinion, from

---

* Whose retainers and secretary the Regent had arrested
and brought to Yedo.

the three great houses to the humblest subject, and give me the result in writing.

"If it is necessary to . . . conclude these treaties" (*i.e.*, if it is impossible to go back from what has been done), "exception must be made of the country in the neighborhood of my imperial city, as we have already directed in our letter, 24th of the 12th month. [The opening of] Hiogo in Sitsu must be excepted if possible.

"The Mikado often considers that he is not safe in his palace at Miako, and he directs the Shiogoon to appoint some powerful Daimios to protect the imperial palace.

"You have thought it well to open the ports to foreigners, but you did not think that foreigners would entangle you with difficulties.

"We would know your opinion in this respect."

This was evidently considered a refusal on the part of the Emperor to accede to the conclusion of a treaty. There is not much appearance of what is by a commentator called "puppetism" in the position of the Emperor when he, standing here almost alone in his council of bribed and intriguing officers, who were all in the pay of the Regent at Yedo, still manfully keeps them all at bay, and, assisted only by his faithful old minister the Taiko, whose attendance he is obliged to command, refuses to accede to the course of expediency pressed upon him by such meanness. He not only refuses, but he warns them from his lofty position of the pit which he foresees they are digging for themselves. The Taiko, probably for his conduct and words at this meeting, was put by the Regent in confinement in his own house, and was only released after the fall of this minister.

Then follows a document, a "Circular from the Shiogoon, the 6th month of 1858, by Kooze yamato no kami.

"The Mikado having been consulted by the Shiogoon's government about the making of treaties with foreigners, he answered that the conclusion of that matter would distress him very much.

"Thereupon the Shiogoon requested all to send their

written opinion upon the subject. Only a short time was required to gather every one's opinion; but, in the meantime, some Russian and American men-of-war came here, bringing the news that in a short time English and French men-of-war would arrive here; that these two nations had fought and won many battles in China; that they would come here in the same warlike spirit, and it would be difficult for us to negotiate with them. The American embassador offered to us, that if we would make a temporary treaty with him, as soon as we should have signed and given him that treaty he would act as mediator between us and the French and English, and could save us from all difficulties.

"It was impossible for us to comply with this without consultation with the Mikado. However, Inoe Sinano no kami, fearing the immediate assault (or breaking out of a war), the results of which might be the same as in China, signed themselves, as men authorized to sign [this expression is somewhat suspicious], the American treaty at Kanagawa, which treaty was given up to the American embassador.

"Necessity compelled the Japanese to do this.

"The Mikado, on hearing of this, was much troubled, but to reassure him we told him we would fortify our shores."

Then further follows a document written by several of the Koongays in Miako:

"At this time there are great changes taking place in our holy country in respect to foreigners. However, it is not for us ignorant people to judge, and for that reason we lately wrote twice to the Mikado. We hoped that he would consider the subject.

"We write to him once more. Since the time of Tensio dai jin the country has been to the present time sublime and flourishing; but friendship with foreigners will be a stain upon it, and an insult to the first Mikado (Zinmu). It will be an everlasting shame for the country to be afraid of those foreigners, and for us to bear patiently their arbitrary and

rough manners; and the time will come when we shall be
subservient to them.   This is the fault of the dynasty of the
Shiogoon.   It is reported that the Shiogoon has sent to Miako
to consult the Mikado about the treaties, but it is impossible
to believe it.   Hotta will return to Yedo and say that the
Mikado has consented to give him a secret authorization,
and he will thus induce the other Daimios to follow the
party of the Shiogoon.   The Shiogoon thus disturbs peace.
If foreigners come to our country they will loudly proclaim
the mutual benefits that trade will produce, but at home
they will think only of vile profit; and when we shall refuse to comply with all their wishes, they will threaten us
with their artillery and men-of-war.   They intend to take
Japan, and to effect this will resort to any kind of deep
scheme in their negotiations.   It is earnestly wished that
the Mikado order that the Daimios from the 'three families' to the lowest give their vote upon the subject."   The
Daimios gave their vote, and they were generally in favor
of exclusion of foreign nations, and of adhering to their
old way.

In 1857, on the 28th day of the 12th month, Hino came
to Yedo from Miako, as bearer of a letter from the Emperor
addressed to the Shiogoon.

"Your duty is to act as Shiogoon; and yet you, being Se
i dai Shiogoon [barbarian-quelling commander-in-chief], are
unable to perform your duties.   You ought to know what
the duties of that office are, and yet our foreign enemies
(eeteki) you are unable to punish.   You have many high
officers with you, and this matter is one of the utmost importance; therefore I wish you to come as soon as you can
to Miako.   If you are unable to come on account of the business of the empire, then you must dispatch some able and
experienced officers, that I may hear myself what is doing.
At the present moment all Daimio, Shomio and Shonin (people) are in perplexity.   Why is this?   It is because the business of the Shiogoon office does not go straight.   On this
account I have every day great trouble, and therefore I

have commanded Koojio Kwanbakku to send Hino, and to communicate orally with you."

(This letter is supposed by some not to have been written by the Emperor, but to have been a forgery by the Koku shiu and higher Daimios.)

Mito, in 1855, had been very active and serviceable in telling the other Daimios that it was all very well to talk of fighting, but that they must first know what means they had. He had been appointed to look after the defenses of the empire. It may be presumed that the more powerful of the opposite party were annoyed with his obtaining this appointment, and with showing them their weaknesses, and had cabaled against him under the headship of Ee Kamong no kami.

On the 29th day of the 12th month of 1857, the letter was given by Hino to the Shiogoon; and the same night a meeting of all Daimios was held in the Siro jo in, a large hall in the castle of Yedo. The deliberations were not over till two o'clock in the morning of the 30th.

In 1858, on the 23d day of the 4th month, Ee Kamong no kami was appointed Regent (Gotairo). He was a Sho sho or major general, and had been brought up while a boy as a Buddhist priest. Probably by this time the Shiogoon was become quite imbecile, and it became necessary to appoint a regent. Ee, being of an age and capacity fit for the situation, had the first claim. He seems to have all along taken a side opposed to Mito, probably arising out of attempts to obtain this office; and as Mito was strenuously opposed to the admission of foreigners, Ee took the opposite side, and declared for the new state of things.

On the 6th day of the 7th month a communication was made to Owarri, the first of the "three families," to the effect that "the Shiogoon regrets to have to notice the conduct of Owarri, and that he cannot longer hold friendly communication with him. It is the will of the Shiogoon that Owarri in future shall confine himself to his house at Toyama in Yedo, and abstain from official business, and that he shall not speak to any one. That, further, all his territories shall be confiscated, and they are handed over to his relative, Matzdaira Setsu no kami," who was then a child.

To Mito a somewhat similar communication was made, and ordering him to confine himself in his house at Koma (ngome near Oji).

These commands, dictated by the Regent, were forthwith carried into execution. The smaller Ometski were appointed to see that such sentences were carried out. One result was that a great number of the poorer retainers of these chiefs were thrown on the country as "floating men," or Ronins, with their two swords to gain themselves a livelihood.

To Hongo Tango no kami, member of the Wakatoshi yori, a similar letter was sent, and he was deprived of the half of his territory and confined to his house.

In addition to these, Ishikawa Tosa no kami was fined the half of his territory, and a doctor to the Shiogoon, Hoka Riki, was turned out of his office and all his property taken from him. But his son was presented with 250 piculs of rice per annum, as he had shown himself on the side of the Regent.

(There is no mention in this work of similar treatment being shown to the great lords, Satsuma, Tosa and Etsizen.)

On the 8th day of the 8th month, the name of Harutaka, son of Kii dainagoon, was changed to Iyay mutchi. This is the boy whom the Regent and his party had put into the place of power, the Shiogoon having been dead for some time. It was given out that he was unwell, and the Regent had been taking means to strengthen his position against Mito. Mito claimed the place for his own son, who had been adopted by Stotsbashi, who was the third son of the ninth Shiogoon. The youth who succeeded was the nearest heir, according to European ideas; and Mito's claim had the defect, that if adoption carried the full consequences which he wished it should, it militated against himself.

The 9th day of the 9th month was the day chosen for the

nominal death of the Shiogoon. Ee Kamong no kami was much with the late Shiogoon before his death, and gave out that he had ordered him to act as Regent during the young man's minority.

Manabay Simosa no kami, one of the Cabinet, was sent by the Regent to carry out his schemes in Miako. He returned in the 12th month, and a few days after his return abdicated his honors and his territory.

Hotta, who had acted as envoy from the Regent to Miako, was degraded. On the 26th day of the 11th month, the two highest officers, Koo jio dono the Kwanbakku, and Ni jio dono Nai dai jin, came to Yedo as envoys from the Emperor.

On the 1st day of the 12th month the title of "Se i dai Shiogoon" was conferred on Se i sho sama Iyaymutchi by the Emperor, by the hands of two chokushi or envoys. The Empress also sent an envoy to the Shiogoon to compliment him upon his obtaining the title, and perhaps also to lay the first proposal as to his marrying the Emperor's younger sister Kadsumia.

During the 12th month, Manabay went down to Miako with orders to Ishigaya Inaba no kami, one of the governors of Miako, to seize the following persons: Ee kai kitchi, the gentleman in charge of Mito's house in Miako, and his son; three gentlemen, retainers in the service of the Kwanbakku Takatskasa dono, and the son of one of them, and a teacher of Chinese in Miako; Matzdaira Tanba no kami, a Daimio, related by marriage to Satsuma. His territory was taken from him and given to a child (Matzdaira Toki no skay). This child's followers were, after the Regent's death, put in charge of the British Legation at Tozenji; also a retainer of this Daimio and his secretary. These were all seized by order of the Regent, and sent to Yedo for trial before the Jeesha boonyo, the judges in the Hio jo sho.

In the 1st month of the following year—*i.e.*, about March, 1859—several of the gentlemen about the court in the service of the members of the imperial family and others of very high rank were arrested. Three of these were retainers of

Sanjio dono, of Arisungawa mia, and of Saiwonji dono respectively. Two retainers of the nephew of the Emperor, the Buddhist high-priest and the secretary of the Kwanbakku, were ordered to be sent up to Yedo. Within two months after this, seven high Koongays and four ladies, with seventeen more of the persons about the court, were all sent to Yedo by orders of Ee Kamong no kami.

In 1859, on the 2d day, 2d month, Itakura Suwo no kami, one of the Jeesha boonyo (temple lords acting as judges) was degraded. His crime was, that, being judge in rotation in the Hio jo sho in Yedo when these prisoners were brought before him, he would not bring them in guilty of anything, as he did not fear the Regent, and he had been requested secretly by the Emperor not to gratify him. At the same time Tsuchiya, governor of Osaka, was degraded and removed. He was an illegitimate son of Mito.

In the year 1858, before these strong measures had been taken by the Regent, Mito had written to the Emperor in the 8th month to the following effect: "Your revenue is not large enough, which is the cause of much sorrow to me. Permit me to present you with a few kobangs; and if it is in your power, please give to the Kwanbakku Koozio dono some additional land, and all the Koongays and those about the court who have titles [I give ?] 20,000 kobangs among them; and as Hirohashi is very diligent and able, I present him with silver."

It may be presumed that with the system of espionage so perfected as it is in Japan, the Regent would soon find out that Mito was intriguing at Miako, and probably got a copy of this letter before he gave orders to seize the persons above named, who were all implicated in these intrigues against him.

In the year 1858, in the 8th month, the Shiogoon (or the Regent more truly) sent three Daimios as envoys to Mito, with a letter to the following effect:

"You, Mito, formerly were anxious to assist Japan in her troubles, and your reasons for so doing were very good. But

the Shiogoon does not approve of your recent conduct."
(Mito had written to the Emperor, with whom he was connected by marriage, to complain of the boy from the Kii
family having been made Shiogoon, on the ground of his
being too young for the office, but in reality to get his own
son appointed by the Emperor to the place.) "You have
spoken to the Emperor too much about the adopted son of
Kii. Further, you have sent letters to the Koongays and
members of the imperial family to gain them over to your
views; and you, a man of rank, have not scrupled to use
low men [Ronins] to carry letters to Miako, inveighing
against the government of Yedo. From these acts of yours
great confusion has arisen. The Emperor has written a letter to the Shiogoon, and low men have been used as the
bearers [? to insult the Yedo government]. You have tried
to stir up a quarrel between the Emperor and the Kubosama,
and have excited discord among the Koongays. It is a most
improper thing for you thus to be acting behind our back,
and in the dark." (Mito had sent many letters to the Fudai
Daimios and Yakonins to gain them over to the side of Stotsbashi.) "You must suffer a severe punishment. But as it
is now the time of Hoji" (*i.e.*, the canonization of the late
Shiogoon), "we are willing to view your crime with leniency. Your punishment is, that you be henceforth imprisoned in your room [cheekio]. This letter I intrust to the
care of your son, to be delivered to you."

At the same time a letter was sent to Mito's son and
heir, of tenor as follows:

"Your father has been carrying on secret intrigues at
Miako. He has sent many of his servants there upon highly
important missions. But all his intrigues have been against
the Shiogoon secretly, and, as it were, behind his back. The
ways of father and son" (*i.e.*, the son cannot help what his
father does) "are different, but I think you may follow a
better way than your father. If you have no better way,
you must send guards to keep your father, and prevent
his carrying on these intrigues. The crime of putting

himself in opposition to the Shiogoon is very great, and merits severe punishment. But you side with your father, and it is natural for you to do so from filial obedience. But for this crime your father must be removed from his position and territory.''

On the 27th day of the 8th month a letter was sent to the principal one of the retainers, the Karo, or minister of Mito. ''Your master has been engaged in very dangerous schemes and intrigues, of which you were ignorant.'' (Mito had written a letter to say that all the Daimios gave themselves up to trifling and debauchery.) ''You were very foolish if you did not know of this business, and you ought on that account to be severely punished. But as Mito, your master, said that this business in which he was engaged was entirely for the good of the empire of Japan, and of the greatest consequence, your punishment shall be mitigated. In future you will take care to look into what your master is doing, and not cause the government of the Shiogoon so much trouble.

''In future, if you do cause trouble, you shall be severely punished.''

It appeared that both parties were trying to gain over the Kwanbakku by bribes—the Regent on the one hand, and Mito on the other. This high officer was perplexed which to side with, but he concealed all from the Emperor.

The Shiogoon commanded a letter to be written to Mito, to inform him that government was aware that many men had come secretly to Yedo from Mito, and warning him of what would be the consequence if any trouble should arise; and at the same time eight Daimios were appointed to guard the approaches to the city.

At this time the Regent was maturing his plans, and having arrested many of the agents of Mito, brought them before the Hio jo sho and judges of Yedo. The personal enmity of the two was working for the opening up of the country to foreign trade.

Many persons, some of whom were connected with the

highest officers in Miako and Yedo, were arrested as being engaged with Mito in intrigues. The head retainer of Mito was kept in confinement, and was commanded to kill himself in prison; * Eekai, the gentleman in charge of Mito's house in Miako, with his third son, the head chamberlain of Mito's establishment, the gentleman in the service of the late Kwanbakku, the Chinese teacher, and a lady about the establishment of Konoyay dono, in Miako, were brought before the judges in the Hio jio sho Hoki no kami, and the two city magistrates, Ishingaya and Ikeda.† Of the prisoners, the three first were beheaded.

On the 8th month, 20th day, the following letter was sent to Nakayama Bizen no kami, who was a Hattamoto in the service of government, resident at Mito's castle to assist him (or to watch him). Officers with the same duties reside at the castles of the other two Sankay, Owarri and Kii:

---

* The mode of suicide common in Japan may be noticed here. It is called by the natives literally to "cut the belly." The name "happy dispatch" seems to have been a felicitous suggestion of some foreigner. It is said to be done by a cut across the abdomen, and sometimes another cut is said to be made in the form of a cross. But any one who knows anything of the subject will think this nearly an impossibility, from the extreme difficulty of making the two other cuts necessary to make a cross. This would be a very butchering and trying job, and would bring on only a lingering death. So far as can be judged from the way it is performed in theaters, the knife, a short well-sharpened instrument, is inserted into the abdomen, and then drawn across the backbone, so as to sever the great blood-vessels, the aorta and ascending vein, which are there of such a size as to allow of death from their division in a few seconds. There seems to be no drawing across the abdomen. What is called swallowing gold leaf in China is in reality inhaling it when rubbed to a sort of flaky powder. It seems to choke the air-vessels, and so produce suffocation.

† Afterward assassinated by his servant, an emissary of Mito, who had got into the office as clerk, and kept Mito informed of all that transpired.

"Your house is a very honorable one, and you are a man of talent and experience. You ought to attend more correctly to do your duty. Now you have been neglecting your duty, while Mito the elder has been intriguing at Miako against me. You are ignorant of what is going on, and show yourself to be very indolent. This is a harsh mode of speaking, but you are still very young. You are hereby ordered to consider yourself under arrest, and remain a prisoner in your own room."

Toki, a colonel of the Household Guards, was degraded from his rank, and his territory confiscated.

To the Sakuji boonyo, Iwase, and to the First Lord of the Admiralty, Nangai, it was ordered that their salaries were to be stopped from that date.

The same punishment was inflicted upon Kawadsi, the keeper of the West Castle. To the Kosho, his eldest grandson, it was written:

"Your grandfather has been guilty of opposing the government, and has been degraded and deprived of his territory, and ordered to confine himself to his room. Therefore it is our will that you take possession of his territory, and also of his office."

It seems to have been the Regent's policy always to put in children in place of those men whom he displaced.

The other keeper of the West Castle was degraded, and deprived both of his territory and office.

To Tayki no skay, commander of the vanguard of the army, son of Oodo, it was written: "Having examined into the offense of your father, I have degraded him; but you are his adopted son, and therefore I give to you his territory and house."

Of other high officers some were beheaded, while others were ordered not to enter a town (Chu tsui ho); others were imprisoned in their own houses (Oshi kome), or in prison; others were put in irons; others confined to one room for life (ay chikio); others were banished to small islands.

All the above, who were themselves persons of some rank,

and connected with the highest in the empire, were brought
to the Hio jo sho, in Yedo, and received their sentences from
the temple lords sitting there.

To Hongo Tango no kami, at that time in the Lower
Cabinet, the Shiogoon wrote:

"Your conduct recently has been very improper. The
Shiogoon has heard of this, and you deserve to be severely
punished; but I will be lenient, and only deprive you of
5,000 koku of revenue, and degrade you." (He had been
made a Daimio, with 10,000 koku of revenue, by the previous Shiogoon.) To his son the Shiogoon wrote as above, but
added: "I will now take the ground I took from your father,
reducing him from a Daimio to a Hattamoto. Your father
must stay in his house, and retire from public life, and give
over his lands and rank to you."

To Ishikawa Tosa no kami a similar letter was written,
depriving him of his honors and territory, which were given
to his son.

The head of the Treasury, Sassaki Sinano no kami, was
degraded.

Iyo no ske, a gentleman in the service of Mito, was transported to Hatchi jio. His son, being only three years of age,
is to be kept till he is fifteen, and then transported also.

Two boys, aged four and two years, sons of Mito's chamberlain, are to be expelled from towns when they arrive at
fifteen years of age.

The Regent, after thus disposing of his enemies, proceeded, in the name of the Shiogoon, to reward his
friends.

He wrote to Matzdaira Idzumi no kami, then the head
of the Cabinet: "I approve of what you have done, and in
testimony I give you twenty-five obangs. [An obang is a
large gold coin worth about thirty-five dollars.] You have
been very diligent in a most difficult and important business.
I am very much satisfied, and will change your territory;
and as that you now possess is very poor, I will give you
better." (He also sent him a sword.)

To the temple lord, Matzdaira Hoki no kami, were given a saddle and six dresses.

To the Owo metski Kowongai were given seven obangs and four dresses.

To the street governor of Yedo, Ikeda, were given seven obangs and five dresses.

To the second street governor, Ishi ngaya, ten obangs and five dresses.

To the treasurer, five obangs and three dresses.

These men had acted as the judges in the Hio jo sho, and had awarded the punishments to the accused. Itakura was degraded because he would not act as the tool of the Regent in executing his vengeance.

In a letter to these officers the Shiogoon expresses satisfaction with the diligence shown by them, and on that account rewards them, at the same time rewarding smaller officers who have been similarly engaged, but without specifying them by name.

To Manabay, who had been formerly Prime Minister, and lately much engaged in ferreting out these intrigues for the Regent, the Shiogoon wrote: "You are now not very strong, and it will be perhaps better that you retire from the weight of public duty."

The Regent and he had a difference as to whether he was right in, or had the power of, punishing these men. The Regent was anxious to get rid of him, but his arguments were strong, and, besides, he was cognizant of all the secrets of the late *coup d'etat*, so that the Regent dared not take a stronger step than simply advise him to withdraw.

The Regent must have been well aware that in acting as he was doing he was playing a dangerous game. He had not been afraid to enter the family of the Emperor himself. The servants of the highest Koongays had been arrested, and themselves insulted and degraded. He had degraded five of the highest Daimios—Owarri, Mito, Satsuma, Tosa, and Etsizen—and had severely punished all of lower rank who had in any way countenanced or assisted those opposed to him. He had put his own protege on the seat of the Shiogoon, in opposition to Stotsbashi, the nominee of Mito. He now felt that he must retain the reins of power in his own hands, as, if he yielded a jot, his enemies would over- throw him, and take away his place and name. The only thing he had now to fear was secret enemies, who might wreak their vengeance by poison or assassination.

The 3d day of the 3d month is a day when a great levee is held at the castle in Yedo, all the Daimios on duty appear- ing in court dresses, with large retinues. At such times it is common for strangers to gather on the broad road or esplanade by the side of the castle moat, to watch the trains of the Daimios going to and returning from court. They often carry with them the small monthly list of officials in which the armorial bearings are given, by which the train of each Daimio may be at once recognized. In the Daimios' quarter of the city the guards of the streets and cross streets are the retainers of Daimios. The guard-houses are some- times divided into two when the guard is divided between two neighboring Daimios. Upon days of levee such as this strangers are allowed to loiter about, and are not so readily noticed as at other times.

At the south side of the castle of Yedo is the Soto Saku- rada, or outer Cherry gate, opening from that part of the in- closure in which the residences of the Gorochiu are situated. At this gate the moat is crossed by a bridge which opens upon a wide graveled road—the Tatsu no kutchi—bounded on the one side by the moat, on the other by Daimios' resi- dences, and leading by a gentle ascent to the residence of the Regent, Ee Kamong no kami.

On the 3d day of the 3d month the Shiogoon was to hold this levee, at which the Regent, now that he had put down his enemies, would appear in the plenitude of his power as the real ruler of Japan. He set out in his norimono toward the Sakurada gate, which was at a short distance, and seen from the door of his own residence. He was surrounded by his own retinue in white dresses. Suddenly a rush of men was made at the train. The bearers set down the norimono. Men with drawn swords ordered him to come out. He expostulated. One fired a pistol through the chair, wounding him in the back. He tried to crawl out, but his head was immediately cut off and carried away by the assassins.

The investigation which follows will show what took place.

On the 3d day of the 3d month (March 24, 1860) the Gorochiu wrote to the commander of the guard kept by Matzdaira Segami no kami: "Why did you allow men in disguise, with small sleeves and drawn swords, to pass your guard and loiter about the Tatsu no kutchi?" To this a reply was given: "There was a heavy fall of snow at the time. I noticed the men once, and they disappeared; but I acknowledge my fault—I am much to blame in the matter. But what shall I do now? Shall I cut off my men's heads?"

The same question was put to Matzdaira Daizen no daibu's (Choshiu) guard, who kept the Sakurada gate. He answered: "This morning at nine o'clock many men passed, but whether they were porters or soldiers I cannot tell. Several passed with blood-stained swords in their hands. I was on the point of arresting them, but as there was much snow falling I could not see them distinctly, or where they went to."

The principal gentleman in the late Regent's service, Kimatta Watari, wrote to the Gorochiu as follows: "This morning, while my master was on his way to the shiro to pay his respects to the Shiogoon, an attack was made upon his train. In the scuffle one man was killed, and the servants of Ee brought the body to the house here."

It is a general impression in Yedo that the servants, or some of them, as well as the guards about, and even some of the Daimios living in the neighborhood, were cognizant of the attack about to be made. Some of them gave no assistance to their master.

The same day the Shiogoon sent two Katchi metsuki to Ee Kamong no kami's house to make inquiries.

The servants of Sakkaï oota no kami, guards of the Owo tay, a large gate of the castle, wrote a similar letter to the above. It is a common plan in Japan, even among Daimios, when an investigation is to be made in which many are concerned, for all to write similar letters, to prevent the government seizing one. They added: "One Ronin, between twenty-seven and twenty-eight years of age, cut his throat. He only had his sword-sheath when found, and no sword. We found one wounded by a shot, and seized him."

At Tatsu no kutchi, the men at the cross-street guard-house, occupied by Tajima no kami and Sakkai oota no kami, said to the Gorochiu: "At about eight o'clock this morning a man shot himself through the neck while holding a man's head in his hand. Immediately one of the guard said, 'I will ask the man where he came from.' He said he was a servant of Satsuma. We sent for a surgeon, and he is now under treatment."

Ee Kamong no kami writes himself to the Shiogoon (notwithstanding his having had his head removed several hours previous): "I proposed going to the levee at the palace, and was on my way there; when near the Sakurada gate, and in front of the joint guard of Matzdaira Osumi no kami and Ooyay Soongi, about twenty men were collected. They began to fire pistols, and afterward with swords attacked me in my norimono. My servants thereupon resisted, and killed one of the men—the others ran off and escaped. I having received several wounds, could not pay my intended visit to the Shiogoon, and was obliged to return to my house, and now I send the names of such of my servants as were wounded."

Of these there were in all nineteen, of which number several died.

Upon receiving intelligence of this attack, the Shiogoon sent to the Regent a present of ginseng root, and to inquire more particularly as to his health and condition.

Upon the coats which were left by the assassins pieces of poetry had been worked with the needle; such as, "Let us

take and hoist the silken standard of Japan, and first go and
fight the battles of the Emperor." Upon another was the
following: "My corpse may dry up with the flowers of the
cherry, but how can the spirit of Japan relax?"

The names of eighteen men are given who were engaged
in the assassination of the Regent. Of these—

Arimura Jesayay mong, who is said to have been the
actual perpetrator of the deed, was head servant of Satsuma.—His brother is probably the man who assassinated
Mr. Richardson in 1862.

Sanno take no ske, a servant of Mito.

Seito Kemmootz.

These three, with two others, are said to have died of the
wounds received, on the 7th day of the 3d month, or four
days after his death. Sakkai and Yakushuri, on the part of
the Shiogoon, sent a letter to Ee Kamong no kami, to ask
how he was, and to bestow upon him a present of fish and
sugar, as a mark of regard.

The Cabinet was in difficulty how to act. They were of
the party of the Regent, but were now afraid that the opposite views would prevail, and that power would fall into the
hands of Mito.

On the part of the Gorochiu, Neito Kii no kami wrote to
the servants of Ee Kamong no kami:

"As a severe misfortune has befallen Ee Kamong no
kami, all his servants and relations are liable to be implicated
in the trouble.* If you, in revenge, should raise disturbance
with the followers of Mito, it will occasion much trouble.
I will endeavor to arrange matters for you, and keep things
quiet."

For some time after the assassination, the gates of the
Shiogoon's castle, known as the Sakurada, Babasaki, and

---

* It is a custom in Japan that the territory of a man who
has been killed by assassins is taken from his family, and
the family and retainers of the Regent were afraid of this law
being put in operation against them.

Watakura, were shut. The Tayass gate at Take bashi, the Hanzo and Saymidzu gates, were open during the day and shut at night.

The members of the Cabinet were allowed a guard of sixty men, and those of the lower Cabinet fifty men.

The men now feared by the government, the partisans of Mito, were lurking about Yedo in numbers. It was known that the head of the Regent had been carried off to the city of Mito and put up on a pole, with much abusive writing attached to it.

The Shiogoon gave orders to five Daimios to arrest all suspicious persons from Mito, and to seize the leaders of the movement.

Mito had said, tauntingly, "How can I, a poor Daimio, arrest these men, when you, the Shiogoon, are not able to do so? If you wish to seize these men, send your officers and do it. From Tatsuno kootchi a head was brought, and Ee Kamong no kami's servants are very anxious to get possession of it."

The head of the Cabinet, Neito, wrote to Matzdaira Osumi no kami: "Three days ago a high officer was assassinated before your door. You did not go to his assistance, or prevent the outrage. You were very negligent of your duty, and you are to be punished by the door of your residence being shut for one week, and you are not to go out during that time, but to confine yourself to your own house."

A similar message was sent to Katagiri Iwami no kami, keeper of the Heebiyah gate; and also to Toda stchi no ske (a child), keeper of the Baba saki gate.

At this time the streets of Yedo were placarded with squibs against the party of the late Regent and those in favor of foreigners. One of these accused the late Gotairo of enriching himself by foreign trade at the expense of the people of Japan, and others were obscure allusions to the founder of the family. Another, by turning the characters of his name upside down, makes of it, "A gentleman's head swept away is very good."

(Some of these squibs were what is called "Yabatai" writing. This name is founded on the following: Abe no naka maro in old times was sent as embassador to China. The Chinese Emperor was angry with him, and said that if he could not read a certain piece of writing he would kill him. He failed, and was put to death. Another embassador succeeded, to whom the same alternative was given. While he was musing upon it, and praying to Ten sho go dai jin, a spider dropped from the ceiling upon the paper, and went from word to word showing him how it was to be read. This is called Yabatai, wild-horse writing, now converted into Yabotai, wild-fool writing.)

The following information as to the assassins appears to have been given to the Gorochiu by Hossokawa, the Daimio to whose residence several of the assassins fled, saying that they were men from Mito, and wished to place themselves under his protection. He is supposed to have known all about the affair from the first.

One of the assassins, Mori, said that, about three months before, he had attempted to kill the Regent by shooting him with a pistol. The ball passed through the norimono, and he made his escape. The day they came to Hossokawa's house was very cold, so they were provided with food and wine. There was much snow falling, which furthered the designs of the assassins, as they thought it was assistance given them from heaven. They were all very tired and sleepy. Upon the 18th day of the 2d month they all went to Mito, afterward returning to Yedo; and they met in the morning of the 3d day of the 3d month at Atango yama. They did not sleep there; but the Buddhist priest was cognizant of what was going on.

The government in Yedo had doubtless good cause for alarm at the present crisis, as Mito, on the one hand, and the young Ee, son of the Regent, on the other, were making preparations for a fight. The policy of Iyeyas in compelling the lords to be personally in Yedo with few followers, while their strength in men remained at their provincial seats, prevented any outbreak. Mito was gradually filling his houses in Yedo with men.

On the other side, the family retainers of the Ee Kamong no kami, the lad who had succeeded to his father, fearing what might be the result of the present crisis, brought up ten cannon from his shta yashiki in the suburbs of Yedo, to his kami yashiki. [Every Daimio of any wealth has three houses in Yedo: his own residence, kami yashiki, where his wife and family reside, near the castle; naka yashiki, where concubines, servants, etc., reside; and shta yashiki, where he has a garden, and retainers, servants, and their families reside.] From his lands at Sano, in the province of Simotsuki, he brought up 400 men.

On the same day on which the Regent was killed, an attempt was made by Ronins of Mito to kill Matzdaira Sanuki no kami, who was a near relative of Mito, but a friend and son-in-law of Ee Kamong no kami. He had some suspicion, and was unwell on the day of the levee, and sent his son in his place. The norimono was attacked, but when the son was dragged out, and they discovered their mistake, the assassins let him go. The father did not long escape, however. He had taken as a concubine a girl from Mito, who, during the next month, stabbed him while in bed, and cut off his head, sending it to Mito. Matzdaira Koonaï no ta yu, another friend of the Regent's, and also a relative of Mito, hearing in the palace of the murder of the Regent, escaped by a back way.

The Daimio Hossokawa Etshiu no kami wrote to the government as follows:

"Yesterday morning some men came to my guards at the main gate, and said they were servants of Mito and had killed the Regent, and it was right that they should go to the Gorochiu; but as it is the first time they have come to Yedo, and do not know where the Gorochiu live, they requested me to go with them. I asked them who they were and what they wanted. They answered, that they had been this morning fighting with the Regent at the Sakurada

15

gate; and having first wounded him with a pistol, they pulled him by the right hand out of the kango and cut off his head. There came at first only nine men, but these were followed by a number of others: whence they came I do not know."

Hossokawa accompanied these men to the Hio jo sho, where the judges on duty asked them to give in writing their reasons for killing the Regent. The answer was: "We have good reasons. From the time of Zin mu tenwo to the present day the Japanese nation has never received any insult from a foreign nation; now five foreign nations have made treaties, and all through the empire the people are angry and sorry and vexed, and the Regent did not care. If he does not care for this, he makes himself an enemy to the nation, and therefore we killed him. We have no other reason."

The officers at the Hio jo sho were afraid to ask any more questions.

Mito sent the following letter to the Shiogoon:

"I am told that some men who were formerly in my service, but who were dismissed, have gone this morning to the Sakurada gate and killed Ee Kamong no kami. They appear to have gone to Hossokawa, wishing that he should take them into his employ. A messenger from Hossokawa has brought me this information. I am very sorry for it, and it has caused me much distress. I could not employ so many servants, and therefore was obliged to reduce my establishment, while some men who would not obey me went away of their own accord. On this account I am unable to arrest or punish such men, and must trust to the servants of the Shiogoon doing so, while I must try to find those who have absconded; but the Shiogoon is powerful while I am comparatively powerless; I therefore beg the assistance of the Shiogoon."

The Shiogoon wrote to Mito on the 4th day of the 3d month:

"Yesterday your servants killed the Gotairo, and now I

fear they may attack and kill some of the Gorochiu. It is ordered that your servants from morning to night, all day and all night, are not to move out of the house."

Otta, Hiobu sho, wrote to the Shiogoon:

"This morning about 8 A.M. the men of my guard informed me that two soldiers had passed them wounded and covered with blood. They, when very near my cross guard, committed suicide. I thereupon sent an Ometski to investigate the case. I asked the men standing near whence they had come. They said from the direction of the Heebiyah gate, and that on account of a severe wound of the shoulder one of them was faint and could not walk. He said to his companion, 'I cannot kill myself, as I cannot move my right hand'; the other said, 'If you are weak I will do it for you,' and cut off his head, and immediately after doing so he cut his own throat. We found that one of the swords of these men was bent round like a bow, and on examining the pockets, one had seven boos [coins], and the other seven boos and a half; and besides the money was a crest similar to that used by the Shiogoon [Mito uses the same crest—the awoyee, or three leaves], which had been cut from his coat; and a receipt from the Yebi ya [*i.e.*, lobster inn], a tea-house at the Yosiwarra [the government brothel]—viz., two boos for Tamanyoshi and two for Chittosay, two girls; one boo for a singing-girl; one boo for drink, two boos for fish, and ten tenpos for rice, with half a boo as a present to the servants of the house, with the date, 2d month, 27th day."

The street governor came and examined the corpses, and took them away on the 4th day of the 3d month.

On the 4th day of the 3d month—*i.e.*, the day after the assassination—Satsuma wrote to the Shiogoon:

"A servant of mine, Arimura Yooske, yesterday absconded and has not yet returned. I find that a man who committed suicide yesterday, near the residence of Endo Tajima no kami, was his elder brother. As I am ignorant of what he has been doing, please to order him to be arrested."

On the 3d day of the 3d month the Ronins in the service of Mito who had assisted in the murder wrote out the following statement and gave it to Hossokawa:

"We left our province of Hitatsi on the 18th day of last month; we did not meet together, but stopped at different parts of the town during our stay in Yedo. This morning we all met at the temple on Atango Hill [in the middle of Yedo], and thence we went to the Cherry gate, and waited between the guard-house of Osumi no kami and the Cherry gate. The Gotairo came along with his retinue. All at once we surrounded the kango on both sides. For some time we argued with the Gotairo. We told him that he was a bad man. We spoke to him about foreigners coming to the country, about the export of gold, about his receiving money as bribes from foreigners. He answered, and his men tried to prevent any attack being made upon him. One of our men fired a pistol into the kango (by which shot he was wounded in the back). He crawled out of the kango, but could not rise off his hands and knees quickly. His servants ran away, and one man cut off his head; six or seven others hacked at his body."

In the pocket of Arimura, the servant of Satsuma, who had been killed, was found a "sakiburay," or permit to travel for the Prince of Satsuma, who was at this time a child—"My master to-morrow sets out for Satsuma, and wants at each station coolies and horses." There was also found a piece of poetry:

"This is my body, which belongs to my master;
I will wait in the ground till my name is made greater."

The following is given as information with reference apparently to the men who had banded themselves together to free their country from the presence of foreigners:

"There are sixty honorable men in the service of Mito who are very hard and iron-willed. Why are they so iron-willed? To drive away foreigners according to the wish of the Emperor expressed in his letter of the 28th day of the

12th month. Mito has received a letter from the Emperor. Hikonay [*i.e.*, the Regent, from the name of his castle] gave it to him to tell him he must go to Miako. We have got the Emperor's letter and know his wishes [that foreigners should be driven out of Japan], and if we do not obey him we are rebels. The will of the Emperor we are determined to accomplish."

As further information the following is given: Hotta Bitshiu no kami went to Miako on the part of the Gotairo to speak to the Emperor about the foreign treaties with Japan. The Emperor said to him: "You have made your treaties first, and afterward come to me to tell me of what you have done. I know nothing about it. I know nothing about the business transacted in Kwanto—*i.e.*, in Yedo." Hotta could not answer the Emperor.

The Regent then sent Manabay to Miako to speak to the Emperor. He had an audience of the Emperor, and advised him to wipe out the treaty made at Yedo, and to make an entirely new and proper one. The Emperor replied: "You have fouled my face, and consider me as of no use. From the beginning there was always an Emperor in Japan; but if now the people do not wish it, I will give up my position. But you are trying to sow divisions between the Emperor and the Shiogoon."

Manabay said: "It will be better for us to make their interests one [alluding to the proposal that the Shiogoon should marry the sister of the Emperor]. If we do so, we can afterward unite to brush out foreigners."

The Emperor replied: "Now, at three or four audiences you have brought forward the business of Kwanto, but each time it has been false. Now you speak truth. If you think it right, put out these foreigners now. But my honor has been fouled and broken."

Manabay said: "At present the government of Japan is difficult and in a critical position, but let us be quiet and delay."

Manabay had, for the Regent, given large sums of money

to the high Koongays, the Kwanbakku, and others, to bring over the Emperor to his side. The Emperor was then standing alone, the Kwanbakku having been bought over. Manabay, on his return, retired from the Gorochiu to his provincial residence in Etsizen, but he got the credit of having saved Japan at this critical period from a civil war. It was only postponed for a little.

The Gorochiu were in great alarm at this time, and issued orders to all the guards around and in Yedo to be on the watch for disturbances.

At the Hiojosho the following evidence was elicited from one of the guards:

"I am a Gay zammi.* In the open space in front of the gate there were eight or nine men standing—some with rain-coats on, and some holding umbrellas—and looking at the Sode bookang.† I heard a pistol-shot in the open space in front, and several shots were fired at the kango. The bearers ran away. Some men then seized Ee Kamong no kami by the mangay [*i.e.*, the stiff tuft of hair on the top of the head], and dragged him out of the kango. After that I heard loud speaking, quarreling and scolding; and soon after they cut off Ee's head. While the quarreling was going on he was not dead, because I saw him moving his hands. Afterward many of the assassins stamped upon the body, and all kicked it; and they afterward hacked the body all over. They then all ran away."

The Gorochiu immediately sent a letter to the Emperor: "This morning (3d day of 3d month), on the Soto Sakurada, twenty servants of Mito assassinated Kamong no kami. We

---

* These are men at the palace gate who look out for Daimios approaching, and give notice to the guard, that they may know how to salute them, according to their rank. They make money by bribes to give the Daimios higher salutes than they are entitled to.

† The sleeve peerage, as it is called, a little abridgment of the Bookang, with the crests, names, and offices of Daimios, often used by strangers to recognize Daimios passing.

fear that Mito may have a design of sending men down to Miako to seize the Emperor, and gain over the Koongays. Therefore his Majesty's government would do well to keep a strict watch round Miako, and in the six roads leading to the capital.''

Matzdaira Higo no kami wrote to the Gorochiu: "This morning there was a serious disturbance at Soto Sakurada. My soldiers are at your disposal to guard any spot where you may please to order them.''

The Gorochiu answered, by the usual way of attaching a small slip of paper to the letter: "We do not require any more soldiers.''

The Shiogoon ordered Sakkai Sayay mon no jo, who was now, by the death of the Regent, head of the Tay kan no ma, or room of the Fudai Daimios, as follows:

"This morning there was a great disturbance in Soto Sakurada; and afterward there was fighting close to the Shiogoon's residence. You must keep all the soldiers under your command in readiness within your house.''

The Shiogoon also wrote to Higo no kami: "You say you have your soldiers all ready for any duty they may be called to. Your loyalty has given me much satisfaction.''

On the 4th day of the 3d month, Okamoto and Soma, the two principal officers in the late Regent's service, went to the Gorochiu with the following letter: "Our master, Kamong no kami, went out yesterday to go to the castle to pay his respects. When about half-way between his house and the gate of the castle, several miscreants fell upon him and killed him. We have certain information that these assassins were servants of Mito and Satsuma. Yesterday all the officers say to us, 'Wait a little.' But this business cannot wait. We wish to know for what reason these men killed our master. There are, at the present moment, some of these men secreted in the houses of Wakisaka and Hossokawa—two Daimios. We wish to see them, and ascertain from themselves why they killed our master. We desire that these men may be delivered up to us. All the people

of Hikonay [the Regent's territory] wish this, and we trust
you will take pity on them and grant their desire."

To this letter the Gorochiu affixed as answer: "Cannot
do so."

The following letter was addressed to the Shiogoon by the
son and servants of the late Regent on the day of the murder. It was written to ascertain whether the law of Japan
would be acted upon in their case, by which the territory of
any officer who has been assassinated is confiscated. "3d
day, 3d month.—Ee Kamong no kami, when going to the
castle to-day, and when near the Sakurada gate, was attacked by a number of villains. At the time, so much snow
was falling as to make it impossible to see a yard before one.
All the servants of Ee are enraged. There were but few
Ronins and many servants, and they ought to have overpowered the Ronins. The servants are deeply shamed when they
think of Ee nawo massa (the first of the family in the time
of Iyeyas). Whatever is to become of us we care not; but
the retainers and friends of Ee wish to know whether the
house is, according to the old laws of the empire, to be reduced in rank and impoverished, or if it is to be entirely
degraded and removed from the territory. We wish to
understand clearly." This was written in the name of the
young Ee; and was probably written with the view of preparing to defend themselves and party by an appeal to arms
rather than by submission.

The Shiogoon answered to this: "All your father's territory I restore to you his son."

Here terminates the native account of the assassination.
It gives some insight into the working of the government,
and the unscrupulous means to which the highest magnates
of the land will resort to attain their ends. From the general tenor of the statements, the extreme hatred of one party
in Japan to foreign intercourse is brought out, and the slight
which the Emperor considered to have been put upon him
by the conclusion of the treaty without his consent and
against his expressed opinion.

Assassination is the *ultima ratio* of the desperation of party weakness. The act implies that the party which has sanctioned it has no one competent to cope with the individual removed, or to fill the place which it has made vacant.

The position of the government upon the death of the Regent was that of helpless inactivity. The sudden removal of the foremost man of the empire was as the removal of the fly-wheel from a piece of complicated machinery. The whole empire stood aghast, expecting and fearing some great political convulsion. The whole country knew who had been the active agents in the deed; and perhaps there were at heart very few who did not feel more or less satisfaction at the blow given to the party which was responsible for, and instrumental in, bringing foreigners into the country; and a civil war or revolution would certainly have followed, had not every one felt that they were, for the first time in their history, face to face with an enemy, fear of whom concentrated all minor feelings, and consolidated them into one great national determination to rid the land of the hated foreigners. This was the one policy which the Emperor demanded of the Shiogoon, which the people looked to the government to effect, and which the lords and military classes burned to carry into execution. Were the foreigners not a mere handful of men, and were such to be allowed to beard and insult the highest personages in the land with perfect impunity? Now, when the head of the party, who was or pretended to be in favor of such a change of the laws, is struck down, if some representative of the national feelings would only arise and lead them on, they would follow to the death in such a glorious cause. But no such leader appeared. Where was Mito, the rival of the late Regent? and why did he not come forward to carry out his own policy at this juncture? The son of the late Regent was too young and inexperienced to claim his father's office, or to assume the leadership of the party. It was the personal hatred of the two men which had been the moving spring in the daring action of the Regent, and in the underhand plotting of Mito. In all probability the feelings of hostility with which each regarded the foreigner were equally strong. Mito said you must admit foreigners, because you cannot keep them out. Ee thought we can admit foreigners, and, if we see fit, afterward turn them out. But Mito was disliked by the other Daimios, and his name was not sufficient to rally a strong party, while he * and the lately degraded Daimios were now in arrest in their own houses, in territories which had been transferred to the hands of infants. They had thus no opportunity for intriguing, having no common place of meeting out of Yedo, as by law they were prohibited from going to Miako, and could only come to Yedo as Daimios, when called there on duty by the government.

In this crisis the only course for the Cabinet to pursue was to go on quietly, managing the routine of affairs until time should open up some line of action. The Gorochiu, therefore, with Neito at its head, and nominally under Tayass as Regent, continued to carry on the ordinary duties of government.

Events have shown that the Regent was right in his judgment of the men whom he sought to remove from his path as obstacles—Mito, Etsizen, Satsuma, Owarri—as these have all since his death reappeared as leaders of the party opposed to his policy in the Obiroma or council of the Kokushu. Etsizen, afterward known by his retired title Shoongaku, was the first among these magnates who attempted to take a lead in the government of Yedo. He had been removed from his position as Daimio and placed in arrest; but, having subsequently been released, was able to move about and obtain an influence in high places. He obtained from the Emperor a letter [afterward considered a forgery], appointing him and Awa to fill the place of co-regents, under the name of Sosai Shoku or Sodangeite. But the fermentation of revolution had already begun to work, and at such a

---

* Mito is said to have traveled over the empire incog. at this time, to study the feelings of the people.

time the first actors upon the stage seldom play the prominent parts they deem themselves fitted to fill. They generally fail to see the causes of the boiling going on around. Such a man is like an atom in a pot of boiling water, and knows and sees nothing of the fire which is causing all the upturning around him. To even a superficial looker-on at the state of things in Japan, it was evident that such a dual condition of government as that then existing could not long continue to carry on foreign relations. The discord and weakness arising from the permission of an *imperium in imperio* by the exterritoriality clause was greatly increased by the government attempting to carry on foreign relations without the consent or against the will of the higher power in Miako. The two powers must work harmoniously; and so long as the internal affairs of the empire are the only possible cause of rupture, the weaker, though more exalted, will find it to be its interest to be on good terms with the lower but more powerful, the executive. So soon as the latter begins to act as supreme power toward other nations, it places itself in a wrong position, and foreign nations will not treat with such a pretense. The opposition finds a head in the Emperor, and the only way to avert a rupture is for the lower power to give way and to act only as the representative of the head of the empire. If he fails to see this, he sets himself against the Emperor, who is then supported, not only by his own nobility, but also by those powers with whom he has entered into relations. The party of the Shiogoon deserts him, and his only *rôle* is to work with and under the Emperor; or, if he refuses to do this, civil war ensues, and he falls.

After the removal of the Gotairo, the Cabinet was able or permitted to carry on the affairs of State. But while everything seemed smooth, smoldering powers were at work preparing for volcanic action. The Kokushu, and especially those who came to Yedo from the west, were becoming very much irritated about the question of foreigners in the country, and foreign ministers in Yedo. The latter assumed a position of superiority to which these lords were quite unaccustomed. They were occupying temples belonging to great families, situated in cemeteries consecrated by the burial of their ancestors and relatives, but now polluted by intruders hateful to the spirits of the country. The foreign merchants were able to beard these princes on the highroad, and to treat with nonchalance dignitaries who looked for the utmost deference, and who were authorized by law to punish at their own hands any real or supposed insolence or insult. On the other hand, they saw trade pushing its way in the country; silk which had been sold for 100 dollars was now bringing 1,000, and Emperor and lord longed to share in such advantages and participate in the profits. The first object which the more powerful of the Kokushu set themselves to accomplish was to break down this intolerable subjection to the Yedo government. This was not difficult to do, as the power of the empire was in the hands of a delicate lad, and the Emperor, through whom the end was brought about, was promised and hoped that the power would revert to him. The agents in this act were Shoongaku, Shimadzu saburo, Choshiu, and a Koongay Ohara—a distant relative and the unexpected successor of a Koongay, and who had spent his early life hanging about the offices of Yedo. After the boy-Shiogoon had been married to Kadsu mia, sister of the Emperor, Shoongaku, who was always full of the most economical if not parsimonious views, reduced the retinue and court of the Shiogoon till it was brought into contempt with the populace. In October, 1862, these potentates produced a letter (forged, as is generally believed) from the Emperor, putting an end to the routine of the Yedo court; and having the power in their own hands, they immediately proclaimed the edict and carried it into execution. The order was to the effect that the higher Daimios were to visit Yedo only once in seven years, and that the wives and families of all the Daimios were to live at their own provincial seats. This removed from Yedo all the luster of the court. At the same time these lords

filled up the complement of their design by inducing the
Emperor to call most of the higher Daimios who were of
their own views to Miako. The Mikado was swayed hither
and thither as the one party or the other gained the power
in the capital; and so at one time Kanso, the retired lord
of Hizen, had the ear of the Emperor in the interest of the
Shiogoon, while Choshiu appeared to have taken up arms
against his sovereign. But he seems all along to have acted
loyally and patriotically in showing an intense hatred to the
foreigners who were by force of arms thrusting themselves
and their regiments into the country. This act was the
great blow which broke up the power and brought to a
termination the dynasty of Iyeyas. He had foreseen and
made provision for intestine war and revolution, but had not
been able to provide for a treaty with foreign nations and an
exterritoriality clause.

In 1861 the foreign ministers, up to that time resident in
Yedo, retired to Yokohama, and pressed one demand after
another upon the Japanese government, already sufficiently
occupied with complications arising from intestine difficulties. The Cabinet was worried by requests for interviews
upon questions of land, of residences, of money exchanges,
of matters of etiquette in interviews with the Shiogoon, and
other matters which might seem trivial in comparison with
the crisis through which the country was passing in the face
of an internal revolution. These foreign ministers were
now, somewhat unreasonably, all demanding that residences
should be built for them by the Japanese government, and
insisting that these residences should (in the face of an article of the treaty to the contrary) be fortified and furnished
with guns. The recreation ground of the people of Yedo,
Go teng yama, was demanded and given up for this purpose by Ando, then Prime Minister, and a large building
was erected by the Japanese government upon this site;
but the feelings of the people at this unjust appropriation
of a piece of ground which had been set apart for their use
were so much excited that another local *émeute* was threat

ened at Yedo. This was allayed by the burning of the new
building, and by the attempted assassination of the Prime
Minister, who narrowly escaped with the loss of an ear.

By these annoyances occurring in the neighborhood of
Yedo, and through the presence of foreigners, a strong party
was drawn over to the views of the Emperor, and the nation
began to see that he had all along been in the right in opposing the admission of foreigners as detrimental to the quiet of
the country. Satsuma and Choshiu built each a large new
residence in Miako. The Emperor called on twelve of the
wealthiest among the Daimios to keep each a sufficient body
of troops in the city for his protection. The young Shiogoon
was invited or called upon to pay a visit to Miako when
Stotsbashi was intriguing against him. He accordingly
went with Kanso, the retired prince of Hizen, while Higo
was appointed Shugo shoku, or guardian of the palace.
This meeting of the Emperor and the Shiogoon seems to
have opened the eyes of both to the power and intelligence
of foreigners, of which the Emperor and his court seem to
have been ignorant. Some of the Miako nobility went out
on a trip with the Shiogoon in his steamer, and were astonished and converted; and Anega Koji was assassinated for
expressing too plainly and openly his opinions as to the
power and energy of foreigners.

The intercourse between the two heads of the empire
seems to have consolidated the power of the government,
and promised to bring forth fruit in a mutual good understanding and co-operation. Stotsbashi sneaked away to Yedo
in disgrace, and had to run the gantlet of an attack on his
way back, when his chief secretary was assassinated on the
highroad at Saka no shta. Shimadzu and Choshiu retired
from Miako in disgrace to their respective provincial residences, where they brooded over their own position and that
of the empire. They could not but feel that it was the loyalty of their views which had entailed on them their present
disgrace, and the prime cause of this was the foreigners.
They knew well that the feeling of every one of their coun-

trymen was with them, and they seem to have at last determined to throw themselves into the breach by bringing about a quarrel between the government and some foreign nation. Shimadzu, the father of the Daimio, then a minor, determined to carry out the laws of the country irrespective of any exterritoriality clauses. On leaving Yedo, on September 14, 1862, he gave out that he would cut down any foreigners he might chance to meet upon the road; when, as he approached Kanagawa, meeting three gentlemen and a lady, he ordered his retainers to cut them down, and Mr. Richardson, wounded and unable to ride away more than two hundred yards, was set upon, fainting from loss of blood, and brutally murdered. Justice was asked from the Shiogoon's government and the punishment of the offender, who was well known to all Japan. The murder of a merchant by a lord like Satsuma was treated with contempt, and the matter was referred by the British Minister to H.M. government. The subsequent necessary delay of many months, before instructions came out to demand an indemnity and the punishment of the offender, raised the courage of the party opposed to foreigners, and Choshiu determined on his part to carry out the laws of the country according to his instructions. He held a commission from the Emperor as guardian of the Straits of Simo no seki, the narrow western entrance to the "inner sea." He had thereby a right to overhaul all vessels passing through this strait. There is no other sea quite analogous: it resembles, but is much narrower than, the Dardanelles, the Sound, the Straits of Dover, or Tarifa, at all of which places some recognition of the power of the nation to defend a vulnerable point of her territories has been allowed in the exercise of certain surveillance over passing vessels. Choshiu fired upon some foreign vessels passing through this strait. The consequence of this was a combined attack by English, French and Dutch, by which he or one of his relatives (by error) suffered severely in men, ammunition and prestige. The Shiogoon disavowed his proceedings, and to satisfy foreign demands proposed to punish the rebel. This, however, he found to be no easy matter, as the whole troops and populace were in favor of Choshiu and his patriotic attempt, and the Shiogoon was at last obliged to make terms with the Daimio.

Choshiu had presented the following memorial to the government upon the position of Japan in its internal and external relations at this juncture:

"Allow me, notwithstanding your political discussions [with the Mikado's envoys], to give you my opinion respecting the troubles which foreigners have given us of late years in asking all kinds of concessions, in addition to the unexpected troubles which exist in our own country. This combination of difficulties within and without, occurring at the same time, and bringing us to a point when our prosperity or misfortune is decided, keeps my heart day and night in anxiety, and induces me to give you in confidence my own feelings upon these subjects.

"I have long thought that union and concord between the Shiogoon and Mikado, and obedience to the Mikado's orders, are highly necessary in keeping up an intercourse with foreign nations, as I have already said very often.

"But every one knows that since the great council of officers, the Shiogoon and Mikado are disunited, which has occasioned a conflict of parties, and brought with it discord and trouble.

"I think the reason of this is, that although the signing of the treaties was forced upon us by urgent circumstances and pressing events, there are some who maintain that the reopening of relations with foreigners has occasioned a degradation of the people, who were so brave and constant ten years ago, to the state of quiescence and cowardice to which they are now reduced by their fear of war and of the foreign powers. These persons who are of this opinion are therefore in opposition to the acts of the Shiogoon, and say that they will themselves undertake to set aside the treaties and prepare the country for war, declaring that the Mikado still maintains the old laws of our country, which direct the expulsion of foreigners.

"Others persons accept, on the contrary, the reopening of the country, and praise the foreigners, and thus destroy all confidence in ourselves. They say that the foreigners have large forces, and that they have great knowledge of arts and sciences.

"These conflicting opinions trouble the minds of the people. Unity is force and strength, and discord is weakness; therefore it would be imprudent to go to war against powerful and brave enemies with discord in our minds.

"The closing or opening of Japan is a matter of the greatest moment. That which cannot be shut again should not have been opened, and that which cannot be opened should not have been shut.

"The closing of Japan will never be a real closing, and the opening will never be a real opening, so long as our country is not restored to its independence, and as long as it is menaced and despised by foreign countries. Therefore the opening or closing of Japan is dependent upon the restoration of our own powers; if that is effected, then war or peace can be declared.

"The condition upon which this power can be restored to us is the enlightening of the people, and their union.

"I think the only way to bring about national union is by solid union between the Shiogoon and Mikado, acting together as in one body. Should there be war, it can be brought to an end very easily.

"A time is now come very different from the barbarous ages, and arising out of the long peace which has prevailed. Every little child knows the respect it owes to its parents and masters.

"It will therefore rejoice everybody in this advanced age to see the Shiogoon hold the Mikado in great respect; and the whole nation would honor the Shiogoon, and all troubles would cease, and then only we can be restored to our independence and power.

"After our independence is restored, it is urgent and pressing that we reform our military institutions, the naval sciences, as well as all branches of industry. We should find out the great advancements and developments of arts and sciences in other countries. The whole nation must devote life and soul to the benefit of our state, and we must learn and study the interior arrangements of foreign lands, in order that the commerce of our country may flourish in this important age. I think all this ought to have been done long since; but nothing of the kind is to be found in the edicts which have appeared so often during the last seven years.

"Inventions and improvements pass on with rapidity, and the time is now come to make all these changes and improvements; but if our attachment to old customs causes us to postpone these measures of such great importance, if these changes are later suddenly forced by circumstances upon the inhabitants, a very bad impression will be produced, creating disorder and confusion. These are reasons why they should be effected now calmly and gradually. I think that the Mikado will not be disinclined to this, and therefore I wish that the Shiogoon should act under the orders of the Mikado, and not conclude matters by his own authority. He ought to let these designs be known to all the Daimios in the name of the Mikado; then there will be a general quiet restored; then the dormant soul of the whole nation will awake, and will be united in power and in independence; and then it will display its force and strength to the other five portions of the universe without anxiety and fear for our own country.

"I do not write these my sentiments to aid you in your negotiations, as they may be of little or no use to you, and only like a drop of water falling into the ocean; but to show my gratitude for the favors of the Shiogoon, which my ancestors have enjoyed during centuries."

The aim of the party opposed to the policy of the Shiogoon and the admission of foreigners seems to have been to

poison the mind of the Emperor against the young Shiogoon, and to embroil the country in a war, by setting the
one against the other. The letters from the Emperor which
have been obtained prove this.

The following letter was conveyed by Shimadzu Saburo
from the Emperor to the Shiogoon about October, 1862:

"I think that the power of the foreigners [Ee jin, wild
men] at the present time in the country is improper; and
the officers of the Kwanto seem to have lost all knowledge
of the right way, and of all plans of action, causing disturbance all over the empire. All my people [Ban nin, 10,000
men] seem about to fall down into mud as black as charcoal. On this account I, standing between Ten sho go dai
jin and my people, am very deeply distressed. The Bakuri
[Shiogoon's officers] have spoken to me, saying, 'All our people are agitated, and the Shiogoon has no power to hold up
his arm. Therefore please give us your sister in marriage
[to the Shiogoon]. If you can do this, Miako and Yedo will
be at concord, and the whole power of Japan can join together, and we can then brush away the Yee teki' [*i.e.*,
foreigners, wild enemies].

"In answer, I said, 'This is right, and I will give my
sister.'

"At that time the Bakuri said to me, 'In ten years the
foreigners must be brushed away.' This gave me great
pleasure; and I pray to the spirits every day to help Japan.

"I have now been waiting for a long time for your
brushing away. Why are you so slow?

"With my sister Kadsumia I sent Tchikusa shosho and
Iwakura chiujo, and at the same time granted a general
amnesty;* and all the business of the government I gave, as
in former times, to the Shiogoon. But this business about
foreigners [Gway-Ee] is of the first importance to the country. Therefore I said, 'Let all this foreign business come

---

* The Gorochiu would not allow this to be granted, and
never published it.

under my care, and I will settle it.' At the time, all the Yedo officials answered to me that the Emperor's proposal was very important and serious, but a speedy answer cannot be given, and that we must wait a little.

"After this time, several Daimios proposed several different stratagems for driving away foreigners. But of all the Daimios only two—viz., Satsuma and Choshiu—came in person to speak to me; and all the loyal people from San yodo [west of Miako], Nan kaido [island of Sikok], and Sai kaido [island of Kiusiu], came to Miako like bees, and addressed me secretly. All these tell me that the officers of Yedo are all bad, and that they are becoming worse from day to day; and that justice and truth are fallen to the ground; and that they do not hold the Emperor in respect; and they are friends of the foreigners, giving them everything they want—silk, tea, and other things—while the whole country loses. All the people are much vexed about this; and they feel that they are becoming the same as servants of the foreigners, and now their habits cannot change. On this account, these people of San yodo, Nan kaido, and Sai kaido, and Satsuma and Mowori [Choshiu], wish to raise the Emperor's flag. And they say, that if the Emperor with the flag goes to Hakonay, the Bakufu [Shiogoon's office] officers, if bad, must all be punished.

"Some men say that, Japan having been at peace for a long time, the spirits of the people are very lazy and slow; therefore they suggest that a letter should be given to the Daimios and people of the Go ki stchi do [*i.e.*, the districts lying upon the seven roads], ordering that foreigners must be brushed out of the country.

"The Emperor says: 'Throughout the empire there are many loyal and patriotic men, therefore I will speak to Satsuma and Nagato to desire the people to have patience.'

"I gave a letter to Koozay Yamato no kami, requesting an answer, and yet none ever came; and last year I wrote and proclaimed an amnesty, and to this I received no answer. Why has the Shiogoon thus lost the way? I believe

it is **not he**, but his officers. All the Gorochiu do not care.
The Ty jiu [great tree] is but young; but I fear that if I
delay but an instant [till I can stand up], all the empire will
be broken up. Therefore I am every day troubled and weep-
ing. All the officers of the Kwanto [the Shiogoon, Daimios,
etc.] think only of the happiness of a day, and forget the
misery of a hundred years. The holy books thus speak, and
you ought to study them. You ought to keep these virtuous
ideas in your minds, and be ready with your military preparations, and then you will clearly see your way out, and
brush away the power of the foreign enemies. But while
all Japan is in a state of excitement, I will hold to the me-
dium course [*i.e.*, between brushing away immediately and
waiting indefinitely]. Since the Tokungawa family began
[*i.e.*, since Iyeyas], there has not arisen a question of so
much difficulty. I have three plans to propose: The first
is, that I will gradually bring the Shiogoon and Daimios
and Hattamoto to Miako, and will hold a council about the
government of the country and the brushing away of foreigners. If we can do this, the anger of heaven and the
gods will be averted. They will rejoice, and the good minds
of the lower classes will return. Then all people will stand
on a strong foundation, and the empire be as strong as a
large mountain.

"My second plan is, you must lean upon the old laws of
Ho taiko [*i.e.*, Taikosama], and give the laws of the country
and the settlement of the question into the hands of the Tai
hang [*i.e.*, large fence, or the Kokushiu] and the Gotairo
[*i.e.*, five elders]. If we do this, the country can keep out
or push back the pressure of foreigners. All round the
coasts military preparations must be made; and so the country will be strong, and foreigners can be brushed away.

"My third plan is, to order Stotsbashi to assist the Ty jiu
on all internal business, and to give the office of Regent to
Shoongaku, to take charge of the outer relations of the office
at Yedo. In that case both the internal and external business will be well conducted, and we shall not blush to think

that we are servants to foreigners, and that they have obliged us to cross our coats the right over the left side.* For all men fear that in a very little time these foreigners will seize all Japan.

"I think that these three plans should now be considered and settled, and to that end I send an envoy to Kwanto; but if they cannot all three be carried out, I wish the officers of the Shiogoon to examine them and determine on one that can be carried out. All my servants must be very busy going round and round, and there is to be no secrecy about it; but every one is to be diligent, and all must give me a faithful report."

At the time this letter was written both Stotsbashi and Shoongaku were in Miako, whither they had hurried down before the arrival of the Shiogoon. The letter bears some internal evidence of being written at their dictation, especially from the proposal made to appoint the two as Lieutenants and Regent to or over the Shiogoon; and corroborates the advice which Kanso had given the young Shiogoon; viz., that he should repair at once to Miako, where the enemies of his power were trying to subvert him.

Not long after this, four Koongays of Miako having been discovered plotting against the Emperor were degraded and obliged to shave their heads and retire to monasteries. Koonga and his son, and the Empress herself, with two concubines, were said to be implicated in these intrigues. The following reasons of punishment were published: "During the last five years intrigues have been carrying on against the Emperor by the late Gotairo and Sakkye Wakasa no kami. The object of these intrigues has been to get possession of the Emperor's person and banish him to one of the islands (as formerly several were sent by Ashikanga and Hojio). Sakkye was very

---

* The custom in Japan is to bring the left of the dress over the right side in front, "migi yeri"; and it is a common saying that foreigners will soon oblige them to change even this custom, and "hidari yeri," cross it over the left side.

false, and tarnished the bright name of the Emperor, which is a very foul crime. Now their devices have been discovered, and the Emperor has ordered the Sisshay [another name of the Kwanbakku] thus to punish them."

The punishment inflicted by the British government upon Satsuma at Kagosima, on account of the murder of Mr. Richardson, was severe but deserved, and, in a political view, was completely successful. The two most powerful lords in the empire had each tried a fall with foreigners and been worsted. They could no longer press on the government to brush out these intruders, as they knew now by experience how far behind the country was in military and naval tactics and means of warfare. The natural result now followed—they began to quarrel among themselves. Seeing their own weakness, however, they instantly began to take what steps they could to bring themselves up to a higher standing by the education of their people, and they began by seeking to acquire a knowledge of steam and steam-vessels. Choshiu and Satsuma sent young men to England, arms and ammunition were purchased, steam-factories were erected for working in iron, military tactics were studied, professors were appointed in their colleges, and officers were obtained to drill their young men and teach the use of the rifle.

The fruit expected from the intercourse of the Emperor and Shiogoon unfortunately did not ripen. The latter returned to Yedo despoiled of much of the former splendor of his position. His court was broken up. The greater lords paid now no deference to him, and the lesser Daimios began to side with the greater. His party consisted chiefly of the Kamong Daimios, the relatives of the family of Tokungawa. Yedo itself was falling into the position of a fading capital, and, as a place of commercial importance, was dwindling with the departure of its political greatness. A feeble attempt was made to recall the edict and re-establish the old order of things in Yedo; but events rolled on, and things are shaping themselves in totally different order from that proposed by the ruling powers.

The defeat of Satsuma by the English navy at Kagosima separated that Daimio from the party of Choshiu and
others, and his counsels to the Emperor were those of peace.
Shimadzu Saburo paid the indemnity demanded of him, and
gave assurances that the offender should be given up when
discovered, which was perhaps as much as could be expected from one who, while a murder was being committed by hiso rders, was quietly sitting within ten feet of
his victim.

The Shiogoon Iyay mutchi had found nothing but trouble
and anxiety from his elevation to the seat of power in the
year 1859. In 1866 his health began to give way, and he
shortly after died, leaving no children, and the way became
open to his rival, Stotsbashi. The period was critical, and
the ablest man would have found difficulty in steering through
the dangers surrounding the vessel of state. The Daimios
would now have little hesitation in withholding their allegiance to another Kubosama until it should be settled who was
to be the *de facto* ruler of the empire—the Emperor or the
Shiogoon. Many would see that some change must take
place in the internal constitution of the empire now when
the government must deal as one body with foreign nations.
The necessity for dual government was at an end. The
mouthpiece of the nation must be one, and give no uncertain sound. The internal resources must be gathered into
one treasury. The police, the taxes, must be recognized as
national, and not as belonging to one petty chief here and
there. The army and navy required reconstruction; and
the power of the feudal lords would have to be broken down
in order to be reconstituted into one strong state under one
head.

The new Shiogoon, Yoshi hisa, attempted to assume the
power with the position held by his ancestors, but he was
too late. His only true policy was to stand beside and sup·
port the Emperor while the lower chiefs impoverished themselves by fighting. He attempted to take a side against the
Emperor, but not being aided by a strong party, he was

forced in 1867 to give way, and by abdicating retire into temporary obscurity.

To add still more to the critical position of affairs in Japan at this time, the Emperor died, being about thirty-eight years of age, and leaving a young boy as his heir and successor. It does not clearly appear who has been pulling the strings of political action on the part of the boy-Emperor; but there can be little doubt but that the two Daimios to whom Yedo was the most grievous offense, and whose ancestors had smarted from the rise of the Tokungawa family under Iyeyas, Satsuma and Choshiu, have not been idle. On the other hand, the wealthy Daimios from the north—Sendai, and other Kamong or relatives of that family—seemed determined to uphold the position of the family, and carry out the principles of Iyeyas at all hazards. Between these parties the Shiogoon, who is said to be an able man, tried to steer a neutral course until he saw what would turn up. At length he came to think that submission to the Emperor was the true policy for himself and for the empire, and he humbly placed himself at the disposal of the Emperor rather than involve the country in another civil war. His submission was accepted by the Emperor in the following terms:

"The conduct of Tokungawa Yoshi hisa having proceeded to such an extreme as to be properly called an insult to the whole empire, and having caused the deepest pain to the mind of the Emperor, both sea and land forces were sent to punish him. Hearing, however, that he is sincerely penitent, and lives in retirement, the excess of the imperial compassion shall be exhausted, and the following commands be enjoined upon him. Let him be respectfully obedient to them. A period of eleven days is granted him in which to comply with all these orders.

"1st, Yoshi hisa having, on the 12th month of the last year, and afterward, insulted the Emperor, attacked the imperial city, and fired upon the imperial flag, was guilty of a most heinous crime. The army was accordingly sent

16

out to pursue and punish him. But as he has manifested sincere contrition and obedience, has shut himself up in retirement, and begs that his crime may be pardoned: in consideration of the no small merit of his family, which, since the time of his ancestors, for more than two hundred years has administered the affairs of government, and more especially of the accumulated meritorious services of Mito zo Dainagoon [the father of Yoshi hisa, and rival of the Regent]; for these various considerations, of which we are most profoundly sensible, we give him the following commands, which if he obeys we will deal leniently with him, grant that the house of Tokungawa be established [*i.e.*, not destroyed from the list of Daimios], remit the capital punishment his crimes deserve, but command him to go to the castle of Mito, and there live shut up in retirement.

"2d, The castle [of the Shiogoon in Yedo] to be vacated, and delivered over to the Prince of Owarri.

"3d, All the ships of war, cannon and small arms to be delivered up; when a proper proportion shall be returned [to the head of the house of Tokungawa, which is reduced to the rank of an ordinary Daimio].

"4th, The retainers living in the castle shall move out and go into retirement.

"5th, To all those who have aided Yoshi hisa, although their crimes are worthy of the severest punishment, the sentence of death shall be remitted, but they are to receive such other punishment as you shall decide on. Let this be reported to the imperial government. This, however, does not include those persons who have an income of more than 10,000 koku—*i.e.*, Daimios; the imperial government alone will punish such."

An important political step has been taken within the last few months, during the present year 1869. The Daimios appear to have become aware of the weakness which inevitably accompanies division, and of the strength which would be gained to the country by consolidation and unification under one head. The threatening position taken up by some

or all of the foreign nations with whom treaties of friendship
had been concluded brought up the subject at some of the
recent great councils. The crushing defeats which had
fallen upon Satsuma and Choshiu warned individual Daimios of their weakness as units in carrying on operations of
war; the enormous expense entailed upon them in procuring
munitions of war, and in exercise, and in the purchase of
steamers, alarmed these lords in the prospect of annihilation
from exhaustion, and they came to the conclusion that such
expenses could only be borne by the empire as a whole, and
that to gain such an advantage the privileges of the class
must in some degree be given up. The removal of the Shiogoon presented a favorable opportunity for carrying out the
proposal, and they agreed heartily to restore all their fiefs
into the hands of the Emperor, and to give up the exclusive
privileges which each held in his own state, that these might
all be thrown into one government, with one exchequer, one
army, and one navy. The latest accounts confirm this cession of their independent rights—in which cession Satsuma,
the most powerful, but the Daimio who suffered most from
the independent system in the very severe punishment which
he received in loss of men, destruction of steamers, and payment of indemnity, with total loss of prestige and position as
a military power, has been foremost. It is therefore reason-
able to suppose that henceforth there will be only one responsible ruling power in Japan.

CHAPTER XII

EVENTS FOLLOWING THE ABOLITION OF THE SHIOGOONATE

MR. DICKSON'S history was published in 1869. During
the thirty years that have since elapsed we have witnessed
a complete transformation of Japan. To make intelligible
the sequence of events, it may be well to describe more in
detail the incidents which preceded, attended and immedi-

ately followed the downfall of the Tokungawa Shiogoonate which, for more than two and a half centuries, had possessed the substance of power in Japan, only the shadow thereof being retained by the Mikado. Within less than a year after January 6, 1867, when Keiki had been made Shiogoon, much against his will, the Prince of Tosa and many able representatives of the Daimio and Samurai castes urged him to resign and permit a government to be constituted on the principles which had prevailed in the anti-Shiogoon era, namely, before the year A.D. 1200. In November, 1867, Keiki so far yielded to public opinion as to tender his resignation; but, as the Aidzu clan, which was stanchly loyal to him, continued to guard the Mikado's palace, it remained for a time uncertain whether Keiki might not resume his functions. Ultimately, a combination was formed by the Satsuma, Choshiu, Tosa, Etsizen and other clans, whereby the followers of the Tokungawa family were expelled from the imperial palace and an edict was issued in the name of the young Mikado, Mutsuhite, to the effect that the office of Shiogoon was abolished, and that the government of Japan would be henceforth carried on by the Mikado himself. A provisional administration was appointed, and all the important civil and military posts were allotted to unflinching upholders of the prospective regime. The ex-Shiogoon, however, was persuaded by his retainers to retract his resignation, and, at the head of a large force, he undertook to re-enter Kioto [Miako] for the purpose of reasserting his former authority. After a battle, which lasted three days, he was beaten by the loyal troops and was forced to take refuge in his castle, where he announced that he would never again take up arms against the Mikado. Nevertheless, the Tokungawa clan showed, for a time, signs of disaffection; but by July 1, 1869, all vestiges of rebellion had ceased and the Mikado's party was triumphant. The trials of the new government now began. The Kuge, or court nobles, and the whole body of Samurai, or two-sworded men, desired to drive foreigners out of the country, but

Okubo, Goto and Kido, who were conversant with foreign ideas, opposed the execution of the plan and sent a noble of the imperial court to give the Mikado's consent to the treaties and to invite the foreign Ministers to an audience with the Emperor in Kioto. The conversion of the court nobles to the party that desired to see Japan reconstructed on European principles now went on rapidly, and the young Mikado was induced to appear in person before the Council of State and to promise that a deliberative assembly should be eventually formed. Indicative of an intention to revolutionize the mode of government was the Emperor's departure from Kioto, which had been the seat of his ancestors for twenty-five centuries, and his adoption of Yedo, thenceforth called Tokio, for his capital. To a considerable extent, freedom of the press was now guaranteed, and a number of newspapers sprung up. Books expounding European methods of thought and education were published, and many pamphlets advocating the abolition of feudalism appeared. Four of the great Daimios, or feudal lords, advocated the change. They addressed a memorial to the throne offering to restore the registers of their clans and proposing that the Mikado should resume possession of their fiefs. In conformity to this request, an edict was issued in September, 1871, summoning the Daimios to Tokio for the purpose of arranging their retirement to private life. With scarcely an exception, the order was obeyed; even the Daimios who disapproved of the measure were unwilling to oppose the resolute men who had framed the edict. The truth is that, even under the feudal system, the real power in each clan had lain in the hands of able men of inferior rank who ruled their nominal masters. These are the men who, during the last thirty years, have controlled Japan. Having first driven the Shiogoon into private life, they then compelled the Daimios to follow him into retirement. Of the men who have governed the country since 1868, not one is a Daimio by birth, and only two or three are Kuge, or court nobles. Almost all were simple Samurai, or retainers of the territorial lords.

It should be mentioned that, in 1869, the Emperor returned to Kioto for a brief visit, in order to perform certain ceremonies at his father's tomb, and, during his sojourn in the western capital, he married the present Empress, who was a princess of one of the five regent families, from which the highest officers under the Mikado have always been selected, and from which the emperors have habitually chosen their wives.

We have seen that the Emperor had promised to convoke a deliberative assembly. This promise was, at first, kept to the ear, rather than the hope. A so-called Kogisho or Parliament was formed of persons representing each of the Daimiates, and designated for the position by the Daimios. It was a mere debating society, whose function was to give advice to the imperial government. How conservative the advice given by this body was may be measured by the fact that it refused to recommend the abolition of the privilege of hari-kari, or of the custom of wearing swords. This Kogisho lasted only for some months, being dissolved in the autumn of the same year in which it was created.

Soon after the suppression of the feudal system in Japan, the Daimiates, considered as administrative areas, were superseded by Prefectures. At first, the ex-Daimios were appointed Prefects, but most of them were soon found to be unfit for high executive office, and they have been gradually replaced by competent persons drawn from the Samurai class. It should further be noted that the extinction of feudalism imposed some onerous financial obligations. It was decided that each ex-Daimio, and each of the sub-feudatories that had been dependent on him, should receive one-tenth of the income which they had drawn from their fiefs. This income was to be free from any claim for the support of the Samurai who had formed the standing army in each clan. The central government undertook to make all payments to the Samurai for services of any kind. The assumption of this burden compelled the government to borrow $165,000,000. In view of the pensions which they had formerly received, lump sums were given to the Samurai, but these were soon squandered, and much poverty and want were eventually experienced by the ex-feudal retainers. Among other remarkable events which took place in 1871, should be mentioned the removal of the ancient disqualification of the *eta* and *heimin*, whereby these pariah castes were placed on the same legal footing as the rest of the population. In the following year, the first railway in Japan was opened. This was a line between Yokohama and Tokio. In 1873, the European calendar was adopted, so far as the beginning of the year and the beginning of the months are concerned. The year is still reckoned, however, from Jimmu Tenno, which is 1873 of the Christian era, and corresponds to the year 2533 of the Japanese era. Still employed occasionally, also, is the Meiji year-period, which began in 1868.

From the beginning of 1872, the remodeling of the Japanese system of education was undertaken. In April of that year, the Mikado, Mutsuhito, visited the Imperial College, subsequently to be known as the Imperial University. The new buildings consisted of three wings, each 192 feet long, joined to a main edifice 324 feet in length. The students in this institution soon numbered 350, taught by 20 foreign professors. The foreign language school, in which pupils learned English or some other European language, preparatory to entering the college, presently had 600 students and 20 foreign teachers. For educational purposes, the empire was divided into eight districts, in each of which a university was contemplated, which was to be supplied by 210 secondary schools of foreign languages. It was arranged that the elementary vernacular schools should number 53,000, or one for every 600 persons in Japan. To these elementary establishments were to be deputed native teachers trained in normal schools. Before many years had passed, the school attendance was computed at three millions.

During the year 1872, two legations and three consulates were established abroad. Before long, the number was increased to ten. The Japanese press quickly emerged from the realm of experiment and became a powerful civilizing force. In the course of a few years, ten daily newspapers in the capital and 200 publications in the empire, equipped with metal type and printing presses, began to flood the country with information and awaken thought. In the department of jurisprudence, also, great progress was made. Since the restoration of the Mikado to actual power, revised statutes have greatly decreased the list of capital punishments; the condition of the prisons has been ameliorated; legal processes have been improved from the viewpoint of justice, and the use of torture to obtain testimony has been entirely abolished. Law schools were established, and to accused persons was given the assistance of counsel for their defense. By the year 1874, there had been a great change for the better in the diet, clothing, and hygienic protection of the people. In the year named, there were in the empire one government hospital and twenty-one hospitals assisted by government grants, twenty-nine private hospitals, 5,247 physicians practicing according to the principles and methods of Western science, and 5,205 apothecaries. In 1875, there were 325 students in the medical colleges at Tokio and Nagasaki, and there were some twenty-five foreign surgeons and physicians in the employ of the Japanese government. Public decency was improved and the standards of Christendom approached. The sale of orphan female children to brothel keepers, the traffic in native or European obscene pictures, lascivious dances, the exhibition of nude singing girls, the custom of promiscuous bathing in the public baths, and the toleration of nakedness on the part of the rural coolies were brought to an end. Religious persecution ceased. All the native Christians who had been exiled or imprisoned in 1868-69 were set free and restored to their villages. We note, finally, that, as early as 1876, the fulfillment of the promise made by the Mikado in 1868, that "intellect and learning should be sought for throughout the world," had been so far fulfilled that 400 foreigners from many Western countries had been invited to occupy posts in the government civil sevice. In 1870, there had been not ten Protestant Christians in the empire. By May, 1876, there were ten Protestant churches, with a membership of 800 souls. In March of the year just named, Prime Minister Sanjo issued a proclamation abolishing the custom of wearing two swords. This measure, which had been first advocated by Arinori Mori in 1870, now became law throughout the land. It was in August, 1876, that the commutation of the hereditary pensions and life incomes of the Sumarai, which previously had been optional, was made compulsory. This act forced the privileged classes to begin to earn their bread. In the same month, the empire was redivided and the 68 Ken, or Prefectures, were reduced in number to 35. It was to be expected that the progressive course of the Mikado's Ministers would excite some disaffection. There were during this year some insurrections on the part not only of discontented Samurai, but also of the farmers on whom the burdens of taxation mainly fell. It was to redress the grievances of the agricultural class that, in January, 1877, the national land tax was reduced from 3 to 2½ per cent, while the local tax, which had formerly amounted to one-third of the land tax, was cut down to one-fifth. About the same time, the salaries of nearly all the government officers were diminished, several thousand office-holders were discharged, the Department of Revision and the Prefecture of Police were abolished, and their functions were transferred to the Home Department. An annual saving of about eight million dollars was thus effected, and the loss to the Treasury from the curtailment of land taxation was made good. In 1877, however, a great rebellion broke out in Satsuma, instigated by Saigo Takamori, who had been formerly a marshal of the empire. After a contest of some months, the imperial authority was everywhere re-established, and Saigo, at his own request, was beheaded by one of his friends. This insurrection represented the final struggle between the forces of feudalism and misrule against

order and unity.   The contest cost Japan $50,000,000 and
many thousands of lives.   In the ultimate treatment of the
rebels, the government displayed a spirit of leniency worthy
of an enlightened state.   Of upward of 38,000 persons tried
in Kiushiu, only twenty were decapitated, about 1,800 were
condemned to imprisonment, and some 36,000 were pardoned.
During the same year, 1877, the cholera broke out in Japan,
but, owing to the enforcement of sanitary measures, there
were but 6,297 deaths.

The Mikado had now been governing Japan for ten years
by means of an irresponsible Ministry.   The oath which he
had taken at Kioto in 1868 to form a deliberative assembly
had never been fully carried out.   We have seen that the
Kogisho, or advisory body, called into existence in 1868,
had been dissolved in the same year.   Subsequently, in
1875, a Senate had been established and an assembly of the
ken governors, or prefects, held one session.   The meetings
of the latter body, however, were soon indefinitely postponed.   Nevertheless, the era of personal government was
drawing to a close.   On July 22, 1878, a long step was taken
toward representative institutions by an edict convoking provincial parliaments or local assemblies which were to sit once
a year in each ken or province.   Under the supervision of
the Minister of the Interior, these bodies were empowered to
discuss questions of local taxation, and to petition the central
government on other matters of local interest.   There were
both educational and property qualifications of the franchise.
Each voter had to prove his ability to read and write, and he
must have paid an annual land tax of at least five dollars.
In October, 1881, the Mikado announced by a proclamation
that, in 1890, a Parliament would be established.   In June,
1884, an edict was issued readjusting the system of nobility.
In the newly created orders of princes, marquises, counts,
viscounts and barons, were observed the names of many men
who had once belonged to the class of Samurai, or gentry,
but who had earned promotion by distinguished services on
behalf of their country.   Three hundred persons, that may

be described as pertaining to the aristocracy of intellect, were thus ennobled on the score of merit. It was expected that out of these newly created nobles would be constituted the upper house, or Chamber of Notables, in the Parliament which was to come into being in 1890. In December, 1885, the triple premiership, the Privy Council and the Ministries, as they had been hitherto established, came to an end. In their place was created a Cabinet at the head of which was a Minister-President. The old government boards, together with a new board, which was to supervise the post-office, telegraph and railway, were organized in such a way as to discharge many thousand office-holders. All the members of the new Cabinet were men of modern ideas, and such Asiatic features as the government had hitherto retained were now extinguished. By 1886, notable progress had been made in the applications of steam and electricity. Of railroads there were already 265 miles open, 271 miles in course of construction, and 543 miles contemplated. Although these lines were built and equipped on British models, most of the surveying, engineering and constructive work and all of the mechanical labor were performed by natives. The trains and engines were worked by Japanese; such light materials as were made of wood and metal were manufactured in Japan, only the heavy castings, the rails and the engines being brought from Great Britain. The telephone and the electric light were now seen in the large cities, and four cables connected the island empire with the Asiatic mainland. Already the Japan Mail Shipping Company employed a large fleet of steamships and sailing vessels in their coasting, trade and passenger lines. We add that, in 1885, the Postal Department forwarded nearly 100,000,000 letters and packages.

The Japanese had, for some time, recognized that education is the basis of progress, and that their efforts for intellectual advancement were seriously impeded by their use of the Chinese graphic system. They perceived that what they needed most of all was an alphabet. In 1884, the Roma-ji-Kai, or Roman Letter Association, was formed in Tokio, and, within two years, had 6,000 members, native and foreign. As their name implies, their purpose was to supplant the Chinese character and native syllabary by the Roman alphabet, as the vehicle of Japanese thought. It was demonstrated that all possible sounds and vocal combinations could be expressed by using twenty-two Roman letters. It was further proved that, by means of the Roman alphabet, a child could learn to read the colloquial and book language in one-tenth of the time formerly required. Scarcely was the Roman Letter Association under way than it printed a newspaper, edited text-books, and transliterated popular and classic texts in the appropriate characters of the Roman alphabet. By an imperial decree, issued in November, 1884, the English language was made part of the order of study in the common schools. Meanwhile, the progress of Christianity acquired considerable momentum. Not only were many converts made by Catholic missionaries, but, by the end of 1885, there were 200 Protestant churches, with a membership of over 13,000. In December, 1885, the Mikado's Cabinet was reorganized, and, during the next four years, Ito and Inouye were the principal molders of the national policy. In April, 1888, a new body called the Privy Council was created, of which Ito became President, while Kuroda filled the position of Prime Minister. In this body, active debate upon the forthcoming Constitution began in May of the year last-named, and proceeded until February 11, 1889, when the long-awaited instrument was proclaimed. Exactly thirty-five years after the American treaty-ships appeared in sight of Idzu, the Mikado, Mutsuhito, took oath to maintain the government according to the Constitution, the documents defining which he, before an audience of nobles, officials and foreign envoys, handed to Kuroda, the principal Minister of State. On this occasion, for the first time in Japan's history, the Emperor rode beside the Empress in public. The one blot upon the record of the day was the assassination of the Minister of Education, Arinori Mori, by a Shintoist fanatic.

Let us glance at some of the features of Japan's fundamental organic law. The Constitution proper consists of
sixty-six articles, but, simultaneously with it, two hundred
and sixty-six expositionary laws were proclaimed. In the
first place, the Mikado's person was declared sacred and in-
violable. In him continued to be concentrated the rights of
sovereignty, which, however, he was to exercise according
to the provisions of the organic law. A Diet or Parliament
was created to meet once a year, and to be opened, closed,
prorogued and dissolved by the Emperor. Its debates are
public. The Mikado's Ministers may take seats and speak
in either House, but are accountable, not to the Diet, but to
the Emperor alone. Bills raising revenue and appropriating
the same require the consent of the Diet, but certain fixed
expenditures, provided for by the Constitution, cannot be
abolished or curtailed without the concurrence of the Executive. To a large extent, the power over the purse is thus
withheld from the representatives of the people. The tenure
of judges is for good behavior. The Upper House consists
partly of hereditary, partly of elected, and partly of nominated members; the combined number, however, of the members of the two last-named classes is not to exceed that of
those who hold heritable titles of nobility. The House of
Representatives consists of about 300 members, who serve
four years. For them there is a property qualification; they
must pay annually national taxes to the amount of fifteen
yen or dollars. Those who elect them must also pay national taxes to the same amount. Those persons who pay
taxes to the amount of over five yen are entitled to vote for
members of the local assembly. These numbered, in 1887,
about 1,500,000, whereas the electorate of the national House
of Representatives numbered only about 300,000. We observe, lastly, that certain fundamental rights were guaranteed to the Japanese people. They have, for instance, the
right of changing their domicile. Except according to law,
they are not to be arrested, detained or punished. They are
also to enjoy the right of freedom from search, the inviola-

bility of letters, freedom of religious belief and the liberty of speech, petition, writing, publishing, association and public meeting within the limits of laws to be laid down by the national Parliament.

The threefold election—namely, for a fraction of the Upper House, for the whole of the national House of Representatives, and for the local assembly—took place in July, 1890. About eighty-five per cent of eligible voters availed themselves of the franchise, and there was a great superfluity of candidates. It turned out at the ballot-box that to be in any way connected with government employment was to invite almost certain defeat, while, on the other hand, few of the old party leaders were chosen as standard-bearers in the new Parliamentary field. We add that, on April 22, 1890, a new code of civil procedure, and the first portion of a Civil Code, were promulgated; since 1881, a new Criminal Code based on the principles of Western jurisprudence has been in successful operation.

CHAPTER XIII

FOREIGN POLICY OF NEW JAPAN AND WAR WITH CHINA

It will be convenient to consider separately the foreign policy which was gradually evolved after the transformation of Japan that followed the Mikado's resumption of actual power. Scarcely had the Shiogoon been overthrown than the desire of conquest and expansion was reawakened. Representatives of the advanced school of Japanese ideas presently maintained that the national jurisdiction should include not only Yezo, Saghalien and the Bonin islands, but also Corea and the eastern part of Formosa, the last claim being based upon settlements made by the Japanese. The Bonin islands, first occupied by Ogasawara, a Daimio, in 1593, and visited by a party of explorers from Nagasaki in 1675, had been neglected by the Japanese for centuries, though long a noted resort of whalers. In 1878, the islands were formally reoccupied in the name of the Mikado, and a local government established by Japanese officers. Saghalien and the Kurile islands had been a debatable ground between the Japanese and the Russians since 1790, and had been the scene of a good deal of bloodshed. In 1875, Admiral Enomoto concluded at St. Petersburg a convention by which Russia received the whole of Saghalien, while Japan obtained all the Kurile islands. The large island of Yezo was administered by a special department until the year 1882, when it was divided into three ken, or prefectures, which are governed like the rest of the empire. Let us glance, next, at Japan's assumption of sovereignty over the little island kingdom of Riu Kiu, or Loo Choo, an assumption which subjected the relations between China and Japan to severe tension. These islands are strung like a long thread between Japan and Formosa. For many centuries, these islanders sent tribute to both China and Japan. Toward the close of the sixteenth century, Hideyoshi demanded that they should pay tribute to Japan alone; but he never enforced his demands. In 1609, Iyehisa, the Daimio of Satsuma, conquered the islands, and made their chiefs swear allegiance to his house and to the Shiogoon. Between 1611 and 1850, no fewer than fifteen embassies from Riu Kiu visited Yedo to obtain investiture for the island king, or to congratulate a Shiogoon upon his accession to power. The same policy, however, was pursued toward China also. After the revolution of 1868 the Loo Choo islands were made a dependency of the Japanese empire, and the king acknowledged the Mikado for his suzerain. Some five years later, the Japanese reduced the king to the status of a retired Daimio, and transformed Riu Kiu into a ken, or prefecture. To this the islanders objected, and continued to send a tribute-junk to Ningpo, and implored China's interposition. The Pekin government, on its part, considered that Japan, by its annexation of the Loo Choo islands, had wrongfully cut off a fringe of the robe of the Middle Kingdom.

Let us now glance at Japan's connection with Formosa, before examining, somewhat in detail, her much more important relations to Corea. It was toward the end of 1873 that a Loo Choo junk was wrecked on the eastern shore of Formosa; the crew were killed by the savage inhabitants of that region, and, as it was reported, eaten. The Loo Choo islanders appealed to their hereditary suzerain at Satsuma, who referred the matter to Tokio. As it happened, China laid no claim to the eastern part of Formosa, and no trace of it appeared on the maps of the Middle Kingdom. In the spring of 1874, the Mikado dispatched Soyejima as Embassador to Pekin, and his representative there obtained an audience with the Chinese Emperor. The Tsungli Yamen disclaimed responsibility for eastern Formosa, and conceded the right of Japan to chastise the savages there. While Soyejima was absent in China, a Japanese junk was wrecked in Formosa, and its crew were stripped and plundered. On the return of the Embassy, 1,300 Japanese soldiers, under the command of Saigo Yorimichi, were ordered to avenge the outrage, and, after a few skirmishes with savages, they proceeded to occupy the eastern part of Formosa. There they built roads, organized camps, and directed fortifications in accordance with the principles of modern engineering and military art. Incited, it is said, by foreign influence, the Chinese government now began to urge its claims upon the whole of Formosa, and to denounce the Japanese as intruders. For a time war seemed inevitable, but the result of the negotiations, intrusted to Okubo, who was sent to Pekin, was that the Chinese paid an indemnity of $700,000, and the Japanese evacuated the island. The abortive expedition had cost Japan $5,000,000 and seven hundred lives.

Japan's relations with Corea were to have much more momentous consequences. During the Tokungawa period, the so-called Hermit Kingdom had sent regularly embassies conveying homage to Japan; but, not relishing the change which the latter country underwent in 1868, disgusted at the departure of the Mikado's government from traditional ideals, and emboldened by the failure of the French and American expeditions against her own territory, Corea sent to Tokio insulting letters, in which she taunted Japan with slavish truckling to the foreign barbarians, and declared herself an enemy. This incident, which took place in 1872, rendered the project of a war with Corea extremely popular in the Japanese army and navy. Some years, however, were to elapse before an armed contest took place between the two countries. In 1875, Mr. Arinori Mori was dispatched to Pekin, and Kuroda Kiyotaka, at the head of some men-of-war, entered Corean waters. The twofold diplomatic and naval demonstration was crowned with success. A treaty of peace, friendship and commerce was concluded between Japan and Corea on February 27, 1876. In pursuance of this treaty, Japan, in 1876, secured the opening of the port of Fushan to her trade, as compensation for an outrage perpetrated on some of her sailors. In 1880, Chemulpo, the port of Seoul, the Corean capital, was also thrown open to Japanese commerce. The activity of the Japanese gave umbrage to the court of Pekin, and, in 1881, a draft commercial treaty was drawn up by the Chinese authorities, in conjunction with the representatives of the principal Western powers at the Chinese capital, and carried to Seoul for acceptance by the American naval officer, Commodore Schufeldt. The treaty, being recommended by China, was, naturally, accepted by Corea. When the Japanese, however, observed that the Chinese were putting forward a pretension to control exclusively the destinies of the Hermit Kingdom, they determined to assert their old claim to an equal voice with China in the Corean peninsula. They allied themselves with the so-called progressive party in Corea, and thus forced China to link her fortunes with the reactionists.

Except among the reformers, who constituted but a weak minority of the Corean population, the Japanese were far from popular in the Hermit Kingdom, and, in June, 1882, the reactionists attacked the Japanese Legation, murdered some of its inmates and compelled the survivors to flee.

Thereupon, the Japanese sent a force to exact reparation, while the Chinese, on their part, sent a force to restore order. A temporary accommodation was effected, but, for two years, Chinese and Japanese soldiers remained close to one another under the walls of Seoul. In December, 1884, a second collision occurred between the Japanese and Coreans, the latter being aided this time by the Chinese. The first named were compelled to flee. The Tokio government obtained reparation for this fresh outrage, but, not satisfied therewith, it dispatched Count Ito to Pekin to bring about some permanent arrangement. There is no doubt that, at this time, the Chinese occupied a much stronger position in Corea than did the Mikado's subjects, but the advantage was thrown away by an agreement which tied China's hands and had far-reaching consequences.

Li Hung Chang was appointed Plenipotentiary to negotiate with Count Ito, and a convention was signed by them at Tientsin, on April 18, 1885. It provided, first, that both countries should recall their troops from Corea; secondly, that no more officers should be sent by either country to drill Corean soldiers; and, thirdly, that if, at any future time, either of the parties to the convention should decide to send a force to Corea, it must straightway inform the other. By this compact, China acknowledged that Japan's right to control Corea was on a level with her own, and it was henceforth unreasonable for the Pekin authorities to speak of Corea as a vassal State. For nine years after the conclusion of the Tientsin Convention, peace prevailed in the Hermit Kingdom. In the spring of 1894, however, the Tong Haks, a body of religious reformers, broke into open rebellion, and, toward the end of May, obtained a considerable success over the troops of the Corean government. China was at once requested to dispatch a force to save the capital, and, by the 10th of June, 2,000 Chinese soldiers were encamped at Asan, a port some distance to the south of Seoul. A few Chinese men-of-war were also ordered to cruise off the Corean coasts. In pursuance of the terms of the Tientsin Convention, notification of the dispatch of these forces to Corea was given to the Tokio government, which, having had equal rights conceded to it, was resolved to exercise them with promptitude and vigor. Within forty-eight hours after the arrival of the Chinese at Asan, the Japanese had placed a far superior number of soldiers at Seoul, and of ships at Chemulpo. They thus secured complete possession of the capital and of the court, although both had been in thorough sympathy with China. To avert an insurrection in Seoul, it was thought needful to secure the person of the King of Corea, and his palace was, accordingly, captured by the Japanese, and the ruler of the peninsula converted into their tool or ally. He was, forthwith, required to put his seal to a document ordering the Chinese troops, who had come at his invitation, to leave the country. This seizure of the King's person took place on July 23, 1894. Two days later, the Japanese squadron attacked the transport "Kowshing" and some armed vessels which were convoying it. In the ensuing engagement, one Chinese man-of-war was sunk, one was disabled, and 1,200 soldiers went down with the "Kowshing." On the same day, the Japanese General Oshima left Seoul with a small force to attack the Chinese camp, which had been transferred from Asan to Song-hwan, a strongly fortified position. The place was carried on July 29 by a night surprise with a loss to the Chinese of 500 killed and wounded; the remainder of the force then retreated to Pingyang, a town north of Seoul, on the main road to China. These encounters were followed by a reciprocal declaration of war between China and Japan on August 1, 1894. There ensued a lull in hostilities, during which Japan poured her troops into Corea, while the Chinese fleet remained inactive in the harbors of Wei-hai-Wei and Port Arthur. About the beginning of September, a Japanese force of 13,000 men under General Nodzu was ordered to attack the strong position occupied by the Chinese at Pingyang. The assault was delivered on May 15, and the Chinese were compelled to retreat with a loss of 2,000 killed, in addition to the wounded and prisoners. The sturdiness of the defense at certain points was attested by the fact that the victors themselves lost 633 killed, wounded and missing. The capture of Pingyang resulted in the Chinese evacuation of Corea.

While the fighting was taking place on land at Pingyang, the Chinese fleet, under the command of Admiral Ting, was conveying troops to the mouth of the Yalu River, the north-western boundary of Corea, where the Chinese were collecting a second army. Returning from the fulfillment of this task, the fleet was encountered off the island of Hai Yang on September 17, by a Japanese squadron under Admiral Ito. The naval combatants were nearly equal in strength, each numbering ten war vessels; two of the Chinese ships, however, were superior in armament. The result of the action was that five of the Chinese torpedo boats were destroyed, and the total loss of the Chinese in killed and wounded was 1,000, while that of the Japanese was but 265.

The Japanese, having been re-enforced by a considerable body of soldiers under Marshal Yamagata, began their forward movement from Pingyang early in October, 1894, and on the 10th of the month reached the Yalu, where they found a considerable Chinese army posted on the northern bank of the river. After a merely nominal resistance, however, the Chinese officers and soldiers abandoned their fortifications on October 25 and 26, thus allowing the Japanese to capture an enormous quantity of war materials, including seventy-four cannon, over 4,000 rifles and more than 4,000,-000 rounds of ammunition. While Marshal Yamagata was forcing the passage of the Yalu, another Japanese army under Marshal Oyama had landed on the Liau-tung, or Regent's Sword peninsula, with the view of assailing the great naval station of Port Arthur. The natural and artificial strength of this place was great; over 300 guns were in position, and the garrison numbered at least 10,000 men, while the assailants did not exceed 13,000, although, of course, they were materially aided by their fleet. Having landed at the mouth of the Hua-yuan River, about 100 miles north of Port Arthur, the Japanese pushed southward and captured the well-fortified city of Chinchow without losing a man. On the next day, they had a similar experience at Talien-wan, where they found over 120 cannon, 2,500,000 rounds of artillery ammunition, and nearly 34,000,000 rifle cartridges. On November 22, 1894, the Japanese army and fleet made a concerted attack upon Port Arthur, and, with the loss of eighteen men killed and 250 wounded, gained possession of a naval stronghold on which $20,000,000 had been spent. During the following month of December, the force under Marshal Yamagata advanced into Manchuria, but here they were confronted by a fresh Chinese army, which had been assembled to defend Mukden, the old Manchu capital, and which evinced a good deal of courage. In one fight at Kangwasai, the Japanese experienced a loss of 400 men, and the subsequent capture of Kaiping cost them 300 killed and wounded. About the middle of January, 1895, the energies of the Japanese were turned against the naval fortress of Wei-hai-Wei, which is situated on the northern coast of Shantung, opposite Port Arthur, and constitutes, with the last-named place, the keys of the Gulf of Pechihli. After landing, on January 20, at Yungchang, a little west of the place to be attacked, the Japanese, six days later, appeared at the gates of Wei-hai-Wei. The place was defended not only by a semicircular line of forts and batteries and two fortified islands in the bay, but also by the Chinese fleet under Admiral Ting, which comprised nine large vessels, besides six small gunboats and seven large and four small torpedo boats. The attack began on January 29, and continued for three weeks; nor would Admiral Ting, even then, have consented to surrender, had he not received a telegraphed message from Li Hung Chang to the effect that no help need be looked for. After the terms of surrender were agreed upon, the Chinese admiral committed suicide. After the fall of Wei-hai-Wei, the Japanese in Manchuria continued their advance, and captured the twin city of Newchang, thus placing themselves between Mukden and the Chinese capital. When spring was about to open, they possessed an army of 100,000 men, ready to move upon Pekin, and there is no doubt that they could have taken the city speedily and easily. Two months previously, the Chinese had sent to Tokio a pretended peace mission with inadequate powers, but now, the Pekin government, recognizing the impossibility of resistance, appointed Li Hung Chang plenipotentiary, and dispatched him to Shimonoseki, which he reached on March 20, 1895. Luckily for the success of his mission, he was shot in the cheek by a fanatic four days after his arrival, while he was returning from a conference with Count Ito, the representative of Japan. This outrage aroused great sympathy for Li Hung Chang, and, to prove the sincerity of his regret, the Mikado consented to an armistice, and sensibly modified the terms of peace upon which he had originally insisted. On April 17, 1895, the Treaty of Shimonoseki was signed, and, on May 8, the ratifications were exchanged at Chefoo. The provisions of the treaty may be briefly summed up as follows: The Chinese were to surrender the islands of Formosa and the Pescadores, and also, on the Asiatic mainland, the southern part of the province of Shingking, including the Regent's Sword peninsula, and, of course, the naval fortress of Port Arthur. By way of pecuniary indemnity, China was to pay 200,000,000 Kuping taels, or, say, $170,000,000, in eight installments, with interest at the rate of five per cent on those unpaid. The commercial concessions were to include the admission of ships under the Japanese flag to the different rivers and lakes of China and the appointment of consuls; and the Japanese were to retain Wei-hai-Wei until the whole indemnity had been paid and an acceptable commercial treaty had been concluded. These terms were by no means excessive, in view of the completeness of the Japanese triumph, but they gave great umbrage to Russia, which foresaw that the presence of the Japanese on the Regent's Sword peninsula would prove an obstacle to its plans of southward extension through Manchuria, and to the attainment of an ice-free port. Moreover, had the Japanese been suffered to remain on the mainland of Asia, they, instead of the Russians, would have become preponderant at Pekin. Accordingly, the Czar's advisers, having secured the co-operation not only of their French ally, but also of Germany, proceeded to make a diplomatic move, the aim of which was to despoil the Mikado of a part of the fruits of victory. Scarcely was the ink dry on the Treaty of Shimonoseki, when Japan received from the three European powers just named a polite request, which veiled, of course, a threat, that she should waive that part of the Shimonoseki Treaty which provided for the cession of Port Arthur and the Liau-tung peninsula. Japan would doubtless have repelled the demand, had she been assured of Great Britain's support. But no assurance to that effect was forthcoming from Lord Rosebery, then British Prime Minister, and, accordingly, the Mikado consented to resign his claim to the Liau-tung peninsula for the additional indemnity of $30,000,000. The final installment of the indemnity was paid in May, 1898, whereupon Wei-hai-Wei was evacuated by the Japanese, and, soon afterward, was ceded by the Pekin government to Great Britain.

Since the compulsory revision of the Shimonoseki Treaty, the attitude of the Tokio Foreign Office has been marked by much reserve and dignity. Japan has employed the years that have since elapsed, and the money received from China, in prosecuting extensive military and naval reforms. Nor is the time distant when, with the warships built at home or purchased in foreign shipyards, she will have a navy only second to that possessed by Great Britain in the Far East, and will be able to place half a million thoroughly trained and equipped soldiers on the mainland of Asia. In Corea, she has obtained increased freedom of action, Russia having practically waived her claims to ascendency in that country; Japan has turned the opportunity to account by building a railway from Chemulpo to Seoul, which should materially help her to maintain control of the Hermit Kingdom. Whatever may be the Mikado's ultimate intention, he has, as yet, given no conclusive proof of a wish to participate in the game

of partition now being played in China. No protest came
from him when, toward the close of 1897, Germany seized
the harbor of Kiao Chou, or when, on March 27, 1898, a
convention signed at Pekin gave the Russians the usufruct
of Port Arthur and Talien-wan. In September, however,
the Marquis (formerly Count) Ito was dispatched as a special embassador to the Chinese capital, for the purpose, as
it is believed, but not positively known, of arranging an alliance between the Japanese and Chinese empires, which
should put an effectual stop to further encroachments on
the part of Russia. Then occurred the palace revolution at
Pekin, whereby the young Emperor Kwangsu was virtually
dethroned, and the supreme authority usurped by the Empress Dowager, Tsi An. There being, thenceforward, no
hope of effecting the desired arrangement, the Marquis Ito
returned to Japan, soon after which—namely, on October
31—the homogeneous Ministry which had taken office in
June of this year—the first Ministry of the kind, by the
way, since the establishment of the Constitution in 1889—
was compelled to resign, and was succeeded by an eclectic
cabinet even more thoroughly representative of the Japanese
desire to play a great role in the Far East. On November
6, an envoy deputed by the Mikado to present certain gifts
to the Chinese Emperor insisted upon obtaining an audience,
and thus succeeded in discovering that the unfortunate
Kwangsu was still living.

 It remains to note that the Tokio Foreign Office has at
last succeeded in inducing the principal Western powers to
abolish the exterritoriality clauses in their respective treaties,
whereby their subjects were exempted from the jurisdiction
of the Japanese tribunals. With the disappearance of these
clauses, which are still exacted not only in the case of China,
Siam, Persia and Morocco, but also in the case of Turkey
and Egypt, the Mikado's empire may be said to have taken
a recognized place among highly civilized nations.

THE END

www.ingramcontent.com/pod-product-compliance
Lightning Source LLC
Chambersburg PA
CBHW030353030726
47497CB00002B/323